Paths
Of
Chaos

Also by Aaron S. Jones

Flames of Rebellion

A Long Way from Home - A collection of short stories from the world of The Broken Gods (available as an audiobook read by Mark Rice-Oxley)

Paths
Of
Chaos

The Broken Gods:
Book Two

Aaron S. Jones

First edition 2021
Book cover by Mars Dorian

ISBN: 9798577518547

Imprint: Independently published

If you enjoyed this book, please leave a review on Amazon and Goodreads.

Visit **www.aaronsjones.com** for more information. You can sign up to the mailing list to be the first to find out about author events, interviews, and will always be the first to hear of new books from the author.

For Mum,

You might prefer crime novels, but you buy my books anyway! Thanks for the support

COLD

It was cold. Damn cold. The wind howled through the naked birch trees. The soft crunch of snow beneath dirty boots was the only other noise that could be heard in the wild lands. Sly pulled his hood tighter around his head, attempting to cover as much of his bearded and scarred face as possible. His movements were slow but determined. The closer they got to the Borderlands, the more dangerous it would be for the two of them. Who knew what madness had taken hold in his homeland whilst he was away? Weeks away in the United Cities and on the damned boat back had only served to convince him that he should have stayed with the girlie and have some fun with the Barbarians; death, betrayal and regret were all that he had found in those piss-poor lands to the south.

'We're close,' a gruff voice muttered next to him. It was the first thing that Cray had said to him in the last two days. Escaping the city of Archania had been a struggle. The Lower City was complete madness. Fires swept across the wooden buildings lining the cobbled streets and blood flew between soldiers and crazed men and women dressed all in black or red. Couldn't tell who needed an axe in the back. Even the best warriors needed to know when to get the fuck out of there. Otherwise they'd just be bones. Sly wasn't ready for that: he had too much killing left in him.

'Aye. I can smell it in the air. Home,' he answered. That

1

was enough for now. They marched on through the barren lands, cold and silent. Sly rubbed his cold fingers across the axe handle resting in its holster on his hip. He'd carried it all the way from a tavern in that cursed city, using it to cut his way through the guards who had been stupid enough to stand in his way. Thoughts turned to what had happened in the city as he gently rubbed his calloused fingers against the leather.

His imprisonment.

Bane's betrayal.

Raven's death.

And Baldor was Gods know where now. Bane had claimed he was in some labour camp but Sly had no idea where that might be. Best to tell the girlie and let her decide what to do about the big guy.

Fuck.

Fuck. Fuck. Fuck.

He'd known Raven had been up to something: he hadn't been himself, made too many stupid decisions. This was what happened when people ignored their gut: this kind of shit. From now on, Sly followed one man and one alone. His own fucking self. Being pissed about didn't sit right with him – he wanted revenge. He'd send as many of the little shits involved straight through the black gate himself even if it ended up with him as bones. Fuck 'em all.

Sly could take his time. Do it all just right. He'd start on his way back to the Borderlands: once Saul was dealt with for his part in all of this – then he could slope back south if he had the stomach for it – make all the fuckers pay.

Cray had his own reasons for joining him on the way back to the Borderlands. He had his own reasons for wanting Saul wiped from these lands. They had their differences, but right now, their paths were heading in the same direction. The short, stocky warrior plodded on through the snow, each footstep getting him closer to his family, captives of the Borderlands' chief.

A spot of snow drifted onto Sly's face before melting and racing towards his bush of a beard. He looked up to see more of the cold bastards dropping down from the white sky above him. The clouds had cast their white sheet over the lands for the past two days, threatening a blizzard to come. This was just the beginning. It was going to be a bad one. Should've grabbed some horses on the way out of that hellhole – would've been back much quicker. Only problem would've been feeding 'em. Too much hassle. Would have cost too much on that thieving fool's ship too.

He spat and growled at the thought.

The pace of the snowfall increased with Sly's dark thoughts – as though he himself controlled the change in weather. Snowflakes swirled around in the quickening wind biting across the two warriors as they trudged through the ever-growing levels of snow. They were used to it – they were Borderlanders through and through. Used to the cold. The fury of the land. The way it tested everyone. Hardened them. Sharpened them.

Sly allowed a crooked smile on his scarred face – brown eyes widening as he stared into the distance at a familiar, colossal structure. He reached out and slapped Cray's chest, preventing him from taking another step.

This could be fun.

Cray grunted and glanced at the dirty hand preventing him from moving forward with a confused look on his face. He hadn't seen it yet.

'You know where we are?' Sly asked him.

'Must be close to the border now. Gotta pass before this storm gets back. Night soon. Too cold,' came the reply. It made sense. But…

Sly pointed with his chin into the distance, knowing Cray would recognise what was in front of them, peeking out of the mist shrouding them beneath the darkening skies.

A rare smile broke out on the usually grim warrior's face as he saw the temple. He turned his round head to Sly and asked a question, already knowing the answer. 'What's the plan?'

'Kill the fuckers.'

Darkness gripped the North as Sly crept towards the temple. Careful not to make any sound, his toes softly hit the snow first before his heel followed, leaving the faintest of imprints. Best do this as quietly as possible. Who knew how many of the bastards were in there now? No point running in with weapons drawn until they knew what they were up against. People called him a madman – but he wasn't *that* fucking mad.

The snow continued falling, pouring down onto the earth as though the ancestors themselves were throwing buckets of the stuff, making visibility more difficult with each passing moment. Sly liked it. The less anyone saw, the better.

He snuck across the snow and pressed his back up against the stone walls of the temple. Freezing cold. He moved his fingers slowly in and out of his palm before balling his fists and releasing three times. Now wasn't the time for them to freeze; he would need to move quickly if they were to pull this off. A moment of hesitation could be the difference between life and death.

He peered around the corner of the building, looking past the stone pillars at the front of the temple. For a moment, he thought he could see Cray doing the same on the opposite side. Difficult to be certain in this weather. He continued on his path round to the front of the structure before arching his back against the wall. To his left stood a great wooden door, the only entrance into the temple. He pulled the axe out of the holster and gripped it tightly in his two hands. He spotted Cray pausing next to one of the thick, round pillars that held up the roof, sheltering the entrance from the continuing snowfall. Every now and then the biting, swirling wind would push a few drops of the cold stuff towards the door, but it was mainly clear.

Cray gave a grim nod, drawing his weapon slowly.

It was time. Sly banged hard on the wooden door three times with the handle of his axe.

Bang.

Bang.

Bang.

He tried to listen for the sound of footsteps, but it was

impossible with the howling wind attacking the temple. He'd just have to wait, back to the wall, fingers tight around the handle of his axe.

The door creaked open. A head peered out from the gap, looked for any sign of an unwanted guest.

'Who's there?' the head called out into the darkness.

'Me,' Cray replied.

The man took a step into the entrance towards Cray's voice. Sly smiled as Cray waved.

'What are you doing here?' He had a cloak lined with thick fur pulled tight against his thin frame. No armour. No weapon. Defenceless. Idiot.

The axe smashing into his skull cracked above the chaotic wind. His body slumped to the stony ground – Sly crouched, stepping forward with it, unable to relinquish his grip on the handle as the blade was too embedded in the dead man's skull. He lifted a dirty boot and pushed hard against the motionless body whilst pulling hard on the axe. Eventually, it tore loose, blood spraying against the doorway.

'Nice cloak,' Cray said, pausing on his way to the door to grab the warm cloak from the corpse.

'He's not gonna need it anymore. He'll be cold with or without it,' Sly responded with a shrug.

He ducked through the gap in the open door as Cray threw the cloak over his broad shoulders with a grin and followed. The temple was as he remembered it. Lights from the candles on the walls cast long shadows across the wooden benches that sat in two separate rows leading up to the altar at the end of the room. Snow fell through a circular hole in the ceiling. Stupid fucking builders.

'What do you think you're doing here?' Four more men stood at the end of the aisle, pausing in their conversation to look over at the two scruffy warriors. The look on their puzzled faces made it all worth it.

Sly's eyes darted to a glint of metal peering out through the heavy cloak that one of the men was wearing. Finally, some real fun.

'We're two weary travellers, here to bask in the light of your cunty lord. Not gonna kick us out are ya? We wouldn't like that would we Cray?'

'Wouldn't like that at all.'

The scraping of four swords being drawn from was like music to his ears. This'll be better than a good fuck.

'You will leave now – this temple is under the protection of King Asher and the Empress of the East. Leave now or you will suffer the consequences…'

'Consequences? Be gentle boys: this is my first time,' Sly cackled as he raised his axe, baring his yellow teeth at the rushing swordsman.

The room hadn't been built for fighting. The aisle was too narrow for all four of the men to attack at once – instead they were forced into a funnel with only two of them reaching Sly, the others left limp and blunt behind them, unable to do anything but watch for the first attack.

A lazy swing of a sword wasn't going to cause any problems. Sly didn't even block it. He dropped his shoulder and let the blade smack the edge of the wooden bench to his right. Cray's sword pierced through the air and straight through his target's throat. Precision. The soldier who had warned them dropped to the floor; sword forgotten in the wooden bench.

Sly swung his axe up with a measured diagonal thrust. As the axe cut deep into his opponent's neck, he kicked out at the body, not wanting to be stuck for any length of time in this battle. Every second counted when you were outnumbered. Blood splattered across his face as the axe was wrenched free, painting him like a deadly canvas.

Two left.

Easy.

The two remaining swordsmen cast a nervous glance at each other and took a cautious step back, swords pointing forward. Easy to be brave when the numbers are in your favour; completely different when you can look at the whites of the eyes of a warrior in front of you and you're the last line of defence. Bravery is a fickle thing.

'You don't fancy this, boys,' Sly warned, wiping the axe against the sleeve of his cloak as he walked towards them. 'You have a choice. Fight us and die. Or, lower your weapons and live.'

It was an easy decision.

The two of them looked at each other again, fear in their eyes. They didn't have the heart for a battle. They knew the outcome. The swords clanged on the stone floor as the soldiers raised their palms open in surrender.

Idiots.

He buried his axe deep into the chest of the one before him, roaring with glee as Cray thrust his sword straight through the other man's stomach and up and out through his back. Great minds.

The bodies dropped to the ground with a thud.

Beautiful.

He stepped over the bodies and eyed the door at the back of the room. He banged against it, taking a moment to study the intricate golden frame. He knew who was behind it. This was the start of his revenge.

He knocked again. No answer.

Fuck this.

He rammed his shoulder three times against the frame. Third time was the charm. The hinges snapped and the door gave way to a darkened room. One candle. One priestess: kneeling with her back to Sly, head bowed in silence.

'Didn't think we would be meeting so soon,' he said, recognising the long dark hair that fell to the bottom of her back.

She took a moment to finish off her silent conversation with whoever the hells were listening. She rose slowly and turned to face him. Her face was how he remembered: proud, arrogant, beautiful.

'If only we'd met at another time…' Sly said softly with a sad smile.

'You don't understand what you're doing. You need us.'

7

Her voice was as melodic as he remembered. Enchanting. Full of shit.

'Your kind fucked us over. Your daddy did anyway. Call this payback.'

She marched up to him with a confident smile on her face. 'You need us,' she repeated, 'this world is dying. We are the only ones who can save it. Leave here without a backward glance. If not, you will regret it.'

A threat. She was a hard bitch, he had to give her that. Kiras would have liked her.

'I have a different idea,' he said, raising his axe.

Her eyes widened in response, 'A woman, defenceless and on her own. Are you that cold?'

Sly jumped to the side as a flash of light shot past him. For the fourth time that day, he felt the sweet feeling of his axe finding its home inside someone who had wanted him dead.

He looked back towards Cray, standing still, eyes focused on the dagger buried in the wall only inches away from his head. He turned back towards the dead, open eyes of the priestess and spat. 'Time to go.'

He grabbed the candle and looked at the fabrics and wooden statues that filled up the room. 'A goodbye gift.' He dropped the candle and watched for a moment as the flames licked the rug beneath it.

Sly stepped out of the temple, following Cray in his new cloak as they walked past the last corpse. The blizzard had died down. Once again, he could hear the snow crunching beneath him.

'She almost got you with that dagger,' Cray said, darkly chuckling.

'*Almost*,' Sly admitted.

'What's next?'

'Borderlands. And quick. It's fucking cold.'

REVENGE

A cool, refreshing breeze carried the scents of the market along the pathway beside the large canal. The wave of smells hit Katerina Kane at once: fish, fresh bread, cooked meat, sweat. Merchants cried out along the wooden boards, pestering whoever was attempting to enjoy a stroll next to the clear body of water beside the pathways. The knowing locals would just smile and nod before moving inwards towards the centre of the city, to places where they could get the real bargains. Visitors to the city would often be seen engaging with the merchants and paying insane prices for the lower quality wares. This was the way of world, unfortunately. You had to wise up.

There was a glow about the floating city of Causrea that was a sharp contrast to Kane's home of Archania. This city was bright, vibrant and full of life. Lovebirds took lazy trips along the canals in thin, elaborately decorated red boats steered by a single oarsman serenading them; melodic tones echoing down between the small gaps of the old, brick houses either side of the clear blue water. She had to admit, this was a beautiful city.

The air felt fresher than back home, like the stench of regret and sorrow was not following her on her journey to the West. She closed her eyes for a moment and breathed in. The cold, dead face of Ella attacked her faster than any enemy ever could. The air may be different; the city may be different; the people may be different, but she was the same old Katerina Kane.

And she had a job to do.

The mess she had escaped in Archania was too big to clean up quickly. Mason D'Argio was running the whole of the United Cities along with that fool King Asher. There was only death to greet her if she went back now. Mason was the root of the problem in the United Cities. She wanted revenge, but revenge was best given with thought and patience. Kane had enough time to plan revenge. And now, she just needed allies. Allies who knew the dangers that they were facing.

She took another deep breath in. Nothing to fear here. This city was away from the piercing gaze of the Empire of Light, away from Mason D'Argio and his ever-watching guard. Here, no one would recognise her.

'Katerina Kane! Fancy meeting you here!'

Shit.

A young, athletic man bounced down the wooden boards towards her, taking a bite out of an apple he had just procured from an unguarded stall whilst grinning from ear to ear; a wide grin that didn't quite reach his sad eyes. He was hurting. He just didn't know how to show it. Poor kid. He'd already been through so much.

'Aleister. Surely we shouldn't be shouting our names about just yet…?' she muttered to her ally. They may be away from the northern region, but it was never a stupid idea to play things safe. She'd learnt that the hard way.

'This city would sink itself before joining that bastard Empire. Nothing to worry about, old lady. Relax.' He took another great chunk from the apple. His eyes were bloodshot. Kane prayed that it was only from grief and no other reason. The young warrior had a history of taking setbacks poorly, and losing the love of his life was a hell of a lot worse than anything else that he had been through. Cities like Causrea offered a quick fix for fragile young men and women in the form of a faze pipe. Numb the pain for days at a time. She'd seen the destructive effect of the drug and hoped Aleister was strong enough to steer clear of such temptations.

'After what has happened, do you really think I will

relax?' Kane replied bitterly.

'Honestly, I have a small feeling in the pit of my stomach that tells me even in death you would be unable to relax. You'd probably turn into one of those marching zombie creatures that they tell tales of in the South.'

Kane smiled as Aleister's laugh rang out through the market. Louder than usual. Far too loud for him.

'Probably,' she admitted. 'I just keep thinking of Ella…'

Now it was Aleister's face that dropped. It was a shitty thing to do but she needed to know how he was feeling. He blamed himself. She knew that. It wasn't his fault but that made no difference at all.

'She's all I ever think, Kat,' he said, throat swelling as he swallowed hard, the mask of humour fading. 'That's why we need to keep fighting. She wouldn't want us to stop. I know that with all the strength in my body!'

'You're right,' Kane admitted. 'Of course.'

'Come on. Bathos and Ariel are out gathering intel. Let's grab some food and see what drinks this fair city can offer us.'

Kane nodded. Drink was a temptation she could allow for the moment. *We all have our vices.*

Revenge is best planned on a full stomach.

'Let me see. Do you have any of the Eastern Red available?' Aleister asked the waiter, a short, grumpy looking fellow with a constant frown. Kane tried to imagine what it would be like for the man to smile but it was too difficult.

'I'm afraid recent… disagreements, have led to difficulties in anything being imported from the East and through the Heartlands. May I recommend the Flarian Red? It is a favourite in these parts. You will not be disappointed.'

'Sure. Why not?'

'I'll have the same,' Kane said, handing the waiter back the list of drinks with a thankful nod.

Kane took a moment to look around. The colours of the city were intoxicating – a complete contrast to her drab, grey homeland. Pink homes stood happily next to green and yellow. The blue waters of the canals complemented the cloudless sky above. Joyful conversations sang through the air in a myriad of languages and accents. Everything here seemed to work in harmony with each other. It seemed alien to her. Foreign. Unnatural. But, beautiful.

'Enjoying it?'

Kane snapped back to face Aleister, unable to deny the positive effect that the change in location had done for them. 'It's funny isn't it. As soon as you move away from people who want you dead, your happiness increases,' she answered, shoulders dropping and feeling the weight ease from them. A drink. Good company. Fresh air. Such things would help push the horrors of the recent moons into the distance – a welcome distraction and superior to the bottom of a faze pipe...

'This place is a message to all others. This is what can be achieved when the Empire doesn't have its fingers gripped around your throat. This is what can be achieved when people stand up to an oppressive regime. This is what can be achieved with leaders who work for the betterment of its people and not the other way around.'

Kane smiled. It was impossible to not share in her ally's passion, his will to improve the world; to take down a giant evil dominating the world. But she was old. She wouldn't witness too many cycles and she had made one last promise.

'Revolution is for the young, Aleister. For the old, we have only revenge. My aim is to stare into the cold, dark eyes of that monster T'Chai. Then, everything else we get out of this is a plus. But I will be done,' she said, noticing the weariness in her own voice.

'I don't believe you. You're too good of a woman to stand by and watch such a darkness take hold. You'll see T'Chai dead, but that is not the end. Like I said, you can't relax.

Kane chuckled. She ran a hand through her hair. It was the longest she had worn it for many cycles. Since before she met

Braego. Thin waves of silver threaded between the dark blonde. Old lady indeed.

'We'll see Aleister. We'll see.'

The waiter headed back to the table, this time with two glasses of red wine on the golden tray he carried. Kane took a slow sip. Sweet. Good. She took another.

She was grateful that her friend pushed no further. They knew each other's limits; they'd crossed them on many occasions. For now, Aleister was willing to let things go and Kane knew that was for the best. She wasn't one for relaxing, true; but her body could only take so much. She had been lucky to survive her last encounter with T'Chai; she wasn't sure she would make it out of the next one. Revenge could be a tiring business.

'Reckon we could arrange a meeting with the leaders of the city?' she asked after enjoying the pause in conversation.

'Possibly. It's a strange city, not like most others. They follow no king or queen. Instead, it is ruled by a council of peers. No one knows who they are; they can't be bribed or bought. They do what is in the best interests of the city. It is how the Republic operates.'

No-one knew who they were? The lack of transparency could cause problems. Any group hiding in the shadows could behave as they wish; such power is easily abused, surely Aleister knew that?

Aleister jumped in before she could respond. 'I know what you're thinking, old lady. But look around you. Seems to work.'

Kane couldn't disagree. She might have a few reservations about a shadowy council of peers but, as she looked around at the smiling faces and children giggling as they jumped around the courtyard – she just could not argue with Aleister's words.

The sun began to dip below the horizon, swallowed into the great waters surrounding the unique city. A layer of burnt red brushed the sky. It appeared as though the whole land was a painting, created by some incredible artist who had the imagination and audacity to create a city where one should not exist.

The gentle splashing of the water against the wooden banks echoed through the narrow alleys of the floating city. Children raced through darkened gaps between the houses as they headed home, aware of the fading light and whatever consequences that would follow.

The sound of footsteps caught Kane's attention. She turned her head towards the newcomer – a slim figure dressed in a sky-blue dress that finished just beneath her knees. Her blonde hair dropped to her shoulders in waves, framing a glowing face with lips painted a deep red. She had never seen her before.

'It must be my lucky day,' the young woman said, flashing a perfect set of white teeth. 'The fabled leader of the Red Sons and the first female Inspector from the United Cities of Archania: here, in my city!'

Kane's eyes flashed over at Aleister – the look returned told her that he was just as confused as she was.

'I'm afraid you have us at a disadvantage. You are?' Kane said, lowering her hand under the table towards her hidden weapon. You can never be too careful. She was beautiful, but such a thing could be a useful distraction in combat.

The woman's eyes dropped as she caught Kane's movement. 'Why don't we cut the shit. I know who you are. I am no threat,' she informed them. 'My name is Sara Giudice. I represent some powerful people in this city. Very powerful. These friends of mine have watched with increasing apprehension as the Empire of Light have slowly spread like a plague across the land of Takaara. They are not willing to let such a plague reach the West. Perhaps you may be able to help us out. The enemy of my enemy is my friend. Paesus, I believe, said that.'

'How can we trust you?' Aleister asked, eyes narrowing.

She grabbed a chair and spun it around before sitting gracefully upon it, staring each of them in the eye before answering.

'I'm not asking you to trust me. Yet.'

'So, what are you asking us?' Kane was on edge. Too many people had fucked them over recently. She was done with that shit.

Sara's eyes stared straight back, into her very soul. 'Because I can help you to get what you want.'

'And what might that be?' Kane asked, leaning forward and staring straight back. 'More wine?'

'No, no, no…' Sara smiled. 'Something much sweeter than any wine. Revenge.'

LOST AND FORGOTTEN

I t wasn't the world he had known.

Alien.

Strange.

Arden breathed in through his nostrils, taking in the odd scent around him. Slightly stale. Smelled like smoke and burning wood. It had been like that since he had arrived. Couldn't escape it. He was getting used to it. Didn't make him retch at least and that was a good sign.

He breathed in again, deeper this time. A scratch in the back of his throat forced a series of coughs from his frail frame. He covered his mouth with a hand and frowned as he spotted splashes of black on his hand as he moved it away. Didn't look too good. Throughout his whole time in the Borderlands, he'd never heard of a person coughing black shit from their throats. Wasn't time to fret about that now. Sly had once told him that worrying was wasted energy. Shit happens when it happens and you just need to roll with punches and keep fighting.

Arden had been terrified of the wild warrior the first time they had met. Now though, he found himself missing the axe-wielding maniac. Could do with some support here, wherever *here* was.

He pulled his shoulders back and groaned with each pop running down his spine. Been lying down for too long. No idea how long but, by the way he felt, it was definitely *too* long. His mouth tasted dry and stale. It had been a while since he'd drank anything at all. He stretched his tongue out from his mouth and smacked his dry lips together.

Looking around, he couldn't tell where he was. Couldn't remember much either. Remembered being cold. Wasn't cold now though. He'd been staying with Korvus and Socket. That, he remembered.

He pinched the bridge of his nose, attempting to jerk his memory into action.

An escaped prisoner.

Snow.

The lights in the sky.

Blood.

His blood.

It hurt to think of the pain of the attack. Socket, the man he had trusted the most in the Borderlands. Silly thing to think really. The Borderlands wasn't a place where trust should be easily given and Arden had handed it to the one-eyed archer without a second thought. The old man seemed genuine enough. A legend to the men of the Borderlands. Campaigned with Reaver Redbeard himself.

Killed Reaver Redbeard himself too.

Arden let out a dark laugh. Fine company he was in now. Stabbed in the back by Socket, a man he trusted – just like the infamous Reaver Redbeard. Though Arden doubted there would be songs sang about his life and death like there had been about the great chief. Socket had been in the songs too. If only the bards had known about the treachery. The lyrics wouldn't have been so flattering about the archer then. Or maybe they would be. The Borderlands was an odd place. Deceit and treachery seemed the norm even in places where burly men would cry about the importance of honour.

A load of shit.

That's what it was. Just a bunch of fools playing games with one another until the time came for them to pass on to the halls of their ancestors. Bones. That's what they said when they died. Just bones. Happened to everyone.

Arden started to walk. One foot in front of the other.

He supposed he should have found it weird that there was almost complete darkness around him. A pale blue moon watched over him but that was all he could see. No stars. No mountains. No people. Nothing.

Strange thing was… it didn't seem weird. Felt like the most natural thing in the world. There was no sound. No wind. Just silence. He was alone with his thoughts and the strange moon and that was how he liked it. No one there to betray him. No one there to spit on him and curse him for the golden pupils that gave him away as a mage. No one there to care about his existence at all. Just him.

He walked. And walked. And kept on walking.

His bare feet didn't hurt. They should have hurt but they didn't. So he walked some more.

After some time, he thought back to Socket's actions. He pressed a finger against his back where the blade had pierced his skin. There was nothing there. No wound. No tight skin of a scar. Just smooth flesh. It was as though Socket hadn't stabbed him at all.

He shook his head. He wasn't going to work out was what happened now. Best to just keep on moving. No clue where he was moving to, but he was moving.

Could have been walking for days. There was no way of working out time in this place. The blue moon always hung in the same position – above him and to his right – unmoving.

Beneath his feet, Arden could see a blue light responding to each step he took. The light bounced out around his feet as they pressed against the soft ground. He watched, curious as he kept moving forward. After some time, another light sparked to his left. Then to his right. The blue lights grew, thin blue flames growing with each step that Arden took. Twenty paces away either side of him, the flames flickered and danced away, growing with intensity. He couldn't feel any heat from the moving flames. For some reason, he knew they were not dangerous. They would not harm him, no matter how high the flames grew.

The light from the flames cast a blue haze over his surroundings, illuminating the area and allowing Arden a chance to cast a curious eye on the realm.

Dark, rocky cliffs guided his path alongside the flames, and he thought he could spot a series of wide, wooden bridges connecting each side of the cliffs. More dancing flames popped up at the top of the cliffs as Arden looked either side, as though he himself had willed it.

'The more you wish to see, the more you will see,' a strange voice told him from out of nowhere.

Arden didn't jump at the sound. He turned calmly and looked up into the serene, white face of the creature beside him. Eight feet tall at least by Arden's estimation. Long, billowing midnight black cloak. Thin, wiry, white arms. Long, dark, wavy hair. And those eyes. He remembered those eyes.

Black orbs with what looked like the night sky glimmering inside them. How could anyone ever forget those eyes?

'We have been waiting for you,' the being said. 'The journey to the Sky Plane can destroy the body, mind and soul of even the hardiest men and women. To survive is a gift given to a rare few, Arden Leifhand.' The voice was different to any other Arden had heard in Takaara. Like two voices speaking at once, in harmony. A melodic song that called to him like no other.

'I feel good,' Arden admitted. 'Better than good, in all honesty.' He reached again for the wound in his back and found nothing but smooth skin. 'I should be dead.'

'Death can be a gateway to a chosen few. A gateway to rebirth. Though, for many, death becomes a prison. A place to rot and be tormented for all eternity.'

'You still haven't told me who you are.' Arden thought he had an idea but every time he willed the thought back to his mind, it blew away like the clouds in a strong gale. 'You seem to know me. I'd feel even better if we were on the same footing.'

The being grinned, black lips curling up into pale cheeks and exposing their sharp white teeth. 'I go by many names. You may call me Osiron if it makes you feel more comfortable. This is my home. My world. These people are my people, and I would do anything to see their suffering end.'

Arden did feel better. Funny thing, names. Just the mention of one could ease tension or raise it. He knew brave warriors in the Borderlands who would quake with fear at the mention of Sly Stormson or Bane the Ear-Collector. Admittedly, even recently he would feel his heart leap with amazement when telling anyone that he was a member of Raven Redbeard's tribe. Or that he travelled with Socket – the greatest archer in the North. Names meant something.

Always had.

Always will.

The blue flames danced past Osiron and illuminated what looked like a huge, cavernous city before them. Tall, colossal buildings built with some shiny black rock shimmered against the sides of the cavern. They were built into the walls all around Arden. Eyes wide, he stared at the amazing city as the blue flames allowed him to witness this wondrous sight. An endless city that continued far past the horizon. His mind should have warned him that this was all some kind of trick – magic or the like. But again, it all felt so normal. Like it was meant to happen here and that anything different would have been wrong.

'Where am I?' Arden muttered to himself as figures crept out onto the balconies hanging from the sides of the cavernous walls. Men and women poured out from their homes, the now familiar blue haze shining around them as they gazed out at Arden and Osiron who continued their march between the flames.

'You are where the forgotten dead wait patiently. Where those who have left their world with oaths and promises tethering them to Takaara rage on. Where the tortured and scarred come to plan their revenge, their return to the world,' Osiron said, waving gently to the men and women cheering as they passed them. 'Takaara can be a cruel world at times. The people are even crueller. I shepherd those who are lost here. They can regain their strength and contemplate the correct path to take. Many paths open in this realm. I offer guidance to those who feel lost.'

Arden chewed his lip, thinking over the words of the unique being beside him. 'So why am I here?'

'Same reason as all the others. You were taken before your time. You're lost and need guidance. I can help you with that.'

'I was told that I was a Guardian, that I had a power most would kill for.' The words tasted like ash in his mouth.

'You are a Guardian,' Osiron confirmed casually. 'You have the power to aid me in helping the others. To ensure they can finally rest. Their eternal torment can end with your help.'

'And how can I do that?'

'All in good time my new friend,' Osiron grinned, 'They have waited for what feels like an eternity. A bit longer will not hurt.'

Arden accepted the response. They had time. There was no rush. He knew that, somehow. Everything felt different but comforting. Wrong but right. Time itself felt insignificant as he strolled between the flames and smiled up at the whispering crowds of onlookers and admirers.

'Takaara has existed as a world open to all. A world where men and women can make something of themselves. Be anything they wish,' Osiron said, glancing at Arden. 'A whole land open for discovery and wonder. Any individual could traverse the length of it should they wish and choose their own path.' They frowned, thin brows dropping and a small crease forming between them. 'At least, that was how it was supposed to be…'

Arden thought of the Takaara he knew, well, at least the small part of it that he knew. A few men and women would venture to foreign lands, but most stayed in the cold North. The only way for anyone to make something of their life was to fight. Borderlanders were warriors to the core. Blood and war spun the wheel of life in the Borderlands and not much else seemed to matter. From what he'd heard of the South, things weren't so different. Less fighting perhaps, but there was still war, plague, and injustice. Socket had even told him that rulers were born into their position, not chosen on qualities that they possessed. Thrones were often sat upon by lazy fools who had lived their lives shielded from the horrors around them. They were told that they were the greatest thing in Takaara and that their wishes were more important than anyone else's. Arden trusted his eyes and ears and that trust led him to think of the world events as just a collection of random occurrences that happened no matter what. Sure, people could make their own decisions, but complete freedom eluded them. A peasant couldn't rise to be king. The biggest bastards in the Borderlands would always rule. There was no room for the little guy to stand above the rest. He thought about how it would look if he were to rule the Borderlands. He'd have a nice collection of arrows and stab wounds within the first hour, no doubt. Strength and size were everything to the warriors.

'What went wrong?' Arden asked, hoping for an answer but not expecting much.

'So much…' Osiron said, their voice breaking ever so slightly. 'Potential. There was potential for greatness with Takaara. The bitter thing about potential is that there are always two sides to it. There is potential for everything to go as planned: for everything to end up good and wholesome and right. But there is also the potential for failure: for everything to fall in darkness. There are so many moving parts in Takaara, so many people making split second decisions based on a thousand different variables. The potential for error is great, unfortunately.'

Arden silently watched as one of the onlookers stepped cautiously down a battered and worn set of black steps that led down from the wall to his left. An anxious man, frowning, eyes darting around him, headed towards them. His pace quickened as his boots dropped to the level ground and he ignored the flickering flames, stepping through them as though they were not there at all. The newcomer dropped to one knee and lowered his head as he reached them, facing the ground.

Osiron tilted their head to the side and peered down at the man. 'Davrus. Rise, my friend.'

Davrus stood, eyes still unable to meet Osiron's. They briefly flickered to Arden before facing the floor once more. The man was dressed for battle. His chest was covered in what looked like large, silver fish scales interlocking with one another. Black gauntlets matched his greaves and a dark, purple wool cape tied with a silver clasp fell to the back of his ankles. His hair was cropped short though his black beard had been left to grow so that it reached the silver clasp attached to his cape. Dark bags sat beneath both of his brown eyes and Arden could see how gaunt and tired the man looked. His cheekbones were almost poking out of his light brown skin.

'We have been waiting, my Lord, for your return. The preparations are complete. Your chosen guests are ready for your arrival in the Hall of Chaos.' Davrus had a harsh voice, as though he had taken too many blows to the throat.

'Thank you Davrus,' Osiron answered with a soft smile. 'Tell the others that I am grateful, as always, for their assistance. Tell the others that I am on my way and we shan't be long.'

Davrus gave a short bow and rushed off back through the blue flames.

'Do they all serve you?' Arden asked, watching Davrus return up the steps to a larger group of waiting onlookers.

'Serve me?' Osiron repeated, slowly running a long, bony finger down from cheekbone to chin. 'They are aware that the only escape from this existence is to help me. Without me, they are lost forever. They would be forced to exist in a realm that does not want them. A realm that was not created for them to reside in.'

'And I can also help you.'

'You can. By helping me, you are helping every single soul trapped in this hell.'

It was Arden's turn to frown. 'Doesn't seem like a hell to me. I've seen worse.'

Osiron laughed, a sound Arden could only compare to a gentle wind gliding past him in the Borderlands. Slow and long – gentle. It was not mocking in any way. 'Your life has been but a speck of dust resting on the top of the tallest mountain. Smaller in size than the smallest of snowflakes. There are worse things than blood and war, than arrows and swords. The physical pain is brief but the mental, the spiritual, those pains are more torturous than a thousand swords in the back. Time works differently here, these people have endured through countless cycles, always waiting for a chance to return, holding on to the hope that they can finish what they started, that they can right whatever wrongs were done to them. This is a hell, Arden Leifhand, though you may not see it yet.'

Arden didn't know how to respond to that. He couldn't claim to be knowledgeable in the way of the world, let alone the hells. All he could do was listen and learn. He couldn't argue with Osiron. He'd felt the pain of a dagger cutting through him and he knew that wasn't nearly as traumatic as the feeling of betrayal that went with it.

'I think I understand…'

'You don't,' Osiron said. 'But you will. You've been through a lot in a short amount of time. We'll take things slowly.'

Arden nodded, chewing on the inside of his cheek. He had been through a lot. A broken mage living in the Borderlands. Finding out that he should have been a prince of the United Cities of Archania. Discovering he was a Guardian with the power to access other realms. Socket's betrayal…

'All my life I felt like nobody.' He found himself saying the words, but he was unsure why. Why was he opening up to this strange creature who barely knew him? 'Then I finally felt like I was getting somewhere. Part of a tribe. Accepted by the great Raven Redbeard. A Guardian. A lost prince… I was getting *somewhere*,' he said through gritted teeth. 'Then it was all taken away from me. That's pain, Osiron. Worse than any dagger in my back. To finally have what I'd desired within reach only to watch as it slipped through the gaps in my fingers like melting ice turning to water. I want to be somebody, Osiron. I'm sick and tired of being nobody.'

Osiron stopped walked. Or gliding. Or whatever it was they did to move forward. Arden copied, turning to face them and staring up into the starry eyes looking down at him with pity.

'You were *never* nobody, Arden Leifhand. You will *never* be nobody.' The dual voice had taken on a hard edge, urging Arden to pay attention. A long pale hand reached out to his face and he didn't shy away as it brushed against his cheek. There was a warmth in the touch. Much warmer than expected. 'There are

24

thousands, hundreds of thousands of lost and forgotten souls who have been waiting for your arrival. You are the bridge between realms, a Guardian who can open paths to end the torture and pain. With you, they will no longer be lost, they will be found. They will no longer be forgotten but remembered. They will be seen. You are the key that I can use to unlock a whole new future for Takaara. A future that will wipe away the pain and horrors of the past. You are *not* nobody, Arden Leifhand.'

A slow burning starting at the base of his stomach flickered to life, rising slowly to his chest before warming his entire being. He blinked a few times, feeling the hairs on his skin stand as one, every nerve in his body aflame and feeling for the first time since he had met Osiron. He glanced up and saw a colossal castle built into the mountainside, as though giants had carved the building using the rock of the mountain itself.

'I am not nobody,' he muttered to himself. 'What must I do to be somebody? What must I do to help the lost and forgotten?' *What must I do to prevent anyone feeling like I did?*

Osiron dropped an arm around Arden's shoulders and guided him towards the dark castle. 'To help the lost and forgotten. You must end their stay in Chaos. There is only one way for these souls to go where they are meant to be...'

'And what is that?'

Osiron tilted their head to take a better look at Arden, magical eyes judging him as the shining stars raced around the black orbs. 'You must help them die, Arden Leifhand. Only through death, can they all be free.'

A RUDE AWAKENING

Aleister jerked up from his slumber, leaping to his feet and blinking wildly, struggling to understand why his face and hair were drenched.

His darting eyes found the familiar hard frown on his sister's face. In her hands was the evidence he was looking for. The explanation for his current predicament. A large, wooden bucket. Empty now, of course, though still dripping with the remnants of water that had been thrown his way.

His instincts wanted to rage, to scream at Ariel for the rude awakening but he was no fool. There hadn't been many arguments over the years that he'd been able to win with his cunning sister and he felt that this might not be one of the few victories. Instead, he chose to study his surroundings. The room was stuffy and hot. No windows but there was a small circular hole in the ceiling. Stone floor with a red and gold rug and black tassels at the ends. A simple bed, his belongings lay scattered on the end, including his cherished sword. Other than that, there was a small, stone ledge sticking out from one of the walls. On the ledge sat a small pipe, still lightly smoking.

Shit.

This was definitely not an argument he could win.

'A faze pipe?' Ariel snapped, voice higher than usual as she threw the bucket at his feet and stared daggers at him. After everything we've been through, you're back on that shit!' She placed her hands on her hips and gave him her best disappointed scowl. He'd seen it all before, of course, but it always worked. He felt the embarrassing burn on his cheeks as he looked back at Ariel and then at the pipe.

'It helps…' he muttered uselessly. By the way her face turned an unhealthy shade of scarlet, he knew he'd said the wrong thing. Should have just shut the hells up.

'*Helps?*' she repeated, horrified. 'It numbs the pain, makes you forget, but that's it! We've been here before. It all rushes back after the hit and strikes you twice as hard. I'm not going through this again, Aleister, I swear it. I can't handle it again…'

'Ariel…' Aleister started towards his sister but stopped as she jerked away, tears filling her eyes.

'No. We all loved Ella. We grew up with her too. Bathos and I are hurting too and we're struggling with it every single second of the day. But we both know that we have to get our shit together and carry the fuck on. You can waste your life away in one of these dens for all I care, or you can get your miserable ass up and do something that would make her proud. I know what I'm doing…' Ariel wiped her tears on her sleeve and sniffed, looking away from her brother.

Aleister couldn't bear to see her like this. He'd been selfish. Trying to numb his own pain meant he had ignored the pain of those he cared about most.

Ella would have hated him for it.

Words were meaningless now. He strode over to the stone ledge and picked up the pipe. In one swift movement, he flung the pipe against the wall and watched as the instrument smashed into thousands of tiny pieces.

'It might not mean much, but it's a start,' he muttered to his sister, unable to meet her stern gaze. She'd seen it before. He wasn't going to convince her so easily this time. 'Does Katerina know where I've been?'

Ariel shook her head. 'You have one last chance, Aleister. Make it work this time. We've been through too much

27

for you to throw everything away with that shit. Come on, Kane has planned a meeting for us. Clean yourself up and meet me in the main square. Time to start acting like the man you always claim to be…'

Aleister sighed and nodded. He couldn't argue with that.

'Your sister told me that you've been busy scouting out lines of enquiry in the city. Trying to find some more support in our battle against the Empire. Any luck?'

Aleister shifted uncomfortably in his chair and purposely kept his bloodshot eyes away from Katerina's gaze. She was an Inspector not so long ago and in that line of work, you have skills that are never lost. She would know where he had been. She would know what he had been doing. And he could feel the heat of shame rising in his cheeks and making him feel as though he was smaller than the mouse scuttling away in the corner of the grand room they sat in.

He'd not had many positive figures to look up to growing up. He'd searched for them, of course. Orphans in the United Cities were mainly forced to fight to survive, to keep going through sheer will and their own guile and ingenuity. In Kane, he had found someone with honour. Someone who pushed him to be better even when she knew he was happy to bend the rules and live outside of the law, a law that she had loved so dearly. He respected her in a way he hadn't respected many people growing up. He'd seen her put up with so much shit from Lower City thieves and Upper City snobs who still frowned at the fact a woman had forced her way into what they felt was a man's position. She fought through the jeers and attacks thrown her way and shrugged off words that would cripple the strongest. She didn't care where you were from. Didn't care how you looked or what God you followed. She only cared about who you wanted to be. And she was one of the first people to recognise that Aleister wanted to be better.

That's why it hurt so much when he finally looked in her eyes and saw the pity and disappointment lurking there.

If there was one thing he hated, it was disappointing

those who cared for him; the few people who suffered when he let them down.

'Nothing much,' he lied, concentrating his gaze on a painting behind Kane. A familiar scene. The Battle of Watchmen's Hill. A charge of cavalry pouring down a hill to wash over the poorly prepared infantry as a rain of arrows fell from the top of the hill. One of the most one-sided battles in the history of Takaara, apparently. Battle preparation and choosing the land became imperative to any army fighting following that massacre. Aleister loved to speak to new recruits joining the Red Sons about the three factors in winning a battle. Knowing your enemy. Knowing your land. Knowing yourself. The Battle of Watchmen's Hill was an easy way of illustrating all three points.

'I spoke to a few leads, but I doubt we'll get any help,' he continued. 'The Empire is feared, even this far west. No one wants to go up against them, especially with the uncertainty...'

Kane swallowed the lie but only because she cared. Aleister knew that. She didn't have the energy to scold him and she knew that Ariel would have already given him a lashing over his stupidity.

'This Sara better be the real deal then. I've had all the success of a eunuch in a brothel with my leads. All dead ends. I fear that if this doesn't pan out the way we wish, then we may have to leave Causrea and search elsewhere. Riskier cities. Riskier people. Just the way things are,' Kane said scratching her cheek and picking up a cloth beside her to wipe the sweat on her brow.

'Things will work out, Kat,' Aleister replied softly. They had to. He couldn't bear the thought of failure now. Not after everything that had happened in Archania. After...

'I know they will Aleister.' Kane sounded more certain than he had expected, snapping the path of thought away from the darkness. 'Ella's death will not be in vain. She will be watching what we do. *Everything* that we do, Aleister.' She stared into his bloodshot eyes, a silent warning to let him know that she knew everything, though they didn't have to speak about it. 'We will make her proud until the last breath we take.' She leaned forward and squeezed his knee to reassure him. 'Let's just make sure that last breath isn't too soon. Aye?' She winked and he smiled. A real smile this time.

'I've got enough in me to keep going for many more cycles, old lady,' Aleister smirked. 'Death itself wouldn't be able to stop me from making this right. From making sure that she is proud of me. I'd fight The Four themselves if I had to. The Empire of Light doesn't seem so big knowing that.'

Kane dropped back into her chair and raised her eyebrows, letting out a gentle chuckle. 'Well, I certainly hope it doesn't come to that. Not sure I could take on the Gods. I'm more of a street level fighter.'

They laughed together and drifted off into silence. Fighting a grand empire was just as dangerous and ignorant as taking on the Gods themselves in Aleister's mind. Still wasn't going to stop him trying though. He'd faced poor odds before and come out smiling. This time he didn't even care if he came out at all.

'Have I interrupted something?' Aleister turned to see Sara Giudice walking comfortably towards them in red shoes that had a spiked heel taller than anything he had ever seen a woman wear before. *How in the hells can she walk in them?* 'I've walked across graveyards with a livelier mood.'

'It's been a difficult few moons, in truth,' Kane said, rising from her seat before Sara shook her head and waved away the polite gesture.

'No need to stand.' She pulled out her own seat opposite Aleister, brushing down her stunning black dress as she sat and shuffled forwards so that her elbows were resting on the table, her brown eyes jumping between Kane and Aleister. 'We have important business to discuss. I don't want to waste time. The servants will bring some wine shortly. I suggest we get started right away, unless either of you have any objections?'

Aleister blew air out from his cheeks and shook his head, excited to listen to the abrupt woman. Kat just flashed a curious smile and sat forward, mirroring the other woman with her elbows on the table.

'Excellent!' Sara squealed, lips curling up as she glanced at them both. 'Then let us begin. We three are here to discuss the greatest dilemma of our age. The fall of the Empire of Light.'

Kane watched the woman like a hawk. *Plotting the fall of an empire. Shit. Is this what my life has come to?*

She wondered what her younger self would have thought about if she were told that she would one day be drinking wine in the floating city of Causrea discussing taking down an entire empire. Probably would have arrested her and thrown her in the drunk cell to spend the night sleeping off its effects. Wouldn't have blamed her. The whole thing seemed crazy, even now.

'The problem we have at the moment,' Sara was saying to them, 'is that the Empire is growing. Its numbers have increased a hundred-fold over the past few cycles, and they prey on the weak and the downtrodden whilst also appealing to the elite with their views on punishment. Thankfully, times are changing. The last quake brought with it the greatest change to our society since the Breaking of the World. Magic has fled the world of Takaara. Their message of magic elitism and their belief that they are the only ones who can visit the Sky Plane is useless now. They will reform and work this into a better message in time but for now, there is chaos within the Empire. And that is something that we can use to our benefit. It is the reason why my friends are choosing now to act.'

'And who exactly *are* your friends?' Kane wasn't willing to listen to grand ideas and reckless plans without knowing who she was working with. Her time in Archania had taught her that the most dangerous people in a person's life are often close by. If she were to work with others, she wanted to at least know who they were.

'Causrea is a small republic but we are an old and respected nation. The countries in the West listen to us. Where we go, they follow. It has always been the way,' Sara said, shuffling in her seat and grabbing a shiny, red apple from the basket of fresh fruit to her right. She rubbed it against her forearm and took a big bite, chewing loudly in the break of the conversation. 'The Council of Ten rule the West. They have ruled for over three centuries and have overseen the growth of the area. The West has prospered and seen progression even when faced with the plague and silly squabbles between nations. The Council of Ten are the ones who wished for this meeting. They are the ones who have called for action. They are the ones who will not sit idly by as they are threatened from all sides.'

'Threatened from all sides?' Kane repeated, seeking further enlightenment on the Republic's issues. She'd heard of unrest in the Heartlands from time to time and whispers regarding trouble brewing but nothing certain. This was as good a chance as any to gather information.

'The United Cities of Archania is under the Empire's thumb. King Mikkael's death will only increase their hold on that kingdom. The East has one beacon of hope in Darakeche; the Sultan has always hated the Empire and their religion and will fight to his last breath to keep his nation from its grip. The Heartlands are no threat right now, but they send their emissaries with each moon, requesting support to take down the tribes on the outskirts of their land. To the South, we have the Boy King.' Sara sighed and pushed her hair from out of her face. 'A power mad Empress in the East and a boy who considers himself a God to the South. The very world of Takaara is tightening against us, choking us, and threatening to destroy our way of life. The Council of Ten are proactive, not reactive. They do not wish to wait until we are breathing our last breaths to act. They wish to cut the head off the snake before we are bitten. Though, acting without provocation could put the Council in an awkward position. That's where the two of you come in...'

Kane coughed into her fist, using the action to glance at her companion. Aleister looked pale and drawn, dark bags under his eyes worsening. She loved the young bastard, but he was his own worst enemy. She longed to grab him by the shoulders and shake him. To let him know that he had a whole life to live and that he shouldn't spend it rotting away on that faze shit he fell into in dark times. But he didn't need that. He needed purpose and an arm around the shoulder. This Sara girl could provide that. Kane only hoped that Aleister had the energy to do something about it.

'The Empire has caused us pain beyond belief. That can't be denied,' Kane said, staring into Sara's unblinking eyes. 'But to face the Empire, we would need proof that you are willing to fight, lest we become lost and picked off by the bastards.'

Sara nodded and sucked her teeth, the shadow of a smile creeping onto her face at Kane's words. The woman's eyes flickered to Aleister as he broke into a coughing fit, thumping a fist against his chest and silently apologising, eyes watering with the attack.

'You're right,' Sara agreed, confident that Aleister was listening again. 'To fight the Empire and the Boy King would be suicide. Certain death would be the best we could hope for. Therefore the Council has planned to send key messengers on their behalf to the Boy King in the South and the Sultan of Darakeche. The Boy King will be offered a marriage with the Princess of Denbar and lands north of the Amari Desert. In return, we will ask for an alliance between the South and the West. At the very least, we will want a truce, enough time to fight the Empire without having to worry about the Boy King marching his army this way.'

'And to Darakeche?' Aleister asked. 'The Sultan may hate the East but he is petulant and makes rash decisions. What will you be asking of him? The old fool can't be trusted in my opinion.'

Sara snorted and laughed loud and hard. 'I heard about your time in Darakeche. The Sultan has still not forgiven you for your part in his son's exile and the loss of his family's sword. This is why I suggest that you go south to the Boy King with your allies. Katerina, I am asking you to head East, to speak with the Sultan and ask him to prepare his army. The West will extend the hand of friendship to Darakeche and destroy the Empire together. What is left, the Sultan will have the pickings of, like a hungry vulture who has waited in the desert for many cycles. He will lick his lips and salivate at the very thought of ridding that part of the world of the Empress. Be careful that he doesn't bite your hand off!'

Darakeche. The Jewel in the East. Kane had wanted to visit the sultanate for many cycles. The chance had never arisen. Now, she was being asked to head there to prevent the spread of the Empire. Two birds. One stone.

'And will I be travelling alone?' Kane asked, aware that the journey would be a perilous one. 'Darakeche is a long way from here. The capital of Mughabir is a safe city but the towns and cities on the way will be dangerous. Takaara has been chaotic since the magic failed and the quakes are making people uncomfortable. More than usual.'

'You will be travelling with the Sword of Causrea. One of the greatest swordsmen this republic has ever seen. He will ensure that your journey is as comfortable as possible, Katerina.'

Kane bristled at the information. The Sword of Causrea. A famed warrior tasked with protecting the Republic at all costs. A champion who chose a life of servitude and celibacy to devote his life to Causrea with no distractions. Such a companion would be interesting to spend a long journey with, make no mistake.

'I am surprised that the Republic would be willing to let such a figure leave the city…' Kane said, eyebrows still threatening to reach her hairline.

'The Council realise that this task is of utmost importance. Strange times demand difficult decisions to be made. The Sword is leaving Causrea but Causrea never leaves the Sword. He will carry the Republic in his heart every step of the way, such is his life.'

'And what about me?' Aleister asked, sitting up in his chair and rubbing at his tired eyes. 'Will I need any escort to the South?'

'I presume you will want your sister and your friend to journey with you. That is acceptable. The Boy King is not fond of official messengers from the Republic. He sits in the capital city of Ad-Alum in his Kingdom of Zakaria and endlessly plots the downfall of the whole Northern hemisphere. My advice is for you to travel with the merchant caravan leaving at the end of the moon. They will shield you from any unnecessary questions and divert attention away from your mission. The lead merchant, Abdulaziz, is one of the few allowed access to travel south and he has built up an understanding with their people over many cycles. Relationships between the West and the South are strained. There was an attack on the Council recently and we believe that the blame lies at the feet of the Boy King,' Sara explained. 'We can do what we can to minimise the risk but there's only so much we can do. The land is harsh and does not greet strangers with open arms. I trust that you can defend yourselves if it comes to it.'

Aleister shrugged. 'If it comes to it. We're used to the dangers of the road.'

Sara smiled and pushed her chair away from the table. 'Then I believe our work here is done. I will meet the two of you once more before you leave and ensure that you are clear with the arrangements. Until then if you need anything, anything at all, just let me know. The Republic of Causrea, and the West, is in your debt. May The Four guide you.'

Kane grunted in response and turned to Aleister. He offered her a weak smile that didn't reach his tired eyes. She offered a silent prayer in the hope that he would have the energy and the will to complete his important task. Convincing the Boy King to go against his violent impulses would be a job only the very best could pull off. But difficult or not, it had to be done. The fate of Takaara rested on it.

TRAITORS

'This don't feel right. Too deep into the Borderlands for my liking. Hillheim is barely half a day's ride,' Sly muttered to his companion as they surveyed the four lumbering warriors around the fire. Through the trees, he could see that they were well-armed but at ease: settled in for the night with a small tent raised in the clearing beside the heat of the roaring flames. *Too comfortable.* 'Four Barbarians this deep into the Borderlands after we were supposed to have wiped the bastards out up north.'

Cray grunted; his own dark, beady eyes fixed on the men in the clearing. 'Maybe we lost...'

Sly had to catch the laughter in his throat. Never had Cray down as much of a joker. A bit of a clown at times, sure, but not one for outright jokes. The Barbarians were good for a scrap, a skirmish or two. But they had been up against all four tribes and the Borderland warriors had been baying for blood. Some of the greatest names in history had trudged north to finally wipe the stain of the Barbarians from their land once and for all and Sly couldn't entertain the thought that those men and women may have lost. Men and women had fought for Saul, Raven, Bane, and Herick. The four tribes united in their hatred of the simple warriors north of them. The savages would have given it their best shot, but it would have been over by now.

'Cowards,' Sly said, nodding to himself. That made the

most sense. 'Fleeing from their destroyed homeland and getting lost in the Borderlands.' That had to be it. Damn cowards. *Could put them out of their misery.* He unhooked the clasp on his belt to release his axe. Four against two were better odds than he was used to. He couldn't bear the insult of four great oafs blundering around his home. He'd make it quick, at least. Get it over with.

'Wait.' Cray nudged his elbow and pointed to the edge of the clearing. Two more figures walked through the shadow of the watching trees and into the firelight. The Barbarians grunted a greeting to the newcomers as they comfortably took a seat on the wide logs that had been chopped down.

Sly frowned.

Two women. Women he faintly recognised. Women from the Borderlands. From Herick's tribe. They bore his mark on their forearms, clear even from this distance.

'Prisoners?' Sly asked hopefully. The women sat with ease amongst the Barbarians, smiling and laughing as they shared a joke across the heat of the fire. He could see weapons hanging from their belts and a spear within reach of one of them on the ground nearby. They were no prisoners.

'Allies,' Cray croaked.

'*Traitors!*' Sly spat, fighting the urge to scream and run headfirst into the clearing, axes leading the way and weaving a red dance for all to enjoy. He'd have done it too. But you don't live as long as he had in the Borderlands by making rash decisions. No matter what the others might say about him, he knew when a fight was beyond his skill. He knew when to take a step back and regroup. Wouldn't do anyone any good if he was killed out here in the snow by Barbarian and traitor scum. The time for him to be bones wasn't yet at hand. He had business to attend to. He needed to know what the hells was going on in the Borderlands.

Turning to nudge his ally, he blinked and jerked up. The idiot was already running at full speed, darting between the trees, sword pointing its way towards the warriors in the clearing.

Shit.

Stupid move but Sly had to admit, the bastard had balls bigger than the fucking moon. He chased after Cray, whipping out both of his large axes and grinning wider than he had for some time. His cheeks ached with the rare action. Nothing like an unfair scrap to get the blood flowing.

The Barbarians were startled by the mad warrior heading towards them. They jumped to their feet but not fast enough. Cray stabbed methodically through the first one's stomach before kicking at his body and wrenching his blade free in time to slash the weapon across the next warrior's throat, spraying the red stuff across the campsite.

Sly swung with all his might. His axe dug into the back of the Barbarian's skull but he didn't stop there. Pulling his first axe free with a sickening squelch that was music to his ears, he twisted and brought his second axe up and across the shocked warrior's throat, slashing with clinical precision. Without stopping to admire his work, Sly moved on. He dropped to one knee without breaking a sweat and chopped behind the knee of the brute swapping deadly strikes with Cray. Sly smirked as the bastard screamed in anguish and buckled, falling to one knee himself as Sly stood back up. Cray buried his sword straight through the man's open mouth and out of the back of his head. No mercy.

This was the way of the Borderlands.

Four down. Two to go.

Not wasting time, Sly spun, knowing that it was just the two women left for them to deal with.

The odds were now to his liking. The two of them left to face off with the two traitors. Bloodied axe raised in one hand, a second gripped tightly in his left, guarding any strike for his chest, Sly was ready for the fight.

What he wasn't ready for was two women smirking with arrows notched and bowstrings drawn. Judging by the huge muscles glistening with sweat on their drawing arms, this wasn't the first time that the females had used the weapons.

Sly's smirk dropped as he stared into their cold eyes. Bastard of a situation to get themselves into. He'd fight to the death but there wasn't much he would be able to do from this distance against bows. Needed to get nice and close to deal death with these axes. Throwing them was pointless. They'd have enough time to dodge the blow and release the arrows. Not a good way to go.

'Fucking traitors.' Cray hocked up a thick load of green slime from the back of his throat and spat at the women's feet. 'Herick will fucking gut the both of you when he finds out.'

Sly noticed the slight confusion in the women's faces. The way their eyes flicked towards one another and their brows creased ever so slightly.

'Drop your weapons,' the woman closest to Sly commanded. Her blonde hair was tied in an intricate series of knots before falling past her chest. A small, curved scar like a crescent moon sat just beneath her right eye. She'd seen battle. That was clear to him. 'Drop your fucking weapons or this arrow will go straight between your eyes, bastard.'

Sly chuckled. Some might think he was mad for laughing while he had a deadly weapon aimed at his face but if you couldn't laugh at death then what the hells could you laugh at?

'Ask nicely and I'll see what I can do.' He flashed her his winning smile. She grimaced back. She was pretty. Strange thought to pass through his mind but it had been a while since he'd been with a woman. Kiras had always mocked him and said that he'd find a pig pretty in the right clothes and perhaps she had been right. Still, this one seemed fair enough. He'd always felt that an uglier bastard would be the one to kill him. Couldn't complain if this was the last thing he saw.

'Drop your weapons,' she repeated. '*Please.*'

'We drop our weapons and you kill us,' Sly said with a shrug. 'We keep our weapons and you kill us anyway. Though I reckon I could get close enough to do some damage to at least one of you. Might as well die with weapons in hand. It's the way of the Borderlands.'

'The Borderlands are changing,' the warrior at the back snarled. 'Or have you been living under a rock for the past moon? Certainly smells like it…'

Sly sniffed and then chewed the inside of his cheek, mulling over her words. They hadn't been away for too long. But in the Borderlands things could change faster than the fading light in winter. Things had been settled for a while, since Reaver's passing. A few scuffles and harsh words spoken between tribes but nothing more insidious. Maybe the plague of chaos had travelled from the cursed South and up to the icy lands of the North. Stranger things had happened.

'What the fuck are you talking about?' Sly asked, keen to find out what had happened in his absence.

The scarred woman glanced over her shoulder at her companion, arrow still locked on Sly though the string was no longer pulled tight – archers could only pull that string back for so long. Too much effort. The one at the back nodded to the scarred woman who sighed, eyes darting from Sly to Cray and back again, judging the filthy warriors still marked in the blood of the Barbarians and the darker stains from the fight in the temple. They must have looked a right pair of bastards. But strength in battle was respected in the Borderlands. Surely that hadn't changed since he'd been gone?

'The last quake destroyed some of the towns in the Far North. Not many survivors. Herick knew our island would be destroyed soon enough. He made a pact with the Barbarians.'

'What kind of pact?' Sly growled, feeling the anger rise from the pit of his stomach. Any pact with the scum of the Barbarians wouldn't be good for the Borderlands. Herick was a fool.

'A united Borderlands – including the Barbarians. All under Herick's rule. A king of the Borderlands ready to usher in a new age for our people.' The right side of her mouth curled up so far up her face that Sly wondered if she'd torn a muscle.

'I doubt Saul would have been happy about that. The warriors of Raven and Bane's tribes aren't too keen on the Barbarians either. The Borderlands wouldn't just roll over and let this happen.' He said the words, but he wasn't sure if he believed them himself. The Borderlanders were a fickle bunch. Whatever made their life easier usually worked for most. A fair few would hate the idea of the Barbarians living among them but would enough be willing to risk their life on it? He wasn't sure. And that made him fucking uneasy.

'Saul?' The woman repeated, sharing a laugh with her ally and rocking her head back in mirth. 'That big bastard is dead. Sent to see his cursed ancestors. Bones. Nothing but bones now.'

Saul. Bones.

Sly had dreamt of the day. Most of the dreams had involved his axe finding the perfect spot in the chief's throat. Enough to spill the blood but not so much that he would die quickly. He wanted the prick to look him in the eyes and see that he was the better man. Now he wouldn't get that chance. Saul was dead. Bones. *Shit.*

'Bones?' he said again, as though the saying of the word would make it seem more real to him.

'Aye,' the woman at the back said. 'No tears were shed at his passing. Bastard wanted to join us with the South. Made a deal with some southern mage. It was stand with the Barbarians and Herick or stand with Saul and the South. Easy choice for most of us in the end. Raven and Bane fucked off south anyway, their tribes stood with Herick.'

Cray cursed behind Sly and spat in the snow. Seemed like they'd picked the wrong moon to head south.

'Word is that Raven and Bane are dead anyway. And good riddance to them!'

Without thinking about the implications, Sly stepped forward, hands still gripping his weapons. The bowstring tightened once more; arrow aimed straight between his eyes. He stopped and snarled at the bitch.

'Bane can rot in the dirt, but Raven was a good man. Honourable. Strong. He was a good leader, so don't you foul your mouth with shit about Redbeard…'

'Touch a nerve?' the woman chuckled at his unease. She squinted at him and the smirk returned. 'I know who you are. Sly Stormson. Raven's dog.' Sly twitched at the insult but that arrow was awfully close now. 'Herick could use a warrior like you, and your friend here. There's nothing else for you in the Borderlands. It's Herick or death. That's why we were willing to ride with those big brutes.' She motioned towards the dead Barbarians with a cock of her head. 'You can come with us to Hillheim if you'd like.

Then on to the capital to see the new chief himself. He was fond of your big friend, Baldor. Maybe he'll give you a chance. What do you have to lose?'

He thought about it. The only way to find Kiras and discover what kind of mess the Borderlands was in would be to keep breathing. Everything else was secondary.

He turned to Cray who wore that familiar frown and thick, furrowed brows. He wanted to find his family. Again, staying alive was essential to both of their plans.

'We'll join ya.' Sly dropped his axes to the ground and raised his open palms in the air. He'd surrendered a few times before and come out alive. Nothing made him think this was gonna be anything different. 'Be good to see Herick again. Need to tell him about Baldor. Was like a father to him.'

'I'm glad you see sense.' The scarred woman lowered her bow and slipped the arrow back into her quiver. Sly nodded grimly at Cray whose eyes widened as he started forward.

He felt the blow across the side of his head like a horse stamping on his skull. A flash of light crossed his eyes before he fell to the ground, body stiffening as his arms snapped to his side. He could see his dropped axe inches away from his face, but he couldn't move to reach it. Pain surged through his head as brown boots stepped over him. He heard angry voices shouting over him. The females and Cray, arguing back and forth. He could barely make out what they were saying as the sound of the world hit him again like a wave crashing against rocks.

'I know who the fuck he is! That's why I don't trust him. Get him on the horse and keep your damned mouth shut. We're half a day away. The boss can decide what to do with him then.'

'You'll pay for this, girl. Mark my words.' Cray's voice.

'No. I'll *get paid* for this. Mark *my* words, bastard.'

Sly saw the boot coming but he couldn't move. He felt his nose crack and that was the last thing he felt.

Hillheim.

Shitty town.

Shitty people.

Too close to the South for many of the Borderland warriors to give a shit about it. Too close to the North for anyone in the United Cities to give a shit about it. Trapped between people who hated each other and waiting for war to erupt at any moment with the volatile nations. Many of the inhabitants of the small town were families of merchants, carpenters, and smiths – people who thrived off being able to travel between two neighbouring nations to sell their goods and make a bit of profit.

Sitting on one of the highest hills in the Borderlands, the town had been converted into a fort during the war with Archania, anticipating invasion from the South. Never happened but the town still bore the effects of that war. A colossal spiked, wooden wall circled the town of Hillheim, dotted with hastily built lookout towers on the southern side.

Even now the towers were manned. Old men with eyesight worse than bats most likely but manned, nonetheless. The town took pride in being the furthest south – the first line of defence was how they thought of it. Wore that like a dumb badge of honour. Sly scoffed at the notion. If they wanted honour, they should have sent more men in the war instead of the boys and men with one foot in the grave that turned up. *Bastards.*

Sly never thought he'd be back but here he was, riding gagged and bound on a slow-moving horse flanked by two bitches and the bastard Cray. Not exactly a hero's welcome but he was alive and that was something. He'd be leaving this town as soon as he could, hopefully with bloodied axes and two more kills on his list.

The gate to the city was open. Arms wide open to welcome any into the town. No need to lock the place up. Who the fuck would attack this shitty town in the middle of no man's land? A few guards stood on lookout at the gate wearing helmets a size too big and cloaks a size too small. No coin for new clothes for the guards apparently. Surprising in a place like this where the citizens valued their wealth over all else. A trait they'd picked up from the South like a plague, Sly thought.

43

He swayed slightly on the horse, head aching from the earlier blow. He eyed the bitch who had hit him, but she wasn't looking his way. Instead, she was facing the open town, nodding at the guards as she passed them with a smile. They waved back and shouted greetings. The women had been here before, that was certain. He wondered how many of Herick's tribe had known of the deceit to come. Had they prepared for the changes in the Borderlands? He was a clever bastard, Herick the Late. Always put himself first and looked after his tribe over all others. Baldor and Kiras had said good things about him but Sly knew that becoming a chief meant climbing a ladder of weak fools who trusted you too much. To get anywhere in this place, you had to look after number one and Herick was the best of the best where that was concerned. Bastard would turn up late to battles when the fight was almost won (or lost). He'd take the glory of victory or accept the thanks of warriors rescued with his late arrival. Of course, he'd taken a fair amount of abuse over it too but through it all, his tribe had grown. First chief to encourage women to join his tribe too.

Clever bastard, Herick. Clever fucking bastard.

The town had that musky smell most towns seemed to have. A mix of sweat and piss and general life meeting together to form a stench thick enough to taste in the air. Not anywhere near as bad as in the United Cities with their thousands of people all crammed in tight between the walls but enough for any who entered to know they were no longer in the wild, free air.

There wasn't much organisation regarding the buildings in the town. Unlike the United Cities where everything had a place, Hillheim, like so many Borderland towns, was more chaotic and open. Folks had built houses, taverns, shops, temples and everything else you could think of wherever they liked. Sly spotted a butcher cutting meat with a great knife as long as his arm; next to the butcher was an old woman greeting a couple of families as they entered a temple to the Old Gods – animal carvings of all kinds peered over the woman, leaning out of the building's face. No one knew what the Old Gods looked like, so some bright-eyed idiot had thought to have them made as animals. People knew animals. Nice and easy for the architects to build then.

Beside the wooden temple, young children ran through an alleyway, chasing each other with sticks pointed forward like thin rapiers, whipping them through the air and giggling as a couple of ragged old dogs chased them and barked, jumping up at them when they managed to get close to the mocking sticks.

Sly watched curiously as one of the boys stared at the four of them on their horses, eyes wide. He dropped the pretend sword, barely noticing as one of the dogs clutched at it victoriously and ran back down the alleyway in triumph, following closely by its mate, barking wildly with envy.

The boy had cropped red hair and murky, grey eyes that glistened with the threat of tears. He wore a tattered navy shirt that had been ripped on one of its shoulders and his trousers were stained with mud and grass. He was staring right at Cray, unmoving.

'Da?' the boy muttered, a filthy hand reaching over his mouth as his body began to shake.

Sly heard Cray's boots hit the stone street as the warrior rushed from his horse and darted between the others, intent on reaching the boy.

The warrior picked the boy up in both hands and held him tightly, allowing the boy's head to rest on his shoulder as the tears began to stream down his face. Cray ran a hand over his head, unable to speak.

'Thought his family would be dead…' Sly said, his bottom lip sticking out over his top. 'Today is full of surprises.'

His scarred companion looked over from her horse, a crease formed on her forehead. 'His family are here?'

Sly shrugged. 'Must be. Saul had them under his wing. That's why he travelled to the South. Saul's orders. Go against the bastard and the kid would be dead by now.'

Her face softened. 'That was Saul's way. Herick is different. You will see.'

'That's how they all start, girlie. Get the support with promises and comforting whispers in your ear. Then they get a taste of power and they never want to taste anything else. I've seen it before, and I'll see it again. The fires of change can only burn for so long. Sooner or later we get left in the darkness and things are just like they were before. Saul, Reaver, Herick. They're all the same. Or at least they all end up the same. Mark my words.'

The three of them sat in silence, awkwardly glancing over at the unexpected reunion. Cray had wanted nothing more than to get back to his family. He'd done that now. Sly wondered what was next for the grim warrior. Stay here and keep by a warm fire and a comfortable bed? Couldn't blame him if he did. Sly was a warrior through and through, settling down had never been an option. The wild land was his wife and two bloodied axes his children. Wasn't ever gonna change. He'd die in the snow with a song of war on his lips.

Still, wasn't for everyone.

Cray bounced over with a loopy smile on his round face, his son propped up on his shoulders with his filthy boots dangling in front of Cray and slapping him on the chest. Not that the warrior seemed to mind.

'This is my son, Jaap,' Cray said with pride, his chest almost fit to burst. 'Jaap, this is Sly Stormson, a great warrior who helped your Da in the south. These women are friends of Herick's.'

'Frida,' the scarred women said, nodding her head to the boy with an easy smile. 'And this is Hilda.' She motioned to the other warrior with a casual flick of the wrist. Hilda grunted, bringing as much cheer to the day as a cup of piss.

The boy smiled and waved at them all before burying his head against his father, face reddening. How the fuck had Cray made such a thing? Must take after his mother...

'If you don't mind, I'm gonna go find my wife and give her the surprise of her lifetime,' Cray said, grinning as his son laughed along with him. 'Been a long time since we've sat down as a family. Saul is gone and I have my family back. If I have to put up with a Barbarian or two then I can bite my tongue and stay my hand. I can meet up with the three of you this evening.' Great.

Another fucking traitor. Swayed by a family he hadn't seen in half a cycle.

'The guards won't let you leave until you've met with the boss. We'll be in Sofia's Den until sunrise. Join us when you can and the boss will decide if and when you will be able to leave Hillheim.' Frida's words were cold but there was a warmth in her face that hadn't been there the day before. Sly was still bound to the horse but Cray was allowed to play happy little families in the town. His reputation really did precede him.

Cray nodded, eyes lingering on Sly for a moment before he gave a grim smile. Sly knew the warrior wasn't going to leave him to his fate. They'd hated each other for a long time but respect was forged in the fires of battle and they'd been in enough shit the past moon or so for Sly to know that Cray couldn't just slink off into the night. Wouldn't be right.

But then, what did right matter here in the Borderlands?

Frida slapped a hand against Sly's horse to get him moving once more as Cray bounded away with his son still hanging onto his shoulders.

'Sofia's Den you said?' Sly called out to her. 'I've heard of the place.' A brothel and a faze outlet. Every town had one. Not the worst place to spend the evening.

Frida raised an eyebrow and peered back at Sly. 'Don't even think about, Stormson. We have a meeting to attend and nothing more. I doubt the women there would let you get your grubby hands on them.'

'Then I'll have to see the men!' Sly noticed the small curl of Frida's lips at the response. Warming all the time that one. It really had been a long time.

The scarred warrior was looking more appealing by the hour.

Faze laced with lavender filled the small room in the den, clouds of the stuff rising and bouncing around the wooden beams that hung low in the room before settling around the small group of people waiting, some crushing the long and slender purple leaves into the head of pipes ready for the buzz of the infamous drug. Sly had tried the stuff once or twice in his youth. Didn't know many who hadn't tried it. The shit wasn't his thing. Dulled the senses. Slowed a warrior down and made him easy for the taking. Last time he'd taken it he'd been goaded into a fight with a mouthy bastard waving boulders for fists. Sly should have had the slow prick but his mind was filled with the smoke and fog of the faze and so he ended up being beaten within an inch of his life. He rubbed at the scar above his eyebrow, remembering how much blood he had lost. Then and there, he'd vowed never to touch the stuff again.

The two women sat either side of him. Frida had been dumb enough to untie his hands but had still kept his axes from him. Still, a man didn't need a weapon to cause damage. Sly could choke her out before she had a chance to move if he wanted to. He glanced over at the three huge, burly men waiting by the doorway. They'd sure have something to say about it if he caused any commotion. The blades at their sides bore a warning to any who may disturb the sanctuary of the den. Sly wondered how many fools had entered a faze-fuelled rage in the den, only to meet death at the end of one of those blades. Folk aren't too smart when caught in the fog of faze.

No. It would be best to wait and get his revenge on the bitch. Somewhere nice and quiet.

Sly could hear the *thump-thump-thump* of bodies slamming against each other in the adjacent room. A woman's faked screams of pleasure sounded through the thin walls, mixed in with the breathless grunts of some patron who'd had enough coin and balls bursting to the brim. Before too long, the man groaned long and hard, pitch rising with delight as he unloaded. There were a few smirks around the room. Frida snorted.

'Well, I hope he didn't pay too much,' she laughed. 'I've had shits take longer than that.'

'I doubt he gives a damn,' Sly shrugged. 'Did what he needed to.'

'True. Better for her. If she screams any louder, she'll have a sore throat in the morning. Thought she was fucking a banshee for a moment.'

Sly exhaled sharply through his nostrils, grinning at the thought as Frida smiled at him.

His lips parted to respond just as the door behind the guards swung open.

An ashen faced, balding man crept out from the room, nervously playing with a loose string of material sticking out from his navy jacket. He avoided all faces in the room like the plague, making for the exit as his lips quivered, threatening to break out into sobs by the look of it. Whatever had happened in there must have been fun. Sly licked his lips at the dark thoughts crossing his mind. Suddenly, he was really looking forward to heading in.

The three guards shuffled to the side and lowered their heads respectfully. The others in the room all stood, dusting down their ragged clothes and bowing slightly to the open door. Sly snorted and stayed in his seat, raising an eyebrow at the exaggerated welcome for whoever was behind the door. This was the Borderlands. Folk in the Borderlands shouldn't behave like this. The place is too close to the South. Acting like the idiots who placed kings and queens on pedestals for nothing other than being born. Fools.

No one else seemed to share his views though. All had eyes to the floor. If he had his axes, he reckoned he could get through at least half of the room before anyone stopped him.

'Is there something funny, Sly Stormson?' A tall, broad woman strutted into the room, stopping as she passed her guards and staring at Sly with a perfectly plucked raised eyebrow. The whole way she held herself informed Sly that she was a woman who would not suffer fools. An elegant purple dress hugged her curvy frame before flaring out past her knees in silver waves. Her slender fingers bore rings with jewels that could rival those Sly had seen in the South. A black crystal hung on a silver chain around her neck, falling tantalisingly close to her ample cleavage. Her lipstick matched the deep, red hair that fell in waves past her chest. Sly noticed that she wore the faint, pale powder on her face that some of the southern women had worn (and some men) but it suited her better. Or perhaps she had just done it better. She was frighteningly beautiful but more than that, she oozed power and intelligence. Sly met her stern gaze and grinned at her emerald-green eyes.

'Stand up!' Frida hissed over him, flashing her eyes his way but keeping her head lowered.

Sly just continued staring at the woman, caught in a game that neither one wished to lose. The room grew heavy with unease. Eyes darted over at Sly and the immaculately dressed woman, all holding their breath in anticipation for the end of the silent game being played between them. After what felt like an age, the woman flashed her perfectly, white, straight teeth and ran a hand down the muscled arm of one of her guards, fluttering her long eyelashes at Sly.

'No need to stand. Sometimes I feel that we may be going too far with these simple pleasantries. I forget myself and my humble beginnings. My parents would be aghast to find their daughter expecting such actions from others, Gods rest their souls.' Her voice was low and rippled with something Sly couldn't discern. A threat. Or a promise. He shook his head, annoyed with himself.

'I stand for no one. If that hurts anyone's feelings then tough shit,' Sly argued. 'I've never seen you in my life. Respect is earned in my world.'

'Spoken like a true warrior of the Borderlands,' Sofia said, nodding and peering at the back of one of her hands, checking the long, red nails that sprouted out from each like daggers. 'But you're in my world now, Stormson. The least I expect is respect.' She spat the last syllable out through her teeth before suddenly changing back to a smile, laughing a fake laugh and stepping aside, holding an arm out to show Sly the way into her room, like he needed the help.

Frida and Hilda looked up and made to enter the room. A guard marched in front of them as Sofia shook her red mane.

'I'm sorry ladies. I need to speak with Sly on his own. Important matters to discuss.'

Sly almost cracked up at the horror on the women's faces at the unexpected news.

'But... I brought him here. *Sly Stormson,*' Frida argued,

'Sofia, surely—'

'*Lady* Sofia,' the woman snapped, the air tense once more. 'You will be compensated for your effort, of course. This matter is not up for debate, Frida. Enjoy my den, consider the night paid for by me. Have your fill of faze, men and women and enjoy yourself for once.' Sofia clicked her fingers and pointed at the weapons on Frida's belt. 'Leave the axes here. They are not yours.'

Frida nodded beneath dark brows and muttered her thanks. She dropped the axes onto her seat and turned, leaving the room in haste, closely followed by her surly ally.

Sly stood and marched into the empty room, smiling as he passed Sofia. *Lady* Sofia he reminded himself with chuckle. The door closed behind him. It was just the two of them.

'So,' Sly said, spinning slowly on the spot, looking around the room at the signs of luxury hanging on the walls and standing on the tables. 'Why is it so important for you to speak with me alone?' He smacked his lips and jumped back into a chair, looking up at the beautiful woman. It really had been a long time.

Sofia frowned and sighed, taking a seat opposite him. 'I'm glad you're alive. Shocked. But glad. You're the one person who may be able to help me.'

'Help you with what?'

'A mutual ally,' Sofia said, leaning forward in her chair, unblinking. 'Kiras of the Raven tribe.'

A PLAGUE OF HUMANITY

I t felt like an hour since he had been there. Or it felt like a cycle. He couldn't decide. Whenever he thought about it, his head throbbed until his thoughts moved on to something else, something easier to grasp.

He couldn't remember sleeping at all since his arrival, but he felt full of energy. Weariness didn't seem to plague him at all, in fact, he felt better than he had for a long time.

Alone, he walked around a forest. The trees were tall and thin like bones but black as though they had suffered the ravages of fire but survived to stand tall and watch over the land. They were bare and he couldn't see any sign of leaves on the ground. He didn't recognise the trees and they smelled strange to him, the stench hanging in the air as he meandered between them. He had no idea where he was going, he just knew that this was the way to go. It should have been odd that he could see or hear no animals amongst the trees. There was no sign of life. Still, he just kept walking.

Eventually, he found himself clear of the trees. A gentle wind swept across him as he reached the edge of a cliff. He peered over the edge, amazed at how white the cliffs were as they loomed over a thin beach and wild waves of the dark sea. He watched the waves for a moment, listening for their crashing against the jagged rocks at the bottom.

Sitting on the grass, he let his legs dangle over the edge.

He wondered if he should have felt scared sitting there. One small mistake and he'd be over the edge. It didn't bother him. Maybe before. But not now. Now he just felt free.

'It's a good spot, isn't it?' A gentle voice danced in the wind.

'Beautiful,' Arden agreed, not turning from the sight but feeling Osiron behind him. 'Always loved just being outside. It's one of the things that's special about the Borderlands. It's wild land, as it should be.'

'Not all of the world is like the Borderlands, Arden,' Osiron lamented. 'Every day the world becomes smaller, men tearing the land apart in order to build and break and scar the world for their own meagre ambition and needs. Takaara is crying out for a defender. A Guardian. Takaara is crying out for you.'

'You told me that saving the people trapped here will involve death. What did you mean?' The statement had been scratching at the back of his mind, niggling at him like an annoying fly always just out of reach so that Arden couldn't swat it away.

'Come with me,' Osiron said, placing an arm lightly around Arden's shoulder. The action felt comforting. 'There is something that you need to see.'

Arden rose from the ground and followed Osiron. The being glided away to Arden's left, inching closer to the edge of the cliff. Osiron shifted to the side so that Arden could see a stone path – steps carved into the very rock itself winding its way down to the beach. Osiron's lips almost reached their pale ears as they gave Arden room to take the first step, cloak swaying calmly in the wind.

The path was dangerous, wet and slippery in paces and although the stonework was not to be laughed at, cycles of natural erosion had damaged certain parts of the path and Arden had to watch his footing as the edge crumbled away. He assumed that Osiron was behind him, but his new friend didn't make a sound as they followed the secret path down to the sands at the bottom.

Arden felt relief as his boots hit level ground once more.

The crashing of the waves was much louder here. It felt soothing to him. He breathed in the sea air and allowed his lungs to take in as much as they could before he let out a long, slow breath, eyes watching the rhythmic flow of the sea. Angry clouds ambled their way towards him in the darkening sky, promising rain soon enough.

'Where do we go from here?' Arden asked, turning to see Osiron peering out at the water.

'Away from the sea. Into darkness.'

To the left of an archway that had been created by the waves slapping against the coast, Osiron pointed a bony finger to a dark cave – its mouth wide open and drinking in the soft lapping, salty water. Arden headed towards the cave entrance, enjoying the feeling of water against his feet as he stepped into the low sea water. It was cool and refreshing.

He followed the water into the cave, running a hand against the natural wall beside him and glancing around the shelter that had been created by the raging sea. He kept walking, finding that the water was a path heading deeper into the structure. After a while, he stopped. He knew that this was where he needed to be.

A small lake had formed in the centre of the cave. Directly in the middle, Arden could see a stump of land. Streams of light managed to creep in through cracks in the wall of the cave, sunlight shone down through a large hole in the ceiling and right down onto the patch of land, displaying a small, stone basin.

Without asking whether he should, Arden stepped onto the lake. His didn't sink this time.

Another step.

His feet touched the water but would go no further. It was like when the icy winds swept through the Borderlands in the harsh winter, turning the lakes and rivers into ice that the children loved to run and slide across. Dangerous but fun.

He looked up, each step carefully taking him towards the stump in the centre of the cave, guided by the rays of light on his path. Walking on water was a thing of dreams and tales of the past but here it felt completely natural. He reached the stump of earth and pressed his feet against the cool, damp ground. Somehow, Osiron was already there, waiting for him next to the basin. He hadn't seen the being pass him on his own path yet here they were. As they should be.

'There are many paths that we may take in a lifetime. Some lead to the light, others into darkness,' Osiron said, their melodic voice ringing through the cavern. 'People make split-second decisions during their lives that can alter things for better or for worse. From this plane, I have watched them make such decisions. I have watched warriors spare unarmed enemies and become friends. I have watched assassins kill kings and queens and change the lives of entire regions in Takaara. I have watched starving women give their last scraps of food to children. I have also watched a dying king make one final journey to see his long-lost son, only to be met with death and cruelty…'

'My father…' Arden whispered. The king of the United Cities of Archania. The man who sent Arden away to the Borderlands to live out a life in the harshest region of Takaara. To live a life as a broken mage ready to be bullied and cast out by all around him. Well, by most people, anyway.

Osiron nodded sadly, dark creases forming above their brows as they frowned pitifully at Arden. 'Your father. A man not only burdened with the task of ruling a great country, but with the knowledge that he had to send away his beautiful son so that hateful, evil people would not be able to use his gift for their own nefarious means. Whatever you feel for your true father, for King Mikkael of the United Cities of Archania, you should feel pity.'

Arden wasn't sure how he felt towards the man. A stranger. He'd only recently heard the man's name and now he was expected to feel something other than rage for the deception of his entire life? It was impossible.

'He sent me away,' he said, rubbing his eyes and blinking at Osiron. 'He sent me away to the Borderlands because he was scared. Well guess what? *I've* been scared.' He jabbed his thumb against his chest as he spat the words out, feeling the rage boiling up inside like lava willing itself to escape from the cage of the volcano. 'I was scared when the other kids would laugh and beat me because of my weird fucking eyes. I was scared when a warrior held his sharp dagger against my throat whilst his friends sacked my town. I was scared when I was forced to fight in the Borderlands against men three times bigger than me because that's what I was expected to do. That's what a man does, right? This is the Borderlands. That's what everyone said to me. Well fuck the Borderlands. And fuck King Mikkael. I was scared but that's how I found my courage. Maybe he didn't find his.' Arden felt hot tears flowing down his cheeks. It was the first time he had cried since leaving Socket and Korvus. 'I was scared when I realised the one person I trusted more than anyone else was the one who had stabbed me. We're all scared. It's no fucking excuse.'

'The weight of a kingdom breaks the backs of even the greatest rulers,' Osiron argued. 'Adding your situation only made it more difficult for him. Then the loss of your mother. Mikkael did well to keep going, even though he fell into a well of despair most would never have escaped.'

Arden could feel something fighting with his rage. Pity. Just as Osiron had said. But he didn't want to feel pity right now. He had a right to be angry. It infuriated him that that was being taken away from him. *Ironic. The fact I can't be angry is making me angrier.* For the first time since coming to this strange place, he was started to feel. Whether it was the conversation about his father or the seclusion of the cave, he didn't know.

'What did you want to show me?' Arden asked, realising that his fists were clenched and relaxing them by his side, allowing his chest to fall as he exhaled.

'We spoke about paths. They are fragile things. One small, seemingly inconsequential decision can wipe out paths before a person or open up a multitude of them. They are not set in stone, unmoving and fixed for all eternity. They flow like the water around this cave. They crash against rocks and separate into streams of potential depending on a myriad of factors and decisions yet to be made.' Osiron flicked their wrist like a dancer. Water jumped up from the lake and danced in the air between them. It moved and drifted with Osiron's calm, slow motions. 'Each path meanders through the planes of existence, they can be seen by the select few. Even fewer can give them… small *nudges*.' Osiron prodded the water gently with the tip of their pointing finger and a single drop of water broke free from the rest, creating its own stream, heading Arden's way. It broke against his chest, darkening his shirt ever so slightly. 'These nudges are made to guide people. To help them with the big decisions and the small ones. Decisions that affect more than themselves. Decisions that can affect cities, countries, worlds even.'

Arden bit his lip, feeling a sudden chill in the air. 'If those able to prod people in certain directions, lead them onto paths of their own choosing – is that not taking away their free will to make their own decisions. To make their own mistakes?'

'It can be difficult to understand,' Osiron sighed, easing the water in a circle and then allowing it to fall into the basin. 'Left to their own devices, humans have shown an extraordinary skill for destroying gifts given to them in good faith. Without these nudges, the paths set before them all lead to a darkness that would swallow the world of Takaara whole. You felt the quakes. They are just the beginning of the world's wrath. It is only just waking up from its slumber and realising that it has been mistreated in its absence. Worse will follow unless humanity is guided onto a more *acceptable* path.'

'Who decides what is more acceptable?' There was no need to ask, in all honesty. He already knew the answer before the question had passed his dry lips.

'Those who can,' Osiron replied, voice sterner than usual, heavier on the air. Their lips pursed and eyes like the night sky thinned for a moment. The chill suddenly left the cave as Osiron smiled and turned their palms upwards, their laughter relaxing Arden instantly. 'I have been foolish. It has been some time since I have spoken of this to someone of your plane. Let me show you. Often seeing is believing in Takaara. Here it is also true.'

Osiron beckoned Arden over next to them. He joined the strange being, accepting the long, comforting arm around his shoulders again and following those mesmerising eyes towards the basin. Arden gasped as the water spun around the circular stone, increasing in speed with each cycle before stopping all of a sudden. The water was as still as the stone itself, reflecting the sunlight shining from above.

'Humanity was gifted everything it needed to make a paradise. A world where all can live and be free. Let me show you what they did with that gift, Arden. Let me show you how they have treated one another and the world around them.'

A deafening roar dropped Arden to his knees as the water around the cave erupted in a liquid fury. The lake rose and crashed upwards against the dark rock, filling the entire cave but leaving a small shelter surrounding the stump of land in the centre. Arden crept back up, arm raised above his head as the spray from the waves fell upon his face. Osiron just stood there, slight amusement etched on their white face as the starry eyes glanced up at the awesome display of power. They clicked a slender finger and thumb and the noise stopped just as fast as it had arrived.

This time the colours around Arden had changed. The water turned a clear white, familiar shapes dancing in the light against it, images of the past and old faces Arden recognised swimming all around him. The closer he got to the water, the clearer the images became. His first meeting with Socket. Arden felt his heart almost burst with joy at the memory. A reminder of the pride he had felt at the archer's kind words. Sly's scarred face as he spat at Arden, screaming at him to release his arrows away from him. Ovar pleading with Arden to release him, to let him go back to his family… The thud of his head hitting the ground as cheers roared around the Great Hall. Hard memories. Bittersweet reminders of the life he had lived. A short life but full of vivid events and feelings stronger than the will of the Gods in his mind.

'You feel that humans should be left to their own decisions. Both good and bad,' Osiron said, guiding Arden's eyes to violent images of the past displayed on the wall of water around them. 'That is your choice. Your decision. I will say no more on the matter. Instead, let me show you some of the decisions that have been made. Just a few decisions in amongst an infinite number of choices I have watched and suffered through.'

Osiron stepped backwards slowly, melting into the water until Arden could no longer see them. He followed, pressing against the shield of water with one hand. It was cool. The water moulded around his hand like a glove, pulling on his arm and enticing him into the faster swirling images around.

There was no sound. The silence seeped into his skin, clogging his lungs and choking him until he coughed, falling down onto his hands and knees. Falling down onto the cold snow of the Borderlands.

Spitting on the snow beneath him, he breathed in heavily through his mouth, shaking his head to fight the growing ringing in his ears. He stood carefully and looked around. It was as though looking through watery eyes. He could see a short, bald figure barely five paces from him.

Herick the Late.

Arden had seen the tribe chief not long before leaving with Socket and Kiras to the Far North. The chief had laughed and joked with the group, even speaking of Baldor like a father who missed his son. Arden had liked him.

This Herick was different. He had a red gleam in the eye like the mirrored reflection of fire though Arden could see no flames. The warrior strode past him. Each movement seemed as though Herick had been painted in a moving picture that only Arden could see but it had been lost in the rain and the paint was dripping and becoming blurred at the edges.

'Hard decisions must be made in times like these. Tough decisions that no one enjoys. Believe me, I took no joy in the pain of our kin.' Herick's voice echoed around Arden, coming from different directions and unbalancing him for a moment. The voice rose and fell at strange, unnatural points but Arden could understand it all. 'You should have just put your weapons down when I asked the first time. Five of my best warriors are dead and that is on you. I will accept some of the blame. Admittedly, I should have realised that you have been around Raven too long. His rhetoric has corrupted you and blinded you to the cold, hard truth of our people. To survive, we must evolve from what we have been. From what we are. The Barbarians offer us the best chance to keep our way but with added strength. Saul would have sold us off bit by bit to the South. Raven knew what was happening and did nothing. Too soft, like his brother and his father before him.'

'Too soft? Raven Redbeard is ten times the man you are. Cowards stab in the back, Herick,' another voice bellowed, a voice Arden knew only too well. A voice that stopped his heart. 'Raven would have looked Saul in the eye and let him know who the better man was.'

'Raven is dead.' Herick smirked at Kiras, enjoying the pain on her face as the reality hit home. Arden tried to look for her, to follow the sound of her voice but she was nowhere to be seen. All he could find was the blurred outline of Herick turning his back on her. 'The Borderlands is better off under my rule. I am sorry for this. Baldor really did love you and it pains me to hurt something he cares for…'

Herick clicked his fingers and strolled away without looking back. The light followed him, leaving only darkness. Arden heard swords released from their sheathes as Kiras' screams bounced around the darkness. He blocked his ears with his hands and squeezed his eyes tight shut, not wanting to see or hear her pain. When he opened them, another light flickered in the distance.

He slowed his breathing, pressing a hand hard against his pounding chest as he crept towards the light. A voice roared through the fog of uncertainty.

'The boy has done nothing!' Raven's voice.

'No, and that is the problem. We need him to fulfil his potential if Takaara is to be saved.' Bane. The fog faded and Arden saw Sly fall to one knee, staring at his blood-soaked hand after reaching for the back of his head. Armoured guards slammed their shields into Raven, overwhelming the chief as he reached for a dagger, fighting to the end. Baldor stepped forward, eager to come to the aid of his chief.

Arden cried out as Bane rushed forwards and sliced his sword across Baldor's calf and slid behind him, blade resting against the huge warrior's neck. Another man stepped towards Raven, dagger forgotten beside him as he waited on his knees, resigned to his fate. The newcomer drew a curved blade as the guards and another Borderland warrior held Sly and Baldor still. 'Say hi to your brother for me.' An Eastern accent. The curved blade tore across Raven's neck, splattering blood onto Baldor and

Sly.

Arden just watched helplessly as the scene faded, hot tears streaming down his face as he remembered the laughter they had shared during their short time together. Raven – always there to give advice. Baldor – a gentle giant with a heart of gold. Even Sly – a bastard who would kill to protect his tribe.

The next light was brighter than the others. He could see three figures standing in the snow. Beautiful green lights bounced around the sky above in a mesmerising dance of the heavens and a colossal, familiar castle loomed in the background of the scene beside a stunning valley.

He'd been there not so long ago.

Arden could see everything as clear as day in the Borderlands. It felt odd to watch the scene play out from this angle. It felt odd watching himself frown as the dagger found his back. There was no pity on Socket's face. That's what hurt Arden. The archer didn't give a shit about what he had done. Arden looked away, unable to look at the man he had worshipped growing up. The man he had thought was a good friend and ally. The man he had trusted above all others.

Instead, he turned on Korvus.

Blood raced through his veins, his heart thumping harder than Baldor's Warhammer against a Barbarian. All he could hear was the rushing of his blood, the thumping of his heart, the ringing of fury and rage wrapping itself around him. *Korvus. He was the bastard who had done this. He had made Socket do it. Why else would Socket have stabbed him in the back?*

'Herick chose to torture someone who had called him a friend,' Osiron's voice was close to Arden's ear but he couldn't turn to face them. His eyes stayed fixed upon Korvis, the bastard mage who had taken everything from him. 'Bane betrayed and killed those who cared for you and protected you in battle. An outsider himself, he should have done more to better the Borderlands, not destroy it. And Korvus…'

'Korvus is a sick man. A plague that needs to be wiped from the world before he hurts anyone else.' The words ripped from Arden's throat before he had any chance to think. He could almost taste the venom in them as they passed his lips.

'He is. They all share the same sickness. The same corruption,' Osiron agreed. 'It is the plague of humanity. They crave power and will do anything to gain it and hold onto it, sucking the life out of anything that gets in their way. This plague will destroy all in Takaara if left unchallenged.'

He could hear Kiras' screams. See Raven's resigned look and sad eyes as he fell. Smell the blood as it filled his mouth following Socket's betrayal.

'There are others, these are just glimpses of the plague. Many more have suffered like you.'

An image of a young boy burning in white-hot flames flashed into Arden's mind followed by a silver-haired mage laughing with a young prince lying on a throne.

'What can I do?' Pain shot up his arms as he clenched his fists, burying his nails into his palms.

'We must wipe this plague from Takaara. Use your gift to lead those lost in Chaos and onto the path to a better world. You will be the bridge that can lead them from their prison, Arden. I will show you what you must do.'

Arden's eyes burned and he felt the power roaring back through him, a power he had only felt once before. He roared and pushed with all his rage and frustration, closing his eyes and feeling a rushing wind tearing all around him.

Could have been minutes or cycles when it all stopped. Arden had no idea, and he didn't care. He opened his eyes and looked at the army of warriors waiting in front of him, glowing blue flames dancing around their frames as they lowered themselves onto a knee, bowing their heads.

Arden smirked as Osiron gently placed their hands on his shoulders.

'They will follow you wherever you may lead, Arden. The Empire, just like Korvus and Socket, wanted you to come here to defeat me. They wanted you to wipe away the chance of these heroes being given a chance to return to Takaara. You should have been a prince in Takaara but that was taken from you and you were handed a world of pain and misery in return. Lead your citizens back to their home. Lead them and show them a better life. You couldn't be a prince in life, but you will become the greatest prince in death. You will become the Prince of Chaos.'

THE FIRST STEPS

'Luck? Don't believe in that shit,' Aleister laughed. Kane could see the shake in the hand he held out for her. At least that proved that he hadn't been taking faze for a while. No setbacks whilst they had been waiting to leave the city. She'd hardly slept since meeting with Sara, worrying about Aleister and what he would be up to away from her protective gaze.

She slapped his hand away with a smirk and pulled him close for a hug, smiling wider as she felt him relax at the physical contact. His arms wrapped around her as he dropped his head against his shoulder.

'Well, even if you don't believe in it, I'm offering you all the luck in the world on your journey, Aleister. You're a good young man and I hope we see each other soon.'

'No need for the tearful farewell, Kat. We'll see each other again,' Aleister replied, pushing her playfully away but she kept her hands gripped against his arms, keeping him close. 'Can't get rid of me that easily. I'm like an unwanted wart.'

Kat choked back the bile and laughed at the thought. 'Disgusting. As always. But you're never unwanted, Aleister. Know that. The next day we meet will be a joyous occasion, I promise.'

'I'm looking forward to it already, Kat.' Aleister had that

mischievous grin on his face but she could see the truth in his teary eyes. 'I'll miss you. Stay safe.'

'And you, my friend. Look after that beautiful sister of yours. And Bathos.'

'Seriously?' Aleister arched an eyebrow. 'We both know they'll be pulling their hair out trying to ensure I stay out of trouble.'

It was true, but she didn't admit it. He was a better man than he gave himself credit for. Unfortunately, his confidence could fluctuate more than the northern weather and every now and then he needed a reminder of how good he could be.

'Remember who you are Aleister. Remember what you have done. Remember what you are capable of.' Kane lowered Aleister's head and kissed the edge of his hairline softly before finally releasing him. 'I will remember. No matter what happens.'

She waved at the others waiting for him in the shadow of the great library. Ariel and Bathos waved back with huge smiles. She wondered if she would see them all again. The sad thing was, chances were slim. They were each heading off to the far corners of Takaara, across dangerous lands full of turmoil and malice. If she saw them again, it would be a great day indeed.

The three warriors joined up with the passing merchant caravan, greeting their new companions and jumping onto carts pulled by strong horses at the front of the line. It would be safer for them to travel with the traders. Anything else would just cause too much attention and that wasn't what they needed heading south.

She pulled a note out from her breast pocket and read the small, scrawled writing on the front. *The Red Sons.* Kane would be passing by the region where the Red Sons had last been sighted. Aleister needed to let them know what had been going on in his absence. If possible, she would pass on the message and ensure that Aleister could inform his old friends of what must be done. Another item on the list of things to do for the old Inspector.

'A good fighter. Needs to stay off the faze though. That shit messes you up big time.' Sara. The advisor shook her hooded head and clicked her tongue as she watched the caravan head towards the gate out of the city. 'Tried to rid the city of the stuff but the dens pop up somewhere else before too long. Best to take a cut of the profits and keep an eye on the desperate fools willing to use the stuff.'

'An ill-judged mistake from a young man,' Kane replied. 'The ignorance of youth. He has overcome much worse in his life.'

'I know. That's why we want him on our side. He will be better off out of the city and back on the road. He earned his name with the Red Sons. Now he has that name to live up to. I expect the best.' Sara sighed and tightened the black cord around her white robe, twisted it into a knot and pulled the robe tighter against her slender frame. 'You have a name too, Katerina Kane. The Council of Ten have always been impressed with your work. Admired you from afar.'

'I'm honoured.' Kane inclined her head as Sara began to walk towards the dust clouds billowing behind the travelling merchants exiting the city. 'I only hope to do them proud with my work in the East.'

Sara took her arm and carefully guided her down the stone pathway. 'They trust you. Too much depends on it to fail. No pressure, of course.'

'Of course not,' Kane chuckled morbidly. No pressure. Just the fate of the world.

There was only one path out of Causrea. The floating city had one wide bridge that passed a hundred paces over the sparkling blue water. Guarded by three hundred of the city's finest warriors, the bridge could be pulled up from the city's side within minutes if needed. Few armies had tried to take the city by force, but none had come close. Causrea was a unique city on the water where people knew they were safe from the constant worries of nearby nations, especially those in the endless changing Heartlands. Leaving the city felt like accepting that her life was to become forfeit once again. It was the same feeling she had when she had left Archania. Leaving her home was torture but it had to be done. She couldn't have watched that kingdom burn under the fires started by Mason and the fool King Asher. Her only regret was that she hadn't been able to find the other prince. The missing Prince Drayke. Her son.

He was out there somewhere. In the wild. Alive. *Gods I pray that he is alive. Take my life if needed but promise that he is still breathing.*

Word hadn't travelled far about the prince. Asher and Mason would have wanted to have kept it quiet. A kingdom losing a prince didn't look too good. They had already been bruised by the attempted rebellion and the destruction of most of the Lower City. The smoke had still been rising as she had left the city days later under threat of death, the image of her friend Lord Tamir's death still playing on her mind. A quick, sad farewell with General Dustin Grey and that had been it. Out in the wild – just like Drayke, she hoped. In the darkest corners of her mind, she wrestled the thought that her son had been taken to the dungeons by the king. Tortured. Beaten. Killed. She knew what happened in the depths of the dungeons beneath the palace. She'd put enough people behind those bars over the years after all.

Ignoring the thought like she would a persistent merchant shouting in the street, she thought on lighter subjects. 'So, this Sword of Causrea. What is he like?'

Sara snorted as they passed the archway leading onto the great bridge. 'You're in for a treat. That's all I'm willing to say. The surprise is always worth it. Hate to have it spoiled upon a first meeting. Never gets old…'

Kane was intrigued. She knew little of the Sword of Causrea but what she had heard told her that she was acquiring a partner of supreme skill with a blade and impeccable manners. The stories of the Sword had grown wild and larger with each telling, as with all tales but there must be a grain of truth in each of them.

'The Sword lives only half a day's ride from the gate. Close enough to be of service when needed but far enough to enjoy the pleasures of solitude,' Sara explained. Kane could understand that. Peace and quiet. She'd enjoyed the hustle and bustle of city life but with each passing cycle she understood the need for time away and reflection. Her rides to Hangman Hill above the city had become a part of her routine, a chance to step away from the busy markets and endless hum of Archania. In her youth, she dreaded the thought of moving out to the quiet countryside. Now, she couldn't think of much better. She peered out across the edge of the bridge, staring at the seemingly endless deep blue of the sea surrounding the magnificent city. Sunlight danced off the water in a way that it never seemed to up north.

Braego had been tempted to move back to the Borderlands from time to time. He'd missed the wild, open spaces. Whenever he had raised the idea, she had laughed and thought him mad. Now though, she could see why he missed his home. Moving away from the United Cities had barely crossed her mind, even since her retirement. Here, with the cool breeze caressing her in the warm light of the sun and the fresh air always embracing her, wherever she may be, she thought that maybe she could have moved here years ago. She could have been happy. That chance was gone now.

She had a mission.

She had people relying on her.

'How long have you lived in the city?' Kane asked her companion.

'Fifteen cycles, pretty much,' Sara said, clicking her tongue against the roof of her mouth as she thought about it. 'Fifteen cycles next moon if my memory serves me correctly.'

'Where were you before?'

'Born in Causrea. I was taken at the age of five from my bed. Slavers used to use the city as a market before whisking children away on boats. The city eventually sorted the problem out but it was too late for those like me.' Kane tried her best to hold back the shock on her face as the woman nonchalantly explained such a horrifying start to her life. 'Travelled across the Heartlands for a while working for a brute of a woman who had bought me in one of the shadow markets in Turkkanza. One day, I was beaten to within an inch of my life. When I woke up, a sad looking man was sitting opposite me as I lay next to a roaring fire. I can still remember the smell of the blood on his blade and the gentle, slow way he crept towards me, going to great lengths to ensure that he didn't startle me. That's the day my true life began.

He took me back home and treated me like a daughter. I owe him my life. Others weren't so lucky…'

'A plague worse than any other,' Kane said, shaking her head in disgust at the story. She'd met some of the worst humans imaginable. Spoken with rapists, murderers, and traded barbs with men and women before their execution for crimes that would keep most awake at night, even cycles removed from the event. 'Slavers deserve a punishment worse than any that I can dream up.'

'A plague which is slowly being eradicated across Takaara, though some of the more *difficult* nations still seem to enjoy the luxuries that come with such actions. I pray to see the end of it in my lifetime. No one should have to go through what I went through…'

'The first steps are always the most difficult, I've found,' Kane mused though couldn't for the life of her think why. 'We should be glad that those steps have been taken and we are now on the right path at last. Though, there is still a long journey ahead.'

Sara nodded, absently swatting a fly away from her hair. 'A very long journey. There will always be difficult people in the world. Evil is a strong word. A lot of folk like to sling it around as though seeing the world split into two. Those who are good and those who are evil. I just see it as people who are difficult and people who are not. We could never win a fight against all the problems in the world. We just have to do what we must. Try our best and see how the dice lands. What do you think?'

Kane blew out her cheeks, unprepared for such a huge question. 'I've seen some horrors over the cycles in Archania. No one can deny that. People pushed to their limit, pushed to breaking point. They can become dangerous and do horrible things. But evil?' She sighed and frowned, pushing her tongue against the inside of her cheek at some of the worst memories playing in her mind. 'I think I've seen evil. Once or twice. Individuals twisted beyond recognition and capable of acts that haunt anyone who hears of them. I believe there is evil.'

'Do you not just think that they were people pushed too far?' Sara argued. 'Pushed to breaking point?'

'The things I saw them do…' Kane shuddered at the memories. 'To think that such actions were done by people would mean accepting that all men and women are able to do such things. And that would lead down a path darker than I am willing to walk down.'

'But people they were, Katerina Kane. Whether you are willing to acknowledge it or not,' Sara said. 'Sick people. People gone too far. People who have smashed through their breaking point and been put back together in the worst ways like a broken vase fixed by a child. I'm not telling you this to argue. I just want you to understand something Kat.'

'And what is that?' Kane asked, unable to wipe the frown from her face.

'There is light and darkness in the world. One can't exist without the other. You'll see more of that where you are going. Don't let it frighten you. Embrace the two sides and know that Takaara will fall if you don't. Come, I love a ride through the fields before sundown. This really is a beautiful part of the world.'

'How you feeling?'

'Exactly how you would expect.' Aleister hated the concern on his sister's face but he had to be honest with her now. There was no way of travelling together to the South with secrets between them. The withdrawal phase always hit hard. He caught the nervous glance towards his trembling hands and felt the sweat dripping down his forehead. Ariel had watched him battle it before but not this close. He felt naked. His sister could see all the horrors and poor decisions he had made sitting right there in front of her in the small tent.

'How long did it go on for last time?' Bathos asked, rubbing his hands together furiously as he always did when uncomfortable. Aleister silently cursed himself. He could handle putting himself through shit and dealing with the consequences but to put his best friend and his sister through it all was pure torture.

'A moon. I think.' His memories were fuzzy and vague

regarding that period of time. It wasn't something he wished to look back on. A dark period of his life best left in the shadows. 'The shaking and sweating should stop sooner. It's hell, but I've been through it before and made it out the other side. I can do it again.'

'You can,' Ariel agreed, face stern as she nodded. 'You will. We're with you every step of the way.'

'Every step,' Bathos added, reaching a huge hand out and slapping Aleister on the leg.

'Thanks. I'm lucky to have the two of you. Don't deserve it.'

'Of course you don't. We're way too good for you!' Ariel snorted. The three of them laughed together, the tension easing in the tent as the sound bounced around the small space.

Two weeks had passed since leaving the Republic of Causrea. Two weeks of slow but steady travelling. Two weeks of keeping from faze and even drink. Two weeks of shaking, sweating and insomnia. He could feel the weight of the bags pulling the skin under his eyes. He'd kept away from seeing his own reflection. It wasn't necessary. Just the way his sister looked at him warned him that he was looking shit. Ariel tried her best to guard him from the pity she had but he could see through her.

'Abdulaziz said we should reach the first city in another week.' Aleister appreciated his sister changing the conversation. There was only so much that could be said for him in his current state. Best to focus on what was ahead. 'We'll spend a few days in the city and pick up more supplies with the caravan. After that, it's the long haul to the South. It may be the last chance for us to enjoy the sights of civilization before we enter the unknown. We've been to most cities north, east and west but the South… we're going in almost blind.'

'You say that like we've never done that before,' Aleister said, smirking. 'Have you forgotten the old days? Creeping into cities with barely a coin to our name. Remember the first time we went East? We stood out like Archanians at the Festival of the Moon. Hardly slept because we were unsure if we would wake up. The dirty looks, the dark mutterings, the promises of death. We made it through it all.'

'Didn't just make it,' Bathos reminded him. 'We built the greatest mercenary group in Takaara. Kings and queens feared the Red Sons. Songs are sung and people raise tankards to us in the taverns across the land. We should be proud of what we have accomplished.'

'Exactly. And I think this will be good for us,' Aleister said, feeling some of the old life energise him. 'A reminder of who we were in the beginning. A reminder of what we wanted to become. Like starting again. Just the three of us. Like the good old days. We built the Red Sons from scratch, something to be feared and admired by all. Imagine what we can accomplish now we're a little bit older, more experienced.'

'From what I've heard, things will be very different in the South. This Boy King…' Ariel sucked in the air through her teeth and shivered.

'Do you remember the stories we used to hear of the Borderlands? The savages from the North who were made of hair and ice and would come down past the border to steal away children in the night and feed them to their families,' Aleister reminded them. Bathos nodded, stroking the stubble on his chin as Ariel smiled at the tales from their youth. 'Frightening monsters hell-bent on destruction and ensuring that the United Cities would be wiped from the map. We've met people from the Borderlands. Great warriors, yes. But monsters? Did they seem like people who would eat children? I don't think so. It's the same wherever we go. People are frightened of the unknown. I bet once we arrive in the South, all those whispers and rumours will be seen for what they truly are.'

'And what might that be?' Ariel asked, yawning and dropping to the side into the arms of the waiting Bathos.

'What it always is. Bullshit made up by those in power to oppress those beneath them. Designed to whip up fear and distrust. The villains in power stay in power because the citizens beneath them aren't able to unite. What we saw in Archania was the beginning of an awakening. All we need to do is ensure people are ready for the next one. The world is ready for change. We can lead the way.'

'Are *you* ready for that, brother?'

The room swam and Ella's cold, dead eyes stared back at him. 'I have to be. For her…'

His dreams were dark and broken.

Ella reached out for him, eyes pleading with Aleister to pull her towards him. He tried his best, fighting with all his strength to grab her and pull her away from the shadows.

It ended as it always did.

His fingertips brushed against hers. Her golden pupils faded to black as she fell away from him. Strange, dancing, blue flames leapt up from the darkness and swallowed her whole as Aleister screamed until his throat grew bloody and raw with the strain.

He fell to his knees, weeping. All energy left him as he dropped and wrapped his arms uselessly around his sobbing frame. Then, two hands gently dropped onto his shoulders, calming him and ending the pain momentarily.

'Aleister. Leader of the Red Sons.' The voice was unfamiliar. It bounced around him, throwing him off guard and confusing him. 'Orphan. Brother. Warrior. Leader. You have worn many masks over the cycles in your life. Time to wear another. People need you. Takaara needs you. Don't let them down…'

He shot bolt upright from the ground, sweat drenching his thin night clothes. His chest rose and fell in a great repeated motion. Hand pressed against his chest; he could feel the painful thump of his heart. Wild eyes shot around the room. He was still in his tent. Alone.

He closed his eyes and focused on controlling his breathing. Each breath calmed him, reminding him of where he was. With it came the realisation that Ella was still dead. He had failed her. There was nothing more he could do for her. He couldn't reach out and grab her. Couldn't prevent her from falling into those dreaded blue flames.

That voice. He tried hard to remember how it had sounded and what the words had been but, frustratingly, they were lost to him. Only a chill remained, making him shudder and shake his head.

Senses returning, he paused, listening to sounds in the distance. Finally, fully awake, he could hear angry shouts and cries around the tent. Cursing, he leapt from the ground and pulled on his trousers. His belt had already been attached to the hooks when he had thrown them absently to the ground before falling onto the furs. He quickly threw on a black shirt and crimson jacket before picking up the most valuable item he owned. His sword Soulsbane.

Outside of the tent was chaos. A large group of the merchants and traders were gathered around the huge fire to the side of the road. Raised voices barked over the crackling of the flames as Aleister drew nearer. Closer to the light, he could see familiar faces of the merchants arguing with unfamiliar men in mismatched, stained armour. Their bronze chest plates were dented and old but the curved swords in their hands spoke of death. This was no joke.

He held back a laugh as a rather upset man in armour struggled on the ground beneath Bathos' huge boot. Ariel stood beside her partner, dagger pressed against another man's throat as she held the weapon at arm's length to her side. The man had his palms raised out and his eyes were wide open as they darted from Ariel to one of the armoured men by the fire and back again. He was trying to weigh up his chances of surviving the night. By the look on his face, he wasn't giving himself much of a chance.

'We are not fighters. Merely men and women interested in keeping what is ours. We are passing through this land without trouble and mean no harm.' Aleister heard Abdulaziz say to a group of armed men. The merchant was head of the caravan. He oversaw who was and wasn't allowed to join and which path they would take. Aleister liked him. Abdulaziz had welcomed him and the others with open arms, promising to do what he could to ensure safe passage to the south. In return, he had asked for nothing. Though, Aleister felt that the merchant would have been pleased to have three experienced warriors join them on their journey.

'No harm?' one of the armed men scoffed. He wore no helmet, allowing his jet black hair to fall to his shoulders. He was in need of a shave and had wild brown eyes that kept glancing over to where two of his allies were held by Bathos and Ariel. 'You hold two of my men at the edge of a knife. We are working on behalf of the Lord Manuel. These lands are his. You are trespassing. Pay the fine and we will leave you.'

'And if we don't?' Aleister smiled at the balls of the merchant. In his time, he'd known merchants to cower and hand over all their earthly possessions if even the most meagre of bandits attempted to threaten them.

'Then we will have a discussion that I don't think you or your friends will enjoy...' The bandit smirked as he tapped his blade against the armour on his chest, making clear his intentions.

'So be it.' Abdulaziz sighed and placed a hand into his long, grey robes. Aleister stifled another laugh, this time in shock as the merchant drew a long, curved sword that glistened in the firelight. 'You are not the first to attempt to rob this caravan. You will not be the last.'

Aleister chose that moment to step into the light, sneaking into the space beside Abdulaziz and tapping on the sheath of his own blade. 'More bandits, Master Abdulaziz?'

'Sadly...' the merchant said, playing along.

'Third lot this week. I'd only just got the smell of burning flesh from my jacket,' Aleister pressed a fist against his mouth as though in horror at the memory. He dared a quick glance at Ariel who rolled her eyes. Bathos shook with the effort of keeping his own laughter at bay. 'Shall we make it quick this time? It is late and I don't have the stomach for playing with these fools...'

'Stop!' Aleister kept his smirk in check as the man opposite him cried out. 'Perhaps we can allow you to pass. Just this once.'

He shared a look with Abdulaziz. 'What do you think, Master Merchant? My sword is still sheathed, but yours is not.'

'Just this once,' Abdulaziz said to the men. 'I shall allow

75

this indiscretion to pass without bloodshed. This caravan has been travelling the same route for over thirty cycles. We do not enjoy being threatened by men with exaggerated egos and tiny cocks. If I see you or your men again, they will face justice. My justice. Let them go.' He waved a hand to Ariel and Bathos who obliged with a smile and a wave as though saying bye to friends of theirs. The two fortunate men scampered away and into the darkness, leaving their forgotten weapons in the mud.

'Lord Manuel will hear of your… *generosity,* Master Abdulaziz. I shall see to that personally.'

'Such a subtle threat,' Abdulaziz mocked, barking a laugh and placing his sword back in amongst his robes. He stroked his magnificent silver beard and stepped closer to his adversary. 'I know who you are, Jorges Bana. I've walked this land since before you were born. Dare to threaten me or my people again, veiled or not, and I will take that ugly head of yours and send it to your parents. They will thank me for my kindness in returning that much of you and we will then continue with our lives. Do you understand?'

Bana nodded. 'I understand,' he muttered.

'Excellent!' Abdulaziz leaned in so Aleister had to strain to hear the next words. 'Now be a good little boy and kindly fuck back off to where you came from.'

The audience of merchants and traders cheered as the bandits fled in haste, tails between their legs like scolded dogs.

'Quite the display,' Aleister chuckled. 'Didn't expect that from a merchant.'

'Think that's the first time I've had to stand up to some arrogant fool in my life?' Abdulaziz asked, winking back at him. 'I've dealt with much worse than that idiot, believe me. The Gods often see it fit to send me little tests of my patience and faith. Most of the time, I have passed.'

'What about the other times?'

The merchant's eyes lit up with mischief. 'Those times are the ones I like best!'

'Miss Sara told me that the three of you would be good in a fight. And I've heard of the Red Sons – who in the known world hasn't after the shit you pulled in Darakeche?' Abdulaziz laughed as one of his men poured him a glass of wine. Aleister declined his glass, sticking to water. Ariel and Bathos accepted the wine as Abdulaziz continued. 'Jorges may return. With more fighters next time, too. He won't take well to being slighted and Lord Manuel even less. Still, we are nearing the city and there will be nothing that he can do once we are there. Even so, it will not be the last time we are approached by those wishing to do us harm. That is why I have asked you in here, to talk about a few of the rules that Sara may not have mentioned before our leaving.'

The merchant was well respected back in Causrea. Aleister had seen him walking through the city with his chest puffed out and turban wrapped tightly around his head as his dark eyes sparkled at the reaction he received from passers-by. Waves, smiles, even a few bows. He was treated like a noble but unlike most nobles, people seemed to genuinely like the man. And Aleister could see why.

'We're grateful for your assistance in helping us travel to the South. If there's any way we can help then we are here for you,' Ariel said, sipping her wine and shifting to get comfortable on the grand, white chair.

'Fighting. Drawing swords,' Abdulaziz began, swilling his silver cup and watching the circular path of the red liquid. 'These are last resorts whilst with my caravan. The loss of one life would crush me. These people rely on me and expect me to guide them across Takaara. Every loss is a slap across my face and so we must only turn to violence when there is no other option. I have a name that is respected in my world. I cannot have anyone dirtying such a pure thing that I have created.'

'Understood,' Aleister said with a nod. 'We do not wish to turn to violence in any situation.' A slight lie. Sounded good though. 'But we are capable once there is no other alternative.'

Abdulaziz raised an eyebrow incredulously but let it go. He was no fool. 'The next thing I wish to remind you of is something that is very important to me and there will be no second chances. Faze.'

Aleister shuffled in his chair and drank some of his water, feeling the heat rise to his face at the word. He didn't need to look over at Bathos and Ariel to know that they were judging his reaction.

'The drug is a personal bane of mine. I had one son. A beautiful boy gifted by the Gods. Abdulrahman. We named him after my father. So like his mother. Playful, confident. Carefree. Too carefree, in the end.' The merchant frowned and took a gulp of his own wine. 'He used the drug during his seventeenth summer. Still so much life to live. It turned him from a beautiful young boy with the world at his feet into a shell of a man who cared for nothing but his next hit. He died. Weeks away from home in a faze den. Another user did it, I later found out. Never knew why. All I do know is that he wouldn't have been there if it wasn't for that ghastly thing. I'd watched my son try to beat it, after the first stage of him using it. The shakes. The sweats. I know the signs.' Abdulaziz stared intently at Aleister. 'If you need any help in beating it, I am here. But if you use it whilst with this caravan, you will leave and never return. I hope I have made myself clear.'

'Crystal clear, Abdulaziz. I swear, I am over it. The after-effects linger but I will never use the stuff again.' His voice wavered but he meant the words. 'I know what I have to lose. And I'm not sure that I can handle any more loss.'

ALL OVER AGAIN

For a second. Just a second, he felt that the last couple of moons had been a dream. Or rather a nightmare. The Doctors. The failed rebellion. His banishment from Archania. There had been some good bits to cling onto. He could still smell the smoke from the flames. Still hear the screams of the fools as they clashed with trained soldiers. Still see the fear in the eyes of the disgusting bastards stepping in his way. But then he opened his eyes, and his mind awoke to the reality of his surroundings.

Stone walls. A small fire flickering softly in the corner of the simple room. He rolled out from his bed and placed his bare feet on the black, fur rug resting on the wooden floorboards. Smaller than his place back in the Lower City but it would do. Cypher had never been one for the luxuries offered in life. Even when offered fine clothes and opportunities to bask in the life of nobility in the Upper City, he had declined. Such things would chafe on him like an uncomfortable pair of trousers. It would annoy him until he grew frustrated and cast them off in anger. The few things he had accepted had blinded him, dulling the edges of his sharpened mind so that he hadn't seen betrayal and deceit meant for him.

Here he could remind himself of the man he once was. The man who lived as he wanted. The man who took what he wanted. The man who worked alone for no one's good but his

79

own.

This was the first time he had been on the island of Norland. The latest addition to the United Cities of Archania – welcomed into the family with open arms but always with a knife secretly placed against its back. There had been troubles between the mainland and the island. Not everyone felt happy about the union. Understandable. Noorish folk loved their freedoms, their identity, their home. Archania didn't give a shit about any of that. Cypher cared even less…

Three bangs on the door interrupted Cypher as he dressed himself. Peering out of the window, a clear blue sky looked back at him as the howl of the harsh wind continued its relentless assault on the island. He pulled his dark robe close to his thin frame as he answered the door, sliding the iron latch and putting on his best grin for the unwelcome visitor. All visitors were unwelcome, this one even more so.

'Zaif. What a wonderful pleasure. A truly delightful way to start the day!' His voice dripped with sickly sweetness but Zaif knew his true feelings. Cypher had trained the bastard, after all.

'And a good morning to you to, you old cunt.' Zaif thought himself no longer the apprentice. Cypher could have reminded him, but some things were best given at the right time. Patience was a virtue of the Gods, or so he had been told. 'You ready to leave?'

'That depends,' Cypher smirked. 'What exactly do I need to be ready for?'

'We're meeting with the Norland ambassador. King Asher's orders.' Zaif waved a flimsy piece of parchment in the air. 'He can brief us about what's going on in the city and then we can act on the information. Shouldn't be here too long. Shithole like this. Won't take much time to sort it out. Stamped out that mess in Archania. This one will be smaller. Easier to deal with.' *Idiot. Have I taught him nothing? Even the smallest sparks can ignite great wildfires. A single flame could destroy a whole forest.*

'I look forward to dealing with it and moving back to the capital. Serving the new King from Archania will be an honour.' Cypher couldn't think of much worse but the words had to be said. They both knew that.

'Don't rush things, Zellin. If Asher wants, you could be here for a long time. Mason D'Argio isn't exactly keen on you right now.'

'And how is the lovely preacher dealing with his loss of power? It is a shame to not be there to comfort him myself.' *To strangle him and gaze into those pupils, no longer golden, but black like all the rest of us.*

Zaif scratched his head and frowned. 'Lost his *magic*, Cypher. Not his power. That man still pulls the strings, golden eyes or not. This is a temporary blip. Chaotic, but order will soon be in place. Believe me.'

'Must make it harder for him tracking the mages down in the city. The ones who fought against him.' Cypher loved winding folk up. Especially ones who had betrayed him. Even if he did feel a touch of pride in his apprentice's despicable actions.

'Water under the bridge. That's how Mason put it. Try to move forward as a nation.'

'And you believe that?' Cypher raised an eyebrow and stroked his growing beard. 'All it means is action will be taken in the shadows. Did I teach you nothing?'

'Taught me to be careful with my words or I could lose my tongue.' Zaif rolled his jaw and sighed as he heard the familiar click. 'I've not forgotten.'

'Good to know. Now, I believe I am ready. Lead the way, my apprentice.'

The low, stone buildings. The biting wind. The smell of piss. The crowds of stinking peasants wandering around the muddy streets and grunting at one another whilst their children skipped between slow moving carts pulled by weary horses. *Not a million miles from Archania.* In both the literal and figurative sense, Cypher thought.

It was comparable to the Lower City. Haggard men with wild beards stomped the streets and stumbled in and out of the taverns whilst some weary women screeched and hollered from the doorways. Manure decorated the filthy, worn paths between the stone buildings, bundled in stinking clumps and ignored by most of the populace who seemed to have grown accustomed to the stench. Cypher could understand that. He'd seen men and women rotting in cells become used to the smell of their shit and piss in the corner of their tiny, bare rooms. It is incredible what the human body and mind can withstand. Cypher had made it his life's aim to push those boundaries. To see what was possible.

Though comparable to the Lower City, Norland hadn't been designed for peasants to spend their time whoring and drinking their way into ignorance whilst the elite of Archania had their fun. The city had spread out from the centre over many cycles, expanding until it reached even the coasts of the tiny island. Though small, the land produced a proud people, a single city united. *United against Archania for the most part of its history.* He chuckled at the thought. Due to its affiliation with Archania, the island had grown from one of warriors and savages living a free life on their farms and tending to their animals, to one that from the outside looked like a poor man's version of the old city of Archania. It was like watching a shit play based on his homeland by a playgroup who were on their last legs. Too few coins and not enough heart to put on a decent display. He recognised a few elements but laughed at the warped, distorted reality of the situation. No wonder these idiots were angry with the mainland. They were slowly turning into a shittier version of the bastards.

'Guard's house is just up here,' Zaif said, hacking up something foul from the back of his throat and launching it past his lips with a vile sound. Something thick and green flew onto a small patch of grass that was trying its best to show at least a bit of life amongst the otherwise decimated pathway. 'Norland ambassador said he'd meet us in there. One of the best buildings on the island. Mikkael sent a decent amount of money over to have it built. Can't have the guards protecting the king's land without a bit of luxury, eh?'

'Indeed,' Cypher agreed quietly as he peered over to where Zaif's great sausage of a finger pointed. 'Almost palatial in its splendour…' The guard's house sat at the end of the road, just past a tavern that looked like it had been abandoned for the last

century, though on closer inspection, Cypher could see a few
shadowy figures moving past the round windows. Their
destination sat alone behind a small grey wall, the stone chipped
and broken in places but not really in need of repair, unlike most
of the city. The walls either side of the building met in the centre
and rose to create an archway littered with green creeper growing
all over and across it, twisting and turning its way around the
stone and wrapping it in its embrace, squeezing tightly.

Cypher walked through the archway, brushing his hand
against the stone and reading a small plaque placed at head height
to his left.

Unmoving. Unbreakable. United.

*To strengthen the bond between our great cities, this building and its
surrounding gardens are a gift from the King of the United Cities of
Archania. The Unbroken King Mikkael sees Norland and offers this gift as
a sign of the bond between the two great cities.*

*May it last for all eternity. Brothers united as one against all odds. Enemies
turned family until the end of time. The people of Archania welcome Norland
and embrace her now as a part of our great kingdom.*

Opened by King Mikkael – The year 1245 of The Four

These plaques really were always full of shit.

The gardens would have once been splendid indeed.
Lush green with stone fountains either side of a white stone
pathway leading up to the tall, wooden double-doors that stood in
the centre of a colossal castle. A clutch of moody guards peered
down from the battlements on the roof of the building just above
large glass windows perfectly situated on both sides of the castle's
face. A grand building, one that stuck out like a queen in a
whorehouse in this filthy city. It had Archanian fingerprints all
over it. Cypher even thought he spotted a statue of Mikkael in the
distance just past a hedgerow of white roses, but he couldn't be
certain. Archania sure loved to bang its fist against its chest and
shout out about how fucking clever and amazing they were. Must
have cost a fortune to build this useless building here in the
middle of nowhere where no one but filthy, ageing guards could
appreciate its value. A waste of time, money and effort. A barn
could have been erected in a day and it would have given shelter

to the useless guards. *The excess of those in power. The arrogance. The stupidity.* It was all so… frustrating.

'This just a guard's house?' Cypher asked. It would be one of the lesser buildings on the mainland but out here it really was something.

'Yup,' Zaif replied as he knocked on the wooden door with three loud bangs. 'Although, it gets used for everything from playhouse and festival hall, to hospital and indoor market. The Noorish people are flexible. They see the use of such a building in their city. No need to build anything else when you have this much space just sitting right here, hardly being used.'

'Wise. Prudent cities are rare in these strange times. Most want to display their shiny gifts and strut like a peacock to new visitors. Norland doesn't seem like that. The one thing they do have that yells extravagance is also the most useful building on the island. I'm impressed,' Cypher said begrudgingly. It might seem like a poor man's Lower City, but he saw the appeal.

The door opened inwards and a bored, old man squinted his sullen eyes at the pair of them, looking annoyed to have been interrupted in what would most likely be one of the most boring assignments in the world.

'Names,' the old fellow croaked as though he hadn't spoken for some time.

'Zaif Tanson,' Zaif smiled at the guard. He patted Cypher on the back, much to the experienced man's annoyance. 'And this here is Cypher Zellin. You should be expecting us.'

'Boys from big city…' the guard muttered, nodding after a while as he backed away from them, pulling the door further open. 'The ambassador warned me that you would be arriving today. Haven't had visitors from the mainland in quite some time.'

Cypher stepped in after Zaif, craning his neck to take in all the entrance hall. Three chandeliers hung from the ceiling, bouncing the light off into all directions and brightening what otherwise would be a dark and dreary room. A twin staircase curved from the black and white tiles on the ground and ran up either side of the room and finished at the first floor where guards dressed in all the usual finery stood with glistening spears in hand guarding various ornate, wooden doors beyond the sculpted bannisters. Bronze busts watched silently from black, marble plinths.

An impressive room.

Cypher inched closer to one of the statues, an old leader that the people of Norland still worshipped, and ran a finger over the carved, bald head. Pulling his finger away, he smiled at the filthy amount of dust that came with it. The place needed a clean. Like most grand places he had been in, it looked good from afar but upon closer inspection, it was as dirty and disappointing as anywhere else.

'Please wait here whilst I alert the ambassador.' Cypher almost let slip a wry smile as the guard turned his back on them. No chairs. No benches. Nowhere comfortable to wait. A clever tactic used by many leaders. Designed to make guests wait and stare in wonder around the room they were stuck in, steadily growing more and more agitated and annoyed with each passing second. It showed the guests that they were not the ones in control. They were here at the grace of their hosts and must abide by their rules. Powerless. Not very subtle. But effective.

Cypher decided to use the time to scan the room and take in a bit more detail. If this was what they wanted to display to esteemed guests, then he wanted to know why. What made this so special?

He read the plaque beneath another of the busts – this one a female with dead eyes and long hair. Perhaps he was being harsh; eyes always looked dead when carved from stone or marble.

Fianna Byrne

Led the Norland assault against the Barbarians of the Blue Mountains. Defended her homeland until her untimely death. She inspired the people of Norland and showed them what can be done with a full heart and a sharpened spear.

'For Family and Home – until the last breath has left me.'

A true Noorish hero.

Cypher scoffed as he bent down to read the inscription. Probably fought in a couple of battles and got lucky. The poor always loved to create heroes from the lucky who survived. Battles were pure chaos. Anything could happen in them. There was no skill involved. It wasn't anything like what he had done. There was no subtlety. No thrill of working hard to not be seen, to not be caught. It was the difference between being sculpted with a thin, sharp tool like a scalpel and bashing at marble with a sledgehammer. He was more of a hero than this dumb bitch.

He moved to the next one – a large, hooked-nose man with bushy eyebrows. He looked angry with being made into this bodyless bust and being forced to stay all hours on top of the small plinth.

Finn Harkin

Fought valiantly against the invaders from Archania. Killed the Bloody Prince and defended the city until his dying breath. Finn drove the attackers back towards the coast and fought against great odds to hold the invaders at bay.

'Land and Blood.'

Norland will forever remember his sacrifice.

More laughable bullshit.

Cypher had heard the tale of Finn the Sheep-Fucker. That's how he'd been known in Archania. The son of a tribal chief, Finn had fled with a band of followers towards the coast during the invasion and was caught in the middle of the night with his cock inside one of the poor, fluffy animals. His head had been cut off and displayed to the people of Archania, rotting and bloody outside of the palace gates as a sign of the victory over their savage neighbours. Prince Arkas had been known as the Bloody Prince but that was due to his prowess in battle. Some claimed that the prince had killed Finn's father before taking down a hundred others and finally falling to his death thanks to the numerous wounds he had sustained and fought through.

More bullshit, of course. But that was the way of things. There were always two sides to every story. Two sides capable of speaking of the same incident but seeing the events through a different lens. Some would see white where others saw only black. Cypher had decided long ago to search for the shades of grey. There, more often than not, the truth resided.

'Interesting room isn't it?' Zaif said to Cypher, craning over his shoulder to look down and read the plaque with squinted eyes. 'That's the Sheep-Fucker ain't it?'

'It is indeed,' Cypher replied, smirking. 'For some reason, they have decided to leave that particular name off the plaque designed to honour him.' *Can't think of any reason why…*

'Should put a bust of the sheep next to him. Or in front of him, that's how they found the bastard after all. That's what you get for messing with Archania. Still, no such problem now, they're part of the family after all.' Zaif's tone told Cypher that even he found the idea humorous.

'I'm sure we have seen the last of the hostilities between the nations. We are one family now, after all. Brothers and sisters, don't you agree?' Cypher kept himself from laughing but Zaif didn't seem to care. His booming laugh rang out through the cavernous room.

'They were wise to fold. But it won't be long before we're standing on opposite sides. They will never accept the Empire of Light and it is only a matter of time before we are embraced fully into their world. We will see the blood flowing then. Enough blood to turn the seas red.'

'I cannot wait for such a day.' He could wait. Patience was one of the many talents that Cypher prided himself on.

There wasn't much else to do in the room. Zaif paced across the tiles like a trapped wolf, blowing his cheeks out at regular intervals as his stomping grew steadily louder. Cypher couldn't be so easily frustrated. He knew the game and was happy to play it, for the time being. Showing your frustration just proved that you had weaknesses and that wasn't something he wanted strangers to know. Seemed like Zaif still had a thing or two to learn.

'Calm, Zaif,' he breathed to his companion, slowly patting the air in front of him with both hands as the large man snapped his head towards him. 'This is what always happens. A test. Don't rise to such tactics. It is beneath you.'

'It is disrespectful!' Zaif growled, looking thoroughly ticked off with the poor welcome.

'On the contrary,' Cypher argued back. 'It is respect of the highest level. They are wanting to discover our breaking point. Assessing us to judge if we are worthy. Simple, but effective. Especially if you rise to it as you are…'

'Bah! Disrespect is all it is. Can't tell me otherwise.'

Fair enough. There are only so many times a horse can be led to water. If it doesn't drink, then it will die. Cypher was happy for this horse to die if it so wished. No skin off his nose.

'Gentlemen,' a voice finally called from the top of the stairs. The old guard had returned, at last. 'The ambassador is ready for your company. Please, follow me.'

Cypher smirked as Zaif breathed in slowly through his large nostrils as he stared up at the speaker. 'That wasn't so difficult was it, old friend?'

'It is the last time I will be disrespected in Norland. I guarantee it.'

So aggressive. Always ready for the fight. It's why they were a good team. The brain and the brawn. Still, Cypher owed Zaif payback, and he wasn't going to forget that so easily.

'I'm sure it will be, Zaif. After you…' Cypher motioned for the large man to lead the way, still smirking as Zaif pulled his shoulders back and started up the stairs. 'I'm sure it will be.'

'My apologies for the delay, brothers. For so long, I have been twiddling my thumbs and looking for things to do in this grim city but suddenly, I feel like a man in demand! Most strange! I do so miss the tranquillity of ages past when I could fish by the lake and read a book sitting near the edge of the cliff and watch the waves crash against the coast.'

The ambassador had been in demand for less than a month. This was the first time that he had actually been doing any kind of work that was demanded by his role as ambassador to the Noorish people. Yet he had the audacity to complain and yearn for the simpler times when he did fuck all. Cypher almost felt a begrudging level of respect for the idiot. Almost.

'I feel as though the days of tranquillity may have passed. That last quake…' The ambassador shuddered and shook his whole body, as though attempting to rid himself of an evil spirit. 'The days of order and calm seem past. Magic has left the world, for good or ill and such great changes will scar the world for all to see. That is my belief.'

Cypher made a non-committal grunt but Zaif wasn't as composed in keeping his feelings about the ambassador's nonsensical words at bay.

'Mason D'Argio warned us all about this. Too many fools turning away from the Light. From the One. Magic will return, and great will be the wrath of the One. He has spoken of this.' Cypher had never thought the man a zealot. In all the cycles they had spent together in the dungeons, the big man had shown not even a slither of interest in religion of any kind. He had placed his faith in himself and his own abilities, like Cypher. It appeared that time in the East had altered Zaif's perspective on things. *A worrying thought. Religious fools can be dangerous at the best of times but religious fools with Zaif's skills could be frightening…*

Ambassador Ward rubbed his clean-shaven chin and looked across at Zaif from his extravagant seat beside the roaring fire. Some would call it a throne. The ambassador truly had settled into the city and was enjoying the comforts of his position. No wonder he disliked any sign of change. The bastard was living the high life away from any prying eyes of his peers.

'Mason D'Argio. He was the one who sent me here. Had a disagreement regarding my belief in The Four and the next thing I know, the papers had been signed and I was on a ship across the short sea to this blot on the maps of Takaara. Not a man to cross, that one. I heard about the burnings…' The ambassador's eyes glazed over for a moment. Cypher saw the man's knuckles whiten as they clutched tightly onto the wooden arms of the chair. 'I always thought the people here were savage but even they would not burn young men and women. No honour…'

'The *criminals* were punished for breaking the laws of the United Cities of Archania, ambassador,' Zaif admonished the man, snapping him from his trance. 'You would do well to remember that…'

'Of course!' The ambassador chuckled darkly and sat up once more in his chair, forcing a smile onto his face that Cypher felt didn't belong there. 'The King's Justice. That's what it is called. No arguing against it. Though, there will be less burnings I suppose now, with magic dripping from the world. Used to see them all with their golden eyes meeting up by the tall stones on the eastern part of the island at sundown. Now, they are more like us. Same eyes. Same problems. A shame…'

Cypher allowed the edge of a smile onto his face as he listened to the ambassador; his words closely fit to one who would be sympathetic to the cause of magic-users. A strange position to be in when you worked for a nation who had outlawed most uses of magic. Lucky that he was all the way out here or he would have been one of the ones to burn in front of the screaming crowds.

'I believe we were sent here for a reason, Ambassador,' Cypher cut in, spotting the annoyance on Zaif's face and not wanting to watch the ambassador fly out of the window and splatter in the beautiful gardens. Too much paperwork. 'Zaif and I have spent many cycles working with criminals in the palace dungeons and extracting vital information on behalf of the United Cities in the name of justice. Only recently, we saw first-hand the chaos and fury as citizens of the Lower City attempted to cause problems for well-behaved members of society and destroy our beautiful capital all because they felt life was being unkind to them.' Twisted truth. But to Cypher, that was the best kind of truth. It was malleable. A plaything to be moulded to his own devices. 'It was mentioned that there has been dissent and rumblings of trouble in your own city. The quake, the word of rioting in Archania. Ripples in the water of the kingdom that need to be stopped before they spread further. Tell us what has been going on and we will help as best we can.'

The red colour faded from Zaif's face at the reminder of

the work they had been sent here for. Ever the man of duty it seemed. The ambassador nodded and stood up, pacing over to the flames to his left and staring into them as though searching them for the words to respond. It was some time before the man elected to speak.

'This is a peaceful city. Norland has stood alone in this angry sea for centuries. The people are proud and stubborn. Forcing them to become one of the United Cities was like breaking a misbehaving dog. It can go one of two ways. Either that dog is obedient and ends up relying on you and caring for you. Or the dog bites back. That threat has always been there. Now, with the unrest in the capital, the Noorish people are aware that their neighbour over the sea is distracted. It is the perfect time to remind them that this is no broken and tired dog. This land and its people still have a bite or two left in it and they want to see what will happen…'

'A rebellion against the mainland?' Zaif asked, fury etched on his face. Cypher hid his grin as the ambassador turned to face them. *Another rebellion. What fun.*

'You need to see things from their point of view. Norland would have been a willing ally to Archania. They are neighbours. Both wary of the threats from neighbouring nations and both willing to support one another. Queen Laria even contemplated marrying off one of her sons to a pretty, young daughter of a chief of Norland at one point. Her idea was rejected, of course, as soon as the council stepped in. Demeaning. Beneath the Archanian people. That's what they thought. Still, there was a bond. That bond was destroyed when the Bloody Prince decided to hang and gut ten Noorish travellers in a small tavern in the Lower City purely for his own amusement. When Norland demanded justice, the war began. A war that ended with Norland becoming part of the United Cities of Archania. The biggest insult to a proud people but one which had to happen for their survival. The wounds have healed but the scars are there, and its people are fighting fit once again!'

Cypher licked his lips and mulled over the words. It was no surprise. Even with Archania's warped version of events, everyone knew Norland had been bent over and fucked good and proper. 'What exactly has been happening in the city? How are you aware of the rebellion?'

'Meetings,' laughed Ward. 'They're not exactly a secretive bunch. They want to be seen and no one is opposing them. Why would they be opposed? Crimson robes and black masks like those worn by the plague doctors of old. They call for a change in Takaara, not just in our small corner of the world. They call for change.'

'Wait,' Cypher snapped, leaning forward in his chair and staring at Ward, concentrating as best he could. Had he heard it right? 'What masks do they wear?'

'Like a plague doctor.' Ward motioned with his hand out from his nose like a large beak, one Cypher knew only too well. 'Creepy when you see it in the moonlight. No one has been hurt but their numbers are growing. Only a matter of time before something is done.'

The Doctors. Just like before. Haller and Tamir had said they would not stop. The death of one could inspire the many. Seemed they were right.

'These masked men,' Cypher said casually, twisted and rubbing his fingers against his palms. 'How would I arrange a meeting with them? If they are stirring trouble, then we should at least find out what they want. The only way we can do that is by talking to them.'

The ambassador strolled over to his seat and fell back into it, breathing long and hard as he stared into Cypher's eyes, his own sparkling in the firelight. Cypher even thought he caught the shadow of a smile curl at the corner of the man's lips.

'That's the most interesting thing about all of this.' Now the smile grew in full, shadows hanging beneath Ward's eyes as he grinned, enjoying being the one in control. 'Their leader. Only two days ago he asked for us to send one person to speak to him. He only gave one name. One man that he would converse with on this island.'

'What name did he give?' Cypher asked but he already knew the name that would stab out past those dark lips.

'Cypher Zellin.'

SPEAKING WITH THE DEAD

'Bit out of the way, don't you think?' Zaif grumbled. He'd been in a foul mood the whole journey from the city. Trudging around in the cold, muddy bogs isn't so appealing after spending cycles in the sunny lands to the east. Easy to forget the harsh realities of life in the North when you're away from the endless rain and biting winds. The big man's shirt clung to him with the wetness and a slit in the front of his right boot meant the rainwater just filled the thing up and settled around his foot like a cold bath. They couldn't be much farther from the heat of the East and Zaif knew it. 'If I'd have known it was this far, I'd have told the bastard to come to us.'

'You think they would have come?' Cypher asked, pulling his own hood tighter to his face. 'Difficult to escape from the city if things go sideways. Out here, with the open space and the numbers, they have a fighting chance if we decide to turn on them.'

'They have no chance,' Zaif scoffed. 'If we decide to lower the boot, they will be crushed and that will be that.'

'Whose boot will stomp down to crush them? You may not have noticed, Zaif, we are alone on this island. Norland is part of the United Cities in name alone. You heard the ambassador. King Asher would need to send more men to crush any rebellion. The two of us are not enough…'

Cypher grinned at a couple of wild-eyed farmers pausing from their work to stare at the passing entourage. One of them looked him right in the eyes and spat on the ground before returning to his labour. The locals had never set eyes on the mainland. Some would never have seen a true citizen of Archania – unless you counted the men that raided their homes and pillaged their land, shedding the blood of any who stood in their way. They were in hostile territory and needed to tread carefully.

'We are close now,' the ambassador called back to them from the front of the line of soldiers who had been chosen as an escort. 'Just through these trees.'

Cypher stumbled through the cramped forest, cursing as he tripped and almost fell flat in his face, catching himself just in time. The naked trees crept ever closer to one another, stretching out their branches like arms blocking out the weak light of the fading sun. In the distance, tiny lights lit up a pathway in front of the small travelling band.

'I take it that's where we are heading?' he asked Ward, pointing towards the eerie lights.

'We're expected.' Ward smacked his lips together and picked up his face, eager to reach their destination before the last of the light died. 'I'm sure we are to get a royal welcome.'

The forest opened into a circular clearing. Around the boundary of the clearing stood crimson-robed figures as still as statues, all holding lanterns to light the enclosure. Cypher bit his lip as he locked onto the familiar plague doctor masks they all wore under their raised hoods. *Just like those in the Lower City. Just like the one that I wore.* It seemed that the King's answer to the rebellion had not put off copycats. Happened too often. Cypher himself had once spoken to a young man who wished to replicate his crimes. Flattering, if unoriginal.

Three tents were erected in the circle. A large, pyramid like tent flanked by two smaller tents. They were wet with the day's rain but had held up well thanks to the protective enclosure shielding them from the wind. The ambassador stopped ten paces from the main tent's entrance, waiting in silence between two of the soldiers that had marched with them for the journey. Cypher and Zaif joined them, stopping in line and waiting.

'All a bit much, don't you think?' Zaif remarked, taking in the whole enclosure and ensuring that his hand was always close to the hilt of his weapon.

'Mind games,' Cypher said to his younger companion. 'A bit theatrical but it often puts any enemies off balance, keeps them guessing. Even the slightest of advantages can be important, especially to folk like this.'

'If anyone would know, then you would.'

'Cypher knew it was meant as an insult but there was no reason to take it as one. 'Exactly. I would know,' he smirked, eyes falling to the entrance of the tent as a small man bent under the animal skin and marched towards them, dressed just like the others.

'Greetings. We appreciate your haste. Time is of the essence in such matters.' Cypher didn't recognise the muffled voice. Accent seemed like it was from the mainland, but he couldn't be sure with the sound distorted by the mask.

'Of course. In such dark times, a lack of action and a slow response could mean the end of everything.' The ambassador bowed his head ever so slightly as he spoke the words. 'How is she?'

'Unchanged. She is resting. He is with her.'

Cypher frowned, unable to follow the logical route of the conversation beside him.

The masked man approached Cypher, coming to within an inch of his face, close enough to smell the leather on the beak of the mask and see the slow drip of rainwater fall from the curve of the hooked nose. Cypher didn't flinch. It would take more than a mask, a robe, and a lack of space to scare him. A small tilt of the head and then he felt something heavy pushed into his hand before the mask arched over Cypher's shoulder. 'Choose.'

He knew what was in his hand. A familiar weight he would never forget. Didn't even need a moment to think about it. With practised skill and movement, he flicked his arm up, twisting his wrist effortlessly.

Zaif didn't move. Too shocked, most likely. Cypher pulled the blade out from his old apprentice's neck and wiped the blood on the masked man's crimson robe. Good choice of colour. Zaif frowned, confused, and pressed his fingers against the hole in his neck. The blood seeped slowly from the wound and covered his fingers before falling beneath his wet shirt.

'You…' Zaif spat at Cypher, realising what had happened. 'You *fucking* bastard!'

The ambassador leapt forward with surprising agility and ripped Zaif's sword from its sheathe and pushed up, throwing all of his considerable weight into the attack and forcing the weapon out through the large man's shoulders. Cypher stepped forward and watched joylessly as the light faded from Zaif's eyes. He caressed the shocked face and dropped to his knees, bringing the dead body down with him. 'You were one of my finest. I never should have let you leave the dungeons…'

He couldn't keep the disappointment from his voice. Zaif could have been something more. He had everything. The size. The speed. The complete lack of empathy. A pity. He'd known since they left Archania that this would be how it ended between them. One name ticked from the list.

'Could have killed him back in the city,' Cypher said, handing the knife back over to his new ally.

'They wanted to see you do it,' the ambassador shrugged. 'Wouldn't have it any other way. Theatrical, just like you said.'

'Effective, just like I said. Though I could have stabbed either of you. Lucky it turned out the way it did.'

'No.' The ambassador laughed, throwing Zaif's bloody sword next to the corpse and clicking his fingers. The two soldiers that had flanked him began to drag the body away, pulling it across the soil and leaving a path free of brown leaves. 'You are curious, Cypher Zellin. When there are questions, you want answers. And I know you are doing your best to reach out for those answers right now. Only with us alive can you find them. Zaif was the odd man out. He had served his purpose. There was no more need for him.'

The ambassador dropped the earlier pompous attitude and flowery language, instead speaking with clarity and precision.

This was a man who needed to be watched. He wasn't the bumbling buffoon Cypher had thought he would be.

'Who am I to meet in that tent?'

'Our leader. He only wishes to speak with you. It is an honour. I know this may all seem very strange, but he will ensure that it all makes sense before you leave that tent and return to this clearing. That I can promise you.'

Cypher hated that feeling of uncertainty – the lack of control. He'd spent most of his adult life yearning to hone his skills so that he would always be the one in control but now he was to enter the unknown. He'd dealt with the Doctors before but maybe they had changed more than just the colour of their robes.

'Am I to walk in defenceless? Even Zaif was permitted to carry his own sword.' Worth a shot.

'A sword that cut through his stomach and pierced the skin between the back of his shoulders. You are better off entering that tent without the threat of weapons. I would ask you to trust me, but I am no fool. All I will say is that there is no need for weapons in there. If we wanted you dead, you would be.'

The truth of the ambassador's words rang clear. These robed men and women were no rebels. They were backed by the power of Norland. There was no way he would be able to fight his way off the island. He needed to listen to their leader's words and choose his next path wisely, whatever that may be.

'I guess I'll head in and say hello to my biggest fan.'

'Go in with an open mind, Cypher Zellin,' the ambassador recommended. 'Everything is not as it seems.'

Cypher kept the frown from his face and managed a confident smile as he marched towards the tent. He lowered his head and entered under the animal skin, pausing to take in the smell of lavender and honey that smacked his face upon entry. It was a large tent. More room above his head than he thought there would be. A collection of candles circled the room, casting an orange glow and throwing odd shadows from the small, wooden animal statues that stood around the edge of the tent. Another masked man sat in a blood-red robe on a simple chair at the back of the tent, waiting patiently.

'Cypher Zellin,' the man said. 'I knew you'd come.'

'You know my name,' Cypher responded. 'But I don't believe I know yours.'

The masked man stood and walked towards Cypher, stopping only a short distance away. 'I was there when you stoked those flames in the Lower City. I was there when you raised the hopes of the citizens who had lived off the crumbs offered to them by the elite of Archania. I was there with my mask and my sword. I was there when you ran away. Do you know who else was there?' His voice grew agitated, his gloved fists snapping into balls at his side.

'There were a great many people. I do not know them all,' Cypher said, rolling his eyes at the stupid question.

'My wife was there. She is still there.' A dead wife. *Great.* The man took his mask off, brown eyes burning with fury. 'Her name was Ella. She believed in a better world. One where innocence wasn't treated with such contempt. She was more foolish than I ever was, sadly. She died the night of the flames. My name is Matthias. You were there when the flames began Cypher Zellin. Are you ready to see what has been left in the ashes?'

'Do I have a choice?' He'd never even heard of this Matthias, let alone his dead wife. Irritated was an understatement.

Matthias barked a cold laugh and licked his lips. 'No. No, you don't.'

Sitting on the floor was more comfortable than Cypher imagined it would have been. The range of furs covering the ground certainly made things easier and allowed for an appropriate level of comfort. Cypher had lived in far worse conditions, so he wasn't going to complain. Matthias sat opposite him, slightly raised in his chair as he looked down at him. Without the mask, he looked just like any other fool from the mainland. Nothing interesting. The dark shadow of stubble covered his jaw. Messy, dark hair. Watery brown eyes. And the pale skin of the North.

'It still feels strange, not being able to do magic.' Matthias breathed in through his nostrils and exhaled. 'Spending your whole life hiding a truth about yourself creates a prison for the soul. Ever since I was little, I could remember people around me, loved ones, warning me to hide my gift. I was taught to shield the gold from my eyes and blend in, to be just like everyone else. I finally felt like everything was changing. The Doctors wanted us to step into the light, to reveal our true selves without shame to the kingdom. I was ready. Unfortunately, we failed. You were there. You know what happened.'

'What happened was a bunch of ill-prepared men and women attacking a city full of trained soldiers. Needed more support. I expected the mages to do something but all they did was burn…'

Cypher saw the flicker of annoyance cross the former mage's face, but it left as fast as it had arrived. The rebellion had been a bit of fun for Cypher – a 'fuck you' to Mason and the new king for the way he had been treated. There was never any chance of it succeeding.

'However it turned out, things have changed since then,' Matthias continued, only sadness left on his face now. 'After the last quake, we no longer need to hide in the shadows. We're just like everyone else.' His bitter tone informed Cypher of his feelings on that final point.

'Then why the masks? Why the tents in the middle of a forest miles away from any other settlement?' Cypher asked, pulling at the threads Matthias left dangling.

'I was searching. I wanted to end my life. Losing the purpose of improving the lives of my people. Losing my wife… I had nothing else to live for. Then I had a dream.' *Great. Another religious fool following the madness of dreams. What a waste of my time…*

'A dream?' Cypher didn't hide his disappointment. To his credit, Matthias took the ridicule well, smiling and waving his hands in the air.

'I know exactly what you're thinking. I would have thought the very same thing not so long ago. All I ask is that you listen to me.'

'I'm all ears.'

'In the dream, I was visited by a being with many faces. Not man, nor woman. Or at least neither of them on their own. I heard a strange voice. The voice told me to come here. Here I would find a girl with a gift. A girl who would help to pass on a message to others. The voice told me that this wasn't the end, but the end was coming. As a part of The Doctors, our aim was to heal a dying world. We saw a sickness and wanted to do something about it. Now, we see things differently. We're no longer here to heal, but to destroy. From the ashes, a new world can be born. We're The Doctors no longer: now, we are The Plague.'

'And subtlety is obviously still not part of the organisation,' Cypher chuckled to himself. 'I've heard many madmen speak of destroying and rebuilding, never seems to work out that way. There are always obstacles in the way. You couldn't even destroy your own city. What makes you think you will succeed this time?'

'We are guided by someone with the knowledge needed to undertake such a task. Someone who can offer the world on a plate if all we do is put the pieces into place. She has told me what the instructions are. We must follow them. The first was to build our group. The second, to find you.'

'And what is next on this strange list of instructions?' Cypher wanted this over with now. Such foolishness was beneath him.

'Next, we clear the way for their arrival. Once here, they will be able to cleanse the world of Takaara with fire and blood. Then, we can rebuild. Start a new world free from the horrors of yestercycle.'

Cypher marvelled at how Matthias could keep a straight face spouting such utter tripe. Madness really had taken the fool after he had lost his wife. He'd seen it before of course. Those who grieve are often broken and they break in different ways. To cope, this man has created an illusion, a way to give himself further purpose. Just one more question to ask, before Cypher could leave for good.

'Who are you clearing the way for? Who is speaking to this *girl*? Who will destroy Takaara?'

The bags beneath Matthias's eyes grew larger as he lowered his head, eyes still boring into Cypher's as his grin grew unnaturally wide.

'She speaks to the only being capable of such destruction. The God of Chaos.'

Cypher paused, mouth hanging slightly open before he managed to decide on his words. 'Take me to her.'

'That's exactly what she told me you would say...'

A single low, stone house stood next to the cliff, watching out over the endless crashing waves. There was nothing else nearby for as far as the eye could see. Grey clouds fired arrows of rain at the aggressive sea that beat at the jagged rocks by the coast. A depressing sight. Whoever built that small house must have been running away from something. Just standing beside it made Cypher feel as though he had reached the edge of the world. The perfect place to hide someone, or something.

'She's been here for a while now. Kept her out of the way since the quake. That's when it began. She enjoys darkness now. Helps prevent the headaches,' Matthias said, leading their small group to the house. He walked slightly ahead of Cypher. The guards followed, weapons sheathed but close to hand and alert eyes looking in all directions.

'You've not said much about her,' Cypher said to the leader who was wearing his mask once again. 'I feel as though *I* am in the dark at the moment. It's not a feeling I'm accustomed to...'

If Matthias recognised the threat left hanging in the air then he showed no sign of caring. A small shrug of the shoulders and that was it. 'I don't want to give too much away. I know you will most likely think this all complete madness. She is something best experienced than explained.'

More cryptic words. Cypher wondered what he would

find when the door opened into that room. At least he didn't have long to wait. Matthias banged on the door. Two heavy knocks. 'I'm coming in. I've brought him with me,' Matthias called out, loud and clear before pushing the door open. 'After you, Cypher Zellin.'

Cypher nodded and crept forward. A stale smell filled the room as he entered the darkness. No windows. No light except for a candle burning in the corner of the room. He could just about make out a small figure lying on a single bed in front of him, long, dark hair falling down and covering her face, obscuring her features from Cypher's curious gaze. He heard the door shut behind him as Matthias followed him into the strange room.

The three of them waited in the silence. Most people would have been unnerved by the strange atmosphere. The lack of light. The continued waiting. Cypher had done his time in darkness. He had waited far longer and he had survived. This was nothing. Still, he wanted the answers, and he wanted to get back to the mainland. He'd taken Zaif out but Mason D'Argio and that little prick of a king were still breathing.

'I'm sorry for the lack of light.' Her voice was soft and quiet. Cypher had to strain to hear it clearly. 'Since it started, the headaches have been difficult to handle. The darkness soothes them and allows me to rest when I can. But I suppose you don't mind, Cypher Zellin. You, who has lived in the darkness for long enough. More than most humans have managed and yet here you stand.'

Cypher was glad that the girl couldn't see the flicker of annoyance on his face in the darkness. She'd said what he had been thinking, only a moment later. He shook his dark thoughts away and brushed it off as just a coincidence.

'The dungeons of Archania make this place seem like a luxurious mansion. I would envy your abode if I were still locked away down there. Fortunately, I am now free to go where I please,' he answered with a smirk.

'If only that were true,' the girl responded, not missing a beat. 'They're watching you. You have rid yourself of your old apprentice but there are bigger fish to catch in these parts of the world, are there not?'

This time he frowned, unable to keep the discomfort from his face. 'Who are you?'

'My name is Phoebe. Though, that seems irrelevant after all that has happened. Who I am isn't so important. *What* I am is of a more pressing issue.'

'Then *what* are you?' Cypher asked, his anger growing with the constant vague words pouring from everyone around him. 'Does anyone here speak with clarity?'

'Apologies.' There was a hint of humour in her voice this time. 'After what I've seen, I forget how odd my mannerisms can seem to most people. I was a mage. Grew up in Norland, daughter to a fisherman. Not an interesting life, but a happy one. When the quake hit, he was out on his boat with a few others. The waves were strong enough to destroy the wood, breaking the boat into tiny pieces. My father's body washed up on the coast a day later. At the same time, I felt my body seize up. My arms and legs snapped together, and I fell to the ground, shaking. At least, that's what I'm told. I have no clear memory of the incident. All I remember is what I saw.'

'What did you see?' Cypher asked, chewing his lip as he listened to her drone on.

'Flames. Death. Life,' the girl said, her voice quickening. 'Through it all, there was only one thing threading it all together. Chaos. Pure chaos.'

'A cute story. But what does any of this have to do with me?'

'I saw you there, Cypher Zellin. I saw the role you play in what is to come. They spoke to me and I have listened. Now you must listen if this world is to heal through fire and flames.'

'Matthias here said that you need me to clear the path for the God of Chaos.' Cypher felt goosebumps prickling his skin at the thought. 'I'm not a religious man, but if there is one aspect I've always been drawn to, it is chaos. What do you need to tell me? What are you asking me to do?'

Phoebe patted the bed beside her, inviting Cypher to move closer. He glanced at Matthias who nodded his support before taking his mask off and holding it loosely at his side. In the low light, Cypher could still see the worry etched on Matthias' face as he stared over at the small girl lying in the bed. He stepped closer to Phoebe and lowered himself onto the furs keeping her warm. This close, he could see that she was pale, more than normal, even for a girl born this far north. She looked close to death. Cypher had seen enough death to recognise it. Whatever this girl was doing, it was draining the life out of her.

'My new gift has a few, difficult consequences. A sacrifice for the greater good. Vald Sickness is what they call it. A fancy name for a debilitating illness brought on by too much magic flowing through a body. This is a shock, the first time. Matthias took a few days to recover from his first experience. I doubt I have long left.'

'Feels unnatural. There's nothing like it,' Matthias agreed, shivering at the memory.

'Take my hand. They will come and they will speak to you. The message is for you alone.'

Cypher hesitated as the fragile girl held out her clammy hand, shaking ever so slightly. He swallowed and looked from Matthias to the girl, wondering what in the hells he was doing all the way out here in the middle of nowhere, talking of Gods and chaos. He cursed under his breath, taking the girl's hand and steadying his nerves.

His entire body felt aflame. Every part of him burning as though the girl had lit a fire around him. He tried to scream but no sound left his throat. He couldn't move, his arms and legs tensed, snapping together before he felt Phoebe's hands convulsing, taking his own hand and throwing it up and down wildly. The world went black and he was lost in the darkness, blind to everyone and everything.

The agony stopped. A wave of nausea swept over him and he felt the bile burning his throat. He opened his eyes and saw blue flames dancing in a circle around him. He was alone.

'I've waited for your arrival. A key link in the chain of events that has been so long in coming.' The voice sounded far away, like it was being spoken across a vast distance to someone else, but Cypher could still hear the words. An elegant voice, well-spoken and musical. A woman's voice. 'Be calm. Your being here is essential for what is to come. A necessary journey for us all.'

A gap opened in the flames and a tall, beautiful woman strode through with the confidence of a queen. Dark hair fell straight and down past her shapely hips and her eyes were black but sparkled like the stars in the night sky.

'I've waited in the darkness for a long time. Like yourself. We are cut from the same cloth. I need a voice in Takaara, a herald capable of taking my message to all the fools who may think of standing in my way. In *our* way.' Cypher jolted as thousands of grim-faced men and women flashed behind the woman and then disappear just as quickly. 'My flames will destroy. From the ashes, there will rise something new. Something *better*. I can show you.'

Cypher blinked and, suddenly, the world had changed. He recognised the white palace of the Upper City, but it wasn't like he had ever seen the majestic building. Flames roared across every inch of the palace as swarms of bloodthirsty warriors tore through the last defence of the Archanian army. The wall surrounding the city had been broken in two places as more attackers streamed into the city. Archanians ran screaming from the invaders, falling in their haste to be away and never getting up as swords, axes, arrows and spears found them where they lay. The great city was destroyed.

Loud cheers and chanting drew Cypher's attention to the palace gardens. A horde of warriors were pumping their fists and shouting as they dragged two men across the ground, ignoring their cries for mercy. He watched as a vicious looking woman, scars covering her face, pulled King Asher by his hair and shoved his face forward to the vile crowd. They cheered as she drove his head down onto a waiting spike, laughing mercilessly as the blood sprayed across the laughing audience.

The second man had familiar silver hair. Mason D'Argio. His white robe edged with gold had been torn at one shoulder, exposing his right arm and a seeping wound. Blood splattered the once elegant robe and mud had splashed up to the frightened man's knees as he was thrown onto them. For the first time since Cypher had met the preacher, he noticed that there were no jewels hanging around his neck; no gems shining from rings on his slender fingers. The confident, arrogant preacher was now broken and panicked, unused to being out of control.

Cypher smiled as he saw a thin, bald man step up to the mage and stare at the preacher, smirking at the lack of gold in his pupils. *There I am. Doing what I have only dreamed of.* He gave a holler of his own as they tied Mason to a wooden pole and cheered as the other Cypher slowly lit the base of contraption. The flames took their time to work their way up. He could smell the burning flesh. Could hear the screams of the preacher. Could see the terror in his eyes. Revenge. Pure, cold, lovely revenge.

'You are offering me this.' Cypher rubbed the growing beard on his chin, lapping up the beautiful scene below him.

'And so much more. This is a mere snapshot of what will be done,' the God of Chaos answered, resting her hands on his shoulders.

'I'll be your herald. Hells, I'll be your dog if it means I get to watch that bastard burn. Just tell me what I need to do.' The flames rose higher and Cypher basked in the comforting heat.

FATHERS AND SONS

A rden lay on his back, listening to the lapping of the waves. He stared up at the ceiling of the cave, his eyes following a bat flapping around trapped and alone. Its leathery wings flapped furiously as it flew this way and that, colliding against the walls and searching for its place in the world.

He sighed, bored with the sight of the bat struggling and ambled towards the pool. It was quiet inside the cave. Peaceful. He was left alone with his thoughts and it brought a calm tranquillity that he needed. He'd had time to think on Osiron's words. A prince. The Prince of Chaos. It sounded stupid. A tad over-dramatic. Sly would have laughed his head off at the title and even Kiras would have fought back a snigger or two. Still, wasn't it what he deserved? After all that had happened, didn't he deserve something good? Power. Control. A chance to show people that he wasn't the foolish, young boy that could be pulled one way or another by people acting like he was just a plaything. He was a man now and he needed to show them all. Korvus and Socket especially.

Arden dropped his naked body into the relaxingly warm water and continued until his shoulders were submerged beneath the still liquid. He groaned with pleasure; his whole body soothed by the healing waters. The bat still flapped around, snapping Arden from his reverie as his eye twitched with annoyance. The animal flew back to an outcrop in the rock and hung upside down from the ledge.

He ignored it, content that it would be no more bother, not today at least. Allowing his head to rest back against the pool's edge, he closed his eyes and listened to the waves still crashing outside of the cave. There was nowhere else like it in the world. Nowhere else he could just be still and embrace the world's music.

'I'm glad you like it here,' Osiron's voice echoed around the cave. Arden kept his eyes shut, smiling to acknowledge his new friend's words. 'Calm waters. Darkness. Warmth. I designed it myself.'

'You should be proud. I could spend the rest of my existence in this pool,' Arden said, letting his legs float up to the top of the pool and pushing away from the edge. He floated across the water slowly, loving the feeling of weightlessness.

'I hate to steal you from such a tranquil scene,' Osiron said, pity vibrating through their strange voice. 'But there is someone I wish for you to talk to. Someone I believe you have been wanted to speak to for a long time. If you are to become a prince, you must meet him and put the past to rest. Only then can we shape the future.'

'Who do you wish for me to speak to?' Arden asked, finally opening his eyes to see the damned bat flying in circles around Osiron who stood patiently, barely noticing the flying beast as it flapped around their head.

'It would be better for you to see him before I speak his name. There is a power in names. You will see.'

The same eyes. Green circling the black pupils. The same colour hair though his was streaked with silver, especially above his ears. Gave him a distinguished look that suited the man. Pale, wrinkled skin. He held his shoulders back and stood tall, head tilted slightly to the side as he peered down at Arden. Eventually, he gave a satisfied nod and even cracked the slightest of smiles.

'I've been waiting my entire life for this moment. Dreamt of it. I've ran this scenario around in my head since before I can even remember,' Arden's voice sped up as he stumbled over his words, face heating up as the blood rushed to his cheeks. 'Have to admit, this isn't how I had it pictured in any of those thoughts.'

King Mikkael cleared his throat and ran a hand through his silver hair. Arden recognised the same movement as the one he did when he was nervous. Strange, the things you notice at a time like this.

'A meeting that should have happened many cycles ago.' A powerful voice. Deep and regal but tinged with a weary sadness. 'I remember the last time I saw you. Your mother held you in her arms and gave you one last kiss on that little head. I've thought about that kiss every day of my life. And every day since…' he added with a stern look at Osiron before his eyes softened and turned back to Arden. 'I tried to see you, before the end. Thought I'd get a chance to apologise in person and ask for your forgiveness, if that was possible.'

Arden thought in silence for a moment, staring at the regret in his father's eyes. Forgiveness. He was unsure if he had it in him. His whole life had been a lie. Born a prince and sent to live in the wild Borderlands with cutthroats and killers. He'd shit in the middle of a freezing forest and dug a damn hole and, for all that time, he was a prince who should have had servants and maids taking care of him. Did he have the capacity to forgive such a thing?

'I forgive you, Father.' The words slipped out between his lips without much thought preceding them. 'I wish we had time in life. It seems we are only able to speak in death.'

'A cruel joke of the Gods…' Another purposeful glance to Osiron from the king. 'That is their way, I am afraid. In the eyes of the Gods, kings and peasants alike are just the pieces on the board being played in a game that even they don't care too much about.'

'What happened?' Arden asked. 'When you left to meet me in the Borderlands. What happened?'

Mikkael blew out his cheeks and rubbed his temples, staring at the floor before raising his head and wincing in pain. He ran a hand across his neck, clearly agitated by the memory. 'I was… betrayed. I left my kingdom in the hands of my eldest son. Your brother, Asher. A few old friends promised to look after him and guide his path – leading a kingdom can be tougher than finding your way through a labyrinth with a blindfold and everything around you on fire.' He laughed nervously. 'I trusted a man I shouldn't have trusted. My misplaced faith led to a dagger in the back and one across the throat. I was days away from seeing you and instead, I lay on the cold snow of the North as my blood left my body. The leers of paid killers were the last things I saw as I stared up at the night sky. All I could think of was what a huge, damned mess I'd made of things…'

Arden felt the anger boiling, his body tense at his father's words. Murdered as he made one last journey to find his lost son. It was just as Osiron had told him. The plague of humanity. They had their chances and they kept throwing them down a fiery hole, casting them away at each attempt.

'You had similar deaths, father and son,' Osiron said, glancing pitifully at them both. 'Betrayed by those you trusted. Stabbed in the back and left to bleed out in the cold snow. There is a meaning to death, just as there seems to be so many meaningless things in life. Fate has brought the two of you together at last. Your time of leading is over Mikkael. Your son, Arden, is ready to lead now. The Prince of Chaos will take the throne. What do you say to that?'

Mikkael looked at his son and chewed his lip for a second before that impressed nod returned. 'I say that if he leads then I will follow.' The king drew his sword and twisted the handle, turning it to Arden and offering it to him. He dropped to a knee as his son took the blade. 'My son. My prince. Lead the way and Chaos will follow. And so will I.'

'Come, Arden.' Osiron pulled him away and turned his body, facing him into the darkness. 'There is one other I would like you to speak with.'

Red hair. Wavy and wild. Sparkling blue eyes that Arden knew so very well though they were edged with more wrinkles than he was used to. One scar ran down from the man's left eye down to his upper lip, cutting a path through part of his infamous beard. A wild, manic beard coloured as flames that fell to his chest and was decorated with braids and bells.

'It is a great honour to meet you, chief.' Arden stuttered over his welcome as he lowered his head respectfully, waiting for the stocky leader to acknowledge him. He was so much like his son. A bit bigger maybe. In both height and width. Bit more of the white flecks and lines in his hair and beard than his son. But Reaver Redbeard still held himself like a king – a man of power. Like his own father, Arden could see the pride and dignity just in how the man stood, surveying all around him with those wise eyes. 'I met your son. Fought alongside him for a while. He was a good man. A man to follow. You would be proud.'

'I *am* proud,' Reaver responded after some time, sniffing with those great nostrils but never moving his eyes from Arden. Like a predator carefully judging his prey, working out when to make its move. 'My son would have been a greater leader than I ever was, given the chance. Sadly, the Gods deemed it necessary to allow him to be taken before his time. He will be sitting with his ancestors in the Hall, raising a horn to his tribe and the Great Raven. I am proud.'

'He died in the United Cities,' Arden informed him. 'He wanted to be there to say the words for his brother, Braego. They both died away from the snows of their home. Away from their tribe.'

'We all pray for the right death. Honour, dignity, and to die with a sword in our hand and a song in our heart.' Reaver sighed and there was sadness in his eyes as he looked away from Arden for the first time. 'There is no right way to die. Kings have died taking shits. Peasants have died fighting off bandits to protect their families. Some folk have died after a slip on the ice. Death embraces them all the same. I sometimes think we have it wrong in the Borderlands. We talk of living with honour, but we stab each other in the back and spend our lives drinking and killing, constantly keeping one eye open in our sleep as we look out for the next bastard with enough balls to show us some steel.

111

Ain't right in my mind. Not now I look back on it all. Socket used to say all this of course. That man saw more with one eye than most folk with two.' The large warrior chuckled and the warmth returned to his face, reddening his cheeks and bringing back the sparkle in his eyes.

Arden frowned as his old friend's name dropped into the conversation. He'd wondered how long it would take for the old archer's name to crop up. 'He stabbed you in the back, didn't he?' Reaver nodded, slowly running a tongue over his lips as though he could taste the memory of his blood leaving his body. 'Did exactly the same with me. I trusted him. One of the few I've ever trusted, in fact. The pain of that blade forcing its way between my ribs was nothing compared to the pain of knowing that he was the one to wield it.'

'Socket always thought he knew best. Often did, to be honest.' Reaver scratched his beard. It was the little mannerisms that caught Arden by surprise. Uncannily like his son. 'I don't hold any hate towards the man. We spent some good cycles side by side fighting together and sharing the light and heat of a fire. One ill move doesn't take all that away in my eyes.'

An unexpected view to take, in Arden's mind. But Reaver always had a reputation for following the path less travelled. Warriors in the Borderlands had killed for just being looked at in a funny way. Yet, here was one of the most famous leaders in their history speaking of forgiveness towards the friend who stabbed him in the back when he was on the cusp of making history.

'I'm not sure that I can be so forgiving,' Arden admitted.

'New wounds hurt the most. Old ones ache a little but don't do much more than remind you of how much you've grown. Of how far you've come. Time heals, they say. I have to agree. You need time.'

Arden grunted, shuffling his feet uncomfortably at the thought. 'I wonder how much time it will take for these wounds to heal…'

'Distractions can help. I never had a chance for such things. You do, by the sound of it.' Reaver's eye flicked to Osiron who waited patiently to the side, hovering near Arden's shoulder. 'You gonna do what they want? Become this Prince of Chaos?'

'What do you think I should do?' Arden asked, eager for his hero's advice on the difficult matter.

Reaver sucked in his breath and exhaled out his nostrils. Hands on hips as he looked up and frowned. He rubbed at his fiery beard and thought a while longer before coming to a decision. 'Not my place to decide for you. It is your choice at the end of the day. Though, I must admit, I have no ties down there now. My boys are dead. Herick leads the Borderlands with Barbarians I fought against all my life. Everything I worked for lies in ruins. If you want my advice, there's only one thing that I can suggest.'

'What do you suggest?' Arden asked.

Reaver stepped closer and clutched Arden's shoulder tightly, almost painfully, as he bent down so that their noses were almost touching. Arden could feel the heat of the warrior's breath on his face.

'Burn it down. Burn everything down. You owe them nothing. Set it alight and dance in the ashes, Arden Leifhand. Burn it all and cause chaos.'

Arden nodded; his mind finally made up.

'I'm ready.' He twisted his neck and caught the smile widening on Osiron's face, those starry eyes shining in blue light as flames erupted all around the trio.

'Then we shall ready the army. We must prepare. Everyone will soon embrace the Chaos...'

SLOW AND PAINFUL

It was an odd building. An odd building for an odd man, Sara had said. It was old and certainly needed a coat of paint or two, but Kane could see the beauty in it. White walls were kissed with the sunlight that seemed to shine down endlessly in this part of the world. Kane wiped the sweat from her forehead and searched for a tissue in her breast pocket before realising that she had lost that earlier in her journey. Instead, she settled on another sip from her water bottle and winced at the warmth of the liquid that had been out in the sun for too long.

'When I said he was odd,' Sara warned. 'I mean he is really odd. Most folk have an image in their head when they meet the Sword of Causrea. Kind of like the knights in your United Cities. All honourable and dignified. Manners and discipline taking precedence over all other things in life. That's not his way…'

Kane struggled to keep her laughter at bay. Knights with honour and dignity. She thought back to Sir Dominic and the way he swanned around Archania living off past glories. Brothels, taverns, and faze dens knew Sir Dominic better than most. He certainly wasn't the most inspiring of individuals. She remembered his feeble attempt at leading soldiers back during the rebellion and shook her head in dismay. He'd ran to the back of the line as soon as he realised that actual fighting would break out. All bluster and fighting words but nothing to back it up. His sword was polished to a shine that blinded any who stared at it too long. She wondered when the last time would have been when that weapon had tasted blood. *Far too long...*

'Perhaps the knights of the United Cities aren't exactly what you think they are, Sara. I found the men with honour were often the ones who spoke few words and were last to draw their blades. There isn't enough recognition for men like that. Knights are the ones who chase glory and that, in my experience, isn't the most honourable of actions.' She thought of Braego and a smile found her lips as she imagined him as a knight of the United Cities. He'd have deserved it. Never would have accepted the damn title though. Too much of a Borderlander to accept such a thing. Fighting was a way of life for him. Not something to be proud of. Just something that happened and that was that.

'Perhaps not. I used to love reading tales of their battles and even the romances of knights and princesses as they sneaked around castles behind their parents' backs. A simpler time, for me.'

Kane thanked Sara as the younger woman pushed open a low, white, wooden fence that ran round the perimeter of the grounds. The garden was wild. A rainbow of various flowers and plants grew with seemingly no order. Oranges and purples mixed with reds and blues and, between them all, dark grass rose tall and forced others into the shade. A thin stone pathway wound its way to the front door. Needed some work. Weeds slipped between cracks and breaks within the stone, thriving with the lack of an opponent to take them out.

'He live on his own?' Kane asked, eyebrows almost meeting as she frowned at the disrepair.

'That obvious?' Sara snorted, following her gaze to the broken pathway. 'He's not overly fond of company. Last person I brought over to tidy up the garden quit on the first day. He's an acquired taste.'

Sara banged on the door and called out a greeting. 'It's me, Sara! Get your ass out here, old man!' She turned to Kane with an embarrassed grin as her greeting was met with nothing but silence. 'Bastard always likes to play these little games...'

Kane smiled back. Maybe he hadn't heard them? They stood outside like awkward merchants trying their best at selling snake oil to annoyed customers wanting none of it. The minutes slipped by before Sara gave up on the front door. 'Come on, there's another entrance to the side.'

Kane shrugged and followed as she made her way round to the side of the house. The grass grew neater as they passed the stonework on the side of the building. Less wild and untamed as the front. A solitary chair sat facing out towards the valley in the distance. She thought there would be a stunning sunset that could be seen from that spot as the sun dipped in the west. Be good to see it if the opportunity arose.

Sara snapped her from her daydream, standing next to another door built into the side of the house. She pulled a long, rusted iron key out from the inside of her robe and slotted it into keyhole. The lock clicked as Sara turned the key gently, pushing the door with an odd uncertainty and peering into a darkened room. Kane followed cautiously, still frowning at the lack of life in the house.

A musty smell clung to the warm air. The place obviously hadn't been cleaned recently. Kane felt the hairs stand up on the back of her neck as walked deeper into the house. Dirty plates lay scattered on a small oak table and a rat scuttled across the floor beside her boots. She'd been in places like this before. More often than not, there'd been a death a few days before and the poor victim had no friends or family to find the body before the decomposition. Always horrible. Horrible smell. Horrible sight. Everything was horrible. She recognised the signs.

Sara reached the next door frame and gave an annoyed sigh. Kane stepped around a chair and looked away for a moment. A muffled scream forced her to look up just in time to see Sara blocked from view by a shadowy figure. Her hand naturally snapped to the hilt of her sword as she raced into the next room, crashes and bangs mixing in with curses from Sara and her attacker.

Kane dashed through the doorway only to feel a fist collide with her jaw. She stumbled to the side, her head going all fuzzy with the impact as her legs shook like branches in the wind.

116

She shook the fuzziness away and swore at herself. *Pull yourself together!* She was ready for the next attack. There wasn't enough time to dodge the tackle, so she allowed the attacker to force her backwards, deciding to use the momentum against them. She wrapped her arm around their lowered head and jumped back with the attack, attempting to drop her assailant onto their head.

She groaned as her back slammed through a wooden chair, legs splintering and shattering in all directions. The air flew from her body, but she'd taken worse hits. Sara pulled the attacker from her as Kane used the chance to roll to the side and jump to her feet as best as she could. Kane cursed as Sara was thrown over the attacker's shoulder and slammed to the floor, screaming as her arm twisted and a large, black boot pushed against her ribs. Kane roared and swung a punch, but the bastard was fast. Too damn fast. She cried out as her fist stopped in its path and her whole shoulder twisted in its socket. She gritted her teeth and launched a boot between the legs. Kick to the fruits always worked.

Again, the attacker dodged with unusual speed and spun Kane's body towards him, pulling a dagger from his belt and pressing it against her throat, warm, calm breath kissing her cheek.

'That's enough!' Sara yelled, brushing the splinters from her hair and coughing as she slowly climbed to her feet. 'You've had your fun!'

'Fun?' A man's voice roared. 'Ha! This is not fun. A test. One in which you both failed. I can taste nothing but disappointment, as usual...'

Kane cursed as the man released her and ushered her away. He pulled a thin, black mask from his face and pushed his short silver hair back, grey eyes piercing Kane.

'You are the worst host I have ever met. This is the last time I bring a friend over,' Sara grumbled.

'Host?' Kane choked, mirroring her opponent's glare and hoping she was displaying just as much anger in that look as he rubbed at her sore neck. 'This is...'

'Istari Vostor,' the man butted in, finally releasing her

from his gaze and turning to Sara, returning the dagger to his belt. 'It is good to see you, daughter. You took the throw better than the last time but you must be better prepared for the attack. How many times must I say this to you? The first strike may also be the last. Know this.'

'Daughter?' Kane repeated as Istari pulled Sara in for a warm hug and kissed the top of her head with love.

'Yes.' Sara looked lovingly from her the man to Kane, beaming from ear to ear. 'Though, not my birth father. Katerina Kane, meet Istari Vostor. The Sword of Causrea.'

Kane felt the skin on her face stretch almost to breaking point as her eyebrows took a journey higher than they had for a long time. 'The Sword of Causrea.'

'The man who saved my life.'

'I'm not going with her.' Istari shook his head and sighed. 'Could have killed her. She failed.' Then he left the room without another word.

'An odd building for an odd man,' Kane muttered, watching him leave.

'I tried to warn you,' Sara laughed, placing an arm around her shoulder and leading her after the man.

'Did you try hard enough?'

'You wouldn't have come if I did.'

'True. Too true…'

***

She sipped on her hot tea, cupping her hands around the flask and doing her very best to ignore the bickering coming from inside. She'd offered to help clean up the decimated room but both Sara and her surrogate father had baulked at the idea. Sara being polite and Istari offended that a foreigner would be touching his stuff.

She'd settled for taking a seat outside and enjoying the view before her. A pink sky dashed with white clouds and a falling red sun dipping below the horizon. A warm evening breeze blew throughout the land as she tasted the strange tea. Sweeter than she was used to back home but not worse for the difference. Sara had made it in between sweeping up the mess her father had caused and apologising multiple times to Kane – always with a cheeky smile on her face as though she had enjoyed the whole thing.

Relaxing in the low chair, Kane could see why Istari lived out here, alone. The peace. The quiet. The beauty of the world around this solitary house. Braego would have loved it here. Bit too warm for his liking maybe, but he would have grown accustomed to it, given time. There were no merchant's calls, no call for prayer, no horses racing over cobbled streets, no crying children angering their ill-equipped parents. Just nature and the beauty of Takaara. The work of the Gods was at hand here for as far as she could see. Humans hadn't the chance to spoil it, yet.

And then the bickering erupted once more.

'I've told you time and time again, I'm done with all of that! I'm happy here. Content even. Leave me be.'

'Happy. Content.' Kane heard Sara scoff. 'You have been a pain in the backside for cycles now. You're not the retiring type. Ignoring all the calls of the Council when they need you. You never used to be like that. And now I offer you an adventure across Takaara and you act like this? I'm not amused.'

'Then it's a good thing that my job is not to amuse you. The Council have been a group of fools pissing in the wind for too long. I'd rather ram daggers into my ears than listen to what that bunch of cretins has to say for themselves. Times have changed, my dear, and, unfortunately, Causrea is a mere shadow of its former self.'

'That is still a damned sight better than what it will become if the Empire heads this way.'

A tense pause hung in the air and Kane felt a sudden chill that had nothing to do with the sun's absence from the sky.

'And what do you think this woman from the North will be able to do? What role will she have to play in this grand drama unfolding across Takaara, eh?' Istari's voice lowered, no longer dripping with the previous amounts of venom and mockery.

Perhaps she had imagined it, projecting her own feelings onto the man but she thought she heard the flicker of fear in his strong voice.

'She can convince Darakeche to stand tall. She can tell the Red Sons to finally make a choice and stop playing soldier in the wild. She can make a difference and prevent the horrors of war from reaching the land you have loved.' A convincing speech. Even Kane felt swayed by it, her own chest puffing out with pride at the words.

'Who taught you to be so bloody good with words?' Istari muttered, his amused voice barely finding its way to Kane through the open door.

'An old fool once told me the sharp mind and trained tongue will end the need for the unsheathed sword.' Even from here, Kane could picture how Sara must be gazing lovingly at her father.

'An old fool indeed,' Istari laughed. 'I'm the Sword of Causrea, not the Mouth of Causrea. I suppose I better speak to our guest. It'll be a long journey. They better be paying me well…'

Kane stood as Istari marched out to the garden and stood before her. Stern face. Judging, grey eyes. Sharp cheekbones that could cut worse than some blades by the look of them.

'Istari Vostor. The Sword of Causrea,' Kane said with a light smile and a respectful drop of the head. 'It's a pleasure to properly meet you.'

Istari snorted and looked over Kane's shoulder to his daughter and then back, his own thin lips curled ever so slightly as the breath rushed from his nostrils. 'I'm sure you've had colder greetings than the one I gave you. First female captain or some shit in the United Cities. Not so accepting up north if I remember correctly.'

'You've been to the United Cities?'

'A few times. Cold. Too cold to stay for long.' His eye twitched at the memory. Not many folks could enjoy the cold, dark nights of winter in the North. Kane had loved it. Offered a chance to curl up in some furs next to a roaring fire and a flask of tea… 'I hope you're up for a bastard of a journey. The East is unforgiving and the heat unbearable at times. I don't drop my pace for anyone. I want this over with as quickly as possible with no moaning.'

'She's not a child,' Sara groaned from behind.

'It's fine,' Kane said, turning to Sara with thanks. She stared back at Istari, not blinking as their eyes locked on one another. 'I have a job to do, Vostor. I pray that you can keep up with me. I don't drop *my* pace for anyone.' It wasn't true but this man valued strength and she'd be damned if he was going to belittle her without a fight.

She felt a flash of pride as Istari blinked and nodded his head. 'We set out tomorrow at first light. Sara will prepare the horses. I'll do the rest. You get some sleep. It'll be the last good one you'll have for a while, Miss Kane. Enjoy it.'

'I'm sure I will.'

Her sleep came in fits and bursts. Away from the bluster in the rally of words between herself and her new companion, Kane knew that sleep was never as enjoyable as it had been in her youth. Too many worries. Too many regrets. Too many memories.

Though the bed had been comfortable, she found herself pacing outside in the garden and listening to the calls of the nocturnal animals and staring off out into the world around her. As far as she could fathom, Sara and Istari had even less sleep than she had. The grumpy man stormed around the house, not trying too hard to keep the noise down as he looked for flasks, clothes, weapons, and food whilst his daughter laughed at him and readied the horses. Once again, Kane found her offer to help useless, drawing more annoyance from Istari and a gentle smile of thanks from Sara.

'We can do this Kat. Believe me, it might not seem it, but this is the best mood I've seen him in for an age!' Kane frowned as Istari cursed, stubbing his toe against one of the wooden legs on the dining room table. He hobbled around the room before pulling a dagger from his belt and stabbing the inanimate object four times, eventually leaving the small blade standing up out from the table, still rocking from side to side.

'I fear to see him in a worse mood...' Kane said with hushed laughter. 'We'll face worse things than tables where we are going.'

'He'll be fine. He's an experienced fighter and he knows what he's doing,' Sara reassured her. 'Though, it may be best if you do all the talking, when you meet folk on the road...' She struggled to contain her own laughter as Istari swore once more and rushed up the stairs to his room.

As the sun rose in the east, they were all packed and ready. Kane busied herself with checking the saddle for the third time on her chestnut-brown horse and scratching the animal on its neck. It allowed a chance for Sara and Istari to say their goodbyes away from an outsider's gaze. When they were done, Kane could sense the sadness lingering in the air between them. As much as they may claim that this was just another journey, they knew the risks involved. Takaara was dangerous at the best of times but things were different since the quake. More volatile. The people seemed as eager to erupt as the land around them.

'It's been good getting to know you in the short time we have spent together, Katerina. I would be happy to have the chance to spend more time with you, on your return.' Sara opened her arms and Kane moved into them, a quick hug to say farewell to a new friend. Kane had lost enough over the years; any new ones were welcome with open arms.

'I look forward to it. Keep safe and we shall share a drink on my return from the East.'

Istari jumped onto his steed with the agility of a man half his age. He clicked his tongue and kicked his heels against the horse, pushing it forward and past the two women without looking back.

'He will be a pain. He will annoy you. He will frustrate you. He's not used to company,' Sara warned, staring off after her father. 'But he will defend you with his life and there is no better swordsman in these lands. That is a promise.'

'I've rode with harsher men than your father,' Kane reassured her. 'If he is the worst thing on the road then I am in for an easy journey.' She squeezed Sara's shoulder and leapt onto her own mount, not as graceful as Istari but better than most. She'd ridden the beasts since she was a little girl, this was just another ride in the light of the rising sun.

Nothing more.

Half a day. Half a day had passed before Istari graced her with words. A few grunts, shakes of the head and a nod or two but that was it. Half a day. The man rode his horse, back straight and frown carved onto his face, immovable and frustrating. Kane had attempted a few conversations but there was no point. It was a waste of time and so she had given up, preferring to enjoy the empty road and the changing of the scenery on her route.

Autumn was a beautiful time of year in these parts. Stunning red leaves shone in the sunlight, both on the trees and coating the ground beneath her. There were a few yellow, oranges and browns but red seemed to swallow all other colours on her path. It didn't feel real. There was nothing in the North that was so red and vivid and full of life. She'd seen paintings of talented artists who had used such stunning colours in their work to portray the beauty of Takaara but had always assumed that they were taking liberties to improve their work, to make the scene more fantastical and enticing to the audience. But as she rode through the fields of red leaves and flowers, she thought that she could have been inside one of those paintings. She hadn't given the artists the credit they so obviously deserved in capturing such beauty.

'Autumn here is stunning,' she called out to Istari.
Grunt.
'You must really love living near such a place.'
Grunt.
She took a breath, struggling to hold her annoyance.

Sara had warned her. It would do no one any good if Kane lost her temper with the man just because he wouldn't speak to her. Let him be immature. She could enjoy her own company, there wasn't any need for her to like the man, was there? Sure, it would make both of their lives easier but this was a business arrangement, something put in place for the betterment of the world. She could hate the man but if he got her to where she needed to go then that was all that was needed.

More silence then.

She'd travelled with worse companions. Sometimes it was the ones who spoke too much that were the most annoying. She recalled having to prevent Braego from lopping the head off one new guard who, in his excitement at passing initiation, spent the whole ride across Five Farms bleating about his life from the moment of birth up until that ride. She laughed at the way Braego had turned a funny shade of red and snapped a spear in his hands, shutting the guard up without speaking a word himself.

She missed riding with the warrior from the Borderlands. He'd brought her joy when she had least expected it. Probably would have got on with *this* cranky warrior well enough, now she thought about it.

'Wait here.' Words. Actual spoken words.

Kane nearly fell from her horse in shock. She watched as Istari dropped gracefully from his horse and untied a small, grey cloth bag from his mount. He made for the hill to their side, following a stone path that was nearly completely covered in the red leaves.

'Where are you going?' Kane shouted, dismounting and following her strange companion.

'Nowhere you need to go. I will only be a moment.'

Kane paused and watched him trudge up the steps and waited, stroking her horse and peering out at the pathway up the hill. It twisted around a large boulder, obscuring Istari from view when he was halfway up. She chewed her lip, contemplating her options. Curiosity may have killed the cat, but she was made of sterner stuff. Tying the horses to a sturdy tree, she fed them apples and cautiously followed the cracked steps up the hill.

It was an old path, lined with small, stone statues depicting various Gods – not just The Four. Unlit candles sat waiting in iron lanterns as she quickened her step, taking them two at a time. The top of the path opened onto a hilltop. Kane stood beside a beaten rock, resting a hand against it as she peered out to the edge of the hill.

Istari knelt on a bamboo mat in front of a larger, stone statue depicting a woman with open palms out to the side. He had lit two candles either side of the statue and was murmuring to himself. Even straining and leaning towards him, she couldn't make out his words. Understanding the intimacy of the scene before her, she crept back down the steps and waited at the bottom of the hill, whispering to the patient horses.

A few minutes later, Istari bounded down the steps, face as stern as always as he nodded her way and leapt back up onto his horse.

'You followed, didn't you.' Not a question. There was no point denying it.

'You were praying. But not to The Four,' Kane said, puzzled.

'What I was doing is not of your business, woman. Know that.' His tone was edgier than normal. He sounded angry as he rode ahead of her.

'I didn't mean to offend you,' Kane said. She'd known people follow different Gods before. No harm in it until there's violence and manipulation involved. Each person had their own path, in her mind. 'I just want to know more about you. As you said before, we have a long journey ahead of us. It will be difficult to do it all in silence.'

Istari stopped his horse and waited for Kane to catch up. Looking forward, staring off into the distance, he spoke in a calm and measured tone. 'I've had no one with me apart from my daughter for many cycles. I was praying up here, not to any God, but to them all. My sword keeps me alive but the world is changing, breaking even. I hate the Gods, whomever they may be, but I'd pray to Gods and Demons for the rest of eternity if it means that there is just a slither of a chance of Sara still being here when I return.'

'That's why you've been quiet?' Kane asked. 'Because you are worried about her.'

'Maybe.' Istari shrugged. 'or maybe it's because since we left the house, there have been four soldiers following our every move. Keep your voice down, woman. Tonight, there will be more of your beautiful red splattered across the ground at your feet. Tonight, you can marvel at the Sword of Causrea.'

They lit a fire. Didn't need it for the warmth but Istari had been successful in his hunt. Green pheasants. After a day of riding without a break, the birds tasted better than anything she could remember after being roasted on the small fire in front of her. She tore into the food with abandon, ripping off large chunks with her teeth and groaning with pleasure.

'You're overdoing it…' Istari muttered, tutting to himself and glaring at her as he bit into his own hard-earned meal. 'They'll stay well away if you ham it up that much.'

Kane held back her smile and continued the meal, listening out for any sounds of movement in the forest behind her. At least four. That's what Istari had said, anyway. Skilled trackers but then again, they hadn't exactly been trying too hard. There was no point running away. Nowhere to run to out here. A meeting was inevitable so the best they could hope for was to pick the ground to fight on. They didn't have the numbers but Kane and Istari could at least be sure they had the ground and the opportunity for the element of surprise.

'How close are they?' she asked Istari.

'Close. When they get here. Do nothing.'

'What?' Kane jerked the foot from her mouth and stared incredulously at him. 'I can fight, Istari. I may not be known as *The Sword* of anywhere, but I've had my fair share of battles and scrapes.' She was more hurt than she cared to admit by Istari's comment.

'That may be true and I have no reason to disbelieve it.'

126

Istari placed the food on the mat beside him and licked his fingers before holding his palms up in defence. 'But I'm asking you to do nothing when they arrive. If we are to make it to the East, you must trust me. I was tasked with defending you on your way, let me defend you.'

'I can defend myself,' Kane said feeling her face tense with anger.

'Then why have I been given the job of ensuring your safety?' Istari responded, standing and looming over her.

She had no answer for that. The journey was hazardous but what could two travellers do that was so much more useful than one. Besides companionship and a chance to share stories and thoughts, she couldn't think of the purpose. It was odd that she had only just thought of it.

'The Sword of Causrea.' Kane leapt to her feet at the voice in the darkness, spinning around and cursing as she saw two of the stalkers standing on the edge of the campfire. 'No need to reach for the weapon, lady. We have everything in hand.' She raised her own in surrender, hoping Istari had something up his sleeve. The speaker held no weapon. His face was obscured by a thin, grey scarf that matched his cloak and hood that covered his head, only allowing a small enough gap for him to look out through with dark, piercing eyes. His partner wore the same. She held a bone longbow in her right hand and a loose arrow casually spinning in her left.

Kane risked a fast look over her shoulder and saw Istari standing calmly opposite two more intruders dressed in similar fashion to the ones bothering her. Both had drawn curved swords pointing towards the Causrea native.

'I'm not really one for new friends,' Istari said with a pained expression on his face, still holding his hands low and looking only as annoyed as Kane might be if she had been bothered by a fly whilst enjoying a good meal outside. 'I recommend putting your toys away and going back home. Stay here, and you will find only death.'

The Eastern warriors shared a laugh, one of them later than the rest. Kane saw how the shorter man next to Istari glanced at the other three before feeling brave enough to laugh along. Young. Inexperienced perhaps.

'The arrogance of Western men,' the archer next to Kane spat, raising her bow and pressing the arrow to the tight string. 'Give me one good reason why I shouldn't end him right now...'

'Because your death will be long and slow and more painful than your darkest nightmares...' Istari replied with an impatient growl.

The swordsman closest to him stepped forward at the threat and Kane heard the bowstring tighten further.

'Bastard,' the woman growled back, stepping closer to Istari and further from Kane. '*I* will make it slow. *I* will make it painful.'

Istari shrugged. 'As you wish...'

The bow released with a twang that made Kane flinch. The next sound was of metal snapping against wood followed by a harmonic thud. She spun to see Istari standing tall, sword in hand and a hard, grim look caught on his face. The archer dropped to the ground in shocked silence, a small blade sticking out from her right eye. Her body twitched on the ground as the warrior closest to Istari dropped in similar fashion.

Kane's jaw opened as she realised what had happened. In the blink of an eye, the infamous warrior had deflected the arrow and flung two hidden blades at his assailants, dropping both with unnerving accuracy. She saw the realisation dawn upon the remaining attackers as they screamed with a cold fury and rushed towards the silver-haired man.

His sword was lightning.

There was no need to block the attacks. In two swift movements, The Sword of Causrea flashed his weapon upwards and tore through his first attacker's face, spraying blood in a beautiful arc in the firelight before twisting his body and thrusting the weapon behind him and straight through the last warrior's stomach. One more forceful push with a grunt and the sword poked out of the Eastern man's back. Two swords clanged onto the ground as the light left their eyes. Istari pulled his weapon free and wiped it on the robe of the nearest victim. As casual as wiping paint from his brush.

Kane felt the volume of the world return as she heard a cough behind her. Blinking, she returned to her senses and walked over to the archer still twitching on the red leaves.

'Leave her,' Istari growled, marching over to the suffering woman. 'She chose her fate.'

He ripped the dagger free from the eye and didn't even flinch at the blood-curdling scream. He pulled the scarf from her face so that her dark skin and thin lips were visible for the first time. The woman had a white marking of a sun branded on her cheek. A sign of the Empire of Light.

'Your Empress will need to send more than four amateurs to end my life.' Istari slowly dug the dagger into the branding, flicking the edge of the blade up just as it pierced the skin. Kane turned away but the screams, the screams she could not hide from. 'If you're squeamish, you may want to go for a walk,' Istari warned her. 'I promised her slow and painful. The Sword of Causrea keeps his promises.'

'The Empress keeps her promises. Mason D'Argio keeps his promises,' the woman said between violent coughs. Blood splattered the ground around her. 'Brother and sister have promised your head for our Empire. And we know who you are, Katerina Kane. Mason D'Argio regrets allowing you to leave of your own accord. It is a mistake he will rectify with your death. I may fall but others will rise in my place. *That* is my promise.'

Kane gathered her senses and calmed her breathing. She remembered a young boy burning on a stage in front of a baying crowd. She remembered the smile of a silver-haired preacher with amber eyes.

She turned her head and strode over to Istari Vostor and looked down at the frightened woman, eyes that begged for mercy even though the tongue had been strong and proud.

'Slow. And painful.'

THE TOUGHEST DECISIONS

L ike a dream. A horrible dream after a few too many jugs of the strong stuff. The Borderlands looked like the same place Sly had grown up in but there was something off about it all.

Barbarians.

The bastards were everywhere.

They smirked and grunted every time Sly caught a look of them from under his low hood and he had to force a smile back and restrain himself from trying to slash at every last one of them with his bloody axes. He was a man of true will power, that was a fact, and no man could deny it. Every time he looked into their eyes, he felt the blood lust grow from deep inside him and had to grab something close by as his fingers twitched, reaching out for his weapons.

One of the colossal cunts walked on past him in the rising snow and winked. *Fucking winked.* He growled and brushed a finger against the tight leather on the grip of his axe. It would be easy. Just one of the bastards. No one would need to know. Just another dead Barbarian lying in the snow. Who would give a shit?

No. Not now.

He cursed and closed his eyes for a long moment. A quick and easy death now could throw everything off. Better to wait and get as many of the bastards as he could later. Kiras' life depended on it. Baldor's too. He could almost hear Raven's voice in his head, scolding him for thinking about rushing the attack. The chief had loved the cautious approach. Fat load of good that did him in the end but Sly had to admit that he felt happier with Redbeard by his side, warts and all.

He turned his neck, watching the Barbarian amble away, snow rising past his ankles and reaching the top of his boots. The white stuff hadn't stopped its descent since the start of the week. Just continued falling from the white sky, covering all of the buildings, offering a pristine look for an otherwise messy world.

'It's like travelling with a new person…' a voice said with a soft chuckle. 'Not so long ago, that Barbarian would be twitching in the snow with an axe in his back.'

'No need to fucking tell me that!' Sly growled, glaring at Cray. His companion smirked at the ire shown and Sly felt the heat rise to his cheeks that the man had got to him so easily. 'You don't even have to be here. Should be wrapped up nice and tight with that nice wife of yours next to a roaring fire. No idea why you'd rather spend your time in the cold with this pretty mug o' mine.'

'Must be the thrilling conversations that I can't get anywhere else.'

Though he hated to admit it, Sly had welcomed the sight of the warrior running after him out of the gates of Hillheim. They had argued, Sly claiming that it would be easier alone, but the stubborn fool wanted none of it. They had made it this far and Cray's family was safe. He wasn't going to sit around twiddling his thumbs whilst Sly was out there having all of the fun. Sly may have grumbled but he was thankful. No chance he'd let the bastard know that.

'Sofia asked for one thing. For us to make sure the girl was safe. She didn't say nothing about how many Barbarians I should or shouldn't have some fun with…'

Cray shrugged and tilted his head. 'Can't deny it. But sure would make our lives a fuck load more difficult if we're cutting through a whole army of the bastards before we even find the girl.'

Sly already knew that. Course he did. He was no fool. As much as he wanted to unleash his axes on the scum occupying his homeland, the action would have only one consequence and he'd be damned if he was going to be bones in the ground thanks to Barbarians and leave them free to do as they please in the Borderlands. A bit of restraint and then his time would come. They would teach the bastards a lesson. Sly. Kiras. Baldor. Even Cray. The snow would turn red with the blood of the damned Barbarians.

'So, where you thinking of heading first?' Cray asked as they kept away from the shelter of the farmhouse to Sly's right. 'Take it people won't take it too kindly to see you wandering around the Borderlands right now. Bound to get recognised sooner or later.'

No denying it. Sly had spent most of his life building his name and becoming one of the deadliest warriors in all the Borderlands. Worked damned hard at it and succeeded. Now, that very fact would work against him. Being recognised now would mean finding trouble and they hadn't the time for that.

'Need to stay in the quieter areas of the Borderlands. Keep away from the bigger towns. There's a tavern a few days to the north. Out of the way. A place for rogues and thieves to hide out away from prying eyes. Too far for most to go just for a drink. Ale tastes like piss there too.' He shook at the memory of the drink and licked his lips. May taste like piss but he could do with a stiff drink about now. 'The guy that runs it is an old friend. If anyone knows where Kiras is, then it will be him.'

'Can we trust him?' A good question. Especially after the last moon that they had survived.

'Can trust him about as much as I trust any bastard in the Borderlands, which is about as much as you can trust the Borderlands' sky to go a day without pissing on us,' Sly croaked. 'Kiras worked for him a while ago. Saved his life. He owes her a debt and he'll know it's time to pay up.'

'And if he doesn't?'

Sly smirked, unable to keep the smile off his face at the thought. 'Then it's time we get bloody once again. Didn't come back home just to scratch my arse, did I?'

'Bloody, aye,' Cray agreed. 'Lead the way…'

Had been a while since he'd been this far in the North. Bit too close to the Barbarian's territory for his liking. Still, the tavern was always quiet and there was a begrudging respect between the inhabitants who braved the harsh conditions and long journey to make it all the way out to the lonely building.

Hadn't changed much. Not from the outside anyway. Needed a lick of paint and was covered in snow thanks to the continued storm. Wasn't too likely that there would be many patrons this evening. Sly could barely see the hand in front of him let alone anything else. Foolish to even attempt the journey. But they had a mission. No time to stop now.

'This the place?' Cray asked.

'Haven't seen another place in over a day, so yeah, I reckon this is the place.'

'Just asking…'

The howl of the wind picked up and whipped around them. Sly ignored it, knowing that there would be a warm fire in the tavern waiting for them. He quickened his pace and stomped through the growing blanket of snow. A fine, soft thing – snow. But enough of it could cause a headache or two. Like water. Useful in manageable amounts but too much would drown a man, make no mistake.

Lights of flames flickered through the windows. The door was barred shut, due to the difficult weather, as always, so he banged as hard as he could, hoping that he would be heard on the inside. A few moments later, the door pulled inwards and a soft, worried, old face stared out into the wild land.

'By The Four!' the old man hissed, clapping his hands together and whistling through his teeth. 'Either these eyes of mine have finally played their last trick on me and given up or I'm looking at the ugly mug of Sly Stormson…'

'You gonna let us in or do I need to start cutting?' Sly

asked with a wide smile.

'Been a long time since I've laid my weary eyes on a familiar face. You're most welcome, Stormson. Most welcome!'

Sly stepped in through the frame of the door, pausing only to pat the innkeeper on his shoulder before shaking the snow from his cloak and undoing the buttons. He pulled it off and threw it onto the nearest table. All were empty. Seemed like they were the only ones in tonight. No surprise there.

'This is Cray. Good fighter.' Sly motioned to his ally and the old innkeeper gave a warm greeting to Cray, offering to grab his coat which was politely declined. 'And this old bastard is Cagen. Ran this tavern all his life. About a hundred years or something, right Cagen?'

The old man chuckled and feigned slapping Sly before marching behind the bar to grab them drinks. 'Not quite a hundred! Built it myself with two brothers of mine. They're bones now – only me left. Doubt anyone will look after the place when I'm gone. Not enough appreciate the peace and quiet of being away from the crowds in the towns of the Borderlands.'

'You think *they* are bad crowds?' Sly scoffed as Cagen shuffled over with two large jugs of ale. 'Should take a visit to one of the cities we've just been to. Wasn't right… too many folk crushed against each other. Whole place smelt of sweat and piss. Didn't have enough air to yourself to breathe.'

Cagen shook his head and clicked his tongue to the roof of his mouth. 'Ain't right. We were made for the free lands. The wild lands. Being cooped up together like animals in a cage can't be good for folk, no matter how much money they end up with. I'm happy out here on my own, no need for anything else.'

'No one wants to spend much time out here with you and your piss-like ale. That's why!' Sly roared, awfully pleased with himself.

'If you don't like it, no one is forcing you to drink that piss! Best ale this far out from the main town. No complaints so far.'

'Well I'm complaining.'

'Tough shit. It's that or actual piss.'

The three of them chuckled together, enjoying the chance to stop and relax for a moment. Hadn't been too many chances to do that lately. Something about wandering around in a land full of Barbarians did that to a person.

'I'm awful happy that you stopped by to keep an old, lonely man company, but why are you really here, Sly? You're not exactly known for your friendly drop-ins…'

Sly swished the weak ale around in his mouth and swallowed, slamming the jug onto the table before wiping the cold snot dripping from his nose and staring into the old man's sad eyes. He knew why they were here. Only one reason for it.

'Kiras.' One word. Didn't need anything more than that. Cagen was prepared for it. She was the only reason Sly would be this far north with everything going on in the Borderlands.

Cagen sighed and rocked back in his chair, rubbing his wrinkled face with both hands before leaning forward and settling with his elbows on the table.

'Do you know where she is? What happened to her after we headed south?' Cray asked, pressing for information. Sly shook his head, stopping any further questions. He didn't need to press Cagen. The old man could be trusted where Kiras was concerned. Wasn't gonna play them like fools. Cagen had suffered enough out here in the harsh lands and knew when it was the time to speak the truth.

'Haven't seen her for some time. Miss her smart mouth and her biting comments about the state of this shithole.' Cagen chuckled to himself and looked off into the fire as if remembering warm days of the past. 'I'd be dead if it wasn't for her. She saved my life. At great risk, too. Her and Baldor. Some thugs had been sent to take their usual protection money. At least, that's what they called it. Without Kiras and the big guy, I wouldn't be seated here with the two of you. I owe her everything. The one thing I have always prayed to The Four is that I would be given the chance to pay that lovely woman back for her kindness. A young woman shouldn't have to fight to defend a weary, old man but she did – and it changed her life whilst saving mine. I reckon, in some small way, my prayers have been answered tonight.'

'The Four have been deaf for as long as I've been alive,' Sly snorted. 'Be a damned miracle if they've finally started to listen.'

'Well, be that as it may, Four or not – I have a chance,' Cagen said. 'When shit hit the storm and Herick lopped off Saul's head, everything turned upside down. Barbarians strode right into the Borderlands with barely a sword raised against them. Never thought I'd see it in my life. Even had a few of the bastards come in here to drink. They fucking loved it. Kept commanding me to get more for them. Couldn't say no. Never been the bravest of men…'

'No point saying no. Can't be of use if you're dead,' Cray explained.

'Too true. Known that my whole life,' Cagen continued. 'Kiras has always been on good terms with Herick's tribe – close to Baldor, and Herick saw that guy as his son. Still, you know what she's like. There was no chance she was going to accept Barbarians stomping across the Borderlands unchecked. Killed a few on her own. Some warriors joined her but Herick found out what had happened and sent a group to sort it out. Slaughtered the lot of them. An old friend dropped in pretty soon after. Shook as he told the tale. Saw it all first-hand with his own eyes. A brutal sight and this man had seen enough brutality in his time, believe me. Left Kiras alive. A token of gratitude to show that Herick remembered that they were allies and that she was a close friend of Baldor's. From what I heard, she spat in his face at that comment.'

'That's Kiras,' Sly banged a fist on the table and licked the scar on his lip. 'That girl don't take shit from nobody.'

'Herick didn't take too kindly to being offended in front of his new friends. Wouldn't let them mess with her, he knows Baldor would rip him apart for that if he ever found out. But he let them beat her to within a second of a meeting with The Four herself. At least, that's what I was told. Wanted to go see her but I'm too old for even that journey and this storm would put me in the grave faster than a sword in the gut.'

Sly bit the inside of his cheek and cracked his head to the side, breathing heavily at the thought of the Barbarians beating on Kiras. They'd had their differences but he wasn't gonna sit here and allow any of those bastards to hurt one of his tribe.

'Raven's tribe. Anyone stand up for her?'

'Slaughtered. Hundreds turned to bones within a day or two,' Cagen said, shaking his head. 'The rest folded. Better to be alive and serving than defiant and dead. They weren't happy with how things panned out but what else could they do?'

'They could fight!' Sly hadn't realised he'd been playing with his dagger until he slammed it point-end down into the table and watched it quake on release. 'Limp fuckers have forgotten what it means to be a warrior of the Borderlands. I'll show them. I'll show them all.'

'We go in swords leading the way and we die,' Cray argued, wiping the sweat from his bald pate. 'We need a plan.'

'I have one. Find Kiras. Kill any fucker in my way,' Sly growled, finishing his drink, standing from his seat and pulling his dagger from the table. 'Where is she, Cagen?'

'The same place where you first met her and the big guy. Reckon you can make it in there?'

Sly grinned. He loved reliving the fun battles of old. The blood, sweat, and blades. It was almost poetic that he'd be returning to where it all started. 'Tofthund. The arse end of fucking nowhere. Got a couple of horses?'

Cagen smiled. 'The Four have sent you here, Sly Stormson. Miracles do happen.'

'If that's right, The Four are bigger cunts than I ever thought and we're in for one hell of a fucking ride.'

The storm continued to rage on. Most warriors would have sheltered for the night but Sly had done the journey before and knew what he was capable of. Cray spent the whole time riding in silence. Kept pace well-enough. Could have fallen behind but he didn't. Every time Sly peeked back over his shoulder, there he was, shoulders hunched and hood held low as they battled through the howling storm and onslaught of snow.

It was a tough journey but here they were.

Tofthund.

The arse end of nowhere.

The old, wooden walls around the city had taken a beating over the years and more than a few places had been broken enough for the whole thing to be useless. Guards were stationed on the gate but this storm tested the spirits of the unfortunate tasked with such a role. Last time he'd been here, there'd been a fair few on the gate but today, he could see only two and they sheltered in the towers looming over the gate. Neither were keeping an eye on anything in particular but that didn't help much – the gate was shut, and it wouldn't be opening until the air was clear and that didn't look like happening any time soon.

That's why he was so happy with the shitty wooden walls and their numerous gaps. Gaps big enough for Sly to slip through. Even Cray would be able to get his width through the gap if he sucked in his belly with enough dedication.

Sly crept through first before checking the area was clear for Cray to get through. He heard his ally slap the horses and the sound of the beasts running towards the gates. They wouldn't make it through but neither of them wanted the animals to die out in the cold. He was a mean bastard but there were limits.

Sly kept a lookout as Cray squeezed through, groaning as he tucked in tightly to push himself through, almost falling as he finally made it but catching himself as Sly cursed.

'For fuck's sake!' he hissed at Cray, eyes darting back and forth. 'Make any more noise and the dead themselves will hear us.'

'We're in ain't we?' Cray snapped back, pulling his coat tighter and spitting on the snow-covered ground. 'Quit your grumblin'.'

Sly hid the grin and started walking. The paths were clear – who in their right mind would want to be out in this weather? Every building displayed the glow of firelight as people huddled close to fires and smartly kept in the warmth. They had a bit of time before the dark of night took over the town but the chill of the storm was bad enough to keep all but the most hardened of folk inside. Wandering the streets would draw attention to them and attention was the last thing they wanted now.

They were there for one thing and one thing only.

Kiras.

'Where do you reckon she is?' Cray asked.

'Only one place people worth anything are kept in this shithole. There's a bit of poetry to it if you're dumb enough to think like that.' Sly peered down the street and caught sight of the biggest building in the town. A tavern. Summed up Tofthund perfectly. The one place people who came here actually gave a shit about. The temple was empty. The market was empty.

But never the tavern.

Drink was the God of the broken and forgotten and they worshipped it daily. Nightly too.

'She's in there.' Sly sniffed and ran a thumb against his sore nostrils. 'Gonna be fucking bloody. Need to be quick and violent. You ready for this?'

Cray licked his lips and threw back his hood, freeing his bald head to the elements. 'Let's kill the fuckers.'

***

The first two dropped fast and easy enough. Axes cut through them with the ease of slicing ham with a sharpened knife.

He heard the screams to his side as Cray got busy. The room was full of patrons and all had their weapons to hand. The foolish pricks that had been stupid enough to jump them following the first cry of Sly's name twitched on the wooden floorboards, bleeding all over the floor and staining the boards, and now the look on the rest of the warriors faces told Sly enough to know that the whole room was contemplating their life choices right about now.

Another couple of drunken Barbarians launched

themselves his way. He dodged the first blow but was too slow to escape the horn smashed over his head. There'd be blood, no doubt, and the dizziness slowed him down but there was no stopping him now. Blindly, he thrust up with his axe and roared. He felt the weapon crunch into something and warm blood trickled down his scalp. Could be his own but who the fuck knew or cared now?

Another swing but the flat of a mighty blade caught it with ease. Lucky Sly had two of the damned things and was able to swing wildly, catching the neck of his opponent and grinning as more blood splashed across his face.

He peered over to Cray and saw a sword slide between ribs and another Barbarian fell into a pile of three others on the floor. The rest of the patrons – mainly Borderlanders – were wide-eyed now and sober enough to understand the consequences of an attack. Only two Barbarians were left standing of their own volition, watching the display with interest but deciding to keep from harm's way. Cowards. Sly knew if they all attacked at once then they wouldn't be strong enough to stop them. Luckily, they were too stupid to realise the same thing.

'Weapons away and we forget this whole fucking business happened…' he growled at the tense audience. They turned as one to their own conversations and drinks and kept their eyes purposely away from the two blood-soaked warriors. The two Barbarians were last to turn away, leaning against the bar and eyeing their jugs of ale after turning from Sly and Cray. They didn't seem to care too much about their dead kin broken, battered and blood-soaked on the ground so why would anyone else?

Sly thought for a moment of stabbing the bastards in the back – a clean sweep of the invaders in the tavern. Then he thought better of it. They were here to do a job and this room had been sorted. A few more seconds of fun could lead to complications and Sly wasn't in the mood to deal with that shit.

'Where now?' Cray asked, stepping into line with Sly as he moved through a curtain at the back of the room.

'Keep moving forward.'

The next room had been designed for the purpose of a hideaway for gambling, smoking, drinking and whoring. A luxurious room with decorations that made Sly wince and thank the Old Gods that he'd never been one for sitting in comfort and talking politics. The walls seemed to have been confused with the floor – a great purple fur-like carpet had been placed along the four walls and was soft to the touch. A large, rectangular mirror broke up the wall at the back and displayed the long oak table that had been used recently for a game of cards judging by the blood-splattered white objects scattered around the room.

Two Barbarians twitched at Sly's feet. One had fallen rather unfortunately – or fortunately depending on how you looked at it – during the first attack and cracked his skull against the edge of the table. His eyes were wide open but he was blind to the world around him. Beside him was the woman who had caught Sly by surprise and damn near tore his throat out with the machete she had dropped to the ground. Four shocked hacks to her chest and neck had seen to her demise.

Cray dealt with the other two. Neat sword work and only a bang to his bald head to show for it. There'd be bruising in the morning, but it would take more than a bash to the head to stop that warrior and Sly was glad for it. Wood lay splintered around the room from where Cray had launched his opponent through the air and onto the expensive looking chair behind the Barbarian. A good shoulder charge followed by a final thrust of the sword and that was the last one dealt with. Both of them were breathing heavily now with all the work but it wasn't over yet.

One more bastard room. Sly knew the place. He'd buried his axe into a jumped-up prick in this very room a few cycles ago. Baldor and Kiras had cleared most of the room but Sly had been the one to cut the head off the snake who had poisoned this town. That was the first day they'd met. Headed off that very day to Raven's gathering of tribes and never looked back. Sly had thought about killing the pair of rookies but decided against it. All in all, he was glad that fate had stayed his hand.

'One more room,' he muttered to himself as reached out

for the bronze handle. He heard Cray tighten the grip on the hilt of his sword, ready for whatever madness awaited them inside.

He pulled the door back quickly and Cray rushed in, sword leading the way.

Sly followed.

The room bore no light, except only what was sent in from the adjoining room as Sly opened the door. His eyes strained at first, struggling to even see shapes in the darkness. As they adjusted, they were drawn to a hunched figure tied to the stone wall.

Wrists pulled high in black chains bolted into the stone wall as a shaven head dropped low. The body's frame was thin but the muscles were lean and stretched as the arms pulled down on the chains. Thin clothes covered the prisoner's modesty, as tattered as they were. Sly had seen prisoners treated worse but the purple and yellow bruises patterned across the visible skin still brought the taste of bile in his mouth as he felt the rage returning.

'I thought you pricks were done for the day. I can take the punches all day – I'm a big girl, believe it or not. And a lot fucking stronger than cowards who hit a girl tied again—'

Kiras drifted off as she looked up, eyes locking on Sly and his bloodied axes.

'You look like fucking shit, girly,' he said, doing his best to smirk in light of the situation.

'I've looked worse,' Kiras sniggered. 'Still look a good deal better than you do. Nice to see your ugly mug, Stormson.'

'Keep the tears away until we're out of this cursed town.'

'I'll get you a blade,' Cray murmured after untying Kiras from the walls. He rushed from the room with a face like thunder as she rubbed the red marks left in the chains' wake.

'Surprised to see the two of you together,' she said, smiling even with a fat lip and swollen jaw. 'Thought one of you would be bones by now. Have a nice time during those lonely nights travelling south?'

'Funny bitch,' Sly laughed, helping her to her feet. 'He ain't so bad after all. Swings a sword better than most and I've needed that since shit turned sour.'

He saw the question left on her face as her blue eyes pleaded with him. 'Baldor…'

'Long story. I'll tell you once we're outta here…'

'Raven?'

'Bones. Again. Long story.'

Kiras nodded reluctantly and muttered a low curse to herself. Cray raced back into the room and threw her a sword which she caught with ease. 'Just the one?' she asked.

'Bit short on options at the moment.'

She shrugged and swung the blade through the air a few times. 'It'll do.'

'Did they…' Sly let his question hang in the air before he cleared his throat.

'Herick wouldn't allow them to do any more than beat the shit outta me. Still soft on Baldor. They're like family, believe it or not. Lucky me!'

'This way…' Cray kicked in the wooden door to Kiras' right and bounded off into the storm. Sly followed with Kiras. He glanced at her once but that was it. If they were gonna make it outta here alive then he needed to trust she could handle herself. No room for the weak in the Borderlands. She would stand and fight or she would die.

Cray found the gap in the fence just as the snow began to slow its descent. He crouched low and pushed through, eager to leave the town and make it back out into the wild lands. Sly allowed Kiras through next, keeping an eye on their rear and sighing with relief as there was no sign of a chase. He pushed through the gap and stood, welcomed by fifteen Borderland warriors and Barbarians.

'Shit,' Sly cursed, staring into Herick's eyes as the bastard held a sword to Cray's throat and three more pointed at Kiras, two at Sly.

'What a merry meeting we have here out in the snow,' Herick said with a smile on his face that could have been worn if he had just bumped into old friends and family. 'This really is a nice surprise. Had eyes on Cagen's tavern for weeks now. Knew you'd turn up there if anywhere. And don't worry, the old man is fine. We go back a long way, me and Cagen. A good man. Better than most, anyway.'

'If you're gonna kill us then do it and get it over with. I'm getting bored,' Sly growled, leaning into the pointed weapon and pressing his open throat against the blade. 'Or even better, face me one-on-one, like a man. Bet you didn't give Saul that honour…'

Herick laughed and looked around at the men and women beside him. 'I didn't. I'm not fucking stupid, Sly. I play to win. Honour means nothing if it leads to me being bones in the earth. Worm food. I use my brain, unlike most in the Borderlands. It's why I saw fit to make an alliance with our northern neighbours,' he said with a nod towards the Barbarians. 'But you're right, I'm not here to kill you. I'm here to offer you a deal.'

'Your words mean shit, Herick,' Kiras spat, launching saliva through the air and chuckling as it landed on the seething man's face. He wiped it off as the blood rushed to his cheeks. 'I'd rather die out here in the snow than spend one more second listening to your shit.'

'Is that right? Haven't you noticed that a dear friend is missing from this lovely meeting of ours in the snow? A big friend who I call my son. A friend who once risked his life to defend you from bandits and thieves. Have you not noticed that Baldor does not walk beside Sly and Cray?'

Kiras' eyes darted to Sly and then back to the chief. 'Course I fucking noticed. What's it to you? He'd have killed you himself if he were standing here right now.'

'He sees me as a father. Pretty much raised him with these bloody hands. Doubt he'd hurt me. The reason my men didn't have too much fun with you all chained up is because I respect Baldor and I know how he would feel about such a mess. You can take a beating, so I allowed it. Nothing more was going to happen. Not while he is still out there…' Herick licked his lips and turned to Sly. 'You know where he is…'

Sly shrugged. 'Perhaps I do.' He didn't. He'd sure as fuck find out though, given the chance. Then he'd bring the big bastard back to bury this prick in the ground, one limb at a time.

'He's in a labour camp not too far from the United Cities of Archania. Back breaking work all day and night and they don't like the big guys. I offer you this.' Herick lowered his sword and sniffed, looking at the three of them in turn. 'You leave the Borderlands. You return to the United Cities and you get my son out of that camp. It is no place for a future chief and believe me, that is Baldor's future. Raven and Bane died down there but if they kill him, I'll wipe that shitty kingdom from the map of Takaara and piss on the crown itself.'

'And what happens if we save him?' Kiras asked, voice stern and even. She must have been worried inside for her friend, but she was a hard bitch. She could handle herself. Sly knew that. 'If we get him out of that labour camp in the South. What then?'

Herick lifted his sword and slapped it gently against her face. Then he did the same to Cray, and finally, to Sly. It took all of Sly's strength to ignore the mockery but even he knew when the odds were against him. It was a tough decision to make, to not raise an axe and bury this bastard here and now but the toughest decisions are often the most important.

'You get him out and send him my way. Then, you never step foot in the Borderlands again. Every bastard in the Borderlands – Barbarian or not – will be searching for it and they will know that there will be gold aplenty for the warrior who brings me your heads. Especially your pretty one, Stormson.'

Sly looked over at Kiras who nodded grimly. Cray just shrugged, obviously not giving a shit either way. He was just up for the fight. Sly loved it.

'We'll go get Baldor. That was the plan anyway,' Sly said with a smirk. 'If we see each other again, you better hope I'm a corpse. If not, I'll send you to the hells and piss on your bones.'

'I wasn't going to do this, but...' Herick rubbed his jaw and thought for a moment. He clicked his fingers and turned his back on the three of them. Sly could just about hear him over the returning howl of the wind. 'Teach him a lesson. Leave the girl and the silent cunt. Just Stormson…'

Sly grinned as the first fist slammed into his face. He rocked back but didn't try to reach for his axes. A tough decision. But the best ones usually are.

'Sofia will pay for releasing you too,' Herick hissed, eyes flaring. 'Got a spare set of chains waiting for her…'

Five more strikes and Sly's eyes finally closed for the night.

NEW FACES AND OLD

Kane allowed her shoulders to fall beneath the water's surface and breathed a sigh of relief. The river's cool water revitalised her. A reminder of times when she hadn't been cursing her luck for being sent on a mission to one of the hottest spots in the whole of Takaara. The lush reds and greens of Causrea were a distant memory now: replaced with the orange and beige dunes as she wandered further east with her strange ally.

Istari seemed comfortable enough. He had wrapped a black and green cloth around his mouth and the back of his head and wore a similar scarf on the top of his head. His bright eyes sparkled out between the two pieces of material as he washed his dirty clothing from the days before in the river. He claimed that such items protected him from the howling winds that drew in harsh sands that could be biting on the face and eyes especially. Kane had been fortunate enough not to have the theory tested so far but she knew it was only a matter of time. Desert storms in the East were the stuff of legend back home. Merchants and traders would sit back beside roaring fires and tell frightening stories of the sandstorms as eager listeners plied them with drinks aplenty, each tale becoming bolder by the jug.

Her face still stung with the heat beating down from the relentless sun. She couldn't remember the last time she'd seen anything but blue in the sky and clouds had become a distant memory – at times she found herself wondering if she had hallucinated the whites and greys of the floating matter. They seemed almost too good to be true after such a long ride in the desert. Floating support that offered free water from the heavens. Surely such a thing could only be dreamed of by some delusional fool crying out for a drink or two in this maddening heat?

But here she was, gently swaying in the cool river and following its meander with her eyes as it glistened with the light of her recent enemy. She cupped her hands and splashed the water against her face, cooling it instantly and pushing away the sweat and filth from the ride. Istari, she noticed, purposefully looked away from her, eager to ensure that she knew he would not stare at her naked body. He needn't have bothered. She was comfortable enough and travellers on long journeys would have to get used to such sights. It was imperative to be clean and refresh oneself and that meant nudity. Still, she was thankful for the man's tact and respect. The old warrior was a difficult man to judge – she never knew from one moment to the next how he would behave. Stomping out fires one moment and screaming at her that it would draw enemies from the distant land, to laughing and winking at her as he shared a story from his youth when he fell from the ramparts of a castle and into the surrounding moat, much to the amusement of his fellow trainees. An odd man, indeed.

According to the warrior, they weren't too far from the border of Darakeche. Istari claimed that it would barely be a half day's ride until they entered the first village. The land thrived close to the river, the source of growth and protection for the Eastern people. Two more greater rivers lay further east but Kane still marvelled at the width and length of the one she bathed in now. She could barely see the opposite riverbank from her position – feeling that it was more a small sea than a large river.

'Falls down from the mountains in the distance,' Istari had told her, pointing off to the row of jagged spikes stabbing into the blue sky. 'Brings the water down from the heavens and winds its way around like a giant blue snake. Beautiful thing, really.'

It was. Beautiful. A lone source of water in the otherwise

sparse land. The rivers in the north could freeze for months at a time but she doubted this one ever would. She had even heard rumours before that parts of the river dried up in the more difficult, dry summers over the cycles. A terrifying thought.

She dipped her whole body and head below the water and shut out the sounds of the world. It felt like being in another realm, a dimension away from Takaara. Just her, all alone as the gentle current drifted past her. As she broke the water once more, she rubbed at her eyes and opened them. With a jolt of surprise, her eyes landed on dark spots on the horizon – dark spots slowly heading towards her.

'Might need that sword of yours,' Istari called over to her, staring out at the same ominous shadows in the distance with a look of mild amusement. 'More friends by the looks of it…'

Kane rushed from the water, ignoring the embarrassed look that crossed Istari's face as he caught himself glancing over at her before purposely looking anywhere else. 'Better put my clothes back on too then, eh?'

'Might be a good idea,' the old warrior grumbled back.

She was enjoying this.

As they drew nearer, Kane could see the three figures better and marvelled at the strange beasts they rode. Camels, Istari had called them. She'd never seen the like though she had once read a book about the animals and studied a few crude illustrations. Such things didn't do them justice.

Sand-coloured to blend in with their environment. Wide hooves to distribute weight better that allowed transport across the shifting sands with ease. Long, dark eyelashes that would prevent the continuous sands from flying into their eyes in a storm. And most amazingly of all, two large humps on their backs that Kane had read allowed for the storage of fat or water – texts hadn't agreed on which was correct. Either way, these beasts had been designed by the Gods to survive this harsh climate and land and she was pleased to have met them in person, even if she had to glance warily at the three warriors peering down at her from on top.

'Westerners, right?' the closest man said from his camel. All three of them wore light, silver armour that protected their torso but nothing on their arms. Blood-red scarves covered their head and most of their faces apart from the eyes – just like Istari. Curved swords were sheathed at their hips, white handles gleaming for all to see – a warning, or a threat.

Kane studied the speaker – his black skin glistening with sweat. Her eyes narrowed as she caught sight of a familiar marking on the man's bulging bicep. A red sun, a blood circle with various waves running from the centre.

'From the West, yes,' she replied with palms raised in the air, ignoring the sound of steel slipping from its sheathe. Istari didn't seem like a good talker and was quick to shed blood. Perhaps it wasn't needed in this instance. 'In fact, I believe we may have a mutual friend…'

The warrior pursed his lips and gave his allies a quick look of curiosity. Both had the bronzed skin of the East and dark, brown eyes that fell on Kane now.

'A mutual friend?' the lead warrior asked, pulling the scarf down from his face and showing a hooked, white scar on his cheek, like the crescent moon in the night sky. 'We're listening. Not many friends out here in this part of the world.'

Kane glared at Istari but he wasn't paying attention to her. Not openly anyway. He kept his sword ready in his hand and stared straight at the scarred warrior barely ten paces away.

'That tattoo, one of my closest and oldest friends has one the very same. You are members of the Red Sons, yes?' It was a guess but one filled with hope and logic. Aleister had told her that the group were roaming around the deserts, a barrier to the East in the event of all-out war. The tattoo was just another piece of evidence that meant a piece in the puzzle. By the flicker of recognition at the name, she drew confidence in her assumption. 'I remember chasing a boy, his sister and their good friend around the streets of Archania – little rascals who had the dream of one day leading their own company of mercenaries. That boy made a name for himself out here, Aleister. Aleister of the Red Sons. He has a message for the group. If you are affiliated with them, as I believe, then we would be very grateful if you could take us to whomever is in charge.'

The warrior muttered something to his allies in a harsh language Kane didn't recognise. He glanced at the sword in Istari's hand and finally turned back to Kane. 'It's been a while since Aleister was seen in these parts. Darakeche isn't exactly open to him after what happened last time...' The three of them laughed together, sharing a joke that was lost on Kane and her statue-like companion. 'We'll take you to our leader. Half a day's ride. It's a small town but free from any connection to the bickering leaders of the region. Free from the iron fist of politics that chokes the breath from the world. What are your names, friends of Aleister?'

'Katerina Kane from the United Cities of Archania. And this is—'

'Tammaz Lirland, from the West,' Istari interrupted, offering a small nod as Kane did her best to keep her eyebrows from becoming lost in her hairline in surprise. Up to him, she guessed. If he wanted to hide his identity then she wasn't going to argue about it.

'Ben Odash. This is Marek Duhail and Maz Duhail. It's good to meet allies of our old leader. There will be time to speak of the great three as we ride. The Red Sons welcome you to the East, Katerina Kane and *Tammaz Lirland.*' The way Ben spoke the name gave Kane the impression that he knew Istari was lying, but he didn't give anything else away.

'He was the one who brought us out here in the first place,' Ben said with a soft smile, scarf now tied around his waist and falling from his hip though he kept his head covered with a small, red hat shaped to his skull. 'Promises of treasure, coin, drink, friendship and, most importantly, freedom. Freedom from corruption, from leaders who knew only greed, freedom from the shackles of our past. The Red Sons represent a new life for those who wear the red.'

'He always did have a way with words,' Kane chuckled and shook her head as she accepted a chipped, clay cup from her host. The tent they sat in was simple, enough to shield them from any storm and with no luxuries. 'I told him he could sell sand to the East and he told me to think of a more difficult task! A confident kid who was always getting into trouble. Always getting *out* of trouble too. Cheeky smile and a sparkle in the eye. And the girls…'

'Ooohhh,' Ben clapped his hands together and threw back his head, 'the girls. That never changed then. Left a trail of broken hearts in the desert. Always attracted to the wrong ones, Aleister. Kept mentioning a girl from back home, don't think he ever got over her…'

A flash of green eyes – and golden pupils – popped into Kane's mind. The light left them and she felt her heart stop for an instant. Ella. The most beautiful young woman she had ever known and just as kind and intelligent to boot. A young woman who had died on the cobbled streets of the Lower City in Archania as flames tore through the wooden buildings and screams blended with the crack of thunder.

'No, I don't think he did…' she croaked, coughing to clear her throat which felt suddenly restricted and full. 'I don't think he ever did.'

Ben's face dropped in the uncomfortable silence, aware that he had upset his guest but not knowing how. 'If there is something that I have said…' he appealed to her, motioning forward.

Kat stood and backed away, hand covering her lips as she stumbled to the exit. 'It's fine. I just need some air.' She pushed the animal skin aside and rushed out into the warm evening. Thousands of tents stood in rows across the sandy desert. Ben had explained that The Red Sons had chosen to set up camp here half a cycle ago following a particularly nasty quake. They kept an eye on the town nearby and provided the people with support following the deaths and injuries of many of its people. The Sultan had ignored their cries for help and shunned them following the Red Sons arrival. A deep wound still bled and the Sultan wasn't ready to ignore it, even to the detriment of his people.

A few of the mercenaries looked her way as she stumbled away from the tents, eager for open space and freedom to catch her breath. It had been a while since she had thought of Ella; the guilt clawed at her chest. She'd lost so many friends over the cycles that she wondered if there would be a time when some would be forgotten. Her first husband had been killed by Cypher Zellin. Braego killed by Mason's right hand – T'Chai. Elder Morgan died in front of her, another victim of the Empire of Light. Lord Tamir. Ella. Her son, Drayke was said to be lost after running from his homeland too. How many more people would she have to lose?

'You're pretty easy to sneak up on, you know?' a calm voice said with mirth behind her. Kane spun on her heels and scanned the woman who was staring at her with a smile. A faint memory tugged at the back of her mind. 'That's twice I've managed it. Thought you were the experienced one…'

Blood-red hair fell down in waves to the woman's hips. Her skin had been darkened by the Eastern sun to a light bronze that suited her. Her accent was familiar. Archanian. Kane licked the inside of her cheek as recognition hit her like a bolt of lightning.

'The assassin by the docks,' Kane pointed a finger at her, nodding as the memory returned in full. 'You saved me from the shadowed figure in the night. Payback from Aleister if I remember correctly.'

The woman gave a short bow and laughed. 'That's right. I am Zaina. Aleister sent me out here to speak with Jax and the others. Tried to get them to head off to Archania and help with the rebellion. You don't need to be a seer to see that I failed miserably. Bastards ended up shuffling closer to Darakeche. A dumb move if you ask me.'

'Aleister is their leader,' Kane said, puzzled. 'Why would they not do as he asked of them?'

'It's been a while since Aleister did anything for the group. Too easily distracted and off on his own little missions and journeys. That's not what a group like this need. They need a leader with focus, with strong will. Aleister changes his mind with the shift of the wind and that makes folk restless. Some of the new members haven't even seen him. He's like a legend. One that we still hold in a good light, but legends don't put food on the table.'

'So, who is running the place now?'

Zaina offered a non-committal shrug. 'Depends on who you ask. Jax was the one Aleister left in charge. A placeholder to keep the fort standing until his return. But Jax has been – odd – of late. Odd makes folk restless too. Since then, some have been more likely to listen to Adnan Yil-Youssef. Guy knows his way around the place and he is trusted by Ben, who is well-respected and one of the old guard.'

Kane stopped for a moment, running the names over in her head and doing her best to work out why she knew them. 'Adnan Yil-Youssef...'

'I'm fairly sure you know the name...' Zaina smirked, enjoying the shock clear on Kane's face. 'The Sultan's estranged, hated son is now lining up a push to run as leader of The Red Sons. Welcome to the East, Katerina Kane, you're in for one hell of a time.'

Sly stared at the incomplete map of the North and scrunched up his face in puzzlement. Never been one for maps. He could get where he wanted to and make it back the same way. He knew the Borderlands and had enough knowledge of the North to know he could make it home if he needed. That was all. He'd travelled to Archania before and he'd go the same way again – easy enough. He stared at the squiggles and lines and tiny pictures and felt a painful pulsing building between his eyes.

'You've not been this place before,' Kiras argued. 'The place where they are keeping Baldor is new. We can't waste any time if we are planning on getting to him while the big man is still breathing. Can't waste seconds on pride.'

That's what Raven used to say to 'em.

'Sounding more 'n more like him when you speak, girlie.'

154

'That a bad thing?'

'You know it's not,' Sly grumbled. 'But he's bones now. You can have all the best sayings in the world and it means nothing at the end of the day. Still bones for us all.'

'Now you're the one sounding like him…'

Sly threw a half-eaten bone her way but she dodged it easily enough, chuckled along with the action as Sly sniffed and grabbed for more meat cooking over the small fire. 'We'll make it to Baldor. Big man is too stupid to die. Map or no map – we'll make it to him. Mark my words.'

'Consider them marked.'

They sat together, chomping on the rabbits Kiras had caught for them earlier in the day. Cray stalked somewhere in the darkness, eager to keep guard in what was now an unfriendly land. Always been unfriendly in Sly's mind. Just now there were even more bastards out there who wanted him dead. They'd been lucky with Herick's offer, even if the proud warrior hadn't liked to admit it. More often than not, folks held at sword point ended up as bones, like Raven Redbeard.

'You think that was the end for us, back there?' he asked the girl as the flames sent dancing lights in her tired eyes. 'Surprised Herick didn't just put an end to the three of us there and then. 'Specially with those Barbarians watching. Could've made a statement.'

Kiras watched the flames a while longer before she responded. 'He cares for Baldor. Truly cares for him. Believe it or not, he also likes us.' She frowned as Sly laughed in defiance and spat next to the fire before raising her voice a little louder. 'Hear me out! He hated Saul, maybe more than us. Always getting put down and belittled in front of his tribe by the big prick. No respect there. The Barbarians offered him revenge and power. Might seem horrible to us but Herick did what he thought was best for him and his tribe – he's never felt strong links to the rest of the Borderlands. He's too far out in the wild on that island. Closest thing he has to family is Baldor and Baldor is as good as blood to us. He might have thought about killing us as it would be easy, but he has a small slither of honour left in him. At least, that's what I reckon.'

'Then what you reckon is shit,' Sly spat again. 'Bastard sold the Borderlands for his own benefit and pissed all over the ashes after watching it burn. How'd do you think Raven would have taken it?'

Kiras shrugged and pursed her lips. 'Not here to ask, is he?'

Sly nodded and sighed, throwing his last bone into the flames and leaning back onto his palms. 'All have to go sooner or later. That's the way of things. Still, would have loved to have seen the look on his face once he found Herick had the balls to do what he did…'

They shared another laugh and fell into silence once again.

'Sly, Kiras…' A whisper from the shadows. Cray. 'Weapons. Trouble nearby. Barbarians, I reckon. Seen the flames.'

'No point putting them out,' Sly muttered. 'Use it to draw 'em in.'

'Aye,' Kiras whispered back, 'We should get to the shadows, they've probably already seen Cray.'

Cray nodded his agreement with the plan and slipped his sword from its sheath and turned his back on them as they made for the edges of the light. Sly crept to the left of the fire, keeping to the thin, bare trees and looking out for any sign of movement.

The Barbarians weren't quiet. Four of them altogether. No need for silence when you think you outnumber your enemy four to one. Can be as loud as you'd fucking like. And they were. Big boots crunching the twigs and snow on the ground and not thinking to keep their volume down as they chatted and laughed together before stepping into the light, swords drawn and ready, though hanging low and pointing at the snow.

Cray stood motionless, his own weapon mirroring the Barbarians'.

'Alone in the woods at this time?' the lead Barbarian said, scratching the stubble on his cheek and cracking his neck to the side. Ugly bastard. Half his right ear had been torn off and his nose was bent in more ways than one. Not his first fight. Though Sly promised himself it would be his last. The other three just leered and glanced at each other, lank hair swaying with their movement before they stared back at Cray, shoulders hunched over as they leaned towards their enemy, ready for the fight to begin. 'Could probably use some company. Now our kind stand with the Borderlands, we should share the fire and some food.'

'Already had food. Don't need the company,' Cray grunted. The fake smile dropped from the Barbarian's face at the words and he glanced at his allies, readying them for the next move.

'Now, that ain't so nice of ya. Herick wouldn't be too pleased to hear one of his men ain't being nice to his new friends.'

'Fuck him. I'm not Herick's man. I'm my own man. Don't like that, well,' Cray sniffed and shrugged his shoulders, 'fuck you, too.'

He moved faster than a broad man should, did Cray. Sly allowed him a moment to dodge the first attack, ducking low under a wild swing of the sword by the screaming Barbarian before jumping into the fray himself. Almost caught the next one unawares with the axe but a sword snapped up to greet it before it landed in Sly's preferred destination.

'Fucking Borderlander!' the Barbarian screeched through gritted teeth as he tried his best to force Sly's axe back with his sword. The sound of metal on metal rang through the small clearing as the battle heated up. Sly caught sight of another of the bastards heading his way so he released the trapped warrior in front of him and rolled to his left and away from a thrusted blade. His axe snapped up to meet the oncoming Barbarian's sword. The Barbarian's snarl twisted to a shocked intake of breath as Sly slipped a small dagger between his ribs. Worked more often than not. The smallest of blades can end a man's life. He knew that. His adversary's body tensed before relaxing as he realised what had happened, eyes drifting down to the blood seeping from the wound. Sly took the opportunity given to raise his axe and crack it down as hard as he could on the fool's skull, slicing it from hairline to nose. Right between the eyes.

A perfect hit.

Still, no time to appreciate his handywork. A scream to his right told him that his first opponent was ready for round two. Cray was busy trading punches with a Barbarian almost a foot taller than him – swords lay forgotten in the dirt beside them. Kiras darted this way and that, escaping what would be killing blows as a colossal sword swung after her each time. She'd drawn blood with her twin swords. A cut bled freely from the Barbarian's forearm and he was limping on his left leg.

But Sly had to focus on his own predicament.

He parried the first lunge with his bloodied axe and jumped backwards, allowing the Barbarian to feel in control. The fool was lunging wildly, off balance and likely to fall. Sly smirked as he saw a winning smile flash across the young warrior's face, already sensing victory. He stopped and waited for the next attack. Moving swiftly, he stepped to the side of the thrust and launched himself forward. The Barbarian was taller but his lunge had sent him off balance on his front foot and his face now met in line with Sly's.

Still smirking, Sly closed his eyes and slammed his forehead into the Barbarian's face, groaning with pleasure as he felt the crack of bone and teeth on impact. He gripped his opponent's sword hand tightly to prevent any last-ditch attack and launched his head forward again. And again. And again. And again. And again.

He released the hand and shook his head as the limp, lifeless body dropped to the floor, face an unrecognisable bloody mess. Even the lad's mother wouldn't have been able to pick her son out if she were here. That's a damn fact.

Kiras had her own adversary on his knees and defenceless. She finished him with a double slice of her blades and turned away before the headless body fell. Cray was a bloody mess, trading blows that were becoming slower and slower with each turn. He was breathing heavily, motioning with both hands for the Barbarian to bring on the next attack, eager for more.

The Barbarian roared and snapped his fist back. Sly heard a whistle of something fast fly through the air followed by an unnatural halt of the man's roar. Looking over at the Barbarian, Sly spotted a lone arrow sticking out of his throat. His eyes blinked a few times, peering down as his weak hands uselessly pawed at the reason for his demise. The Barbarian fell awkwardly against a tree, breathing ragged and fast.

Cray stepped forward and slammed his knee into the man's face, finishing the battle with one brutal attack.

'You do choose your damned moments, don't ya?' Kiras chuckled, wiping the filthy swords on her trousers and looking past Sly into the darkness. There was only one man who could have hit a shot so well outside of the light.

'Pick his moments?' Sly snorted. 'Bet he was standing there waiting for us to finish the rest of them before he did that. Could have saved us some time if he'd have stepped in earlier…'

'And where's the fun in that?' Socket ambled into the light with a smirk of his own, twirling a bone bow in his hand and staring at the mess they had made. 'Besides, I only just got here…'

Sly peered around the archer, looking for any sign of company. 'Where's the kid?' he asked, though fearing the answer.

'Didn't make it,' Socket said, voice soaked with sadness. They'd been close. Sly knew Arden was a weak bastard but he'd shown some talent. A few more cycles and the Borderlands would have shaped him into one of them, that was a fact. 'I heard about Raven, and Bane. Shit times.'

'Shit times,' Kiras agreed. 'Baldor is alive. Fancy saving his big ass from the Southern fuckers?'

'Hmm…' Socket smacked his lips and looked around at the three bloody warriors. Kiras standing with her twin swords ready. Sly twisting the axe and wide-eyed, eager for another kill. And Cray, standing casually beside the Barbarian he had just defeated. 'Nothing better to do. Would be good to see the big fella again. To the South it is.'

Sly holstered his weapons and smacked his hands together before trudging towards the old archer. He slapped him on the back and turned to Kiras, a tired smile on her bloody face as she too welcomed him back.

'Shame about the kid, I liked him,' she said softly.

159

'Aye, me too.' Socket nodded, frowning. 'Gone too soon.'

'We'll make 'em pay,' Sly promised, eyeing each of them in turn. 'Once we have Baldor, we'll return and the Borderlands will be ours. Nothing will get in our way.'

THE JOURNEY SOUTH

'The Bridge of Ukufa-Umday,' Abdualaziz said, flashing his eyes and smiling wide at Aleister, enjoying the man's discomfort. 'The Tall Death. One of the oldest bridges in Takaara. Fastest way to the South. We could travel many miles east and follow the sloping hills but this way saves us days of travel. We have travelled across it many times – still takes my breath away when I look upon its ancient majesty.'

Aleister took a deep breath and swallowed as he looked out across the bridge. A fog had settled over the land, obscuring the distant end of the stone bridge so that it seemed they would be passing into another world itself. A colossal chasm opened its mouth beneath the bridge – a physical symbol separating the north and south of Takaara. Legend told of the reason for such a huge scar on the land. Fighting magi. A land ripped in two. From his vantage point at the edge of the cliff, Aleister couldn't see the bottom of the canyon but he could hear the rush of water beneath him. A river that journeyed all away to the Western Sea. At equal points along the bridge, huge stone supports ran all the way down from the bridge to the land at the foot of the canyon.

'When I look upon it, I just feel sick.'

Abdulaziz laughed and slapped Aleister on the back, forcing him to catch himself and pressing a hand against his chest in fear of falling.

'This bridge can hold much larger weights. There is no

need to fear the crossing.'

Aleister blew out his cheeks and nodded to the merchant but he wasn't sure he had the same confidence as the eastern man. The grey stone bridge was wide, enough for four carts to cross side by side. On either side, rope ran the length of the bridge and offered a small barrier prevented a deadly fall. Still, Aleister couldn't help but picture himself falling over and becoming lost to a watery grave below.

The first group of horses and carts crossed the arched, wooden threshold that signalled the entrance to the bridge. No longer were they walking across God-made earth but instead trusting to the ability and design of man. Aleister took a tentative first step under Abdulaziz's mirthful guidance.

The hard, chipped stone held with his boots pressing against them.

A sigh of relief.

'Big chicken. If it holds Bathos then you'll be fine,' Ariel called over, stepping with ease onto the bridge with her partner and openly mocking her brother.

Bolstered by embarrassment, Aleister looked up and followed her, repeatedly reminding himself that the bridge had held for hundreds of years. Why would today be any different?

'I'll push you over the side and then we will see who is fine…' he threatened as he pulled his sister in for a tight hug, squeezing the breath from her before releasing her. 'Things like this aren't natural…'

'I have to admit,' Bathos boomed over the two of them, 'even after everything we've seen, this is pretty special…'

'Aye,' Aleister agreed. 'Bloody special…'

'Has to be magic,' Ariel muttered.

'Aye – can smell it in the air around the stone.' A woman piped into the conversation. She rode slowly on her pony, laden with a multitude of bags on either side of her beast of burden. 'Makes me nauseas being around such a strong smell of the stuff.'

Aleister frowned. 'You can smell it?'

The woman offered a sad smile and tugged at her head scarf, ensuring her hair was covered. Her wrinkled and bronzed skin told a tale of a traveller, one who had spent large amounts of time out in the elements. 'Never used to be able to. Spent my whole life around the stuff and it smelt just like anything else. Since my pupils turned black every time I am near old magic I almost choke on the stuff. Used to do all I could to hide that I was a mage. Now I'd do anything to have that feeling back. It's like being crippled without it. Like I've lost an arm or a leg…'

Aleister glanced at his sister and Bathos, pleading with his eyes for them to step in as an uncomfortable silence hung in the air.

'It must have been a dreadful experience to live through…' Bathos said, nodding sadly. Aleister bit his lip. Not exactly the soothing response he had been hoping for.

Thankfully, the woman smiled. 'Yes. But I have lived through it. Others were not so lucky. Many magi spent their lives wishing to be more like everyone else, to blend in and be just another soul trying to make it on this world. We never thought that we would have that wish granted. We certainly didn't think it would hurt this much.' She looked off into the distance, lost in tragic thoughts. Her pony bristled and she woke, as if from a dream. 'Best be keeping up with the others. I hope we have time to speak again. Enjoy the journey.'

Aleister waved and forced a smile onto his face, praying it looked genuine enough to the broken woman. He wondered if Ella would have felt the same, had she lived through the failed rebellion. Would she have been grateful for the life she had or wished for the power that she had lost? His heart paused as he realised that he would never know how she would feel. He'd never know anything new about her ever again…

'You okay, Aleister?' Ariel asked, head tilted as she tried to snap him from his daydream. 'Away with the Gods there, aren't you?'

'Something like that,' he replied, shaking the dark thoughts away. 'Come on, let's cross this damned bridge.'

Aleister felt like kissing the rocky ground as he finally felt his boots leave the stone of the bridge behind. Silently, he made a promise that he would take the longer way round on the way back. Never again would he cross that cursed bridge. He'd spent the whole journey speaking with Ariel. With Bathos. With Abdualaziz. With random merchants and families. Once, even with a horse who seemed annoyed with his insistent chatter. Anything to take his mind off the fact he was placing his faith in a stone structure so tall that he couldn't see the bottom.

Still, he'd made it. That was something. And now it was done with.

'Wasn't as nerve-wracking as you may have first thought, eh, Aleister of The Red Sons?' Abdulaziz patted him on the back and smiled. The light of the moon and stars caught a tiny diamond on one of the merchant's teeth.

'Easy. Could stroll across it for all eternity if I had to,' Aleister lied with a grin of his own. Abdulaziz's loud laughter proved that the merchant wasn't so convinced with the answer but Aleister didn't mind. Had to be scared of things from time to time. Fear is what built bravery. Without fear, a man is stupid and prone to mistakes.

'You're telling yourself that fear thing again, aren't you?' Ariel snorted. 'Doesn't work for bridges, brother. That's just sad…' She dodged his light-hearted slap and skipped away after the carts, away from Aleister's curses.

This side of the bridge there was a calm wind – warm and relaxing. Similar to the air in the East, but thicker. Breathing in felt more of a chore than it used to be. Perhaps he was just imagining things after the wearying march across the Tall Death.

They marched on into the night, until Aleister felt his legs ache and his eyes blink slower each time they moved. Just as he felt that he could go on no longer without rest, the caravan halted their movement. Moments later, Abdulaziz and his closest allies moved along the caravan, passing on the message that they would be setting up the tents for the night.

'How far are we?' Aleister asked when the merchant

reached him. Bathos was setting up a small fire whilst Ariel busied herself with assisting with the tents.

'A day's ride to the nearest village. Just into the shelter of the forest. I will go on ahead and ensure that we will be welcomed by the inhabitants. A small formality that must be done. We are in their land, after all,' Abdulaziz said, stifling a yawn with a jewelled fist.

'And after that?'

'After that, we will leave the village and head onto a slightly larger town deeper into the trees. You and those who are following will split from the caravan at this point. I will send one other with you to assist in making it to the capital but that is all I am willing to do. I cannot risk the respectability of my caravan over this. I'm sure you understand.'

'Of course,' Aleister said, reassuring the merchant. 'You have done more than enough for us. We wouldn't wish to bring harm on you or your caravan.'

Abdulaziz nodded his thanks and pressed on, checking on his various guests and colleagues. Aleister shifted over to the small fire Bathos had manged to get going. They certainly didn't need it for heat – even with the sun long gone, the land was warm and Aleister felt sticky with sweat. In the East, when the sun had left for the night, the temperature would drop with it but out here it seemed the heat was here to stay. Sun or no sun.

'We can cook something small and then get our heads down for the night,' Bathos said, blowing on the embers. 'I take it that we will be splitting from the caravan soon enough?'

Aleister nodded, watching the growing flames. 'Abdulaziz said he will offer someone to guide us into the city but that will be it. Up to us from there on.'

Bathos sat back from the flames, pleased with his efforts. 'As it should be. Just like in the beginning. The three of us working together to do what is right. We'll need to careful though. The tales I've heard of this Boy King...' Bathos blew some air from his cheeks and shook his head nervously. A strange thing for the usually unrattled warrior. 'Not many things can give me nightmares but if the tales are true...'

'You know what tales are like. They grow taller with each telling.'

'Taller than that bridge?'

'Nothing is taller than the cursed bridge,' Aleister said, pointing at Bathos and his stupid grin as if daring him to challenge his statement.

They listened to the crackle of the flames for a while before Ariel returned, silently crouching low and leaning against Bathos who easily accepted her weight. She allowed the silence to linger, embracing its comfort.

'How are you feeling?' she asked after a while longer, eyes looking up at the stars shining in the cloudless sky.

Aleister held out both of his hands. 'See. No shaking.'

Ariel turned her head and gave a proud smile mirrored by Bathos. 'That's good brother.'

'Better than good,' Bathos agreed.

'Aye.' Aleister cleared his throat. 'I'm sorry that I make the two of you worry over me. With all we had going on, neither of you deserved that.'

'You were grieving. *Are* grieving,' Bathos said. 'We know how much she means to you. She was our friend too. And we didn't have many of those growing up where we did.'

'You just need to let us know when things get too tough,' Ariel implored. 'That's what we're here for. No point pissing about and acting like the big man all the time. You hurt the same as the rest of us. Kings and peasants bleed the same. And jumped-up pricks like you even more so…'

The three of them shared a laugh and allowed the silence to return. Aleister used the time to think about the journey they had been on. Three orphans growing up in the Lower City of Archania. They'd been all across the North. All across the East and West. The only places they'd never been to were the South and the Borderlands. Not bad for three annoying, little orphans.

'I appreciate everything you do for me. Both of you,' Aleister said, unable to look at the two of them in case he lost his nerve with what he was about to say. 'I know I get a lot of the credit for what we do but without you two, I'd be dead. I can be an arrogant, annoying prick at times but I want you both to know that I know what you do for me. And I'm grateful.'

'Soppy little bastard isn't he, from time to time?' Ariel muttered to Bathos who chuckled back.

'Aleister – Leader of The Red Sons. One of the greatest mercenary groups in the history of Takaara. And here he is thanking little old you and me…' Bathos put on a shocked voice and fluttered his eyelashes.

'Bastards.' Aleister pulled his muddy boot from his foot and threw it at the pair of them. They screamed in shock and delight as he laughed along with them. 'That's the last time I ever try and be nice to the two of you. Remember that!'

'We will!' Ariel cried, brushing her dark hair away from her face before settling back down and wiping joyful tears from her eyes. 'You just remember that we're a team. We rise and fall together. We live and die together. No remorse. No regrets. That's our way. Ain't nothing gonna change that, brother.'

***

The night was just as hot when Aleister woke. The song of crickets permeated the night but he could sense a disturbance somewhere close by. Nothing he could see. Nothing he could hear, even. But he had been in enough dangerous parts of the world to know to trust his gut when it was telling him to wake the fuck up and be wary.

He pulled on his trousers and buckled his belt. Finally, he wrapped his fingers around the hilt of his sword and prayed he would not need to trap more souls within the unique weapon. Crouching low, he snuck out from under the exit of his small tent and poked a head through to his neighbours'.

'Psst…' Ariel was lying flat on Bathos' hairy barrel-like chest as it rose and fell with each booming snore. 'Wake up!' he screeched, careful to ensure that his voice was too low for anyone but the two of them to hear. With a practised effort, the two of them leapt up, eyes blinking furiously at the intrusion.

'You should knock…' Bathos growled, never happy to be woken from his slumber. 'We could have been—'

'Knock on what exactly? It's a fucking tent.' Aleister whispered. 'Something's up. Weapons and stay together,' he commanded, whirling away confident that they would follow without argument.

They followed his simple instruction without debate, trusting him as they always had.

Aleister led them away from the tent and into the darkness of the night. He could see the outline of the rainforest in the distance, a black shadow looming on the horizon. In the other direction lay flat land broken up only by the rows of tents that had been erected by those travelling in the caravan. There were a few lights glowing due to torches standing outside of tents but not many. Most of the travellers were too weary to be up at such a time. Still, there had to be guards on the lookout. Abdulaziz had explained that he kept a lookout for his people at all times of day and night on their journey. He knew that danger lurked around every corner. So where were the guards?

'You two, stay together and check Abdulaziz's tent. Make sure he's in there and he's safe,' Aleister commanded, eyes peering everywhere in the darkness. 'I'll run along the caravan and find out where the guards are.'

Not waiting for an answer, he rushed off, keeping low and turning his head to search for any sign of trouble. As his eyes adjusted to the lack of light, he spotted a shadow on the ground. Still and lifeless. Cursing, he sprinted to the scene, hoping it wasn't what he thought it was.

No luck.

He pressed two fingers against the victim's neck but there was no sign of life. The guard's sword still lay in its sheath and there was blood staining the ground and the woman's throat. He wiped the wet blood from his fingers onto his trousers and searched for any clue as to where the culprits had fled. Listening carefully, he heard voices in the distance.

'Wanted to catch up with you before the bridge. My men ain't too fond of the thing if truth be told. Don't matter much now though, does it. I did warn you. My master isn't keen on being embarrassed and that's what you lot did when you crossed his land without permission.'

'Lord Manuel has leave of his senses if he thinks such an act will go unpunished. Believe me Jorges, there will be trouble.' Abdulaziz tried to sound stern and confident but Aleister could hear the edge of fear in his voice.

He recognised the man standing in front of Abdulaziz as the bandit who had been scolded earlier in their journey. The bastard wore a pleased look on his face as he stood in front of thirty armoured men. Two of his cronies held Abdulaziz by his elbows as two motionless bodies lay forgotten to the side. Revenge for the earlier meeting. Aleister cursed. There was no way they would be able to take down such a force.

'Ah but you see, dear friend,' Jorges Bana cried. He placed his hands on the merchant's robe and brushed off some of the dust from the night, as though speaking to a close ally. 'That's the beauty of it. We're in the South now. What happens here will not be known in the West. We can blame it on the damned savages who live in the trees around here. No one would care to argue. Lord Manuel can even say that he sent some of his best men to investigate and they too were lost, sacrificing themselves in the name of justice. It all works in his favour, Master Merchant.'

Bana whipped his open hand across the merchant's face, catching him with the back of his knuckles. Abdulaziz took the blow without a sound. He spat what Aleister thought may be blood out of his mouth at Bana's feet but that was all.

'You're stronger than you look, you sand dogs. But when the time comes, we will wipe all of your kind from Takaara and the world will be a better place for it.'

'I've been slapped harder by my wife when I'm out of line,' Abdulaziz replied to sniggers from the soldiers watching, much to the distaste of Bana. 'Do not mistake your weakness for my strength.'

Bana lunged, sword leading the way and thrust the weapon up through the merchant's chest. Abdulaziz fell into an awkward embrace, caught by his killer. 'Then do not mistake this quick death for mercy, you Eastern dog.'

Unable to watch anymore, Aleister leapt into action, sword already gripped in hand as he roared forward. Too late to save Abdulaziz, now he was bent only on destruction and bloodshed.

Two bodies hit the floor before anyone realised what was happening. Aleister couldn't see the red of his blade in the dim night light but he could feel the warm spray of blood on his bare torso as he settled into the groove of the fight, swinging with an experienced focus and ease – jabbing, thrusting, and cutting any in his path.

Bana grabbed the nearest soldier to his right and threw the man forward, blocking Aleister's preferred path to the bastard as Abdulaziz dropped at his feet. Two parries but then Aleister upped the pace and twirled, snapping his opponent's blade to the side and spinning his sword low to his side and behind him, thrusting it through the man's ribs before twisting once more and pulling the blade free so he could swing it with all his might, taking off the head clean from the shoulders. The sword screamed with delight as more souls made their dark journey into the blade, trapped forever.

The shock of the sudden battle had worn away and now the remaining men stood prepared for a fight; all with swords or spears ready, a few raising their shields to protect from an attack. Aleister felt the initial adrenaline of battle give way to logic and thought. Defeating them all would be nigh on impossible.

Thankfully, he wasn't alone.

Bathos ripped through the back of the line with his greatsword, tearing across two of the surprised soldiers before finishing them with fatal jabs as he bellowed into the night. Ariel spun a spear with ease and elegance, jabbing straight up underneath the jaw of a soldier as he turned to face her. Caught between three deadly warriors, the group panicked, unsure who to attack first. The chaos would only be to their advantage momentarily. Aleister knew that. He chose his next victim with care and precision.

'He didn't deserve death, not like that…' Aleister said, pacing forward, sword leading the way.

'Shit on him,' Jorges Bana spat back, eyes darting everywhere as he searched for an escape route. 'War is coming and then all Eastern scum will be purged from this world. He had an easier death than most of the dogs will.'

He was faster than Aleister would have thought. A cowardly man, willing to stab an unarmed opponent and look for a way out of a fight, but he was experienced with the blade nonetheless. He blocked Aleister's first strike and jumped back, pleased to find that no one stood in his way.

Aleister rushed forward again, knowing that every moment was vital. If any of the others had the brains to step forward and attack then he would struggle to make it out alive. Another block. This time, Bana led the dance. Three quick strikes. Low. Low. High. He finished with a kick out at Aleister, catching him on his thigh and forcing him to stumble backwards.

Sensing an opening, Bana attacked with all haste.

Aleister smiled at his trick. Allowing his opponent the chance to see victory in their grasp was a favourite of his. He feigned a dead leg before whipping forward, twisting his body inside of the attack and slamming his elbow into Bana's face. The soldier reeled back and struggled to find his footing, stumbling backwards, arms wide open in shock.

Aleister slid his blade through Bana's chest far enough for their faces to meet, close enough to kiss. 'Do not mistake this for mercy…' he growled before twisting the sword and watching the light leave the bastard's eyes.

Any sense of victory was short-lived. He backed away from the oncoming soldiers. They had regrouped and realised that they had the numbers. Clever fighting would see victory in their hands tonight. They had enough about them to know that now. Ariel and Bathos stepped into line with him, standing either side in a defensive stance with their weapons facing the row of enemies.

'Surrendering isn't an option is it?' Ariel muttered from out of the corner of her mouth.

'Reckon that disappeared as an option the moment we killed their friends…' Aleister said, peering around at their deadly display.

'Take as many as you can, fewer of them left means more chance the travellers have of overcoming them,' Bathos said, giving them both a grim nod. 'It's been fun…'

'Who's the soppy one now?' Aleister laughed, spinning the sword in his hands, hoping his feigned confidence would give him even a split second extra to defeat his enemies.

Bathos didn't have a chance to answer.

Arrows whipped through the air and took down five of the soldiers in one hit. Strange cries rang out in the night as the sound of feet running across the ground reached Aleister's ears. He turned to see spears glistening in the moonlight as fifty or more men and women, all with black skin and wide eyes rush towards them. They circled the merry gathering, spear points aimed at throats – at Bana's men, Aleister, Ariel, and Bathos.

The newcomers wore light armour, Aleister could see as they drew closer. The women standing closest glared at him. Her head was shaved and her eyebrows cut into thin streaks. Her armour was painted black but cut off at the shoulders and knees. Like the rest of them, she wore nothing on her feet. Small, silver hoops twisted all the way up her right ear and one through her left nostril. She was an interesting sight, but beautiful. And deadly, Aleister reminded himself.

One of the warriors, a broad-shouldered woman with sparkling eyes that shot fire out at all who looked upon her, stepped forward and kicked over the corpses, inspecting each one carefully. Eventually, she reached Abdulaziz. She bent low and stared into his dead eyes.

'Who is responsible, for this?' she said in a clear tongue Aleister understood.

'He was our friend,' Aleister said, still holding his sword in his hand, unwilling to let it go. He pointed towards the huddle of soldiers that had been drawing closer to them. 'They killed him. Their aim was to blame it on you. Abdulaziz was a good man.'

The woman stood back up with a sigh and marched over to Aleister. She stabbed her spear into the ground and drew closer. She took his jaw in her hand and squeezed tightly. 'Pale. You are from the North. I've not seen you before. What are you doing in our land? And why shouldn't I kill you?' She released his jaw, allowing him to speak.

'We were working with Abdulaziz, looking after his caravan.'

'You failed. He is dead.'

'You don't need to remind me…'

The woman sniffed and said something to her allies in their own language. Spears thrust forward as one, killing all of Bana's men and impaling them on the sharp weapons. Aleister was relieved to see that his allies had been left. The three of them stood still, alive.

'He is dead. Our pact is gone with him. You work for us now.'

Before Aleister could argue, the butt of a spear smashed across his head. His hands pawed at the wet ground beneath him. Blood. Another blow to the head and his night was over.

THE FOLLY OF MYOPIA

'When do we leave? Surely everything is ready now?' Arden looked into Osiron's starry eyes and waited patiently for the answer. He'd waited patiently for a long while now. Osiron had promised much and now it was time that things were delivered. Arden had spoken with the people he needed to and understood what had to be done to save the unfortunate trapped people of the Chaos Plane. It would be difficult, but he knew that he had the support of those around him. The support of those who truly believed he was the prince they had been waiting for. Even his father…

'Everything is ready. The moon is full and the lights of the North dance across the night sky. It's beautiful,' Osiron answered with their usual disconnected voices intersecting over each other. Arden was used to it now. It calmed him.

'That's how we do it. How we cross back.' He said it more to himself than anyone else, running through the idea once again.

'Something like that. You know what you have to do once we arrive. For all the others to be able to cross back into Takaara, the barrier must fall. You must—'

'I know.' Arden interrupted, not wanting to think about it until it had to be done. 'When the time comes, I'll be ready. No hesitation. And once it's done…'

'We can lead the others into Takaara. You, as the Prince of Chaos – taking your rightful place as a leader in the task of purifying the land once again.'

Osiron always had an interesting way of presenting even the most difficult of scenarios. Arden nodded, calmed by the words and ready for what they were about to do. He faced Osiron and pushed his arms out, opening them for the chaotic embrace. Osiron glided forward and slipped inside Arden's arms, wrapping their own around Arden. Tighter. Tighter. Arden struggled for breath as the grip squeezed ever tighter.

He arched his back, feet pulled from off the ground. His mouth opened with the strain of the impact as he felt Osiron pull closer to him. Those strange, calming eyes stared without emotion into his. Unblinking and cold – ignoring Arden's squirms and panic. The eyes drew closer to his until all Arden could see was the black with specks of light. It surrounded him as he struggled. Then, slowly at first, before growing in speed, purple and green waves of light swayed across the darkness. The lights drifted towards Arden, drawing nearer, almost blinding him. The lights wrapped around him. Danced through him. Entered his body and took hold. They filled his lungs, opening his airwaves and allowing him to take a breath, revelling in the air that crashed through his body.

Arden closed his eyes, overwhelmed with the intensity of the invasion. He felt his body drop to the ground and bent over, resting on his knees, eyes still closed as his whole frame shook, convulsing as a shrill ringing grew louder and louder in his ears. He wrapped his hands around ears, hoping to block out the deafening noise. No use. Another convulsion and this time he felt the bile rush up from the pit of his stomach and tear through his chest and throat before crashing out of his mouth, burning his teeth on the way.

Unable to move his muscles, he stumbled onto his side and felt the soft familiar wetness of snow beneath him. Eventually, he managed to roll onto his back, the wet snow pressing against his back. It grounded him. Focused him on where he was and what he had to do. He opened his eyes and looked up into a clear night sky. The moon was full and the stars twinkled above. Purple and green lights swept across the sky. Every nerve in his body burned, as though being used for the first time. He lay there, waiting patiently. He was good at that now.

He wouldn't have to wait much longer.

The castle hadn't changed much during his time away. Darker. The candles were no longer lit in their sconces but that didn't matter now. He enjoyed the darkness. The shadows cloaked him like a comforting blanket, shrouding him as he stalked the wide, open corridors and ran his fingers down the dark wooden panels on the walls. He'd arrived here with a feeling of wonder and awe, hoping that he would learn the truths about himself and what he was. Instead, he'd been stabbed in the back and thrown into the snow like scraps of meat for rabid dogs.

This time was going to be different. This time he would not be thrown into the snow. This time he would leave on his own terms.

The tapestries were darker than before. The colour had drained from them since he had last walked these corridors. The images were the same but grey and twisted like angry storm clouds. The silence was different to last time. There had been a hum radiating through the castle before. Arden had thought it was silence that choked the air but it was nothing like the silence that gripped the building now. This was a silence where he could hear the blood rushing around his body. The scratching of his nails on skin as he ran them across his chin, surprised to find the fuzz of a beard waiting for him.

He remembered the paths of the corridors. The red carpet, now black. The stone floor, now broken and chipped. Korvus hadn't been looking after the castle, allowing it to fall into disrepair. If he had not known better, Arden would have thought that it had been many cycles since anyone had cared for the building. He found the door he was looking for and waited. Just a simple wooden door. Different to the last time he'd seen it but that didn't faze him. The door opened without him raising a hand. He stepped in calmly, gazing around the bare room in wonder. All the books, the knowledge, the learning – all of it had gone. The shelves were bare and filled with dust and cobwebs. A single table stood in the centre of the room. Two chairs. Simple, mahogany chairs, nothing fancy or luxurious. They faced each other at either end. In the middle, Arden spotted a full bottle of red wine waiting for him. An old mage sat patiently on one of the chairs. He seemed to have aged a great deal since their last meeting. Creases branched out from the corner of his dark, cold eyes – so very different to the golden pupils that had stared over Arden's lifeless body in the snow. A silver shirt lined with black lace and deep blue trousers were different to the dark robes Arden had seen him wear. Today must be important to him.

'The place has changed a bit since last time,' Arden said, pulling the chair from under the table and taking his seat, staring across at Korvus who gave a resigned smile in return. 'Can't say that I like the improvements but it's bold. Feels a bit, *lifeless,* without the books and the colour on the walls.' He remembered the last time he had sat at the table, eating his food and doing his best to follow Korvus's strict tutelage. 'I suppose I understand a bit about that now.'

'Osiron is playing you for a fool,' Korvus chuckled, leaning over and grabbing the bottle of wine. He slowly poured the red liquid into two plain glasses and offered one to Arden, handing it to him after a gentle nod. 'It's what I had always feared. We needed more time but the fact is, no matter how many lives you have in this world, there is never enough of the bastard stuff. Slips through your fingers as you try your best to squeeze it tight – like sand searching for the cracks to escape as you desperately try to cling on for more.'

'Playing me for a fool?' Arden struggled to hold back the laughter at the thought. 'You and Socket were the ones who played me for a fool. You made me believe that you wanted what was best for me but, in the end, he stuck a dagger in me like I was a piece of meat and you both watched me bleed out in the snow.' He sipped his wine – the same colour as blood. A strong fruity taste, not Korvus's usual kind but it was good stuff, nonetheless. 'Or did you forget that?'

The muscles in Korvus's face twitched at the last

question. 'I have forgotten nothing, Arden Leifhand. We were doing what we thought was best for all of Takaara. Your power was generated through trauma – through your anger, your sadness, your frustration, your fear. We believed such an act would unleash the power of the Guardian inside you. A last-ditch attempt at saving Takaara. It would take time; we knew that. After the first week, the warmth of the castle faded. The colour drained from the walls and everything inside that had been a part of the Sky Plane faded. Only the greatest of disturbances could have done such a thing. You've aligned with them.' Korvus shook his head and downed half of his glass before gasping long and hard, swilling the rest around before looking back at Arden. 'Your eyes. I recognise them now. Osiron can be one convincing bastard, I know that. I just didn't expect you to fall for the parlour tricks. I thought you had more of a moral compass, one stronger than mine at least. I was wrong.'

'Wrong?' Arden spat, throwing his wine onto the rug next to him, feeling the rage coursing through his veins. 'You were wrong in many things but not with that. You betrayed me! You *killed* me! How dare you speak of a moral compass. *I'm* the one who is trying to save Takaara. Save it from the disgusting leeches like you.'

'There isn't enough time to explain it all,' Korvus said sadly, finishing the rest of his drink and exhaling before chucking his glass onto the floor, mirroring Arden's actions. The glass shattered into tiny pieces, reflecting the low light of the lanterns hanging on the bare walls. 'Find Socket. He cares for you, even if you don't see that now.'

'He cared enough to put the dagger through me and end my life. He cared enough to watch me die.'

'He will explain. Too late now, but he will want you to know…'

'I know enough…' Arden stood and pulled a curved dagger from his belt, marching towards Korvus who sat waiting calmly.

'If only you did…' The old mage muttered absently, glancing up at Arden and staring into his eyes. 'Like a clear night sky…' he said to himself before his eyes fell on the dagger. He didn't attempt to move or try to defend himself. He just sat there, watching. 'The Gods abandoned us many cycles ago. You are a pretender wishing to sit on an empty throne, Osiron. The five hells are waiting you and all who follow your paths.'

Arden's body convulsed, his fingers gripping the dagger tighter than ever. For a moment, it felt as though he was watching the scene play from afar, a low growling ripping through his body as the dagger inched closer to Korvus. '*You fall, old man. As will all the others. There is nothing you can do to stop us.*'

'I suppose not. Not now...'

Arden whipped the dagger across the throat with surgical precision, not even blinking as the scarlet blood flashed and splattered all over the fancy silver shirt, staining it forever. Korvus's head lolled forward and banged onto the table, like falling asleep in a drunken stupor as the wild men of the Borderlands had been prone to do after one too many drinks.

Arden ran a hand softly through the old man's thin hair as he marched past him and towards the exit. 'Where next?' Thunder boomed around the castle and the ground beneath Arden shook. A crack opened up straight through the centre of the library, stretching the two sides apart and pushing them away, creating a division twenty paces wide. Arden watched as stone and wood cracked and broke and the castle began to tear itself apart with the impact of the quake.

He shook, head jerking to the side as he heard a soft crack and felt his stomach lurch. '*The United Cities of Archania. The kingdom that should be yours. A message is being delivered. Once it arrives, it will be time for you to see your brother...*'

Brother. Arden grinned, ignoring the chaos unfurling around him. Time for another family reunion.

***

The smell of the docks was best left in the forgotten parts of memory. The sweat of the sailors and workmen. The salt smell of the sea as the waves lapped against the wooden piers. Piss, vomit, and blood. Wasn't one of the cleanest places in Takaara but why would docks be clean? Always in a state of transition as merchants, mercenaries and folk just wishing to start a new life passed through on the way to their next job or adventure.

He was pleased to feel the hard, wooden boards beneath his wet boots as he stepped onto the docks and away from the drifting ship he had travelled on for the last couple of days. Norland wasn't too far away but the winds had been moody as the hells and had fun playing with the ship and its occupants. A few of the sailors had chucked up their guts on the way, younger ones not used to the rocking and swaying, as the older ones chuckled but still cast nervous glances up at the darkening skies. Cypher was past caring about the oddness of the weather. Used to be a time when you could work out what it would be like depending on the season but now it was all over the place. Bright, beaming sunshine in the morning and angry, black clouds with a touch of lightning in the afternoon. Made no sense but Cypher didn't want to waste energy caring.

A burly worker carrying a large barrel on his shoulder spat on the floor next to Cypher and stared him in the eyes. Cypher smirked and stared back, unwilling to be intimidated by the muscled dock worker.

'Afternoon,' he said. 'Such a lovely day…'

The worker grunted, stern face switching to a frown, clearly confused by the bright greeting. The idiots didn't understand manners and politeness. Always knocked them for a loop. The fool probably would have preferred a curse or a snarl from Cypher. That was precisely why he wouldn't offer it to him.

He took his time and ambled through the docks, dodging the numerous workers and whistling on his way. He'd had the whole journey to think about his next course of action. What had originally been a frightening meeting with a presumed God was now most likely a hallucinogenic event brought on by smokes and incense in that small hut by the cliff. The girl was probably crazy, driven mad by some herbs or mushrooms and the sort. He'd heard of that kind of thing out in the wilder parts of the world. Nothing for the commoners to do but enter a trance and imagine that their world was more interesting than it actually was. A form of escape from the shit day-to-day existence that greeting them every time they woke up.

Every time Cypher thought he had convinced himself it was all a fucked-up dream, an unwanted image flashed into his mind. Clearer than the workers marching past him. Clearer than the gulls flying overhead, looking out for scraps of food. Clearer than the barking dog bounding past his feet.

An image of a being with unreal eyes that showed the blackness of the night sky with specks of light like stars that shone deep into his soul…

Cypher shivered, unnerved by the reminder of his visit to the hut. *Damned prick!* He scolded himself. It had been real. He knew that. Every time he tried to ignore it, it became clearer in his mind, reminding him of his mission.

Matthias would be on his way soon enough. With him would be the those calling themselves The Plague. They would reinforce Cypher's message to Mason and Asher. A message sent by the God of Chaos.

'Cypher Zellin.' An Eastern voice. Cypher knew that sly drawl anywhere.

'T'Chai. It's good to see you without a lead around your neck. Mason must have trained you better than the other dogs he has.'

If T'Chai was in any way offended, then he was damned good at not displaying it.

'Certainly. You arrive back in Archania, yet you left with Zaif. Zaif was the superior on your mission. Why have you returned without him?' T'Chai sounded slightly annoyed but his face was impassive, arms folded calmly across his chest as he searched over Cypher with his keen, brown eyes.

'I see nothing escapes you and your master,' Cypher said with a small, mocking bow. 'My dear friend Zaif,' he pressed a hand against his chest and scrunched up his face in mock pain, pretending that each word was a stab to his heart. 'My dear, dear friend Zaif. He is dead. Gone. Deceased. Lifeless.' Cypher sighed, amused to see the flicker of shock cross the Eastern native's face. 'He shall be missed, that is certain. The problems in Norland persist. I, myself barely escaped with my life! Zaif practically sacrificed himself to save me. In fact, it wouldn't surprise me to one day see a statue of the hero standing in the Upper City.'

'Quit your humour, Cypher Zellin,' T'Chai snapped. 'And tell me what happened.'

Cypher grinned, pleased with the sudden outburst. He loved finding those nerves and prodding away. 'Zaif was killed by a rebel group in Norland. I have information but it includes a message only for the ears of the king and Mason himself. I would tell you, but messages to dogs have the habit of becoming lost in translation. Too much difficulty in the barking, I believe…'

T'Chai's face had reverted to his original rock-like unbending state. 'Follow me.'

Moving from the docks and into the Lower City allowed Cypher a chance to witness the changes since he had last passed through the region. People were still taking hammers to the charred wreckage left behind as a reminder of the failed revolt. The burned homes and buildings still standing were being dismantled by grim and sad-looking men and women. The same men and women who had most likely believed that a new life was right around the corner for them. A new life where they had the opportunity to rise above the filth they were mired in now. One positive was that the city seemed more open, less claustrophobic than before. Cypher had enjoyed the closeness of the streets and buildings but destruction allowed him to view the city with a new perspective. Less shadows and places for hiding which could be a pain but it gave the city more of a welcoming feel. Some bastard would love that, no doubt. He'd enjoyed the maze-like paths and the unknown. Thinking that with any corner turned you could step in front of a fucker wanting to kill you. Gave him a thrill like nothing else.

There were more folks sitting on the streets. Filthy and unwashed, holding out torn hats or pressing their grubby, little hands forwards in the hope that a few idiots would throw some coin their way. Cypher spat on one of them – a young woman with a dead look in her eyes. Wastes of space, the lot of them. Why couldn't they get up off their lazy backsides and do something if they wanted coin and food? Life doesn't give you anything good for free, so you best do something about it. That's what he'd done. Rob, steal and kill if you need to. But don't just sit there begging and acting like life isn't shit for everyone. What made them so special?

'Seems to be more of them than before,' Cypher said, more to himself than to his quiet companion. 'The king not thinking about doing anything about it? Makes the place look... untidy.'

Another beggar, an old man with swollen gums and no teeth, crawled on his hands and knees and clutched at Cypher's robe. A quick, sharp backhand across the face threw the man back towards the street side, hands now clutching his aching cheek. Cypher glared at him until he looked away. They had to be taught a lesson. Just like training dogs. The stick was a useful tool for these kinds of people. For most kinds of people really.

'King Asher is dealing with many things right now,' T'Chai responded curtly. 'Rebuilding the Lower City is on his list. He has offered support to any magi struggling with the loss of their power after the last quake. The Upper City has many large buildings and grounds where the king has offered to care for those who are having difficulties with such a sudden and overwhelming change.'

'A surprising move,' Cypher scratched his head and tried to catch a glance at the Eastern warrior's dark eyes and black pupils. 'I'd have just killed the lot of them. Easier. Less expensive. Still, I guess your kind are having those same difficulties...'

'A temporary setback. The Empire's power never lay in its use of magic. We saw the problems with overuse of magic and warned others about the dangers they would face if it were used incorrectly by untrained fools. What has happened is proof that we were right all along.'

'Or maybe you caused it all by using your magic to mess with the Sky Plane,' Cypher said, knowing the theory would frustrate the patriotic warrior. 'Ever think of that?'

'The Empress knows what she is doing, Cypher Zellin. Unlike you, I listen to those better informed and follow their instructions without hesitation.'

'Even a dog has the intelligence to bite back every once

in a while. Blind loyalty doesn't work, my Eastern puppy. Remember that.'

'And you remember who you are working for…'

Cypher shrugged and left it at that. He had wound up the warrior enough for now, anyway. They walked together through the rest of the Lower City in silence. The market was back up and running at least; a small crowd had gathered to buy food and other items, each buyer haggling in an attempt to lower some of the unrealistic prices called out by the merchants talented in ripping off their customers. Some things never changed.

The gate separating the upper and lower halves of Archania had changed.

Three lines of guards armed with shining spears and bright white cloaks over silver armour stood on either side of a spiked, iron gate. Two new towers stood in the middle of construction, ladders all over the place and materials scattered on the other side of the gate to Cypher. King Asher may be acting like the kind, helpful king but this display proved that there was fear in the king's court. Triple the security. Two new watchtowers. Brand new armour and weapons for the guards. The divide between the two parts of the city had been clear before but now it was as subtle as an animal in heat. Asher feared what the Lower City could do, even after stamping out the rebellion.

'An interesting decision from our wise leader…' Cypher said, glancing up at the towers and hoping that one of the workers might fall to their deaths whilst he was there.

'A necessary decision,' T'Chai explained to him. 'The Lower City rose up against the king and his allies. They threatened treason and there are consequences for such rash actions.'

'Dividing the city in two probably ain't the best idea. Of course, just my humble opinion. What would I know? I'm only one of the few to have lived and breathed on both sides of this damned border…'

T'Chai ignored the statement, instead choosing to have his own, short conversation with one of the guards. Cypher noticed that the new uniform had that insignia of the white sun stitched into the shoulders. They were no longer just the King's Guard. They were part of the Empire of Light. That was clearer than day to any who passed through the city. Archania welcomed the Empire's embrace and was suckled up to its big sister in the East. Asher had been the last piece of the puzzle.

Once the gate was opened, the guards parted, allowing the two of them to pass whilst keeping an eye on a few of the citizens inching closer to the gate, as if daring themselves to make a run through it whilst it was open. They must have thought better of it as Cypher heard the gate close behind him without any commotion.

Like the Lower City, the Upper City had not been unaffected by the rebellion. Cypher spotted large groups of guards swarmed around particular buildings or fenced-off grounds. He peered at them in curiosity, remembering T'Chai's words from earlier. These must be the places where Asher was said to have helped the citizens suffering from their loss of magic or caught up in the events from the night of the rebellion. These camps were well away from the centre of the Upper City, away from the important people in Archania. They were all situated on the outskirts of the city with high security in place. Cypher grinned at the genius of it all. Mason's work no doubt. Asher was too much of an idiot for such brilliance.

In the eyes of the Lower City's citizens, Asher was the benevolent leader. He was offering support at a time when they needed it most. He was giving up land in the Upper City to help them and give them shelter from the harsh realities of an unstable world. But giving them free reign would piss off many of the posh bastards in the Upper City who would never agree to sacrificing anything to support anyone beneath them. Instead, they were trapped in these prisons, safely away from the important members of society and in a place where Mason and his men could see which individuals had lost their magic. Most likely they were writing down names for the future and possibly even testing them to find a solution to the problem. Victims who could be thrown away with ease if anything went wrong and no one would give a shit.

He had to hand it to the preacher, the man was ruthless *and* intelligent. A frightening combination.

As they walked through the pristine city, troops of soldiers marched past in disciplined groups. Each step synchronized perfectly as the spears stabbed towards the dark clouds above them. Silver armour glistened in the light of day and the sun crest shone on all their shoulders as their white cloaks billowed in the wind. Cypher hadn't seen such activity from the army in a long while. The rebellion in the Lower City must have really shook things up for the comfortable men and women of the Upper City, living in their blissful ignorance of what real life could be like. He imagined what chaos would have been brought into the city if the Doctors had succeeded, if they had taken the Lower City and defeated King Asher's army the night of the flames. It would have been absolutely splendid in his eyes. And just what all these fools deserved.

'I see the soldiers are out and about today. A rare sighting for Archania's finest, wandering the streets of Archania and displaying their strength,' he said, beating his chest with mock pride. Another group, this one much larger than the first stomped their way after the earlier group. Cypher frowned as he spotted the darker skin tone of the soldiers and the unique helmets that they wore. Spiked helms with white cloth resting down each side of the face. The way they moved made the first group seem like amateurs. They weren't a group of individuals that had learnt to march in time; they were one complete unit. An organism with one heartbeat that marched through the city, promising discipline and compliance and warning of the dangers to anyone who disobeys. 'And I see it is not just Archania's finest…'

It was T'Chai's turn to smile. 'We are part of the Empire of Light now. The Empress has kindly sent some of her own warriors to assist in anything that we need. The perks of being part of something greater than one's self.'

A worrying sign. The East was tightening its grip on the North. All the East had fallen, barring Darakeche. Now the North bent the knee to the Empress.

T'Chai led them to the large temple that had been constructed some cycles ago to allow for the worship of the God of Light.

'Mason not in his office today?' Cypher asked as they turned through the small wooden gate and up the path through the small cemetery, white marble tombstones sticking up through the messy patches of grass on either side of a thin stone pathway that led to the tall, open doors of the temple.

'He spends more time in the temple of late. That way, he is closer to the One God.'

'Should have guessed that myself…' Cypher muttered sarcastically, rolling his eyes behind T'Chai's back.

The temple sparkled. The wooden pews had been polished to a glimmering shine and a new red carpet ran down the centre of the room, running all the way to the steps that jumped up towards the altar and a long stone table. A light shone down through a circle cut in the ceiling, the light beaming down to land onto a silver book that stood on its stand on the table in the light. Every religion seemed to have some kind of book that preachers read from. Couldn't remember the message without it, Cypher surmised.

'Wait here,' T'Chai commanded before stomping between the rows of benches and down towards the altar. He leant into a silver-haired man sitting in silence on the bench at the front before rushing back to Cypher. 'He's ready to see you.'

'How delightful…'

Cypher followed Mason's dog to the front of the temple and turned to face the preacher, smiling and offering the most perfunctory of bows possible. He thought he would be pleased to see the gold missing from the preacher's eyes but if anything, they made him seem more threatening. More dangerous. There was no colour there now, just complete blackness. A black hole ready to swallow any who were unprepared to bend to his will.

'Cypher Zellin,' Mason said, voice tired and weary. Different to the melodic tunes he would sing with confidence prior to Cypher's Norland trip. 'I've been told that you have an important message for me. It must be *most* important as you are back much sooner than expected. And *alone*.'

'Well,' Cypher began, scratching his bald pate and

offering a guilty smile. 'Zaif was a big man. Didn't fancy carrying his corpse all the way back on my own. Gave him a burial befitting of his stature, though. You can be sure of it.' Burnt by plague doctors dressed in red...

'I hope that isn't the only message you have for me today.' Mason's tone warned Cypher that he was not in the mood for games.

'The other message is one that is for both yourself and the king of the United Cities of Archania Our brave, sweet and benevolent King Asher himself.'

'And who is this message from? That fool ambassador? I should have burned him when I had the chance...' Mason cursed himself before staring into Cypher's eyes. 'Speak.'

'The message is from someone much more important,' Cypher said, dropping his smile and putting on his best serious face; eyebrows drawn together and face sucked into the centre. He stood, back straight and proud, one arm across his chest. 'The God of Chaos.'

THE PATH HOME

'I do not trust either of them,' Istari snarled after Kane had updated him on the current situation. To the surprise of no one, he wasn't best pleased with the mercenary group and the distraction they had caused. 'Each and every one of them fight for coin. There is no honour in what they do. Selling their sword to the highest bidder. Where is the trust in that? Even sleeping in this tent makes my skin crawl.' He shook his body and turned from Kat; the back of his neck showed the deep red colour that his face had turned in anger. 'I do not give two shits about who is leading this cursed company. My focus is on taking you safely to Mughabir and allowing you the chance to pass on your message to the Sultan. Anything else is of no concern to me.'

'The Red Sons can be a useful tool in the fight against the Empire. Surely you can see that?' Kane asked as Istari sat down on his emerald green mat and lit the candle in front of him. He closed his eyes and took a deep breath in, allowing his chest to fill fully before taking his time to exhale. Kane pushed on. 'The Empire is stronger than you realise. Paid mercenaries could be the difference. They could tip the balance in our favour when the war comes…'

'And if the Empire pays them more?' Istari asked, legs folded, eyes still shut. 'What then? They will turn on us for gold and coin and we will be ashes, unable to even curse ourselves for the stupidity of trusting such weak-boned traitors. The Empire is not led by fools.'

Kat stomped over and knelt in front of him, the candle burning between them. Still, his eyes were closed, unaffected by her movement. 'They were a company started by three friends. Led by people who I know wanted Takaara to be a better place. A better place for the poor. The oppressed. The broken and damaged. They wanted to be the first people to stand up against the injustices of this world and look after people who cannot be looked after if left alone. Those three people are marching south to a dangerous land in the hope of preventing a war that could tear Takaara apart. In their absence, this company will choose a new leader. Whether it is Jax, Adnan, or some other warrior – the fate of this company, and possibly all of Takaara, could be in their hands. We can play a part in that. Leaving them now would be immoral.'

Istari opened a single eye and raised an eyebrow. He sighed and slapped his hands onto his knees, giving up on his meditation in favour of continuing the discussion at last. '*Immoral?*' he snarled. 'You believe that to be immoral? I hope you are comfortable. I will speak to you of immoral.'

Kane shuffled on her mat, sitting properly and staring intently at Istari, granting him her full attention.

'Immoral. You may have heard stories of The Butcher of Khalos.' The name rang a bell, but Kane could not recall any specific details. 'The Butcher lived in a stunning country nestled in the bosom of the Heartlands, called Khalos. I had been there a few times in my youth and twice as a man. Beautiful white stone buildings, gentle lakes next to green banks where men and women would sit and read and bask in the sunshine. The people were kind. Polite. Welcoming, even. I enjoyed spending time in Khalos.' For a moment, Istari stared into the flame of the candle, eyes following the rhythmic dance, lost in memories. He snapped out of it with a cough before apologising and continuing his tale. 'Its leader, Chief Yoonak, was a dangerous man. He loved his country, but he loved power more. He felt that he understood what was best for his land and its inhabitants. The army believed in him and so did most of the people, truth be told. But he was strict. Anyone deemed not pulling their weight, were executed.

Anyone caught robbing or hurting others, were executed. Anyone drinking alcohol or smoking, were executed. Put a foot wrong…'

'Executed…' Kane muttered, getting the message.

Istari nodded and sighed. 'Harsh rules but most of the people agreed with them. They were enforced consistently and the people of Khalos backed their leader, understanding that he had helped to create a land of progress and safety. They were not at war with any land in the Heartlands, unlike most of their neighbours, and they followed The Four, like most of Takaara. A small, select group of people – mainly families and friends of those who had been executed, started to question the regime. Knowing that they would be unable to do anything about it on their own, they raised money and sought support in their cause. They turned to The Red Sons.'

'It is difficult to see if there is true justice when it is regarding someone you love,' Kane admitted, fearing where this story was heading.

'I agree. Those killed were lawbreakers. They were people who knew the laws in place, yet they still broke them. In their land, it was justice. Nothing more. Nothing less. They told their sorry tales to The Red Sons, begging for support in their tirade against a hateful leader – a butcher who kills and destroys the lives of any who breathes too loudly in his presence. Worked well. Within the moon, The Red Sons had designed papers that were spread around the Heartlands and Khalos itself. These papers warned people about The Butcher of Khalos and his oppressive ways. They sowed seeds of doubt and sparked a war between the neighbouring countries. The Red Sons fought in that war. They played a key part in capturing Chief Yoonak and they watched as the people of Khalos, the people he adored and had worked all his life to serve, they watched as those same people took off his head and threw it into a cheering crowd. Do you know what happened next?'

Kane shook her head, sad eyes locked on Istari.

'The Red Sons left. Their job had been done. They had been paid. They marched out of Khalos without a glance back to check on what they had left.' Istari breathed in, shaking with frustration as he recalled the dark events. 'Khalos has been at war since that very day. The white buildings torn down. The lakes polluted with the blood of its people. The neighbouring nations, like sharks, sensed blood and they did not hesitate. It is a country destroyed all because The Red Sons accepted payment without asking questions. Without taking a day or two to discover the real source of the unrest. They were blinded by coin and in doing so, they killed thousands of innocent people and brought chaos to one of the most beautiful countries in the Heartlands. That, to me, is *immoral…*'

The silence suffocated Kane but she couldn't bring herself to say anything. She'd heard tales of The Red Sons, often they had brought a small smile to her lips as she thought of Aleister and his friends running around and doing their best to right the wrongs of the world, just like they had always planned. She had never thought that the tales of heroism and victory would be shining with a gloss that blinded her to the darkness within. Wars and rebellions meant blood and death, of course. The victors always told the tales and, so conveniently, certain parts would be discarded. It had always been the way. But to think that Aleister, Ariel and Bathos had walked away after destroying a country without realising the damage they had done, that hurt.

'They were young, still are…' she muttered sadly.

'Is that the excuse?' Istari questioned, jolting back and frowning. 'They are young. They were old enough to swing a sword. Old enough to take down the leader of a beautiful country. Do not play that card, not now, not here. Mercenaries owe allegiance to no one and that is why we must leave them to their internal problems and focus on solving our own.'

'And what about you?' Kane snapped back, allowing her sadness to manifest itself in rage. 'You are the Sword of Causrea. If you were commanded to take down a leader, you would do it without a moment's hesitation!'

Istari flashed forwards, barely missing the lit candle as he rushed towards Kane, bulging eyes and red face an inch from hers.

'I am the *Sword of Causrea*,' he growled. 'I fight for my country. Not for some fools sitting in a room talking and calling themselves leaders. I am named so because the people gave me that title when I was defending them against invaders and fighting to ensure my country survived. I have never done anything because I was *commanded*. I act based on how I feel. I act based on how best I can help those I care for. The Council of Ten can go and fuck themselves if they command me to do something that I did not already want to do.'

'Then why are you here?' Kane asked, not backing away from his frothing lips or wide eyes.

Istari's breathing slowed and he leaned back until he was sitting once more, still close enough to touch Kane from his position. 'I am here because my daughter worries that the world is about to break and she feels that I can play some small part in ensuring that it does not. She had a difficult enough childhood. A childhood that was darker than any child should have to live through. I made a promise to myself that I would take her away from that darkness and ensure that she would never suffer like that again. If escorting you to Mughabir means that I put her mind at ease, even just a little bit, then I would give my life for it.'

Kane dropped her chin onto her hand and watched the fire fade from Istari. He was just a worried father, looking out for his daughter. Protecting her from sadness in any way possible. 'If you want to ensure that she doesn't have to watch this world break, then I am begging you to give me just two days here. We will speak with whoever becomes the new leader and we will ask them for their support in what is to come. Then we shall head straight to Mughabir and deliver our message to the Sultan. That, I promise.'

Istari pushed himself from the mat and strode over to the tent's exit, pushing the flap open and showing Kane the open plains of the East and the clear night sky. 'You may see things differently to me. Most people do. But I do believe you to be a woman of honour, Katerina Kane. And my daughter seems to trust you. I will stay with you for two days. Then we will ride with all haste to Mughabir and the Sultan.'

Kane smiled and stood, eager to shake hands and complete the deal. 'Thank you Istari Vostor. Shall we shake on it?' Istari looked at the offered hand with such suspicion as he would if she were holding out a basket of snakes.

'Leave. It is time to rest.'

Kane shrugged and wiped her hand on her shirt. She strode past the warrior and out into the open air.

Two days.

That was all she needed.

'How many have thrown their names into the hat?' Kane asked Zaina from their high vantage point in the open amphitheatre Any member of The Red Sons could choose to place their name in a hat. The names were then drawn out at random and each person would be given an opportunity to speak in front of three hundred of the most experienced fighters. Once all of the candidates had spoken and attempted to persuade their difficult audience, a vote would be cast, and a new leader chosen.

'Only three. Jax. Adnan. And one other, a newbie. Most folk expect Jax and Adnan to get the votes, so it wasn't worth the time or energy for others to throw their name in,' Zaina explained.

'Did you not think of throwing your own name into the mix?' Kane asked, nudging her new ally with her elbow and producing a light chuckle. 'It may be The Red *Sons* but, in my experience, women tend to make cooler decisions when push comes to shove.'

'I would have loved to. Unfortunately, I've been away too long. Too much time in Archania on watch for Aleister and not enough time sharing the difficulties of the road. I wouldn't get the votes the others will. Adnan and Jax have proven their leadership skills and gained the trust of their men. Maybe next time…'

Set in the hills just outside the small town of Doba, the amphitheatre allowed for a cool, gentle breeze to sweep in as the red sun fell beneath the horizon. The horseshoe shaped theatre had rows of tiered stone seating that rose up around the edge to allow for the best views for the audience, no matter where they sat. In the East, they loved to watch plays out in the open air. Tragedies, comedies, and anything in between could be played out in front of a rising sun or a watchful full moon to allow for the correct atmosphere and tone to improve the setting for the stories displayed by actors on the stage in the centre. It was said that such a theatre originated in the East but most areas Kane had visited over the years had claimed to be the first with such a design. Braego had laughed at her when she had explained that to him. 'The Borderlands will never make such a claim. Never seen such a thing!' he had cried through joyful tears. The memory brought the shadow of a smile to her face.

Zaina had led Kat to seats near the higher tiers, away from the general rabble of mercenaries sitting closer to the front and sharing stories and greetings with each other. 'It's best if we keep you away from them for now. These events can be quite full on and you're an outsider – some of the men might not look too kindly on you being allowed access to such a meeting,' Zaina had explained to her.

Kane didn't mind. She understood the way these things worked and was honoured to be allowed a place at all. If that meant sitting alone for the entire thing, so be it. If you can't be happy in your own company, when can you be happy?

'Right, I better head down there. Enjoy the show!' Zaina bounded down the steps, red hair bounding majestically in their waves as she took the steps two at a time. She passed a familiar, grumpy face on her way down.

'Istari Vostor,' Kane said with genuine surprise. 'What a pleasure to see you here.'

Istari looked over his shoulder and then glared daggers at Kane before taking a seat beside her. 'That name must not be uttered amongst these people. I would prefer them to not know my real name…'

'My apologies, Tammaz Lirland,' she said with a wink, glad that she had remembered the fake name. 'I will work harder to not forget. Though, you do know that these people don't care who you are.'

'Of course they do,' he grumbled back. 'Probably sell me

to the highest bidder, given the chance.'

'People would only bid if they were guaranteed time away from you. No one would pay to have you near them, my dear. It's the sad truth.' Kane thought for a second that she spotted a curl at the corner of his lips but perhaps it was just wishful thinking.

'They would pay to have my head on a spike in any land in Takaara, believe me,' Istari insisted, jabbing a finger against Kane's shoulder before lifting his right leg across his left and looking down at the scene before him. 'Strange way of doing things. A vote. Too open for problems. Votes can be bought. A corrupt candidate with a bit of intelligence and less than a slither of honour can win by a landslide. Not the best way to go, in my opinion.'

Kane rolled her tongue over the back of her teeth, mulling over Istari's thoughts. She hadn't thought about the problems with such a method. In fact, she'd quite liked the idea. 'But it allows everyone a chance to be involved. It means the leader is someone chosen by the people who they will be leading. Surely that is a powerful thing?'

Istari blew his nose on a small piece of cloth and threw the filthy rag to his side. 'If it worked properly.' He shrugged. 'Those clawing at the robes of power are not often people who can be trusted in my humble opinion. With such an open system, the possibility for abuse is too great for it to work as it is planned to do.'

'Then what would you suggest is a better system to employ? Being born into power like kings and queens?'

'Not suggesting anything. Just making an observation. That's why I live on my own away from any cities or towns, Katerina Kane. Away from the problems of the world so that I may have my own peace. Why do you think I'm so pissed off at being dragged on this merry mission all the way out here?'

The hum of the crowd died down and Kane looked over to see that everyone had taken their places in the audience. A hush fell over the theatre as Ben stepped out into the centre of the stage, smiling broadly at his colleagues.

'Here we go,' muttered Istari, leaning back and frowning down at the stage, obviously not too pleased with the show.

'You be quiet,' Kane hushed him up with a smile, looking out the corner of her eye at the experienced warrior and then back at Ben who was calling for his audience's attention.

'My brothers and sisters,' Ben began, 'we gather here on this beautiful night for an important occasion. An historic occasion for The Red Sons, the greatest mercenary company in all of Takaaran history!' Cheers erupted at that as men and women clapped hands in the air and hollered at one another, proud to be a part of the infamous group. Ben smiled and allowed the chaos for a moment before calming them down with patting hands. 'That's right, the greatest company in the history of the world. I am proud to fight beside you. I am proud to drink beside you. I am proud to know that one day I will die beside you!' More cheers and wails. Istari rolled his eyes and mimed puking until Kane nudged him with her elbow.

'Don't be rude,' she whispered to him, though she needn't have bothered with the caution due to the high volume of yells inside the theatre. It died down once again and Ben continued.

'Aleister, Ariel, and Bathos started out as three friends dreaming big. They built what we have today. They tore down corrupt systems. They robbed the corrupt rich and defended the weak. They are the reason we are where we are today.' Ben paused, holding the audience in the palm of his hand. 'But every great company must welcome change. Not a change in values, no. But a chance to move forward. A chance to grow and improve. That time lies before us this night. We will listen to our candidates and hear how they plan to follow on from our great leader who is continuing our cause far away from here. They will inform us of their intentions before we decide if we are to lie in bed with them!' Whistles and laughs from the crowd now. Kane found herself sniggering and even Istari coughed to hide his own amusement. 'Listen to their words and make your decision. We are The Red Sons.'

Zaina stepped onto the stage with a large hat and held it out, upside down, towards Ben. He reached into the hat and pulled out a small piece of parchment. He stared at the name, twisting it in the light of the candles that lit the stage until he could see it clearly. 'Adnan Yil-Youssef!' he called to wild cheers and applause from the audience.

A young, dashing man leapt onto the stage, waving at the cheering audience. A golden feather stood elegantly out from a silver turban wrapped tightly around his head. The Sultan's son. That's what Zaina had told Kane. He certainly held himself like royalty. An off-shoulder crimson cape held with a silver clasp swept over the left side of his silver mail. His smile was whiter than the sands on the Bone Coast. Kane worried for a moment that the smile would blind someone in the audience, but the fear passed with a snigger that caught in the back of her throat.

'Yil-Youssef?' Istari muttered, stroking his chin and leaning forward to get a better look at the candidate. 'The estranged son of the Sultan... I'd wondered where he had got to. Rumour had him somewhere in the Mines of Golotha searching for diamonds. Didn't think he would be foolish enough to stay this close to home...'

If anything, Adnan Yil-Youssef certainly had Istari Vostor interested. And in Kane's eyes, that had to be a good thing.

'My brothers and sisters of the Sons,' Adnan said once the cheers had calmed down and all were listening. He paced across the stage, taking his time, drawing them in. 'We are gathered here tonight to begin the next phase of our great journey. A journey started by Aleister. By Ariel. By Bathos.' He paused to let the roars of appreciation erupt from the crowd. 'I may not have been here for long, but I have fought alongside each of you. I have stood side-by-side in battle and I have bled for you!' He thumped his chest with a bare hand, numerous rings shimmering on his fingers as he lapped up the attention.

'We have settled in the East, a land I know better than any in this company. I left the luxuries and ease of life as the son of the Sultan of Darakeche and I chose to join this company as I saw the potential of what we could become. I saw that we could start something that would change the landscape of this region forever. My father is not long for this world and my brother Arif is weaker than the old man. Accept me as your leader and I will guide this company through a prosperous era of hope and justice. We will free Darakeche from the tyranny of the Sultan and ensure that every man, woman, and child is able to live a free life under the red sun of the East.'

Kane balked at the deafening response of the audience. Men and women stood on their benches and roared whilst pumping their fists and slapping each other on the back. Throughout it all, Adnan just calmly nodded, grinning at each and every one of his allies.

'He speaks well,' she admitted, impressed so far.

Istari grunted, obviously not sharing her opinion. 'You would speak as well if you had been raised as the son of a Sultan. Two hours a day speech training and extra during special seasons. He has been raised to speak in front of a large and usually hostile audience. In front of these fools, he is barely breaking a sweat.'

Kane let the remark go without response, eager to listen to more of the skilled orator, no matter how he had managed to gain such a skill.

'We have spent a long time in the sands, looking after the towns on the edge of the East, ensuring they are not forgotten as the rest of the world turns a blind eye to the growing power of the Empire of Light and the harsh regime of my father. We have been defending this land and who better than us to lead this region of Takaara into a new age.' A considered hush had fallen over the listeners now. They all knew that they were listening to something special, something that could have an impact on their company for cycles to come. 'My father, for all his faults, has never bowed to the Empire. One of the few things I have respected him for. But he has also never entertained the thought of taking the fight to the Empire, of halting their rise with the sword and the bow. For too long, Darakeche has been pleased with being the shield, just like us. But in that time, the Empress grew cunning. She sent her preachers to the far lands and slid them through the gaps in that shield. The disease of the East has spread in spite of the Darakeche shield and that is why we, The Red Sons, must take a stand and turn the shield into the sword and stab at the Empire with all our might.'

No cheers now. Just intent listeners judging the powerful words and attempting to work out if this were something that would work in their favour.

'They realise that under his leadership, they would be tasked with doing something most nations have been too scared to do,' Istari muttered, leaning over to Kane but keeping his eyes on Adnan. 'Ask too much of your men and they will question their loyalty. One must hit them in the sweet spot. Not too much. Not too little. Nothing like the risk of death to turn a man off following a new leader. Need to gain their trust before throwing shit like this out…'

Adnan stopped his pacing and stood in the centre of the stage, at the very front, as close to his friends as he could be. He threw his arms out in front and turned them so that his palms faced the Sky Plane, offering himself to his people. 'I know the dangers that lie on this path. But I also know the strength and determination that lies within you all. We have been the travelling mercenaries for long enough. Now is the time to leave a lasting impression on Takaara. Now is the time for us to be more than the odd song sang by drunken bards in taverns. Now, we step up and change the world for the better. I ask a lot because I know that all of you are capable of delivering. Together, we can do anything. Whatever happens, we know who we are. The Red Sons.'

The charismatic man bowed low to the ringing of cheers and whistles from his adoring crowd before sweeping his cloak aside and marching from the stage and past Ben who squeezed his shoulder as they crossed paths.

'A great warrior, a proud man, and a dear friend. Could Adnan Yil-Youssef be the next leader of The Red Sons?' Ben laughed as the roars began once more; clearly the soldiers weren't tired yet. 'Now to our second candidate. A man who has the stamp of approval of our great founder himself. Experienced and charismatic, this man has fought almost since the very beginning of our company. Jaxsin Mortella!'

Jaxsin strode onto the stage with the confidence of a warrior facing a tied-up opponent in a fight to the death. His chest seemed to be at least two paces ahead of the rest of his body as he pushed it out to its peak whilst staring out at adoring fans. The lithe man brought a grin to Kane's face. He was unusual for a warrior.

On his head sat a large black tricorn lined with gold. A lavishly large green feather fled from the rim of the hat and trailed the rest as he danced towards the front of the stage. A red cloak drifted elegantly down past his knees and a golden sash ran from his right shoulder all the way down past his left hip. Long, black, heeled boots clipped on the stage as their golden buckles attracted the light of the lanterns. He had a lithe figure, different to many of the muscular, burly warriors Kane spotted in the crowd. A magnificent moustache wriggled above his lip and ran to the sides of his mouth and down, drifting below his chin. Such a wonderful piece of facial hair reminded her of General Grey. Her smile faded as she remembered the last time she had seen Grey. The moment was too closely linked with the death of his lover and her friend, Lord Tamir, for her to feel anything but pain. She struggled to bat away the gaping void of sadness threatening to grip her chest, choosing to take five quick breaths to steady herself.

'Are you well?'

Kane was shocked to see a crease of worry on Istari's head as he gazed at her furiously tapping foot. She stopped the tapping and bit the inside of her cheek, praying for the sudden wave of loss to pass, as it always did.

'I'm fine,' was all she could say to him. Istari fell silent but he was not appeased by the answer, continuing to watch her out of the corner of his eye. 'Really, I am,' she insisted to no avail, considering the groan from her companion. She was thankful to hear Jaxsin Mortella speak, a distraction from the uncomfortable moment.

'Darlings,' Jax licked his lips and peered out at the crowd, blowing a kiss to a few who had chuckled at the start, 'you all know *me*. Jaxsin Mortella. Jax. Or Sin. Depends what time of day or night you catch me…' He winked to raucous laughter, obviously an in-joke for the company. 'I have danced the sweet dance of this company for many a cycle. I remember the shitty days of no food for a week and taking jobs that meagre peasants

would turn down. The early days are steeped in nostalgia and a
rosy shimmer but I was there and the stench of that first cycle will
never leave these perfectly plucked nostrils, believe me.' More
laughter. 'We took on fights most would flee from screaming. We
had to. What other choices did we have? We needed coin. We
needed to make a name for ourselves. In the beginning, people
would frown in confusion or laugh in jest when the name of The
Red Sons was mentioned. It has been a hard path to stand here
before you, but I have taken every bloody step along the way and
I have taken it with pride!'

The loudest cheer yet. Kane turned to Istari but the man
just sat there unblinking, eyes focused on second candidate.

Jax whipped off his hat and flicked his long, black hair
back, running a hand through it before facing his calmed audience
again. He brushed some of the hair from his shoulder and sniffed,
calmer than anyone else in the whole open theatre, it seemed.
'You see, I remember the hard times. I remember the blood. The
hunger. The thirst. Aleister. Ariel. Bathos. Good people. Great,
even. They had a dream and they fought so that we may stand
here today and make this decision. But they all moved on. The
Red Sons grew beyond their early expectations and now we are
too great for them to reign. Instead, they cross Takaara, leaving us
to fend for ourselves.' A few dark mutterings echoed through the
audience at the last comment; this wasn't what they had expected.
But Kane spotted a few short nods in agreement. 'I don't blame
them. They were young and idealistic. Three friends banding
together to do some good in the world. And they have. Now, it is
time for us to continue the legacy. To build on the foundations
they put in place. In that regard, I agree with my dear friend,
Adnan Yil-Youssef. But, a slight word of caution…'

Jax held up one long, thin finger – a huge sapphire hung
from it, sparkling in the light.

'Another good speaker,' Istari whispered, eyes still fixed
on Jax. 'Though less trained. Raw.'

'Adnan wants us to stand up against the Empire of
Light,' Jax scoffed, throwing his arms out wide and imploring to
his audience to see the folly in those words. 'An *Empire*. There are
whole nations, whole *regions* of Takaara who shake in fear at

taking on the behemoth from the East. The United Cities of Archania have now fallen to the plague of the Empire. But dear Adnan wants us to battle daddy and then stand up to this unfathomable beast.' Jax flashed his own winning smile and shook his head, tutting and waving his finger left to right and back again. 'This is madness. A beautiful, glorious madness. But madness, nonetheless. By all means, we can take Darakeche. The people living in the towns on the outskirts of the land love us as their own anyway, they know what we have done for them. The capital of Mughabir will fall with the right push. But to then turn to the Empire? That would lead us down one path. Destruction.' Jax glared at them all, letting them know that he was in no mood to jest. 'Small steps. Easy steps. That is the way for The Red Sons to make progress. Race too fast and we will trip and fall. No remorse. No regrets. Remember the words, my darlings. Remember who we are…'

The crowd clapped their approval, more subdued now that they had two sides of the argument to ponder. Urgent mutterings broke out as small debates erupted within the audience. Jax gave a flamboyant bow, nose almost hitting the floor and danced from the stage.

'And what about him?' Kane asked, eager to hear Istari's thoughts.

'Interesting.' One word. That was all.

Ben calmed the crowd one final time, blowing out his cheeks and shaking his head. 'Such an interesting contest so far. No matter what happens, we are blessed to have such people in our company, that is for sure.' Polite applause. 'Now we have one final candidate, a newcomer to our cause. This young man only recently joined us. In fact, I've barely said two words to the guy!' Tired laughter. They had seen all they wanted to see. They had no time for this newcomer, that was plain to see. 'He wishes to only go by the name, *The Prince*.' Ben struggled to keep the mocking tone from his voice but was unsuccessful. An increase in laughter now and Ben didn't even bother to stem it. 'Welcome The Prince, my friends.'

A hooded figure walked in from the shadows and onto the stage as Ben left, still laughing and shaking his head. The figure moved carefully, black boots slapping on the stage. In fact, the final candidate was dressed all in black, as though in mourning. Black studded leather armour covered his torso and a black cape ran down to the ground, with the hood still up and shielding his face from the fading light. Silver clasps on the front of the cloak were the only bits of colour Kane could see. A touch dramatic, she felt.

The newcomer stopped in the centre of the stage. The wind stopped its gentle wave, unnerving the mercenaries in attendance. A few called out, annoyed and frustrated and wanting this display over and done with.

'Say your piece and fuck off!'

'Come on you bastard! Speak!'

'Wasted our Gods' damned time!'

'Prick!'

Kane rolled her eyes and leant back, unamused by the strange display. She was surprised to see Istari leaning closer, his chest rising and falling slowly as he ignored all of the shouting below him.

The Prince raised a black gloved hand, instilling an uneasy silence on the audience.

They waited.

And waited.

And then he spoke in a stern, but calm, even voice. A voice Kane felt that she remembered from a long-forgotten dream.

'The Red Sons. The famous mercenary group known around Takaara for freeing the lost and damned and supporting those who cannot support themselves,' The Prince said. 'The birth of your company is well-known. The seeds of this company grew in the shittiest parts of the United Cities of Archania, ignoring the darkness and finding the light in an area of the worlds where justice and truth had been seemingly discarded. Such beauty born in such an ugly place. But Archania wasn't always that way. A sickness lies on the land and you may be the only ones who can cure it.'

Kane's lips parted as the pieces fell into place. 'That son of a bitch…' she said to herself, feeling the edges of her lips widen.

'I am not standing here to take over your company. I am asking you to follow me this one time. For a good cause. For the people who feel that they are lost and damned. For the people who feel that they are forgotten. I am asking you to return home to Archania. Free your brothers and sisters and settle in the North if you want a true home, a chance to end the constant travelling and difficulties of the road. I am asking you to purge Archania of the plague of The Empire of Light. You will have support, of that, I can promise you.'

'And how can you promise that?' someone called from the benches, to the agreement of others.

The Prince paused, waiting for the shouting to die down. Then he threw down his hood, his young, pale face clear for all to see. Kane gasped and threw a hand over her open mouth, her suspicions confirmed.

'Because I am no weary traveller. I am Prince Drayke of the United Cities of Archania.' The crowd burst into shocked murmurs as Kane felt tears burning at the back of her eyes. Drayke grinned. 'And I want to take back my home. *Our* home.'

'That's bound to ruffle some feathers…' Istari chuckled, pleased with the turn of events.

'Indeed,' Kane said, heart still racing. She felt as though at any moment it would burst from her chest, clear for all to see. 'He is my son.'

JUSTICE

The madness of a moot in the Borderlands paled in comparison to the general day-to-day activities in the Lower City of Archania. Arden remembered shrinking back into the shadows in the Borderlands, trying to escape the bustle of warriors crammed in between the buildings as they stomped through the snow between taverns and halls, shouting and barking at each other and always teetering on the edge of a brawl. He had felt out of place and found it difficult to find space for himself, to find somewhere to breathe and be away from all the vibrancy and life in what was usually a calm and open land.

Yet here, in the Lower City, Arden found himself longing for those moments back home. The busiest of days in the Borderlands were nothing in comparison to the crush of the Lower City. Wave upon wave of people rushed by, eager to get to Gods knew where and they weren't stopping for anything. He even caught sight of an elderly woman thump a young man on the back of his head with a large bag as he crossed in front of her path. The man barely flinched, marching along the cobbled road with a frown and a rub of his head before shaking it off and ignoring his attacker. In the Borderlands, that old woman would have paid for her reaction with a knife in the back.

Or the front, in all honesty.

The city seemed to take on a life of its own. It had a variety of smells: some Arden was unfortunately familiar with and others which woke in him a longing for something new. New smells, new sounds, new tastes in the air, even. Everything just seemed so fresh and alive. He was caught between wanting to experience everything at once and wanting to rush back to the wilderness and live alone as a hermit, as Socket had often done in the past. The reminder of the old man stung. He told himself that he would need to make a stone of his heart if he was to succeed with his mission and so he pushed the thought to the back of his mind and pressed on through the throng of moving people.

The sheer number of people overwhelmed him. Filthy, dirty people covered in the demands of the day as they shuffled miserably along their way, grumbling and grunting if bothered by anyone else who dared to interrupt their grim journey. These people seemed even less jovial than the warriors in the Borderlands. Arden had never thought such a thing possible. The crush of the people intensified for a moment as the road narrowed. He felt suffocated, needing a moment to gather himself but he hadn't had the time since he had slipped into the city through the Western Gate. Osiron had explained what must be done. The messenger would have spoken to the leaders of the United Cities by now. It was up to Arden to place his boot on their neck and ensure that they knew that they meant business. This wasn't some empty threat. It was a promise of what was to come. A new future for all Takaara.

Arden pressed forwards towards the north of the city, walking over the cobbled streets and breathing a sigh of relief as the crowds gradually dispersed into the alleys and markets either side of the main road. He was intrigued to see that some of the buildings bore marks of a recent fire. There were large gaps dotted randomly on his path where foundations of buildings had been left but the rest of the building had been torn down. Osiron had told him that a failed rebellion had recently taken place in the city. A sign of the unrest of Takaara and further proof that what they needed to do was right and just.

He kept his hood up as he reached the gate. Construction was under way as several white-cloaked soldiers guarded two new towers and a black, iron gate separating the lower and upper parts of Archania. They looked at Arden with suspicion, peering under their shining helms and furrowed brows. Arden grinned confidently back at them. The old Arden would have been intimidated. The new one had been through death and Chaos to stand here. Mere soldiers with spears and armour were nothing in comparison.

'What's your business?' a soldier asked, raising an eyebrow as Arden paused by the gate.

'Cypher Zellin' Arden answered, remembering the name he had been told to ask for.

'Destination?' the soldier asked, sounding bored more than curious.

'The Halls of Justice.'

The soldier's eyebrow raised a step further at that and his eyes searched Arden up and down, all the way along his black cloak trimmed with midnight purple silk. Arden had no memory of ever receiving the cloak, but he knew it was the most comfortable thing he had ever slipped into. He opened it with his right hand, displaying the lack of weapons for the soldier.

'No need for any of that, Mister Barrow,' a voice called from the other side of the gate. 'This one is with me…'

'Just doing my job, Zellin. Nothing wrong with that,' the guard grunted, giving Arden one last look before sliding to the side as other guards came to pull the bolts away and open the gate.

'Indeed. Such a remarkable work ethic is to be treasured and welcomed in today's fickle climate.'

Arden passed through the gate and raised his own eyebrows in mild surprise. Though only a small gate separated the two parts of the city, it was like walking into another world. Gone were the uneven, cobbled streets littered with rubbish, piss, shit, and filth-ridden civilians. In their place were tall, stone buildings that shone even in the low light of the cloudy day. The streets were even and lined with colourful plants and flowers. The people walked past in twos and threes, enjoying the space afforded to them as they skipped on their way wearing clothes with an overabundance of lace and frilly material in various places. Their clothes were a smattering of bright colours to match the flowers around them and all the people Arden looked at wore smiles showcasing teeth brighter than the Borderland snows.

All except one.

'Arden Leifhand, I presume.' A low, gravelly voice full of mischief. 'It's a pleasure to meet you. Cypher. Cypher Zellin. Seems I'll be your escort through the city today. Help you to see the delights of the Upper City of Archania.'

Cypher was bald, middle-aged and wore the shadow of a beard around his jawline. His dark eyes seemed to twinkle with malevolence that forced Arden to hesitate before making his response. He nodded at first, allowing himself time to clear his throat and find his words.

'You have passed on your message?' Straight to business. It was the first thing that popped into Arden's mind.

'That's right. Come on. I'll tell you all about it on the way…'

The roads were wide enough for many carts to amble past, led by strong, well-fed horses trotting through the Upper City as well-dressed drivers in comically large hats held the reigns and kept their backs straight whilst Arden presumed men and women relaxed in the strange looking carriages. The gold and silver on display woven around in intricate patterns on the edge of the carriages caused Arden to wince uncomfortably. Such extravagance would cost as much as it would take to feed one of the Borderland villages for a moon or two with a coin to spare.

'King Asher took the throne following the recent death of his father.' Cypher's words jolted Arden from his musing, and he turned his head to face the man, listening carefully to the information. Information about his brother and father. His family. 'Prince Drayke shuffled off after the last big quake and hasn't been seen since. Being kept hush hush, of course. The royals don't want the commoners finding out about Drayke's disappearance. He was well-liked by most. Spent time with the peasants some said. Never got on with his brother so thought he'd leg it after daddy passed on. Wise decision if you ask me.'

'What do they think of King Asher?' Arden asked, eager to find out more about his family and its current situation. 'Is he well-liked?'

'He is… feared,' Cypher replied cautiously, drawing out the word. 'A new king, especially a young one, causes a people to become wary. They need to see how he treats them before they offer him their love, respect, or disdain… The city has been in turmoil of late and the city of Norland is threatening to break free from the United Cities. It would be an embarrassing blow.'

'Norland,' Arden rolled the word in his mouth as he remembered the name of the city Osiron had spoken of. 'They have chosen to join with us. That is where you were found.'

Cypher nodded. 'They are waiting for the signal.'

'Excellent. Now, tell me, how did your meeting go?'

'Asher may be the king but the real power is a preacher. A nasty piece of work who does everything in the name of the Empire of Light. Came over when this kingdom was at its weakest and dug his claws in. A clever man. A powerful man. A dangerous man. He is the true power here and don't let anyone tell you otherwise.' Arden noticed Cypher scowl at a couple of men striding past, each turning away as they saw who was walking past them.

'Friends of yours?'

'Don't have many of those… where was I?' Cypher said, spitting on the floor and twisting his neck to give one last hateful glance at the men now in the distance. 'That's it. Mason D'Argio. The preacher. He guides the king and basically tells the lad what to do. Anyone who dares to go up against him ends up charred and smoking. They love a good burning in this city.'

'You have seen this?'

Cypher shrugged casually and nodded. 'Course. I was his chief torturer. Made the bastards squeal myself.' Arden held back the numerous questions racing through his head and motioned for Cypher to continue. 'Anyway. I met Mason the other day and passed on the message. The Empire is powerful and less likely to sway thanks to my words than the statue of old King Borris is to sway in a gentle wind. He listened but seemed distracted. Something has happened recently and he either didn't give a shit what I was saying or he didn't believe a word I said.'

'Have you ever fallen out with him before or given him reason to not believe you?'

'Threatened to kill him once or twice before,' Cypher laughed, as though it was something everyone would say to someone that they worked closely with. 'And he's said the same. We'd both like to see the other one charred and smoking if we had our own way. I have never met a bigger prick in all of this kingdom and, believe me, I've seen some things…' Cypher winked and then flashed his eyes before pulling away from Arden and whistling as they carried on their walk through the city.

The strange man reminded Arden of Sly. Both were confident in themselves. Comfortable to say things as they are and always standing in a shadow of violence, ready to erupt. Arden wondered what dark things this man had done over the cycles but then kept himself from shuddering at the thought.

They reached a courtyard, spacious and beautiful. The splash of water from the various exquisite, stone fountains filled the air around Arden as he followed Cypher into the shadow of a colossal, towered building watching over the whole city. His jaw hung loosely as he stared around at the wonders of the Upper City and imagined what it would have been like to have grown up as a boy in this magnificent world.

'That's the palace – quite a sight,' Cypher said, noticing the look of awe on Arden's face. 'Come on, this way.' He led Arden to a row of buildings built into one another – three storeys high with slanted tiles on top to guide the rainwater that started to fall from the increasingly dark clouds. They passed rows of doors painted various bright colours until finally finding one to Cypher's liking. He pushed the door open and stepped in.

'Belongs to one of our friends in Norland. Wife died in the rebellion and he hasn't been back since. Might as well make use of the place. The maid's been in and tidied it all up at least. Gives you a comfortable place to stay until we head to the Halls of Justice. You'll be in for a treat there. Get to watch how justice is meted out in the great United Cities of Archania.'

Arden silently nodded, running a hand over an oak table beside him and frowning at the layer of dust that he wiped away.

'I'm sure you have stayed in worse places up in the Borderlands. Heard tales about the harsh winters up there. There's a bed and I'll send some food your way this evening. I'll be round bright and early tomorrow, justice wakes with the sun.'

'I'll be ready,' Arden muttered, glancing around at the odd statues and paintings that decorated the small room. 'Don't worry about food. I will be fine.'

Cypher gave him a nervous eye before heading back the way they came in. 'Get some rest,' he called back to Arden. 'You'll need it.'

Arden slammed the door shut and stared at the back of it for a moment, taking a deep breath and slowly releasing it from his chest. 'I sincerely doubt it.'

The Halls of Justice were as packed as they always were on such occasions. Only the Upper City elite had been invited for today's events – a new clampdown on allowing Lower City citizens into the region prevented any from gaining access to the trials. A move suggested by the new king who sat up on the balcony in the newly redecorated room. The last quake had destroyed one side of the building but a quick response from the king and his council meant that the place was now looking better than ever. Appearances were everything, after all, in the United Cities.

Asher looked his usual grumpy self as he gazed down at the empty stage. Beside him, Lord Balen was attempting to engage the young royal in conversation but the king showed no interest in the old man's words. Probably blathering on about the state of the treasury or some boring topic. On Balen's other side sat General Grey. The soldier looked as though he had aged another decade in the time Cypher had spent away from the city. The general had been getting on a bit but now his eyes were bloodshot and sat on top of deep bags threatening to pull his face down towards his lips. His hair was streaked liberally with more dashes of the colour of his namesake. He looked like a man defeated. Perhaps the king and Mason had not forgotten about the rebellion and Grey's dithering. The rest of the seats on the balcony were filled with dark-skinned men and women wearing blindingly white cloaks. Subjects of the Empire, no doubt.

They were all subjects of the Empire now, he realised. Just another nation sucked into the endless shadow of the East.

But not for long.

He peered out of the corner of his eye at the strange man beside him. Arden's eyes stared at the stage before them, waiting patiently. Not many things could unnerve Cypher but he had to admit, this young man gave him the shivers. His eyes would shift from a normal white with blue rings around black pupils to a disturbing blackness only speckled with small dashes of white. Just like a clear night sky. Just like, *those* eyes. The eyes Cypher had seen in Norland. The eyes that visited him whenever he closed his own.

The Eyes of Chaos.

'Always said, the Empire is welcome in this city. Doing great things in the East, that's certain. Keeping that dog Sultan on his leash, that's for sure!' Cypher turned his head to look out for the annoying voice shouting over the general hub of noise in the room. Sir Dominic swayed in his seat as he spoke to his usual group of hangers-on, his eyes peering over to those in white cloaks as he raised his voice further, hoping they would catch his words, no doubt. 'Most welcome, they are. In fact, I'm not sure why we haven't aligned ourselves with the Empire in the past. I used to speak with my dear friend, our recently departed King Mikkael – Gods guide him – I used to tell dear Mikky that there is wisdom in such an alliance. Of course, I was ahead of my time, as is so often the case. And dear Mikkael had a lot on his plate. It's good to see that his son Asher has seen the sense in the partnership.'

Cypher licked his lips and turned away, shaking his head in disgust. It did not surprise him though. Sir Dominic was the walking embodiment of all that was wrong with this world. Too many fools in high places. Fools with a voice that others would too readily listen to. The knight had been the loudest opponent to the Empire barely a moon before, threatening to lead a group of soldiers and take the East himself.

What a prick.

Still, the sycophants lapped up his words and nodded along, speaking words of agreement whenever he chose to pause – usually after slurring his words in his constant drunken state.

'I know that man…'

Cypher snapped his gaze on Arden at the mutterings, then following the man's eyes to the incoming party. Mason D'Argio led a team of men and women. T'Chai was the first in line after the preacher, followed closely by four guards carefully watching two skinny, filthy and beaten prisoners. An old man and a young woman. Cypher noticed the work. Bruises on the cheekbone, swollen lips. Bits of hair torn from skulls. Nasty, amateur work. He clicked his tongue in disgust and rolled his eyes, feeling his anger and frustration rise at the shoddy work. Then he remembered Arden's words and tried to focus on them.

'The preacher, Mason, is at the front. Silver hair and a look on his face like he'd trodden in shit and couldn't escape the smell.'

'I saw him in a dream…'

Cypher ignored the last comment, not knowing what to do with it. 'One after him is T'Chai, Mason's lap dog. Good fighter and tortures with talent. Another I would rather see as a corpse.'

'Ladies and gentlemen of Archania,' Mason bellowed, not needing to call for silence from the watching crowd. 'Let us begin our day of justice…'

Arden kept his eyes on the silver-haired preacher. He had seen the man during his time with Osiron. He felt a fury waiting to erupt within him as the images of what this man had done flashed through his mind. Cypher had said the man was unwilling to listen or care about their message. Arden promised to make him care. By any means necessary.

The clothes may be rich and fancy. The crowd respectfully quiet and restrained. But Arden knew what was happening today. It was what he had seen before. He had been there. He had experienced an execution. Because that's exactly what this was. An execution cloaked in the shroud of justice – just like it had been in the Borderlands when Ovar's head had landed with a thud on the floorboards and the bloodthirsty warriors had erupted with cheers, roaring away as Saul grinned like a boy happy to have pleased his parents. It sickened him. He wondered for a moment if this crowd would jump with delight as the warriors in the Borderlands had once *justice* had been served. He thought they would. He had seen enough of their kind to guess on their actions at such a disturbing act of violence.

'We gather here in the light of the One with righteousness and hope. Hope that we are heading into a better world. Better days for our people. We have joined with the benevolent Empire of Light and are now placing our feet on the smooth path we need to follow to improve this once great kingdom. Under the guidance of King Asher and the Holy Empress, the United Cities of Archania can enter a golden age of wisdom and progress.' The preacher paused, his fake smile dropping into a sad frown. 'But with such progress, there comes setbacks. The path forward is not straight and easy. There are obstacles we must navigate past and one such obstacle continues to rear its ugly head. The quake nearly tore this grand building apart but we have rebuilt and fixed the cracks – ensuring it is now better than ever. Just like we will with this kingdom. To do that, we join here today, looking for ways to rebuild. Ways to fix the cracks. Two citizens stand before you today, accused with disturbing the king's peace and attempting blood magic in Archania.'

Loud roars and screams of hatred emanated from the men and women around Arden, leaving him in no doubt of the similarities of these people and the ones he had left behind up North. They were all the same. All baying for blood and death.

'Burn 'em!'

'Smoke the fucking pigs!'

'Take their fucking heads!'

All the same.

Arden sighed, leaning back on his bench and watching the display, eyes still on the preacher as he appealed for calm.

'My brothers and sisters, I appreciate and welcome the care and strong feelings you have for the justice we fight for. And I promise, justice will be served. Master T'Chai, bring forth the first prisoner…'

The man wore only a filthy rag tied around his waist for modesty. His head had been roughly shaved, judging by the patches of dark hair still visible and the yellow bruising. His jaw hung slightly off centre, clear evidence of a sore beating, yet he still managed a scowl under dark, bushy eyebrows. A multitude of white scars littered his body along with more recent yellow and purple bruises to match his head. Arden certainly respected how the man managed to keep his composure and stand tall, back straight and proud as he glared out at the disgusted audience. There was no whining or begging for his life. He was pissed off with his treatment and he wanted everyone in that room to know it, whether he could speak or not.

'This… *man,* has been charged with the murder of innocent Archanians living to the north of our kingdom. Though offered an olive branch, the Borderlanders proceeded to burn a temple to the God of Light, killing all those trapped inside.' Arden felt a flicker of curiosity pass through him as he heard a quiver in the preacher's voice as he read out the crime. Not what he had expected from the apparently cold, stern man of God. 'The crime showed an unusual level of cruelty, burning men and women, both young and old. Innocent, all. Such brutality and hate have passed without remorse since imprisonment and questioning. Such a crime, in my own opinion, should be answered with only one punishment. Burning.'

The room stamped their feet and shouted in agreement with the preacher. Arden just sat still, watching the scene play out in front of him.

'Never heard this crowd go against the bastard,' Cypher said, leaning over to him. 'Bunch of sheep, go along with whatever they are told to.'

Arden peered up on the balcony and scrutinised his brother. The king wore a silver circlet holding back his flowing dark hair. A white fur cape mixed with gemstones on his silver silken shirt, giving the impression of an actor playing at being a king. Raven had always said that a king can always be seen through his actions, and not their outfit. Asher definitely looked the part in his finery, but he wasn't acting like a king should, in Arden's admittedly inexperienced opinion. Standing on his feet, the king of the United Cities of Archania screeched down at the stage, threatening to fall right over the balcony and onto the unsuspecting crowd below. The old man next to him frantically attempted to pull the king back by his lavish cape but he was fighting a losing battle, eventually admitting defeat and falling back onto his own bench and allowing Arden's brother to shake a fist and let spit fly from his mouth in amongst the continued roars of approval from the baying crowd. An interesting sight, at the very least. But not what Arden had hoped upon first meeting his older brother.

Arden's gaze pulled away from his furious brother as a guard dragged a chair behind Mason D'Argio. The preacher clicked his fingers and two others pulled the silent Borderlander onto the seat and tied his hands around the back of the chair.

The preacher's ally, T'Chai, had procured a long torch from somewhere, the flames lighting up his dark face, illuminating his brown eyes that had been painted around the edges. He handed the torch to Mason without a word and backed away, watching the poor man with a trained gaze, arms folding behind his back – a true soldier. He seemed almost bored with the whole thing.

Mason took the torch with a shaking hand. He muttered something to the man that seemed to enrage the woman being held by the two remaining guards. She thrashed and shook violently, trying her best to reach the preacher, eyes open in hatred and teeth bared as a promise of violence. The guards held her tightly, doing their best to keep her arms from slipping from their grasp. Arden wondered what had enraged her so, but then his attention turned to the torch. The chair had been lit, the flames licking at the wood and finding their way across the thin, filthy cloth of modesty and flickering across his scarred and bruised skin.

The smell. Such a putrid, unearthly smell. It clung to his nostrils, holding tight and refusing to let go. He turned his head in response and winced, eyes still watching the flames do their job. He'd looked away once before when tasked with attending an execution and it had haunted him ever since. He'd passed through his own death since then and become stronger for it. Looking away now would be cowardly. Whether this man deserved this kind of torture or not, Arden knew that he had to watch until the end. The dying deserved that at least. Even a stranger looking on was better than only enemies and fools. Even if he were only remembered in the nightmares of others, at least he would be remembered.

The angry calls and shouts faded. An uncomfortable silence settled over the room, broken only by the cracking of the flames as they swallowed the wooden chair and the man upon it. He took the pain well. As silent in death as he had been in his last moments of life. The pain must have been unbearable. Arden had heard tales of men and women who had hidden herbs under their tongues before such torture in an attempt to numb the pain they knew awaited them. Perhaps this man had been one of the lucky ones successful in such an action. His body was charred and black now, hair stripped away by the hungry flames and pale skin turned either an angry red or a dull black. Arden heard the doors at the back of the room open and then slam shut as a few weaker-stomached watchers in the crowd fled from the scene, clearly unable to hold down their breakfast amidst the sickening torture.

Even the king had settled back down onto his seat. Still leaning forward with a hungry gleam in his eye, he watched the whole thing, never turning away, even for a moment.

'He didn't do a fucking thing, you hear me!' Arden raised his eyebrows, listening to the fury of the woman as she screamed at the preacher over the crackle of the flames. 'He weren't the one who killed your precious little bitch in that temple…'

The warrior with painted eyes dashed forward, snapping the back of his hand across the woman's face and dropping her to the floor, much to the shock of the guards who let her slip. They recovered fast, grabbing her beneath the crease in her arms and pulling her to her feet. A red mark had already begun to form on her right cheekbone. Mason D'Argio glided towards her, stepping between her and her attacker.

'I would keep that forked tongue behind those swollen lips if I were you, my dear. There are worse ways to go than in the flames of the One. My patience is already frayed with your sickening act. Your friends in the North were lucky that they were killed in the fight with my guards. You are the last one breathing out of the criminals who desecrated such a sacred place – such beauty. I could make your death slow and painful. So painful that you would be begging for the flames before long.'

The woman laughed, blood staining her teeth. She leant back and flung her head forward, launching a thick ball of saliva through the air. It splattered against Mason's face and she let out another laugh that echoed around the chamber, mixing with the gasps of shock and disgust.

'Just watched a man burn to death and they laugh at a prisoner spitting at her husband's killer,' Cypher said, grinning as though he had never seen anything funnier in his life. 'This kingdom is more fucked than I gave it credit for.'

Mason wiped the bloody spit away with a handkerchief from his breast pocket. He chucked the used cloth onto the floor, distracting the woman's angry glare for the briefest of seconds. In that moment, Mason jabbed forward, seemingly holding the prisoner in an awkward embrace. Arden glanced at the preacher's elbow and saw it snap back and then thrust forward. Once. Twice. Three times. Four times. Five.

Five times.

The woman's eyes opened in horror, the bloody smile fading from her face. Mason stepped back and turned to the silent crowd, his light robes and ashen face splattered with the woman's blood. In his hand, a small dagger pointed out, soaked in the red stuff. The preacher had a manic gleam in his eye as the woman slumped forward, her head lolling to the side as her eyes closed. The guards guided her down to the floor, looking at each other nervously, unsure what else to do as she bled out on the floor next to the still smoking corpse of her fellow prisoner.

'We offered the Borderlands an easy life. A partnership. A united North for the first time in the history of Takaara.' Mason's voice was steady now. A cold fury keeping it on the straight and narrow. A smatter of hushed whispers broke out around Arden at the preacher's words, he turned his head cautiously, listening for what was being said and trying to gauge the mood.

'The Borderlands?'

'A partnership with those savages? Unthinkable!'

'He's lost his damned mind…'

'King Mikkael never would have…'

Mason ran a hand over his face before pinching the bridge of his nose with finger and thumb, increasing the amount of blood on his already messy face. 'A united North to stand with the Empire against any who dared to raise a hand against us. And what did they do? They spat in our faces. They burned our temple. They *killed my daughter*!' The whispers grew more urgent now, and louder.

'The bastards!'

'Never could trust those wild fuckers. Kill the lot of them I say!'

'What disrespect!'

'Did he say his daughter?'

'Didn't know that he had one…'

'They killed my daughter and spat in our faces. We tried to be the good neighbour. To look for a path away from the darkness of our past but they preferred to stay in the shadows,' Mason said, voice now shaking, a large blue vein throbbing clearly on his forehead. 'Well, I stand before you, my brothers and sisters and I say this: They will not be offered such an olive branch again. Not whilst I am a part of this great kingdom. Not whilst the great and merciful King Asher sits on the throne. Instead, I say we offer them the points of our swords, our spears and we offer them all the hatred we can muster. In the Light of the One, I vow that I will make each and every Borderlander standing in our way pay for what they have done. We shall wipe them from

Takaara so that not even the trees will whisper of their existence as the Northern wind blows through. I ask, are you with me?'

The whole room rose as one, shouting, cheering, barking madness. Arden sat unmoved next to a smiling Cypher. He glanced up at the balcony and shook his head as his brother beat his chest with a fist and clapped his hands vigorously.

'Seems like Archania is going to war…' Cypher muttered, sucking his teeth and nodding around at the still roaring men and women in the Halls of Justice.

'They are,' Arden agreed. 'They just don't know it yet…'

Aaron S. Jones

NOT OUR FIGHT

The town of Barnham sat close to one of the smaller rivers in the North. Looking down from his vantage point on the hill, Sly thought the town didn't look too different to some of the villages back in the Borderlands. Many of the wooden buildings were two-levels high with sloping rooves to guide the falling rain onto the muddy streets below. There was no wall separating the town from the wild, green lands around it. Good farming land sat close by in perfect rectangles ready to be ploughed in the autumn season. Tall hedges were in the middle of their cut and a patch of purple aster flowers grew on the east side of the town, giving the land a necessary dash of colour. A large, fenced square kept in the roaming sheep as they grazed. A sleepy town. No sign of any danger.

'Reckon we'll be met with smiles or swords?' Sly asked Kiras. He picked up his boot and dragged the bottom of it against the jagged rock next to him, slicing away the cow shit he had stepped in on the way up the hill.

'Can't remember the last time we were welcomed with smiles,' Kiras said, scratching a bruise on her cheek and scanning the horizon. 'I'd be happy with a thin frown and somewhere warm to sleep. This constant rain is beginning to get on my nerves.'

'Better than the heat,' Sly informed her. 'Had a river of sweat in my pits and other places beside at all times of day and night when we were in that cursed city. I'd take the cold and wet rain any day of the week over such hell.' Heading back south, Sly feared the ominous threat of the heat. Thankfully, such fears had been washed away by the steady rainfall. He welcomed it. It was familiar. He'd take the soggy boots and trudging through the sludge of mud and shit over the oppressive heat he had experienced in Archania. Men weren't built for such things.

'Sounds like you didn't have the best of times on your little trip...' Kiras laughed but there was no joy in the action. 'Almost like you missed it back home.'

'Didn't wanna fucking go in the first place,' Sly growled. 'Rather have stayed a fought the Barbarians or gone with the kid and the old man. Better than the little scrap we had down south and spending time in their shitty dungeons.'

Kiras cleared her throat and bit into her bottom lip, a clear sign that she was building up to say something important. Sly had been around her enough to know that. 'Speaking of the kid...'

Sly peered at her from under his wild eyebrows, watching the way she rubbed one of her boots against her leg. Nervous. 'What about it?'

'Socket don't seem in the mood to talk much about what happened. Headed to the Far North to see an old friend who could help the kid and then they meet Barbarians on the way and Arden is killed in battle. Socket makes it out and heads back. You believe all that?' The way she cocked her head to the side and frowned told him that she wasn't buying the story.

Sly shrugged. 'Folk die all the time. Remember Arlo? Shit, Raven and Bane died after some poxy argument down south and Baldor has been taken by the bastards. The kid wasn't ready so, yeah, I believe the old man. No idea how he survived it, but you've seen what he's like with the bow. Probably shot his way out and fled once the kid was done for. No point hanging around after that. He's no fool. Not gonna stand there and fight them all.'

Kiras sighed, defeated by the logic. 'You're right. I think I'm just in a foul mood with all that has happened. We've gone from fighting with Raven and fending off the Barbarians to fleeing our home and its invaders to help one of the few remaining living friends I have. Just feels shit.'

'Always feels shit. Life is shit,' Sly responded with no sympathy. 'You've always known that girlie.'

'Yeah,' she said, voice fading as she began her descent from their lookout position. 'Come on, let's tell the others about the town. A warm bed for the night will do us no harm.'

Sly trudged back down after her, grinning all the way. 'I hope you weren't classing me amongst your friends a moment ago…'

'Nah,' Kiras called back, still facing forward with her hood up to hide her head from the rain. 'You're still a cunt.'

***

They received a few curious stares but nothing worse than that. He'd expected worse, for sure. A few folk frowned their way but most were too busy rushing to escape the rain and making their way inside the buildings scattered around Barnham. Sly sniffed at the air and caught a wave of freshly caught fish. He sniffed again as his eyes followed the smell. A wide cart pulled past carrying a large net filled with the stuff. Freshly caught from the nearby river, no doubt. His stomach groaned and lurched. Some nice, fresh, cooked fish would settle his stomach down and put a smile on his face.

'Could do with a bite to eat.' It was Cray who said what Sly had been thinking.

'You've had enough already,' Sly joked, tapping a hand on the warrior's large stomach. 'I'll have your fill.' Cray just smiled slightly in response, used to Sly now after their time together. The bastard wasn't so bad.

'We'll head to an inn. Grab some food and sort beds out for the night. Then we can start asking questions before heading off towards the camp.' Socket knew what to do. The old man may only have the one eye, but he had seen it all before. That was probably why he seemed so bored all the time.

'We stay for one night,' Kiras commanded, voice stern and offering no room for discussion. 'Baldor needs us, and he needs us as soon as possible. We rest. We eat. We move on.'

The trio nodded in agreement, knowing how much the big guy meant to her.

'We know the mission, girlie,' Sly responded, staring her in the eyes so that she knew he was being serious. 'We ain't letting the big man rot down here. One night. We move on.'

Kiras agreed with a silent flick of her forehead towards the darkening heavens. The woman was struggling with her best friend being imprisoned so far from help. If anything happened to the big man, Sly knew that Kiras would tear a path of fire and fury through any who brought such pain upon her. She'd burn the entire North if it would help Baldor. Part of him longed to see such a thing. A bloody Kiras lighting up this shitty world would be something that Sly could get on board with. But Baldor had always had his back in a fight. And Sly wasn't gonna forget that in a heartbeat.

The inn had seen better days. At least that's what Sly presumed as they stepped into the building. Three buckets stood in their path to the counter where a broad-shouldered woman sat in her chair, snoring softly. Rainwater leaked down from the ceiling and hit the buckets with a small splash. Sly peered up past the oak beams and chuckled to himself as he gazed through a large hole, straight into one of the rooms.

'Greetings!' Kiras bellowed, slamming her palm onto the counter to wake up the innkeeper. Even Cray smiled, though only slightly, as the woman jolted up from her slumber and stood to attention, eyes wildly glaring in all directions to identify the disturbance. They landed on Kiras and the rest of them as she sobered up, finally coming to her senses. Must be a slow day. She wiped the drool from her chin and the corner of her mouth and offered them a warm smile, finally ready to greet them.

'Must've dozed off!' the woman chuckled, smacking her lips together and frowning for a moment. 'The rain always puts me to sleep. What can I do for ya?'

'Two rooms. One for me. One for the three fellas here.

225

Don't need to be nothing fancy. Just a bed will do,' Kiras stated. 'How much?'

The innkeeper scrunched her face up, humming to herself and taping her fingers on the counter as she worked out the cost and probably how much she was going to try to get out of the obvious outsiders. 'Five pieces of copper,' she eventually decided on. 'I'll throw in a hot meal for six.'

'Perfect.' Kiras responded by grabbing the necessary coins from a small bag and tying it back up and attaching it back on her belt. 'Know anywhere we can grab a decent drink?'

'Only one place around here,' the innkeeper said, pointed a stubby finger to the east. 'The Ram's Head. About two hundred paces down and turn left at the crossroads. Easy enough to find. Decent ales but steer clear of the wine. Tastes like goat piss. I'll get your rooms ready for when you return.'

They nodded their thanks and turned away, all eager to grab a drink and take the weight off their feet for the first time that day. It was a long journey from the Borderlands and they had further to go. Breaking Baldor out of whatever hole he was in wasn't going to be easy and they would need to be ready for anything.

'All seems a bit too easy so far,' Sly said as they left the inn and found themselves once again out in a downpour. 'Don't get me wrong; I'm not asking for difficulties but my guts are telling me something is wrong. This kingdom is in a mess but we're getting help as easy as anything.'

'What do you expect us to do?' Socket asked.

'Stay on your guard. There'll be blood by the end of the night, mark my words.'

The ale was good. Better than piss-like wine anyway. Not like the drink devoured in the Borderlands but good enough for now. Sly cracked the muscles in his back and stared out from the corner of the room as the others sat in silence and enjoyed their drinks, just happy to have a chance to pause for a moment. Sly never paused. He was on the edge, like an arrow waiting on a string, pulled back, eyes fixed on its flight path.

Smoke clouded the room as men and women puffed away on pipes and argued with one another; slamming fists on the wooden tables and throwing cards down in fits of frustration after losing an important hand. Felt as Northern as it could in here. Only difference Sly could see was that the tavern had winding, wooden stairs that led to more seating upstairs and the staff working in the tavern were all dressed in clothes Sly would expect royalty to be wearing. Shining golden buttons glimmered in the light of the room's many lanterns. Black waistcoats covered pristine white shirts and all the staff rushed around with a small pad of paper on which they wrote down orders as they fled from one table to another.

'I'm impressed,' Kiras said, sticking out her bottom lip and nodding as she glanced around the room. 'Not bad for a Southern tavern. I expected worse. Almost feels like home.'

'One major difference,' Sly said, searching the Southerners and then shaking his head. 'Aside from the quality of drink.'

'And what's that?' Socket asked, sipping his own and releasing a slow breath.

'Weapons,' Sly answered calmly. The other three turned to look out for confirmation of Sly's words. 'None of them are carrying weapons. Do that back home and you're a damned fool. Here, I haven't seen one, apart from when we passed the butcher's shop...'

'You're right,' Kiras agreed. 'Probably don't get many people like you out here. Fishermen and farmers. No need for weapons. What they gonna disagree about?'

'Always somethin' to disagree about; you know that. Even if it's about the state of the fish or someone's fucking sheep going missing. Always something to get the blood boiling before it begins to flow. In our nature.' Sly sniffed and gave his best smug smile, loving his feeling of superior intellect.

'Not gonna argue with you there. Seen enough shit in my time to agree with you...' Socket said, waving a waiter over and pointing at his now empty jug. 'Four more,' he croaked, waving at the rest of them. No need to ask. They'd be in here for a while.

Laughter pierced the general buzz of conversation in the room as the drinks kept flowing. The mood in the tavern lacked the tension that Sly usually found himself in. These people seemed to get on with each other; to enjoy being together, laughing, joking, playing cards, and generally just sharing conversations. Strange. No signs of bloodshed at all. Not even a raised voice or a shaking fist of threat. It was all so… boring.

He wanted the excuse for a fist in the face. A broken chair over the back. Even a push in anger would be something. This place was soft. Not for the first time, he found himself marvelling at how such a nation could have halted the advance of the Borderlands and drove them back home.

'How did we ever lose to these fools?' he wondered out loud.

'You were young; don't remember what it was like,' Socket answered. He nodded his thanks to the returning waiter with their drinks and handed them out to each of them in turn. 'They were well-drilled. Better armour, better weapons. And more men to fight for them than we have snowflakes in the Borderlands. We won our fair share of battles but every time we killed one of 'em, another three would pop up to replace 'em. Soft they may be, but such numbers could suffocate even the most intelligent and hardened of warriors. The truce came at the right time. Any longer and the Borderlands would have been devastated. The Barbarians would have just been able to walk right in and put their feet under the table.'

'And after all of the fighting and the blood, it happened anyway,' Sly spat, hating the thought. 'Should have went further north and wiped those fuckers out before this happened. Instead, we went south and paid the price. Hindsight is a bitch.'

Cray grunting. Sly thought it was to agree with him but he wasn't certain. The stocky warrior wasn't one for giving too much away.

From his position, Sly's eyes found a newcomer to the tavern. A tall woman. Blood-red cloak that fell to the floor and tight, black trousers. She wore a black shirt that matched the wavy hair falling to her chest and she scanned the room with dark green eyes, looking for someone, or something. Those eyes fell on Sly and his allies and they widened. Seemed that she had found what she was looking for.

'On your guard,' Sly growled as the woman marched over to them and placed her long, slender fingers onto the back of the lone, empty chair around their table. If she was intimidated by four warriors staring at her in silence, then she sure wasn't showing it.

'Is this seat taken?' she asked, giving each of them a hopeful look. Sly flashed his infamous grin but it had no effect on her at all. Interesting.

'You blind?' he responded, waiting for her reaction. She twisted the chair and sat down, not waiting for further words.

'I was informed by a friend of mine at the inn that four armed warriors from the Borderlands had arrived in our sleepy, little town. We're not too far from your home but it's a rare sight even so.'

'What's your point?' Kiras asked, swishing the ale around her mouth and swallowing hard. She leant in towards the woman and kept her gaze, unblinking and daring the woman to blink first. She held her own for long enough; eventually a smile broke out and she blinked.

'Barnham is a town in the middle of nowhere. Most of the folk living here moved here because we wanted to be away from prying eyes and dumb laws. We're a part of the United Cities but we don't intend to be suffocated by such an association. We live out here and farm the land. We drink. We smoke. We talk. We care for each other,' the woman said, hitting a straightened hand out on the table to enforce her words. Still hadn't got to the point, though.

'And what the hells does this have to do with us?' Sly asked, rubbing his scratchy beard.

'We're a sleepy town. Not much happens. Then, the quake hit. The world shook and something odd happened.'

'You're all mages. Magic users.' Sly turned to Socket as

the old man just sat there, calm as you like as he said the words, sipping his ale as though he hadn't said a thing. The woman raised her eyebrows, clearly shocked at the response. Her mouth moved but it was Socket who made a sound first. 'Can smell the stuff. Reeks of it in here. You live out here because such activities are frowned upon in the capital. I hear burnings are all the rage.'

The woman's face tightened at the last phrase. 'Burnings,' she spat and made a strange sign across her heart with one hand. 'We moved away so that we could live our lives in peace, away from their watchful eyes and iron fist. Archania sits in the Empire now. They sent white-cloaked soldiers here half a moon ago. Took three innocent folk and claimed that they had been working against the Empire as mages and must be punished.'

'What's that got to do with us?' Kiras asked.

'You are fighters. We are not. Without magic, we're as useful as cow shit. Might as well send the sheep into battle. Those soldiers are returning in two days. We want you to kill them.'

'And why would we do that?' Sly wondered, taking his time with his drink. 'Got nothing to do with us.'

'Kill them and we will help you with whatever you need. Borderlanders don't idly wander this far from their homeland. Tell us what you want and we can sort something out.'

Sly shared a pointed look with Kiras and then Socket and Cray. They could use support in getting Baldor from the camp. What little they knew about his predicament wasn't enough right now.

'Killing them won't solve anything,' Socket said, groaning as he placed his elbows on the table and looked at the woman. 'There's always more. They'll just send others in the wake of their deaths.'

'We know.' The woman paused, again looking at each of them before glancing over her shoulder. The room had fallen silent without Sly being aware. All eyes in the room looked in their direction. Clearly, this woman meant something to them. 'We want you to kill them. Once that is done, we are marching towards Archania. We have had word from our brothers and sisters in Norland. War is coming to the United Cities. We intend to take down the kingdom and drive the Empire from our land.'

'I was there when some idiots tried doing that before. Didn't work out as planned,' Sly warned her. 'And they had weapons.'

'We won't be alone,' the woman argued. 'There will be a whole army marching alongside us.'

'And what army is this?' Kiras laughed. 'The Borderlands have their own troubles and the kingdom has aligned with the East. What army is willing to stand side-by-side with a town of broken magi?'

'There's only one army I can think of,' Socket moaned into his cup, a pained expression on his old face. He looked more ancient than Sly had ever seen him, as though he had aged years in their short time in the tavern. 'The army of Chaos.'

Sly gave an incredulous laugh. 'You're joking right? Chaos? Even if I play along for the punch line, this is not our fight. We're here to save a friend and leave. This is *not* our fight.'

Socket sighed and gave Sly his best one-eyed glare. 'But it *will* be.'

LIQUID COURAGE

'I feel that enough time has passed for my next question so I'm going to go ahead and just get it out there.' Kane knew what was coming. Istari had been polite enough to leave her alone for the night and the following day. Now the sun had finished its watch for the day, Istari was in no mood to wait any longer to hear the answers to his questions. 'How in the five hells are you the mother to the second in line to the throne of the United Cities of Archania?' Istari paused and shook his head for a moment as though shaking away cobwebs in his mind. 'I'll rephrase that. Is Prince Drayke actually your son? And is the recently deceased King Mikkael his father?'

Smarter than he looked. Two questions that got straight to the heart of the matter. Two questions that proved Istari had put some thought into it. He didn't believe that Katerina Kane had slept with the king of the United Cities of Archania. But he did believe that Drayke was her son. That left only one option. There was a long answer. And a short answer. Kane struggled to decide which one would be more appropriate.

'It is… complicated.' That was the best she could muster, along with a regretful sigh. Judging by Istari's mocking laughter and disbelieving open mouth, he wasn't going to leave it at that.

'The blind warriors of Sago Island could see that! *Complicated*! Of course it is complicated! Now,' he pulled a chair towards her and patted the seat before sitting down on the purple rug in front, gazing up at her with eager eyes and a wide smile. 'Tell me everything.'

'Where do I begin?' Kane said, shoulders sagging in defeat as she sat on the offered seat. She rubbed her temples and closed her eyes, fighting away the impending headache.

'I find the beginning is often the best place.'

'I was married, a long time ago. I loved him and he was good to me. Then he was murdered.' She found herself rushing through the words, keeping her eyes on a small, black rock statue of an elephant just behind Istari, unwilling to look at him as the words poured out from her. It had been a long time since she had spoken to anyone about this. Braego had always been her sounding board. Since his death, she had no one she could tell. No one she could trust. Odd, that she was telling the story to this strange, detached man. 'My role meant that I was on the case. I was the one who was meant to be stopping murderers and criminals in the United Cities but I couldn't even stop the bastard killing my husband. In my grief, I turned to a warrior from the Borderlands. A strange man who found himself away from home and in need of support. We fell in love.' Hot tears rolled down her cheeks but she ignored them. Instead she cleared the lump in her throat with a couple of short coughs and a beat of her chest. 'Excuse me.'

'There is nothing to excuse. Please, take your time.'

Kane pushed a hand against her shaking leg, stopping the rapid tapping. She breathed in and blinked away the tears. 'I fell pregnant. In my role I had struck up a friendship with King Mikkael. He had shown faith in me when no one else had. I informed him of my… condition. He knew that all I had worked for would be dashed if word got out that I had fallen pregnant with a warrior from the Borderlands. I should have been grieving and not opening my legs for some warrior from a land we had only recently fought a war against. I would have been shunned by all in my Archania.

'We decided that it would be best if I went away and had the baby in secret. A beautiful baby boy. The queen had fallen pregnant at the same time, as luck would have it. Word reached me from Mikkael that there was a problem with the boy. At the time, I believed their second son was breathing his last breaths. To help them – and understanding that Braego and I would never be able to live as a happy family in Archania – I offered them my son. To raise in the palace and to show to the United Cities in the hope that this new baby would unite them and bring them together. Mikkael and the queen accepted the deal and they raised Drayke as their own. The plague killed the queen along with many others in the kingdom. Mikkael raised Asher and Drayke as brothers and no one else knew the truth.'

She sniffed and wiped away the tears, feeling a weight rise from her chest. It felt good to get it out. Even to someone she considered almost a stranger.

'I've heard some crazy stories over my lifetime. Been a part of a fair few myself,' Istari chuckled, uncrossing his legs and leaning back onto his palms. 'But that is worthy of a prize. Sleeping with the enemy and swapping your child into a royal bloodline almost as old as Takaara itself.'

'It's not just a tale,' Kane pleaded, her brow creasing in frustration. 'It's all true.'

'I believe you. Do not confuse my amazement for distrust,' Istari said, standing with a groan and stretching his arms behind his back. 'True or not, this tale deserves a reward. How about a drink?'

Kane blew her cheeks out and nodded in relief. 'I damn sure need a drink.'

'Great!' Istari clapped his hands and patted Kane on the shoulder, looking happier than he had since leaving his home. 'A drink or two to salute your story and then onto more important things.'

'More important things?' Kane repeated, confused.

'Yep. I'm taking you to meet your son. I do so enjoy family reunions.'

'This is a bad idea. This is a really bad idea.'

'This is a great idea,' Istari insisted. Of course, he had refrained from drinking more than one glass of wine, preferring to move onto water. "This damn place is too hot to sit here drinking wine. Need to stay fresh." That was what he had told her. She had ignored that advice, of course. Should have stopped by the third glass but it had helped her with the nerves and the tapping leg. Calmed her by the fifth glass. Sixth was maybe one too many. The way her stomach lurched and her head pounded told her that perhaps even the fourth may have been one too many. A lie down would have been the best option but she had to trust Istari whilst the world swam in front of her eyes.

'Braego had always promised to catch me when my legs began to wobble like this,' she spoke more to herself than anything as she tripped and lunged to the side, catching herself with a strong hand against the rocky wall.

'Well I'm not promising anything,' Istari warned her. You fall over and I will piss myself laughing until you get your own backside up off the floor. You chose to drink that much so you can deal with the consequences.'

'*You! You! You* were the one who suggested a drink!' Kane reminded him, incredulously waving her arms high and wide.

'*A* drink,' Istari said, raising a single finger. 'Not two damn bottles! You're speaking to your son who has no idea he is your son. A little tipple for courage, sure, but this much is madness…'

'So I *should* just go to sleep. This is a bad idea.'

'No. It is still a good idea. I will make sure you do not embarrass yourself too much. But it has been too long and you never know when you may get such a chance. Believe me. Life is fleeting and such chances do not come by too often. Tell him the truth and tell him you care. He may have difficulty with it at first because the truth is like a rose. Difficult and beautiful. The thorns may cut you, but the flower will fill your heart.'

'I'm still not sure,' Kane said, leaning over for a moment and taking deep breaths to prevent the vomit from rising from the pit of her stomach. Felt much worse, drinking this much in such heat. The cold wind of the North would always wake her up and drag her to her senses. Not so much in the warm Eastern heat.

'Of course you are not sure,' Istari reasoned. 'You are pissed. Let me do the thinking for you. Now, where is his tent? So many of the damned things. Need a sign or something...' he muttered to himself, weaving between the tents and peering into a couple in search of Drayke.

Kane stumbled towards the sound of raised voices; years of training kicking in through the fog of inebriation. She pressed a finger against her lips and tapped her ear three times, hoping Istari had some sort of idea of what she was getting at. He nodded solemnly in response, creeping over with cautious footsteps.

Kane pressed against the animal skin separating her from the frustrated voices, trying her best to get a clearer sound.

'I have been with this group for many cycles. My blood, sweat and fucking tears have been spent in the name of improving the lives of our brothers and sisters. Yet this *boy* wonders in and weeks later feels that he is in a position to be judged as a leader of The Red Sons? It's complete and utter madness, Ben. Surely you can see that?' Kane recognised the strained voice. Jax had been calm and collected on the stage but behind the tent's exterior, the experienced warrior appeared to be losing his cool.

'You have been with us a long time, Jax,' Ben's calming voice agreed. 'As such, you are aware of the values we based this group on. Values that you have helped to water from a seed and have been lucky enough to watch grow into a whole, beautiful wood. Everyone is given an opportunity, regardless of birth, nationality, status, or past. We judge each and every person on what they can bring to the Red Sons. Whether you have served for ten cycles or ten days, we need to make the right decision.'

'I know that,' Jax spat. As though knowing it and agreeing it were two things standing on opposite sides of a great mountain, never to meet. 'And I know that if this kid gets voted in then we are in for some shit. We don't even know if he really is a prince of the United Cities. Has anyone bothered to double check? Could be a spy sent in to look for our weaknesses; take us down from the inside.'

'I remember your doubts when we accepted Adnan into the fold,' Ben chuckled at the memory. 'You felt this company needed to distance itself from royalty.'

'Well, that's the other thing.' Jax's voice rose a level as he regained some of his bluster. A second wind at the reminder of a past injustice, no doubt. 'There are three candidates going for this position. A position of great value. To be the leader of The *fucking Red Sons!* Two of them are princes. The son of a sultan and the son of a king. Nations standing either side of us geographically. Then there's me. This group was meant to mean something. We were meant to spark hope in the common man. To show them that it didn't matter what the circumstances of your birth were; The Red Sons were proof that you could rise up and make a fucking difference. Be somebody in this corrupt fucking world. Let either one of them stand as leader and we will be pissing in the wind. The people of Takaara will turn their backs on us, realising that we're just a bunch of fucking sell-outs like everyone else.'

'Well, I certainly don't wanna end up covered in my own piss. Or anyone else's for that matter,' Ben said, still doing his best to lighten the mood in the tent. 'I hear your words, Jax, truly I do. But if birth is of no consequence to us, then we must allow Drayke and Adnan the same allowances as you. *That,* will prove that we are following our values. Go get some rest. The leader will be announced tomorrow, once all the votes are counted.'

Ben's tone left no room for a retort or even a final remark. Kane heard the stomp of boots followed by the swish of the tent's entrance flap being pushed aside in haste. Jax was done for the night, it seemed.

'Doesn't sound best pleased, that one…' Istari muttered to her as they finally moved away, continuing their search. 'Should keep an eye on him.'

'He's just annoyed that some new faces are stepping over him to stand at front of the line. Nothing unexpected,' Kane answered with a shrug, feeling the drama of the conversation washing away the wine-induced haze. 'Anyway, I can prove to them that Drayke is who he says he is. I'm from the United Cities.'

'If anything,' Istari began ominously, raising a single eyebrow in her direction, 'you are proof that he is no prince of the United Cities. You are his mother and his father was no king.'

Kane allowed that uncomfortable truth to slide without response, instead focusing on their original mission. She pressed forward in the low lantern light and peeked through any gaps she could find. Most occupants slept soundly whilst one left her a deep shade of red – stretching in the nude in the middle of the night seemed to be his choice of meditation before a good night's sleep.

Finally, she stumbled upon the correct tent.

'The last time you snuck out of the palace it was to see the sights of the Lower City,' Kane couldn't help but laugh at the complete surprise breaking out on the young man's features as he turned to face the intruder in his tent. 'This time, I feel that you may have travelled a bit further…'

'Katerina Kane…' Drayke mumbled to himself as though his eyes had landed on a ghost. His face turned whiter than a sheet and those sharp, intelligent eyes widened just like his father's used to when she had caught him unawares – something that didn't happen too often. 'What in the hells are you doing here?'

'Such a greeting isn't becoming of a prince of Archania,' Kane said with a bow. 'More of an outlaw on the run…'

Without another word, he rushed towards her and threw himself into her arms, so pleased was he to see a familiar face. She held him close and marvelled at the way he had seemed to grow so much in the short time since she had last seen him. His shoulders were broad, just like Braego's, capable of carrying heavy loads, no doubt. She pushed him away and realised that she now had to peer up to look into his glistening eyes. They filled slowly with tears as he flashed her a row of white teeth. Teeth that shone amid a dark, growing beard. So like his father. His true father.

'Sit, please!' Drayke said as he left her embrace, motioning to the piles of cushions sitting on a purple and gold rug in the centre of the tent. So different to what he had been used to growing up in the palace. Yet he seemed so comfortable here, as though it was something he was born for. Braego would have been proud to have seen him like this. A man unbroken by the harsh road. Drayke had made it all the way here from the United Cities and he had done it with just his wit and skill. All alone. The thought made her heart skip a beat. 'You must tell me why you are here. And how you found me.'

Kane glanced over her shoulder and found herself frowning as she realised that Istari was nowhere to be seen. Her lips curled in a knowing smile as she realised that this is what the bastard had planned all along. A solitary meeting of mother and son untainted by strange onlookers.

'Found you? My prince, I stumbled upon you on my way to the nation of Darakeche. I have journeyed from Causrea on a mission of great importance. The fact you are here is the greatest of coincidences and one which brings such joy to my heart!'

'Praise The Four!' Drayke bellowed as he reached out for a bottle of wine, threatening to pour it into a glass before Kane vehemently waved it away. She needed a clear head now. The confidence – or stupidity – brought on by alcohol was not needed here. 'They have guided us together at last. When did you arrive?'

'A few days ago. I must admit, I was very impressed with your speech. Your father would have been so proud.' Kane realised the slip of her tongue and quickly added, 'And your mother, of course.'

'Father always said that a leader must fight with words before raising a sword. A tree growing in a field of thought is greater than one born of blood. He had loads of odd sayings like that. I miss them greatly.' The young man's face dropped as he thought of his recently passed father. Or the man he knew as his father.

'He did,' Kane agreed, remembering the great friend that she had lost. 'Your brother has made quite the impact in your time away,' she said, keen to get the young prince's views on what he left behind. 'Joined the Empire of Light and attempted to unify the North. Busier than he's ever been by the sound of that.'

'I'm not sure I agree with that,' Drayke said with a smile full of mischief lighting up his face. 'He was always busy. Busy whoring, bullying and befouling the palace with his horrid actions and mood. I've no idea how our parents managed to create two such different sons.' Kane hesitated, her face dropping at Drayke's words. The intelligent prince spotted the misstep and narrowed his eyes, clearly thinking and attempting to resolve the thoughts in his head. 'Did I say something I shouldn't have?'

Kane shook her head. She sniffed and cleared her throat, her mouth suddenly dry as she felt the need for another drink. 'You have only ever spoken clear and true, my prince. It is I, who have spoken words of deceit. Words spoken as a shield to protect you. The Four work in strange ways and I must say, I have carried a burden for such a long time, our meeting here, against all odds feels a little bit like fate. Though I may lose a friendship that I have cherished greatly, I feel that you finally deserve to know the truth.' Kane felt her shoulders sag as Drayke's frown grew more pronounced. 'At the very least, I owe you that.'

'What are you saying, Kat?' Sweat began to pool around his forehead, whether it was the oppressive heat or nerves, Kane had no way of knowing.

'I've watched you grow into a fine young man,' Kane began, tearing her eyes from her son and focusing on a small, silver net that dangled from a line of string that ran across the tent. If she looked at him now, her resolve would fall apart like a weak dam broken by the relentless crush of the river. 'Braego trained you and did his best to instil in you values and beliefs that he held dear. The king was burdened with the grief of his wife's passing and so we took it upon ourselves to support you, when it was needed. We were both so proud of the young man you grew into. Even more so seeing you here now, standing on your own two feet and attempting to take leadership of the most infamous mercenary group the world has seen in an effort to take back your home.

'We swore at first to stay away, just in case people noticed. It was too tough a task for me. He didn't care, of course, you know what Braego was like. Did things on his terms and fuck the rest if they didn't like it,' she chuckled at the bittersweet memory. 'He really loved you. Every day he spent training with you was a blessing in his eyes. A gift from the Gods.'

'Kat,' Drayke's voice was low and wary, as if he knew what was coming and feared it more than anything else. She'd gone too far now; there was no turning back. 'What are you saying?' He peered at her as though she was a snake, slowly uncoiling herself in front of him.

'I think I better have that drink. You see,' Kane gulped and forced herself to meet his sad, confused eyes. 'You are my son.'

BEHIND BARS

A plan. That's what Aleister always needed. A good, strong, reliable plan that would solve the problem and get them on the right path once more. He'd always had a plan. Even the times when it felt to others as though he didn't. There was always a plan. Sometimes made on the fly with the wind blasting his face and heart thumping out of his chest but still – there was always a plan.

Now, his head hurt far too much for a damned plan. He just lay in the suffocating heat of the night and groaned softly to himself as the sweat dripped over his body and through his clothes. The sound of a slow, lazy river met his ears as he slapped at the tiny flies buzzing around his neck. He slapped one and scowled as he stared at the mess left on his hand. He brushed the remains against his trousers and sat up, closing his eyes to still the swaying world. There had been enough times in the past where he had been whacked on the head; he knew that he needed to take things slowly. Still, the lack of a plan itched at him worse than the annoying bugs attempting to devour his flesh and blood. Nasty, frustrating, little bastards. They just kept coming back for more.

He rubbed his eyes and winced as he pushed some of the sweat into them, inadvertently burning his eyes. They stung for a moment, blurring his vision. He wiped his hands on his shirt, finding one of the areas less affected by his body's natural cooling system and tried again. This time, his vision returned with more clarity.

The prison he found himself in was more of an animal cage. Rusted iron bars with a rectangular base and roof. There was nowhere specific to piss or shit and no sign of food or drink left by his captors. He looked out from behind the bars and took a deep breath. Even in his current predicament, the sight before him was a thing of beauty that couldn't go without a momentary pause of acknowledgement. There were prisons and cages in the world where Aleister would pray to The Four that he would never find himself in. Some places were so reviled and spoken of in such hushed, fearful tones by strong and usually brave warriors that Aleister would have preferred death.

This was not one of those places.

Strange, vivid and beautiful plants and flowers of all colours fought each other for the light creeping in through the canopy of tall tress watching overhead. Past the cluster of odd trees with their wide trunks, Aleister spotted the gentle meander of the river travelling past. Pushing himself onto his feet, he strode over to his bars and wrapped his fingers around them, pressing his head between two of them to get a better look at the opposite bank. It was here that he could see a row of simple, wooden houses standing on tall, wide wooden poles that sank into the muddy bank and held the house up in a way that reminded Aleister of the jesters who marched on stilts in some of the parades in Causrea and Archania. They would march and smile their way through the parade and every time Aleister saw them, he would marvel at the way they were able to maintain their balance. Each time he would secretly wish for one of them to fall. These houses weren't going to fall though. He guessed they were designed in preparation for a downpour; a flood that would raise the level of water in the river and threaten the homes. In the oppressive heat, he wondered if it would ever rain such an amount down here for those poles to be necessary.

Further down the river, he spotted a few men washing some sheets, the water up to their knees. One of them, clearly finished with the laundry, ambled out of the river and over to a makeshift washing line and flung the wet sheet over before stretching the corners so that it was splayed out to its extremities.

Aleister thought such things must dry quickly down here in the constant heat. Not like back home when you would spend most of the day praying that a sudden rain wouldn't destroy all the work of the rare heat from the sun.

A small wooden boat floated by the bank of the river, tied to a post sticking out near one of the strange houses. Not too far away from the boat, a grassy island sat alone in the middle of the river, diverting its water to either side before it continued its journey. Aleister's forehead creased with worry and confusion as his eyes locked on a beast that he had never seen before. Its body was at least the length of three men lying down. It had the toughened dark green that Aleister had seen illustrated in books fantasising about the existence of dragons and long, yellow and black teeth that interlocked along a long, powerful jaw. Black, cold eyes watched the men standing in the river barely forty paces from where it lay alone on the island. Aleister had a sudden pang in his chest and he crossed his fingers, hoping that the terrifying animal was unable to swim. A stupid thought. It had somehow made it on the island. It must have a way of getting off. The only way would be to swim. Unless it was capable of growing wings like the dragons it looked so similar to.

He thought for a moment of calling out to the men, of warning them about the danger that lurked nearby. Then he saw one of the men look up in the direction of the beast. The man just turned away and carried on with his washing. Obviously, that took priority over his own life. Madness.

'Such a majestic beast,' a voice said behind Aleister. He spun away from the bars and found himself looking at the woman who had ordered his capture. She wore a thin shirt cut off at the sleeves and trousers that ended just above her knees, showing as much of her shining, dark skin as was respectable. Silver rings curled around her neck almost up to her chin, keeping her frame tight and to attention. The same silver could be seen ringed in her nose and all the way up her right ear. Different to the styles Aleister had seen on his travels but no less beautiful. 'We have an understanding with the crocodiles.'

'What understanding is that?' Aleister asked, curious.

'We stay away from them; they don't eat us…' She

flashed a wicked smile, showing off her brilliant, white teeth.

'I will be going nowhere near it, that is for sure,' Aleister said, moving as close to the woman as he dared and kicking at the iron bars to emphasise his point.

'I agree with you,' she smirked back but Aleister was unsure if she was trying to be humorous and failing or just unpleasant. 'Do you know what it was like in the South when your kind first travelled here, claiming to have *discovered* us?' Aleister shook his head, knowing when a question had been posed for the speaker to elaborate on instead of allowing for a real response. 'They called us *savages*. Mocked our homes and our culture. Mocked our way of life and claimed that they had the better way of things in the land of the half-sun. They reached the river-villages on the outskirts of our land and believed they had found the centre of our civilization. They never got within a moon of stepping foot in the Kingdom of Zakaria and were even further from its heart; the city of Ad-Alum. They had seen enough and were tired already of their pink, peeling skin and dripping sweat ruining their fancy clothes.

'They attempted to steal men, women and children from our land to sell across the Gods' Bridge. Some succeeded. A small amount. Most died the most painful deaths we could imagine. We had welcomed them into the outskirts of our world and they repaid us with such an insult. Ever since then, we have never trusted your kind. Pink men with small brains and smaller ideas. Tell me, why should I ever allow you and your friends to leave the cages we built for dangerous animals?'

Aleister rolled his tongue around the front of his teeth, swallowing hard as he tasted the stale, unclean flavour of his mouth. He needed a good wash; was that a good enough reason? Two minutes in the river would be an improvement. Just as long as he stayed away from that animal from hell…

'Honestly,' he began, pursing his lips and putting his hand to his chest, 'I understand why you have placed me in this cage. I look nothing like your people. I look exactly like the pricks who treated you with disrespect. You've never met me before and so you have nothing to go off except those who have come before me and that is no good thing.' His captor nodded at that, her bottom lip sticking out as she listened. 'But you trusted Abdulaziz. He was one of the rare outsiders allowed into your land and he trusted me. I'm not here to steal, to hurt, to conquer. I'm here to act as a bridge between two people who I feel need to stand together as a darkness sweeps over all of Takaara. You might not like us pinks and in all honesty, we've acted like the ultimate cunts towards your people and so it is deserved. But soon, when the darkness comes, you will see that we share a common enemy and pink, brown, or black, that enemy knows no distinctions. Consider it a colour-blind evil intent on destroying everything you love. If we don't convince your king to at least hold off on any notions of invasion, then we are all doomed.'

The warrior snapped her spear up from the ground by kicking it on the one side, catching it deftly with her right hand and spinning it; an obvious display of skill to show him that she was no inexperienced fool. 'Our king has longed for the chance to enact his dream of revenge on your people. A world that bows to him. That is the goal.'

'If he moves now, there will be no one left to bow to him,' Aleister warned, face as stern as he could manage. The sweat was now dripping into his beard, salty, as he ran his tongue around his dry and cracked lips.

The woman stepped forward, her face giving no sign of her emotions. She placed a dark hand on one of the bars and pulled. The door swung open along with Aleister's mouth.

'It wasn't locked?' he asked, amazed and wondering why he hadn't tried the door.

His captor laughed, a beautiful song that called out to the forest around her. 'Your friends were out within minutes of waking up.'

'Then why keep us in a cage?'

'For fun. For your own safety.' She shrugged and waved a hand to Aleister before turning her back on him and leading him away from the river. 'Do you know why those men in the river continue as they do, even with the danger of that animal lurking nearby?'

'No idea,' Aleister replied. 'I'd be running as far as I

could to get away from it…'

'You cannot outrun it. We have a saying down here in the South. I'm not clear on its translation in your tongue.' She paused and bit her lip, trying to work it out. At last she spoke, slowly and carefully, trying to find the right words. '*A danger seen is a danger that can be faced. It is the unseen danger that causes fear.* We like those animals being close by. We know where they are. It is when they drop under the waters and hide from view that we become nervous. Remember that when we keep you and your allies close. We are always watching. One false move and we will not hesitate to kill you.'

'I see you have spoken to Buhle. I like her,' Ariel said, munching on an unidentifiable piece of meat. Aleister's stomach growled, warning him not to ask questions as Bathos passed over another slab for him to chew on. Tough. But not bad. 'You were in that cage for a while. Enjoying the time alone? A bit of *me time*?' she snorted with laughter at her own mockery and dipped her body to the side, banging into Bathos who shared her mirth.

'Funny. Real funny,' Aleister retorted breaking into a smile of his own. He was too relieved to be alive to feel shame for his stupidity. 'Glad to see you two have been filling your faces whilst I was passed out in an iron cage.'

'An *unlocked* iron cage,' Bathos reminded him, nearly choking on his food as he held back more laughter. Ariel clapped him on the back, barely able to restrain her own chuckle as she found joy in both of her friends' misfortune.

Aleister used the chance to gather his senses and take in the terrain and their position. They sat in a patch of the jungle where the trees grew further apart, each gaining enough light to grow and prosper without having to battle each other for every foot of earth. Just like near the river, the plants and flowers here were breath-taking. A myriad of colours created a floral rainbow that threatened to take Aleister out of reality; it was so far from the drear browns and greens of back home. A world where the sky always seemed grey or black and rain fell like it had a personal vendetta against all the inhabitants of Archania. Here, the sky was a vivid blue and the rainbow had fled from the skies to make home amongst the lucky Southern people as they ambled between the trees, laughing and playing with children and going about their chores with a whistle and smiles on their faces. They were happy out here. The only reason for a scowl or a stern look was when the people of the forest stared their way, at the *strange pinks*, as they liked to say, not bothering to keep their voices down as they spoke of them with suspicion. Bathos in particular bore most of the unnerved stares. His broad shoulders could carry such a burden. He was used to standing out in the crowd. Aleister had to hide a smirk when he noticed that many of the woman continued to look over at the big warrior, mostly with interested glances and licked lips. Ariel hadn't noticed yet. He prayed that he would be there when she did. A bit of fun out here was needed after the chaos of the other night and their near-death experience with Bana's men.

'What's the next step?' Ariel asked him, finishing her food and chucking the leftovers into a small, wooden bowl that had been carved with various animals for decoration – most that Aleister couldn't recognise. A skinny dog padded over, breathing heavily, its tongue lolling out of its mouth as it eyed the prize in the bowl. It gently lifted the remains of Ariel's food out of the bowl and scampered away, afraid that someone would realise what was happening and attempt a challenge.

'Find out as much as we can about the people,' Aleister advised, still gazing around and trying to burn everything he saw into his mind. Even the slightest of details could become important later. He studied the strange houses. Oval shaped and built with a stone base and supported with wide wooden planks. The rooves were thatched; thick bunches of grass tied together with string to shield the buildings from rainwater. There was no door to the buildings, just a rectangular hole that allowed for easy entrance and exit. Two children, each dressed in what looked like grass skirts, chased another stray dog into one of the buildings and then back out again, giggling profusely and almost falling over in their joyous delirium. Aleister found himself smiling along with them.

'And then what?' his sister pestered him, snapping him from the moment. He shook his head and tried to focus on creating a plan.

'The goal stays the same. Things just become more difficult. We still need to work out a way for passage into the capital. That is what we must focus on. After that, we find a way of contacting the Boy King and convincing him that a truce with Causrea is in the best interests of Takaara, including the South.'

'Sounds easy.' Bathos worked his jaw, stretching it wide and rubbing at the hinge. 'Convince a king to hold off a war or an invasion when his target is at its weakest…'

'What other choice do we have?' Aleister sighed, grabbing his cup of water and downing it in one go. He'd crossed the deserts in the East but this heat was a different kind; sticky and suffocating.

'We do have another choice,' Ariel said, glancing either side before leaning in close. 'Something that we know has worked in the past…'

'Are you sure you're not the male sibling?' Aleister asked, leaning forward and copying his sister's suspicious actions. ''Cause you've got some fucking balls just for suggesting that out here. I'm not keen on this pretty head ending up on a pike as a warning to the folly of pinks.'

Ariel sat back and stuck her lips out, raising and lowering one of her eyebrows. 'I think you have forgotten the dangers we have faced before, brother. Most plans we have involve the distinct possibility of our heads ending up on pikes. If we fail in this mission, we're dead anyway. I know that none of us have spoken that truth out loud but it's true and you both know it. We've been in battles before but at the moment, we're on a straight track to a war that would consume most of Takaara. Think about that.'

He did think about that. They had been through the hells before and fallen out the other side with just a few scrapes and bruises. They were still young, but they had been forced to grow up fast. Old warriors in young bodies. The inexperience of youth had thrown them into situations that even just a couple of cycles later, Aleister shuddered at the stupidity. But it had all worked out, hadn't it?

The scrape of steel as the sword was deflected and stabbed through Ella's stomach filled his mind. Her beautiful, open, hunting eyes stared out at him in the rain as the flames burned all around them – a light display for the end of all things in his heart.

He shook the dark memory away and found that his sister and Bathos were giving him that worried look they had mastered over the cycles. He rolled his eyes, blocking their worries with the exaggerated action.

'We have been through a lot. We can see that as we are indestructible or we can see it that we have been using up all of the luck we were gifted and our time is coming soon. Either way, any decision we make will need to be thought through and analysed. We are not the young fools who left Archania,' he reminded them.

'Agreed,' Ariel said, a stubborn look on her face as she crossed her arms, 'we are experienced mercenaries who have done more in a few cycles than most fuckers do in a lifetime. With that, we must be confident in our actions. The rebellion in Archania went balls up because we were not leading it. We were the supporting cast in a big shit show organised by fools who had no right in leading such a thing.' She unfolded her arms and softened slightly, her whole body easing as the tension left her. 'Every time we have worked together with a clear goal, we have been successful. The three of us. Fuck everybody else. If our goal is to ensure the South doesn't invade then we will make sure it doesn't fucking happen. Right?'

'Right.' Aleister gave her a sad smile. It was all he could manage. Too many reminders of the incident in the Lower City. It sapped him of his energy, made him want a drink and other things besides. Even in this uncomfortable heat, a bit of Firewhiskey or some wine would go down a treat.

'We can discuss this later,' Bathos said, nodding his head to something behind Aleister. 'Looks like we got company.'

Buhle strode confidently amongst her people. They

paused as she passed them, silently bowing their heads and holding a fist to their lips until she acknowledged them with a smile or a quick word of greeting. Every single one of them did this action, respectfully stopping whatever they were doing to welcome her. Even the children stopped in their games, much to the relief of the poor, puffing and panting dog. They copied their elders' actions, giggling slightly as Buhle knelt and pressed her head to theirs and pushed them on their way. They searched for the escaped dog before choosing the most likely direction and bounding away.

'Takes a lot to earn such respect,' Aleister said as Buhle stood over them.

'These people know what I would do for them, what I do for them. What I have done for them. Respect is earned. Rest easy knowing that I have earned it, pink man,' Buhle answered him, eyes flashing with the mocking phrase at the end. 'I have been in discussion with the people of the village. They wish for you to stand before The Wise Women. They live a short walk from the village. Once they have judged you, we will either send you on your way back where you came from. Or we will help you in your mission. Their word is law.'

'The Wise Women?' Aleister repeated, sounding out the phrase and wondering what such characters would look like out here. 'Take us to them.'

'I warn you, any sign of mockery or disrespect towards them will be taken harshly. Even the slightest indiscretion in such matters will lead to death.'

Buhle clicked her fingers as Aleister rose to his feet. Bathos and Ariel flanked him as two men scrambled towards Buhle. They stood tall, each almost able to look at Bathos in his dark eyes without needing to crane their necks.

'Your weapons,' Buhle stated as the men pulled the weapons from the baskets tied to their backs.

Aleister released a long breath as he felt the leather against his fingers and palm. It was as though he had spent the whole time away from the weapon with his breath held in tight to his chest. He relaxed and buckled the belt around his waist, relieved to feel the extra weight of the sword at his hip. He softly ran his fingers across the golden falcon at the head of the hilt and exhaled. Ariel and Bathos grinned like kids given their first birthday toys by their parents. They swung their own swords in the air, enjoying the familiar feel of the weapons gliding in front of them.

'Thank you,' Aleister said, hoping that Buhle understood the significance of such a gesture. 'This weapon is dearer to me than my own sister.' He smiled at the angry tut aimed in his direction.

'Some argued that you should not have them returned,' Buhle explained. 'Wisdom prevailed. The Wise Women have interesting ways of judgement and they love a good fight. They may even ask you to fight each other...' Aleister looked out of the corner of his eyes and noticed that Bathos and Ariel had stopped swinging their weapons and were now glancing nervously at each other and then back to Buhle as she turned her back on them, arms folded behind her slender frame. 'Come, we must reach them before sundown. The beasts by the river really are quite the challenge in the darkness...'

'I think I want to go back behind the bars,' Aleister muttered to his friends.

'You might not be able to see them anymore,' Ariel warned him through gritted teeth, 'but we're still behind them. Mark my words. We're still behind them.'

YOU SCRATCH MY BACK

'Smells like fucking trouble. The whole thing smells like fucking trouble.'

'Of course it smells like trouble,' Kiras snorted. 'Everywhere right now is in the shit and the only thing around is trouble. Borderlands has always been a mess but this is a new level of mess, even for us lot. Ain't anywhere in the whole of Takaara that ain't in trouble right now so we just need to choose which trouble we're gonna dive headfirst into.'

Sly didn't like it. Didn't like much, in fairness, but that weren't the point. They had a target and that didn't involve helping a bunch of weirdos dressed in strange outfits. Last time he had seen such fools they had almost burned their whole city to the ground and then got crushed by a bunch of soft Southern cunts. He wasn't gonna be caught up in that shit again. No way.

'They'll help us get Baldor. Anyway they said we can have free drinks for life…' Socket argued.

Maybe he could get caught up in it again. Just a little.

'Why didn't you open with that, you dumb shit? Must be going senile, old man,' Sly growled.

'I wish I were. Means I'd be able to forget about you…' Socket muttered back in jest. At least Sly thought it was in jest. Maybe not. Who gave a shit anyway?

The four of them strode through the rain, not bothering

to quicken their pace. The weather would need to work harder than that to put them off a walk in the open. The cold rain had nothing on the biting wind or the hailstones as big as small dogs falling from the angry skies in the Borderlands. They just kept on going, following the instructions given to them the day before in the tavern.

'Still, free drinks or not,' Sly carried on as they walked over an arched stone bridge keeping them from the gentle stream running through the town, 'these people are a bunch of weirdos. And yes,' he added as he saw Kiras raise her eyebrows in his direction, 'I understand the irony in what I'm telling ya!'

The poor weather held a shadow over the town. Sly growled as the empty paths soon became filled with rows of figures dressed in long, flowing, leather, red cloaks. They lined either side of the path running up to the largest building in the city – the home of the town's Elder – a converted temple from the earlier days of the town's history. Each of the guarding figures wore the dumb black masks with red eyes that Sly had seen worn in Archania the night of the flames. They lit up the path with lanterns held in gloved hands. All of them kept silent, pointed beaks facing their opposite number on the other side of the road. They seemed less bothered by the rain than the Borderlanders.

Sly thought he'd test their resolve. He crept up closer to the nearest one and peered right up against the mask. 'Boo,' he murmured as he stared into those ominous blood-red eyes. He chuckled as the guard kept still. Impressive. He thought about jolting forward and forcing a response but thought better of it. Not worth it. There would be time for fun and games after they had Baldor.

The former temple looked old. Bits of green grew through the gaps in the grey stone and the coloured windows looked as though they needed a bit of a clean. They had Four windows. Four statues standing on the corners of the slanted roof. Each statue a sign of the faith in each God. The Four had been worshipped here since the city's inception it seemed.

Two of the masked guards opened the large creaking, arched, wooden doors. Kiras led the way in. Socket frowned up at two of the watching statues above him before following her in.

Cray paused for a moment, hesitating.

'Having second thoughts?' Sly nudged him as he passed the stoic warrior. 'Can always head back to the family. No one is keeping you here.' He said the words but it was safe to say he only half meant them. Cray had proven himself a strong ally and handy in a tight spot too.

'I told you before, not a fan of religion. This old temple reeks of corruption.'

'So you did,' Sly recalled. 'You got faith in that sword of yours. I've faith in this bloody axe,' he said, patting his weapon like a well-behaved pet. 'Things go tits up and we'll cut our fucking way out of the mess. Just like last time.'

Cray nodded, not entirely convinced but enough to inch towards the entrance. Sly waited for him, chuckling as his ally made it past him and the door closed slowly behind.

The ground floor of the building was large and mostly empty. A dual staircase ran up either side of the room to the next floor, a dark blue rug tracing its path and softening the harshness of the dark wood. On both the eastern and western walls, long, wide paintings filled up most of the room. Painted with dark, grim oils, they each portrayed an intense and bloody battle. Armoured men fled from hunched shadows with vicious claws that ripped through flesh and sprayed blood all around a muddy battlefield. The artist showed the human warriors with a look of fear in their eyes that Sly knew all too well. He had seen such sights as he got up close to his unfortunate victims in their last moments. The pure whites of their eyes before they took in the last light of their lives. The paintings were not created by some fool with a passing idea of war. The way they caught the horror, the excitement, the pure chaos of battle was something only someone who had been up close and personal to the bloody scene could have conveyed. The shadow warriors seemed a touch dramatic but Sly could understand the purpose to add a little entertainment and awe to such a bloody scene.

'Guests of the Borderlands!' a voice called down from the floor above. Same blood-red cloak as the others but no plague mask. Sly was happy to see that as this woman had stunning green eyes and raven-black hair that fell in small curls onto her shoulders. Much better to look at than those masked fools outside in his mind. 'We welcome you to the Grand House of Barnham and thank you for your decision in joining us today. Please, join me and I will lead you into our Elder's meeting room.'

Kiras shrugged to the rest of them and leapt up the stairs, taking them two at a time. The rest followed, Sly bringing up the rear and checking over his shoulder. You never can be too careful…

The greeter led them down the corridor towards the eastern wing of the large house. The door was carved with small, intricate details and beasts that Sly had never seen before sticking out around the frame. The woodworker was a talented bastard with a lot of spare time, apparently. The greeter opened the door and held the silver handle whilst nodding and smiling to let them know that it was time to enter.

Sly could smell her flowery scent as he edged past her and gave Kiras as wink as she caught him eyeing up the woman. He shrugged as his ally rolled her eyes and marched further into the room.

This room was all dark wood and red carpets. A fire roared at the back beneath a painting of some king – most likely a dead one. Folk down here always seemed to worship the dead ones more than the ones breathing. The walls, once again, were adorned with scenes of a horrific battle, shadowed monsters tearing through the ill-prepared warriors unable to stem the dark tide. Shields and spears lay broken and scattered amidst the blood and dirt of the battleground. Sly followed the scene around to its end; a tall, skeletal figure in a ripped, black cloak smiled, its black lips reaching each ear as the being towered over the piles of dismembered bodies and pools of blood.

Seemed like a character Sly could get on board with.

He caught Cray frowning at the same image and wondered what the superstitious warrior was thinking. Not much probably. Or some weird shit about religion. The bastard loved to moan about religion. That's what happens when a guy doesn't have a hobby. Sly patted his axe again at the thought. Everyone needs a hobby. Else the mind wanders and creates weird shit to focus on.

'It has been some time since I have welcomed guests from the Borderlands,' a voice croaked from the centre of the room. 'Forgive me if I do not stand. My mind and heart have always been willing but the body fights against my urges of late. It is why I value comfortable chairs more than anything else nowadays,' an old man chuckled from his cushioned seat at the centre of a long table. Like the others, he wore the red cloak but had chosen to leave his unusual mask on the wooden table next to a lit candle. His face bore more wrinkles than Sly's shirt had creases after a long journey. A warm smile greeted each of them beneath a crooked nose. Lastly, Sly noticed the old man's eyes. Milky white like two moons sat in the middle of a wrinkled, pale sky.

Blind as the table in between them.

The woman who had greeted them circled around them and took a seat next to the old man. 'Please, sit.' She waved her hand at the four empty seats opposite the blind Elder.

Once all four were taken, Socket was the first to speak. 'It ain't often we're welcomed into such a fine home and we appreciate it. But I'm speaking for all of us when I say we have something important that needs to get done and time is an issue. We've spoken to those in the tavern and were told you could help us. If help is what you're offering, we need it quick. If not, we'll be on our way.'

The blind man rocked back in his chair and laughed lightly, joined by his glamorous assistant in the humour. 'Just what I would expect from the North. Straight to the point. I've been in the United Cities a long time and let me tell you, the officials down here know a thousand ways to drag out their words; a one-hour meeting for you and I could last a moon for those people. I welcome the chance to speak with honesty and clarity.'

'Then tell us,' Sly commanded, finding a piece of meat stuck in his teeth and pausing to wrestle it out with his tongue. 'Why the fuck are we here?'

The woman frowned at the harsh language but the Elder placed a reassuring hand on hers and she relaxed. 'First, let me introduce myself. I am Elder Hogan. I offered my life to The

257

Four from a young age and served the Gods as all in my family have before me. This is my assistant, my eyes in the dark you could say. Alexa Kandor.' The woman gave a curt nod. Sly tried to catch her eye but she was determined to look anywhere but at him. Shame. He sniffed at one of his pits and jerked back with a surprised, bitter grin – slightly impressed with the acrid smell. It had certainly been a while. 'We lead this sleepy town and protect its people. We live out of the way and have shielded those who require it from the harms of the world around us. I have been told that some of you witnessed the chaos in Archania recently. My own brother, Elder Morgan lost his life in the disturbance. A victim of the oppressive Empire of Light that threatens to strangle the life out of the North.'

'Folk got pissed with their masters and were taught a lesson by those in charge. They soon backed off when they realised it weren't an even fight...' Sly said, scratching at his itchy beard.

'They were ill-prepared,' Hogan agreed, nodding. 'Even one as blind as me can see that. My brother was anxious. He grew impatient and acted before everything was in place, as did the rest of them. Still, it is hard to sit on your hands and watch as the flames rise around you.'

'If I recall correctly, it was those in the little masks that caused the flames,' Sly informed him, poking at the plague mask with a filthy finger. 'Didn't anyone ever warn them about the dangers of fire?'

'They knew the dangers. We all knew the dangers. Desperate people do desperate things,' Hogan sighed helplessly. 'I cannot speak for their mindset as their home burned around them and their loved ones fell to the bloody swords and spears of the very soldiers who had sworn oaths to protect them. That is something for the historians looking back with clear eyes and better sight than mine. My role is a different one. Alexa.'

The woman cleared her throat and rested her elbows on the table, looking at the four dirty warriors each in turn. 'Our town has welcomed mages since its inception. Archania used to be home to the most powerful of our kind. That seems to have been forgotten in many places but not here. Here, we are a refuge for those who need it. The last quake disrupted the flow of energy in Takaara. Something went wrong and now our path to magic is blocked. But as one path closes, another opens.'

'The body cannot access magic but the mind works on a level that none of us truly understand, not yet anyway,' Hogan continued as though they had planned this speech and practised it before the meeting. 'The talented men and women of this town have been experiencing visions, strange dreams since they lost the gift they had been born with. As the gold in their pupils faded, another treasure awoke inside them. We saw your coming, Borderlanders, and we know you need help breaking your large friend out from the camp south of here. Decency and manners dictate that I ask you to help us and then we will help you.'

'You scratch our back and we scratch yours,' Sly muttered, a crease forming just above his eyes.

'Exactly,' Hogan said with a wide grin. 'Decency may dictate that but I already know how this pans out. It has been seen.'

'You'll have to understand, old man,' Sly growled, 'we might not be too keen on trusting the vision of a blind man. We're gonna need more.'

'Of course.' Alexa stepped in. 'Your friend is being held in a highly guarded camp during a time of great unrest in the nation. The four of you may be great fighters but you would need to be The Four to get your friend out without loss of life. We can help.'

'How?' Kiras asked, eyes boring a hole into Alexa. She wanted Baldor free more than any of them and she wasn't going to be tricked by some crippled mages.

'In this town we have a small army of fighters. Dependable people who have been training for the war to come. They will assist you in getting Baldor free.'

'And in return?' Socket questioned.

Alexa's lips curled at the thought. 'You have been led to believe we need help protecting ourselves from the returning guards. This is a not the truth. Instead, we ask for something much bigger. One of you will kill the king of the United Cities of

Archania.'

Sly returned her grin with one of his best. 'Where do I sign?'

'Eager, just as I saw,' Hogan muttered. 'I have seen the king lying dead in his bed at the hands of a Borderland warrior. All we need to do is move the piece into place.'

A knock at the door interrupted the conversation. Alexa leapt from her seat and pulled open the door. Another red-cloaked man stepped in after a small bow to the woman.

'My apologies for such tardiness,' the newcomer said, raising a hand in greeting to all in the room and striding around the table with the confidence of someone who knew the place well. 'Only a fool believes he may judge the seas with any level of certainty; the journey from Norland was more challenging than expected.' He placed a hand on the Elder's shoulder and planted a light kiss on his forehead. 'It is good to see you looking so well, Elder Hogan.'

'If my current state brings you joy, then you should have seen me thirty cycles ago!' the older man laughed, squeezing his guest's hand as the man took a seat beside him. Alexa sat back down in hers, the three of them facing the four outsiders. 'It is wonderful to hear your voice, Matthias. I trust that things in Norland are going well?'

'Everything is in place,' Matthias informed him, brushing dark hair from his brown eyes and sinking back into his chair. 'The ships are ready to bring the people of Norland across the sea. We await the signal.' Matthias's eyes dropped and he brushed his lap as though concerned with something. 'Phoebe passed away two days before my departure. The Vald Sickness has no cure. Such a young girl couldn't handle what was being asked of her. We held a day of mourning to show our respect for what she has allowed us to do. She will be with us when we move. That is certain.'

Sly frowned the whole way through the conversation, lost from when the newcomer had started speaking. He wanted more talk of violence. King-killing would do nicely.

'A great loss. She had the strength of The Four within

her.' Hogan grew solemn with the words, falling silent for a moment as they spoke of the death of someone Sly had never heard of.

'We're on a bit of a tight schedule,' he interrupted, licking his lips and narrowing his eyes towards Matthias. A flash of recognition shot through the man's eyes but Sly had no idea why. Maybe he'd killed someone the man knew. Happened often enough. 'You can grieve for the dead in your own time. We need Baldor. And if you wanna help, we gotta go tomorrow at the latest.'

Hogan shuffled in his seat and smacked his own lips together. Matthias and Alexa just sat still and stared daggers at Sly for what they obviously saw as a complete lack of respect. Good. It was intentional and they got the message.

'I understand time is of the essence,' Hogan exhaled and patted Matthias on the thigh. 'Please, my friend, would you be able to explain our current situation in a bit more detail for our esteemed guests?'

Matthias nodded and cleared his throat. 'When the last quake hit, the world of Takaara changed in the flap of a wing. Those of who have used magic all our lives found it impossible to even light a flame. Tears, confusion, frustration, anger. We felt it all. The world had flipped on its head and we were unsure of what path lay in front of us. Then, some of us started receiving strange messages in our dreams. A path opened up before us and gave us hope for what may come.'

'Strange dreams?' Socket repeated, suddenly more invested in where this was heading. Sly spotted Kiras frown at the sudden interest as the old archer leant forward onto the table and lined his good eye directly on Matthias. Cray just sat there, eyes dazed as he stared at the swaying flames in the fireplace. He might not have listened to a word of any of it since they had passed through the door. There was a small chance he didn't even know that Matthias had entered. Sly found himself laughing at the thought before Socket pressed further. 'What kind of strange dreams?'

Matthias shared an uneasy glance with Alexa before turning to answer Socket. 'Visions from the Sky Plane. A guide for what is to come.'

'And what is to come, exactly?' Socket growled, growing increasingly agitated with each word. Sly hadn't seen the old man like this in a while. He liked it. Still had a bit of fire to him.

'An army of Chaos,' Matthias claimed, his own face lighting up with a sudden fire. 'An army that can burn away the corruption and hate in this world. An army that could allow us to start again, to grow Takaara and bring hope and joy to every man, woman and child breathing.'

'When did people start having these *visions*?' Socket asked, spitting the final word out like a curse.

'Just after the quake. Maybe a day or two.' Matthias frowned. 'Why do you ask?'

Socket sat back in his seat and placed a hand over his mouth, frowning intently into space, lost in his thoughts. 'He wouldn't have… would he?' Sly thought he heard the archer mutter to himself.

'Socket…' Kiras said, trying to snap him from his own mind. 'Wanna share something with the rest of us?'

He looked up at her, biting his lip before cursing to himself. 'Korvus said it would close the bridge forever… not open it wider. If he was wrong… *fuck*.'

'You're starting to worry us now, old man,' Kiras said, her voice trembling slightly.

'I killed the kid.' Socket's voice was stern and even, guarded from emotion. 'Thought it was the right thing to do. Cut off access to the Sky Plane with his blood. Without it, we thought the Empire of Light would have to fight battles on a level-playing field.'

Sly blinked and leant closer to Socket, trying to make sure that he had heard right. 'You killed the kid? *Arden*. You killed him?' he asked, wanting to make sure he was right. He stuck a dirty finger into his ear and rummaged around for a moment, digging out as much crap as he could and wiped it on his trousers. 'You fucking *killed* him?' The room fell silent, a deadly silence that wrapped itself around all of those sitting at the table. He heard the creak of the chairs as Cray and Kiras shifted slightly, ready for a fight to break out. Sly had no idea what the three cunts opposite him were doing and he didn't care. 'You said it were Barbarians… but no, it was you, you killed him…'

Socket raised his palms and the action just infuriated Sly even more. 'I thought it was for the best. Korvus is a wise mage, one of the greatest—'

'I don't give a fuck if the Gods themselves told you to do it!' Sly roared, leaping to his feet and kicking his chair away. Kiras and Cray were on their feet in a second; Cray pressing a hand against Sly's chest as Kiras stood in front of Socket, shielding the old man as he sat there, shoulders hunched as he muttered to himself, defeated. 'He was one of us and he was a fucking kid.'

'You were the one saying that we should treat him as a man, as a warrior of the Borderlands,' Socket eventually snapped, rubbing his forehead and looking as though he would rather be anywhere but here. 'You've done worse…'

It was all he could do to not draw his axe there and then. Instead, Sly settled for a roar before bellowing at one of his oldest allies, 'Done worse? I've done what I've had to do. Enjoyed it most of the time too. Still, never stabbed those in my tribe. The kid was one of us. Bet you stabbed him in the fucking back, too.' Sly paused, the rage growing from a seed in his stomach and threatening to take over his whole body, controlling his mind and actions. He knew he shouldn't say it but there was no way of stopping it. 'Just like you did to Reaver Redbeard.'

Socket's eye flashed wide open and bore into Sly, angrier than he had ever seen him. Cray and Kiras were no longer trying to prevent a fight, they stared slack-jawed at the old archer.

'Socket…' Kiras muttered, towering over him. 'Is this true?'

'You swore a damned blood oath, you fucking prick!' Socket yelled at Sly, answering the question.

Sly burst into a wild laugh. 'Piss on your fucking blood oath. You're a fucking traitor and that's all there is to it.' He turned to the three bemused Archanians and drew his axe. No one moved. 'You want us to fight for you and kill this king, fine.

I'll do it.' He pointed his axe at Socket. 'Just keep this fucking snake away from us and you got yourself a deal.' He screamed and slammed the axe into the table before turning and storming from the room without caring if anyone followed.

The cold wind hit him as he marched away from the manor, blood pumping in his head and deafening him as he searched for the way towards the tavern.

'Drink?' a voice called from behind him. He didn't break his stride, just kept walking until Cray caught up with him.

'Aye, a drink.'

'You're getting this round,' another said to his left.

'Thought they were free?'

Kiras laughed and squeezed his shoulder. 'Gotta kill the king first. Then we have all the drinks we can manage.'

'Let's get Baldor out of this shit land. Help or no help,' Sly growled. 'Then we kill the king of the United fucking Cities.'

DEATH IN THE FAMILY

A rden waited for the guard to finish his third walk of the perimeter. The guard had started the night on alert, searching for any sign of trouble in amongst even the darkest of shadows. Now though, the man appeared to be growing bored with his role and had slipped into over-confidence. Arden could use that to his advantage.

There seemed to be some confusion amongst the palace guards. Arden spotted moments of friction between those who bore the white sun on their shoulder – guards of Archania – and those who bore the white sun on their breast – soldiers sent from the East to bolster the city's defences in light of the recent disturbances. There was confusion as to who had dominance in the palace's defences and this led to gaps in the patrol – gaps Arden welcomed.

Cypher had told him where Mason and Asher would be. Arden had memorised the route as best he could and felt confident that he would be able to reach them. All he had to do was make it past the first obstacle.

As the soldier inspected his reflection in the shiny plaque bolted to a pillar beside him, Arden slipped past with ease, gliding through the shadows and creeping towards the single door left ajar on the eastern side of the palace. If Cypher's information was correct, this was the least guarded route of the palace. Through the kitchens and the servants' quarters and then up through a thin passage kept away from most guests who prefer the more majestic and grand tour of the heart of Archanian royalty. Arden cared not for the gold and silver ornaments and precious relics and statues. He had a destination in mind and how he got there was of no importance to him.

It was late but the kitchens were still staffed with a few cooks. Two men and one woman dressed all in white, stains from the evening's work clear on their sleeves and chests. The marks forced Arden to take a second look, almost tricked into thinking the red marks were the sign of some attack and not a sauce that the king probably enjoyed. They laughed together as they put away their instruments and tools, not expecting an uninvited guest. Arden crouched, keeping low next to the metal tables and ensuring that he was out of sight of any of the workers. One of the cooks excused himself and peered towards the still open door that Arden had used to enter the large room. The cook strode over to the door just as Arden grasped for something, anything, on the table next to him. A metal pan. He flung the pan across the room and it clattered against a wall, the rattling echoing around the kitchen and diverting everyone's gaze. Seizing the fleeting opportunity, he sped towards the next door, not looking back and just praying that the diversion had worked well enough. He heard a curse being him and held his breath but kept moving. There was no stopping now.

'What in the hells was that?' he heard just as he crept through the door and squeezed through and away from any curious eyes.

He closed his eyes as his heartbeat returned to normality. His breathing slowed to its usual steady rhythm and then he allowed himself to open his eyes again.

The room was grander than Arden would have thought. Cypher had told him it was a room for servants to eat their food and spend time during breaks away from the guests within the palace; a place to let off some steam. He was expecting bare and minimal but what he found was lavish and opulent decorations and ornaments. Paintings larger than any he had ever seen adorned each of the four walls and depicted great scenes of battle with proud, victorious warriors holding high poles with waving flags. Everyone always seemed so fascinated with flags. Arden had never seen the appeal. In the middle of the room there was a dark wooden table with a white cloth that ran its length. Three candles sitting on the cloth gave off enough light for Arden to see clearly in the room.

To see a small, sweating, trembling man dressed in black with small lenses on the edge of his long nose. A man who was staring at him like he had seen a ghost.

'Please, don't hurt me…' the man's voice quivered. Arden peered down and saw that the man's trousers had darkened around his crotch. Pissed himself. Strange, Arden had never had such an effect before. Sly and Baldor were the ones who could strike such fear but not young Arden. An invader in this man's home, dressed in a dark robe but with no visible weapon. It seemed strange. But Arden wasn't going to let that stop him on his mission.

He swept forward and pulled a shining dagger from beneath his cloak. He found himself stroking the man's face as he whimpered and began to cry, tears streaming down his tired and worn face.

'Those eyes…' the man said, breathless as his own widened in horror. 'Those eyes…'

'Be at peace, my friend,' Arden heard a soothing voice tell the man. *'Your sacrifice is recognised.'*

Then he punched the dagger straight through the servant's heart.

He pulled it free, still holding the body like a lover as light drained from the eyes. He glanced around and found a tall, wooden closet. Big enough for a body, Arden guessed. He grabbed the servant's wrist and dragged him over to the closet.

His dark work done, Arden rubbed his hands together and was pleased to see that there was no sign of a struggle. No blood or broken furniture. A clean death.

As it should be.

The servant's passage was all old stonework and broken steps. Cypher had told him that most royals wouldn't be seen dead in the darker passages of the palace but Asher had enjoyed sneaking around as a prince and having his fun with the very people who had vowed to serve him. The virginity of maids and the dignity of servants. Those were the things he enjoyed playing with. Such hidden passages were a blessing to one with Asher's particular tastes. Arden had scowled at the tales but he wasn't above moving through the shadows and using the passages that his brother had used to his own advantage. The fewer people who witnessed him in here, the better it would be for Archania.

The stairs spiralled as they grew higher, reaching the tallest levels of the palace. Every now and then, the floor would level out and there would be a single wooden door, often opposite a hole with a thin shutter. In the hole, Arden would see a long rope that seemed to run from the basement of the building all the way to the tallest tower. A way of moving goods within the palace without impeding the life of the royals no doubt.

He had reached one such level when he found what he was looking for. A single, black door with a white sun painted at the top.

Arden was relieved to see that the corridor past the door was empty. Lanterns lit the wide path lined with tall paintings of grand looking men dressed in clothing that Arden felt seemed too hot and bothersome to be comfortable. Tassels fell from small medals pinned to the breasts of wide jackets and bits of material dropped from the edges of the cuffs and lining of the jacket. It looked strange and Arden couldn't think of its purpose unless it was to show that these men had more money than sense. Speaking of which, they all wore the same odd crown perched on their head. All the men bore a similar stern and determined expression and strong jawline. Perhaps, like Arden had thought, they were not comfortable in such lavish clothing. Their expressions told the tale of men who were not given a life of joy and happiness. *The burden of leading could crush a man.* That's what Raven had once said to him. *You need broad shoulders and thick skin to survive when the lives of men and women are in your hands. Anything else and you will end up as bones, and nothing more.* He missed the bearded warrior. He wondered what would have happened if Raven had been able to speak to him before heading south. To have had the chance to tell him the truth of his lineage. How would things have differed?

Too late for any of that now.

Arden recalled Cypher's instructions. The door he needed stood just past the fifth king's painting, a rather wide-eyed, moustachioed man with striking blonde hair that was cut almost to the skin on the sides. He glanced around and found no onlookers. It was as he had been told, the arrogance of Mason and his bodyguard mixed with suspicion of those around them meant that security wasn't what it should be.

The room he entered was shrouded in darkness. No lanterns were lit and floor-to-ceiling curtains blocked out any light from the large windows that usually would have allowed at least a glimmer of light from the moon and stars to creep in. The walls were filled with glass bottles with liquids of various colours, more than Arden had ever seen in any of the taverns in the Borderlands. Seemed that the king had more choice than all of taverns in the North combined. The luxuries of the position.

At the far end of the room, the next door lay open a crack and light from that room slithered in along with the sounds of voices. Exactly what Arden was looking for. He crouched low and moved with all haste to stand behind one of the colossal curtains, ensuring that he was close enough to hear what was being said.

'It was no idle threat, General Grey.' Arden recognised the preacher's slimy voice. 'I vowed to wipe those savages from the map and so that is what we will do. They *burned* my daughter. MY DAUGHTER!' A loud bang followed by the shaking of glass and something falling against the floor with a thud. 'How would you react if someone dear to you was killed in such a way?'

'It would haunt me for the rest of my life…' an unfamiliar voice replied. A male's voice. Deep. Sounded tired and sad. 'I would want revenge but I would also be keenly aware that such actions do not return the dead from their resting place. War with the Borderlands will take a lot of resources and effort. We do not know what this Herick is after. And at the same time, there is unease in Causrea, the Boy King of Zakaria is eager for war, and the Heartlands continue to fight amongst themselves.'

'Chaos. Chaos everywhere, General Grey,' Mason replied. 'Our old friend Cypher Zellin returned yesterday from his sojourn in Norland. He claims that a great war is coming, the God of Chaos itself will set foot in Takaara.'

'The God of Chaos?' came a snort from another. 'Losing his role in the palace dungeons must have unhinged the killer. Lost his final marbles.'

'I agree, Your Majesty,' Mason said. 'Cypher cannot be trusted. He wants revenge for losing his precious role and being sent away. I will send T'Chai to deal with him once and for all.'

'Such things are not done in the United Cities,' General Grey warned. A bit of steel hardening his voice now. 'A trial, then the punishment. That is how we do things now.'

'How we do things, is how I decide, General.'

'Yes, Your Majesty.'

An uncomfortable silence followed the warning.

'I must say,' Mason mused, ending the uneasy quiet, the sound of footsteps adding to his snake-like voice. Arden was surprised to hear the steps instead of the slither that would go with his serpentine voice. 'Ever since the small revolt in the Lower City, you have not been the same. The deaths of those caught up in the regrettable struggle weigh heavily on your old shoulders.'

'*Regrettable?*' Grey snapped back, incredulous. 'Men, women and children lost their lives. Sons and daughters of Archania caught up in the fire and blood. They loved their country but were disgusted with how *you* and your Eastern allies have tainted this once great nation. When I sleep, I still see the flames; I still smell the smoke and burnt flesh. How do you sleep, Mason D'Argio?'

'As easy as ever,' Mason answered calmly. 'And even better once we have made one small change to the structure of this nation's security. My King?'

'This kingdom thanks you for your wonderful service,

General Grey,' Asher declared with no hint of emotion. 'We wish you the best in all your future endeavours. Your services will no longer be required. Master T'Chai will be taking your post as of tomorrow morning.'

There was some huffing and puffing. A line of indecipherable sounds uttering from the General as he struggled to comprehend what had just happened. Finally, he found the words he was looking for.

'It has been an honour serving this nation,' Grey managed to say, voice rising in pitch. 'Your father was a great man. Your parents were two of the kindest people I could ever wish to meet and I consider myself lucky to have called them friends. Her death allowed this *poison* to enter Archania. One day, I hope to find the cure.'

'That will be all, Dustin Grey. I would stop now, before your thoughtless words land you in a cell.' Arden could almost picture the sneer on Mason's face as he spoke the words.

'It is a pity you were born first, King Asher. Your brother would have been just what this kingdom needed.'

'Leave now, Grey, or I will have you burned!' Asher roared. 'Speak another word of my treacherous brother and I will give you the slowest death I can imagine and place your head on a spike for all to see.'

Arden pulled himself tighter to the wall as Grey rushed past. He peeked past the curtain as the now former general reached the door leading out to the corridor. At the last, Grey turned and peered into the dark corner where Arden stood, motionless. For a second, their eyes locked. Grey sighed and pulled the door wide open, marching away without a word.

Arden grinned.

The bedroom was larger than most buildings in the Borderlands. The ceiling arched from one side to the other and was adorned with many colourful images of swords, crowns, and suns that repeated themselves throughout the room. Two long, blunt swords crossed against one wall, completely useless if danger were to present itself in the middle of the night. A small fire flickered in the corner of the room and offered the only light and warmth available to the sleeping king. Arden crept closer to his brother and marvelled at the bed. Big enough to sleep six and with four posts that stood on each corner, holding up a purple sheet that sheltered the snoring king.

Sheltered him from what, Arden had no idea.

A wooden chair filled with vulgar cushions stood next to the bed. Arden sat on it and smiled as the chair rocked back and forth on its two, curved legs. Amusing. Being a king definitely had its advantages.

Asher rolled over in his bed until he was facing Arden. His eyes flashed open and he bolted up into a seated position. To his credit, the king did not shout out or scream for assistance. Instead, he reached under his pillow and drew out a sharp, jewel-encrusted dagger. This one looked a bit stupid but it would do the job, if needed, at least.

'We have the same eyes,' Arden said, craning his neck to the side and studying his brother. This was the closest they had ever been since his birth. It was slightly unnerving to spot the similarities between them. 'Mine were golden, once,' he added wistfully. Not that he had ever enjoyed that aspect of himself. Caused him nothing but trouble.

'A fucking mage,' Asher spat. 'One of those loons who believe they deserve more from their betters. You've got some balls coming in here but I assure you, I will enjoy carving the flesh from your bones in punishment for such an attack.'

Not the greeting Arden had longed for from his brother but certainly the one he had expected. 'It's strange. You'd think that I would feel some kind of bond. A connection to you. Since finding out the truth, I've often wondered how I would feel when we came face to face. I thought I would feel a desire to... be closer to you... or something.' Arden frowned, puzzled as he stared into the furious face of the final living member of his family. 'Instead, I feel nothing.'

'Who are you?' Asher queried, lowering his dagger ever so slightly.

'My name is Arden Leifhand. Our parents named me. Arden, that is. Leifhand is from my adoptive mother.'

'*Our* parents?'

'Yes.' Arden felt a swelling of sadness growing inside him. 'You are my brother, though I was sent away days after my birth and replaced with another.'

'Drayke... I always knew he wasn't of my blood,' Asher spat in rage. 'But I don't give a shit who you are, this is my throne and I'm not letting anyone take it.'

'Your throne?' Arden laughed, cheeks hurting as his smile widened. A flicker of fear crossed Asher's eyes. 'I'm not after your throne. I have one of my own. One that is far greater.'

'Then what do you want?'

Arden stood from the chair and moved forward. Closer. Closer. Until his chest pressed against the point of the dagger. He closed his eyes as he felt the blade pierce his skin. 'I'm here to see my older brother.' He opened his eyes and grinned wider. '*And to pass on a message to those who dare to stand against me. Chaos is coming. And one Empire will not stand in its way...*'

'Your eyes...' Asher squealed in terror. Your *eyes!*

Arden grabbed the blade with ease and chucked it over his shoulder. He pressed his hands around the king's throat and squeezed. Tighter. He squeezed until the face in front of him turned purple. Those eyes that had looked so similar to his own now bulged and grew red with the strain. Asher's hands clawed desperately at Arden's but to no avail.

Arden gritted his teeth and arched himself forward, towering over the thrashing royal.

A shame. Things could have been so different.

The thrashing slowed and eventually stopped. Arden took a deep breath and released his grip from his older brother. He stroked the dead king's face and closed the eyelids with care.

He took one last look around the room, taking it all in. Such an extravagant room full of useless things all created for the comfort of one man. If such efforts went into all things, perhaps more people in Takaara would be happy and there would be less talk of rebellion.

He was the sole remaining heir now. The last in the line of true kings of the United Cities of Archania. The throne was his if he so wished.

But he had more important tasks ahead of him.

There was a plan for him. You killing him was not what we discussed. We had plans. We had people who should have done that for us…' Osiron's voice echoed through Arden's mind, knocking him to the side with the disturbance.

'Plans change. His time was now.' Arden grimaced and slammed a palm against the side of his head, fighting against the aches and pains. 'It doesn't matter if anyone sits on the throne of Archania. The kingdom will be swept aside soon enough. A message to any who dare to defy. To any who dare to stand against us.' The pain and nausea faded and the voice in his head calmed to a soothing tone that relaxed him and eased the tension he had felt.

'Chaos is coming…

Cypher sat in the tavern, waiting for his companion. That strange bastard Arden had strolled in without a word of warning and muttered one phrase into his ear.

'The king is dead.'

With that, he had glided away.

Cypher felt better now that he was gone. Not many folk gave him the shivers but that bastard sure did. He drank his Firewhiskey and kept close to the corner, ensuring he had a good view of the tavern and its bawdy patrons. He remembered smashing the face of one of those plague doctor fools not so long ago in this place. Simpler times. Before Gods and magi decided to interfere in his life. He wanted to go back to the old days. Where he could drink, torture and kill without worrying about the grander scheme behind it all. Perhaps he had bitten off more than he could chew?

As if on cue, a familiar face walked into the tavern,

lowering his hood and unbuttoning his wet jacket before hanging it on the wooden post. He swept his dark, soaking hair from his face and greeted Cypher with a grim nod.

'You found your way back then?' Cypher said, nudging a glass of the harsh drink towards the fellow.

'This isn't a place of fond memories for me,' Matthias said, accepting the drink and sipping it. He blew out his cheeks and gasped. The first one always hit hard. 'Norland is ready and we have recruited further allies to our cause. How did your meeting go?'

Cypher chuckled and spun his glass around on the table, watching the liquid swirl around inside. 'Mason didn't believe me. Too concerned with his daughter's death. They crave war with the Borderlands.'

'And the king? Did Arden speak to the king? Did it go as planned?'

Cypher downed the rest of the drink and welcomed the fire swirl inside his body. 'Depends on what was planned. The king is dead.'

Matthias frowned. 'That doesn't make any sense. He was supposed to speak to him, to warn him of what was to come. There were others, others who had been placed in the position to kill the king if needed.'

'No better warning than a murder. I know that better than any. The king's dead. The Borderlands want war. The prince is missing. The Empire rules the North. You were right all along.'

'I was?'

'Yep. Chaos is coming.' Cypher stood from his seat and slapped a hand on Matthias's shoulder. 'Don't think it matters which side you're on, or what the sides even are. Best thing to do would be to stay the hells out of it.'

SMOKE AND RIDDLES

The wooden rowboat was large enough for eight travellers. Two sitting beside each other and long enough for four lines of seated passengers. Bathos being as big as he was, took up room for two anyway, so there were seven passengers altogether as the rowboat gently made its way along the wide river.

Aleister pulled his long oar through the waters, listening for the call from his host as she tracked the appropriate rhythm needed for maximum efficiency in their method of travel. Buhle sat at the head of the boat, sheltered from the sweltering heat by a small white sheet tied to four wooden poles standing on the edge of the structure. Large enough to shelter two passengers but of no help whatsoever to Aleister, Ariel, and Bathos and their increasingly pink skin.

'Easy,' Buhle called to them and they pulled the oars into the boat and Aleister took the moment to splash his hot face whilst Buhle rummaged in a bag for something beyond his sight. 'Here.' She threw something at his face. He pulled open the folded cloth as Ariel and Bathos caught their own gifts. 'Put it on your head and tie it with this.' She threw a small black, circular band to each of them. Aleister had worn something similar in the East to keep the Sun's unrepentant gaze from burning his sensitive skin. He pulled the cloth around his head and ensured that his neck and forehead were covered before tying the band around it to keep it in place. Ariel and Bathos did the same. 'I forget that outsiders aren't used to it.'

'We lived in the Eastern deserts for some time,' Ariel replied. 'But this feels like a different heat.'

'More aggressive,' Aleister admitted, wiping more sweat away from his forehead. 'Intense.'

'Welcome to the South,' Buhle laughed, before speaking to her people in their own tongue. The three other passengers, two men and one woman, relaxed on the boat, used to the journey down the river. Aleister found himself looking out for the dragon-like beasts that he had seen on his arrival but thankfully they were nowhere to be seen.

Buhle reached for her bag again and handed each of the passengers a jar of what looked like milk. Aleister sniffed his before taking a sip.

'Goat's milk,' Buhle informed him, noticing his curiosity. 'A personal favourite of mine.'

Aleister gulped it down. Not what he was used to but his body welcomed the drink as Buhle watched him with curiosity.

'How much farther do we have until we reach the shaman?' he asked her, taking advantage of the lull in rowing and conversation. Ariel was leaning on Bathos' broad shoulder, resting while she could. The big man gazed around at the beautiful colours of the forest on either side of the river, admiring the foreign scenery and breathing it all in.

'Not too far now. Soon you will see the smoke of the God Falls and that's when you know you are close.'

'The God Falls?'

'Ah,' Buhle exhaled in sharply and smacked her lips together. 'The greatest sight known to man or woman. Once you've lain eyes on the God Falls, you may die a happy man, Aleister of the Red Sons.'

'I'm not so sure about that. Still got a lot left to do whilst I'm alive,' he argued.

'Once you've witnessed the glory of the Falls, nothing will compare,' Buhle told him, her eyes glistening as she pictured them in her mind. 'There are stories of men who have taken their lives moments after seeing such majesty, understanding that their life would be nothing more than attempting the futile, attempting to discover something, anything that could compare.'

'I think I know of at least one such thing,' Aleister replied wistfully. He lost himself in the memory of Ella's eyes. Of her voice that made his breath catch in his throat. Her scent that made his heart stop for just a moment. Her lips…

'You okay brother?' Ariel asked, prodding his leg with a finger and looking into his dazed eyes. He shook himself and smiled, pulling himself back to reality.

'All good. It is a beautiful land, truly.' He dabbed the corners of his eyes and busied himself with staring at the strange and unfamiliar fruit hanging from the branches of the trees growing by the river. Purple, orange, yellow. Strange colours for strange fruit.

'An *uthana* has caught your eye,' Buhle said as Aleister's eyes focused on the round purple fruit. Each one was the size of his head. 'Or the love berry, in your language. It is said that the *uthana* that grows under a full moon has the power to infuse passion and love within a soul if it is cut and treated correctly. The Tale of Kimbo and the Uthana was one of my favourites growing up. Kimbo loved a woman from afar and promised himself that one day she would love him too. He brought her gifts and sang songs of love but each time he asked for her hand in union, she turned him away. So he found the *uthana*. It grew under the full moon and he cut it how he had been told by a local shaman. He presented it to her and asked for her to be his.'

'And they lived happily ever after…' Aleister muttered, rolling his eyes.

'No,' Buhle frowned, confused. 'A woman's heart is stronger than a fruit and worth so much more. She turned him down one final time and told him to leave her alone as she had fallen for another.'

'And what did Kimbo do?' Aleister asked, intrigued by the twist.

'Jumped from the God Falls and was never seen again.

They say his songs can still be heard by those who listen by the falls under a full moon. We have many stories such as this.'

'I would like to hear more sometime.'

Buhle cautiously watched him from the corner of her eye. 'I would like to tell them to you. If you survive long enough.'

Aleister viewed his life as one of joy clutched from the jaws of the difficulties handed to him. He'd been lucky enough to see some wonders in the places he had travelled. He'd seen the march of the wildebeest. He'd set eyes on the Temple of Sorrow. He'd tasted the 300-year-old wine from the ancient vineyards of Florenzia. He'd seen more than most and counted himself lucky for that. But for all the wonder and awe that his travels had brought him, nothing came close to the sight in front of him now.

Standing on a small island on the lip of the falls, Aleister peered over the seething cauldron beneath him and marvelled at the sheer ferocity of noise that greeted him. The water crashed down below and smashed into the river at the bottom of the falls with enough force to crush any structure he could think of. A thick mist rose from the crashing of the water and hung in the air. The *smoke and smash*, Buhle had called it earlier with a wry smile. Aleister attempted to speak to his sister but she just shook her head and pointed at her ears. It was impossible to hear anything over the noise of the falls. If ever there were proof of the existence of Gods, then this surely was it.

The misty water vapour soaked his skin. He accepted the cool mist and opened his arms wide, closing his eyes and breathing in slowly. He opened his eyes and smiled at the rainbows seen through the mist as the light of the sun peered on the majestic landmark.

'Smoke and smash,' Buhle chuckled, shouting over the noise of the falls. Aleister nodded, not daring to attempt to talk over the deafening waves. The Falls dropped water into the river that flowed between two sides of a wide canyon. Buhle had told them before the journey that their destination lay in that very canyon. Glancing tentatively down, he was unsure how such a

279

destination could be reached.

Buhle spoke to her companions in their own tongue and caught some coils of rope. She marched over to a single tree standing on their lone island and began trying one of the coils around its base. Once done, she peered over the edge of the falls and shrugged.

Then she threw the remaining length over the side.

Aleister shook his head as Buhle tied another around her waist and hooked it onto the first piece. She pulled on the rope and felt it tighten. Pleased with the result, she headed over to the edge as her fellow Southerners sat by the tree and grasped the rope in their hands, adding a layer of security to the madness. It was clear what she was attempting to do, Aleister just didn't know why she had such a longing for death. Perhaps such a sight really did turn people to madness.

He looked for some kind of support from Bathos and Ariel but they too stood frozen as they watched Buhle cock her head to the side and offer them a wave.

Then she jumped backwards.

Aleister rushed as close to the edge as he could, expecting to see Buhle's body smashing against the falls and making the long and lonely journey to a watery grave at the bottom.

Instead, he saw the grinning woman bouncing her feet against the cliff face beside the crushing waves and giving him the thumbs up. He shook his head in disbelief but couldn't keep a smile from his face at the sheer audacity of the move. The woman held no sign of self-preservation. He watched her descent with a thrilled curiosity. Ariel and Bathos joined him, child-like grins on their faces as they too shook their heads and blew their cheeks out at the madness. It took a lot to shock all three of them. This was definitely worthy.

Ariel placed an arm around his shoulder and pressed her face close to his ear, close enough for her warm breath to tickle his ear. 'You're next, brother.'

His skin prickled with goosebumps as his sister twisted him around so that he could see the Southerner waiting for him with a rope and a smile that had mischief written all over it. The others sat by the tree, still clinging to Buhle's rope but relaxed enough to grin at the fear and panic that must have been obvious on his face.

He tried to protest but there was no way he could be heard over the falls. A strong hand gripped his shoulder as Bathos stood next to him, enjoying the worry in his friend's movements. Bastard would never let him live it down if he backed out now. Buhle had done it. It must be safe. Right?

Once all the checks had been made, and Aleister ensured they were done multiple times, much to the amusement of his darker skinned carers, he took his place on the edge and worked hard on steadying his breathing and suddenly racing heart. His knuckles were white with the effort he was putting into holding onto the rope and he hadn't even moved yet. After much encouragement and what looked like laughter, he shuffled back, still not far enough for the jump. He peered back over his shoulder and could see Buhle waiting patiently for him, as though this was something she did every day.

A hand caught him on the chest and there was nothing he could do but go with the motion, falling back with what he hoped was a manly scream, not that it would matter with the volume of the falls but the mind thinks weird things at times like these. The air rushed around him and the spray of the water splashed against his face and bare arms. His feet crashed against something solid and his fingers burned as they pulled at the rope for dear life. The one around his waist tightened and caught him, stopping his fall, much to his relief.

Heart thumping fast enough for him to hear its beat in his ears, he thanked The Four and slowly shuffled down the cliff face, hoping that Ariel and Bathos would have such an eventful beginning to their drop.

It took longer than he would have thought to scale the cliff face. By the time he reached Buhle, his whole body was aching and his head thumped with the relentless crash of water around him. Closer to the impact, it was overwhelming.

Eventually, he felt a tap on his back and Buhle pointed to a cave entrance next to the rush of falling water. She pressed her feet against the cliff face and bent her knees before springing magnificently back, arcing towards the gap in the cliff. She tied her rope to a sharp rocky outcrop and motioned for Aleister to do the same.

The first attempt ended with his face smashing against the side of the cliff.

So much for magnificent.

He'd settle for passable at this rate. Another three tries and he was on his backside looking up at Buhle as she suppressed her laughter.

'You pinks aren't meant for the outdoors. Best to sit in your castles and palaces in your fancy clothes,' she mocked him as he tied his own rope over hers.

'We are talented at a good many things,' Aleister huffed, blinking to right himself and pushing his fingers into his ears until he felt that his hearing was back to a good standard. 'You've just not been in a position to witness such greatness yet.'

'I long for the day for such an honour,' Buhle bowed, still enjoying her position of power.

'You know, you speak our tongue better than most. How do you know it?'

'All of our people are taught the common tongues of Takaara. Makes trade easier, when we are able to do such things. Also, we are less likely to be deceived if we can speak the tongues of our enemies. To know a man's language is to be one step closing to understanding your enemy. Only when something is understood can it truly be defeated.'

'Paesus...' Aleister muttered to himself, recognising the phrase from a book he used to read with his sister when they were kids.

He was slightly annoyed when Ariel made it inside on her first try. Less graceful than Buhle but a good deal better than his own entrance. Bathos' fumbled attempts improved his mood. Three efforts and one where his knee banged painfully against the edge of the cave's entrance. Aleister held back his joy at not being the only poor student when he saw the way the warrior hobbled over to him, wincing with each step.

'You pinks do make me laugh…' Buhle shook her head and smiled. 'Come, they will be waiting.'

The passage led further into the cave, away from the booming noise of the God Falls. The only light beamed from a torch Buhle held above her head. The rough texture of the walls and lining of the cave eventually smoothed out and twisted into an archway that watched over their heads. Aleister caught markings on the walls, small images of men and women. Some looked as though they were farming, others were clearly battles depicted on the cave walls. Some were only outlines carved in chalk whilst others were a myriad of colours that shone bright even in the dim light of the single torch.

'What is this place?' Bathos boomed, his voice echoing along the passage.

'A place of comfort, of retreat at the darkest of times. A complex series of subterranean paths and corridors that were built in a time we have forgotten,' Buhle answered.

'Glad that's cleared up.' Ariel punched Aleister in the shoulder for that one and glared at him. Sometimes she forgot that she was the younger one.

'There have been dangers in the history of Takaara. Dangers that are worse than the battles and skirmishes you would have seen. The burnings, the rebellions. Dangers that would make the great leaders of the Red Sons quake in their fancy boots.' Aleister looked down and twisted his ankle to get a better look at his filthy boots. Covered in mud and soaking wet. Not so fancy anymore, at least. 'The tales of old say that the world shook in a great quake once. Most people remember the quake, but they do not know what happened before it.'

'And what *did* happen before it?' Ariel inquired, shooting Aleister one last warning look to keep his mouth shut.

'Darkness. Terror. Shadows with teeth sharper than the greatest swords. Claws that could rip the skin of women to shreds in seconds. Red eyes that would stop the hearts of men in an instant.'

'Tales for old women to tell their children when they misbehave,' Aleister said, stifling a yawn. 'Every culture has them. We were told that the giants of the Far North would snatch us from our beds if we didn't listen to our Elders. Soon, we grew up and realised such things were nothing but warning tales.'

Buhle stopped and marched to Aleister, glaring at him straight into his eyes. Her own were not angry, more a mix of worry and pity. 'All tales bear the mark of truth, especially the ones that have outlived generations of intelligent men and women. Do not be so quick to judge such stories as fantasy. One day you may meet the very things that you have dismissed as madness. On that day, I hope you are ready, Aleister of The Red Sons.'

Aleister cleared his throat, averting his gaze from hers and finding something, anything else, to look at. He decided to focus on his chipped fingernails. Boring. But normal. 'I'll remember that...' he muttered pathetically.

'Good. We are here. Speak when you are spoken to. The wise women of our tribe are not to be mocked or joked with,' she warned.

Buhle turned and made her way down steps that had been carved out of the rocky cave structure. They ran down to a wide circular opening far beneath them. Aleister followed, raising his arms in guilt at his sister's silent reprimand and Bathos' amused chuckle. At the base of the opening, larger than the palace in Archania, Aleister feasted his eyes upon the home of the Wise Women. Lanterns lit the circular boundary and at the back of the vast space, a colossal golden head watched silently over the scene.

Aleister planted his foot on the first step and whistled. 'I thought the Falls were something. This place just doesn't let up on the awe and wonder. That thing is worth more than all the jewels in the East...'

'Just remember why we are here brother,' Ariel nudged him with her elbow, passing him on the steps as he stood frozen to the spot, staring at the mammoth treasure. 'I feel that they may treat thieves unkindly down here.'

The Wise Women were a small group of hooded women bunched around strange items. They sat amongst the candles in a ring of golden leaves. Each wore a black dress with the hood up. Around the hood, they had a tight crown of what looked like golden roses that matched the golden interlocking patterns of fabric and jewels that masked their forehead and eyes from view. Their lips were painted gold, to the surprise of none of their guests. The colour scheme was consistent at least, that had to be commended in Aleister's view.

The five women sat on black and gold cushions. Black marble stabbed up from the ground, shaped into tall chairs that kept them in their tight, upright positions. At their bare feet lay an assortment of items, some more familiar to Aleister than others.

A deck of gold-leafed cards.

Ebony daggers with intricate golden threaded patterns swirling along the handle and blade.

A small vial of what looked disturbingly like blood.

A thick piece of rope running through small bones.

Another, thinner piece of string that held together a collection of human ears.

And last, but certainly not least, a single eyeball; white with a brown circle hugging tight to the black centre.

'We have been waiting for this day for some time, Buhle Tunya.' The woman in the middle said, her voice dancing through the circle towards them. She had wrinkles beneath the golden mask and around her lips. An elder of the tribe, no doubt. 'The Sun fades behind the horizon and the threat of night creeps towards the world of Takaara. The second such night in the history of our land and one which carries the promise of more destruction and misery than the first.'

'Mother Ake,' Buhle said, dropping to a knee, bending her head and slapping her chest with an open palm. 'These are the ones you asked for. They come from the North and turn pink in the sun but claim to be of the Red tribe, just as you said.'

Mother Ake turned and smiled, yellow teeth peeking out from the golden lips. The others just sat as still as statues, waiting for their turn to speak. 'You, girl.' Ake pointed at Ariel with a long, wrinkled, bony finger. Ariel looked around at Aleister and Bathos, confused as she pointed to herself and looked back at the old woman. 'Yes, you. Come to Mother Ake. Let me take a closer look at you.'

Ariel crept forward and knelt in front of the wise woman, her throat bulging as she gulped and then wiped her clammy hands on her trousers.

'You look frightened, child,' Ake breathed. 'Do not be frightened of the Wise Women of Zakaria. There are more terrifying things to come than us.'

'That's not exactly reassuring,' Ariel said, stifling a nervous chuckle.

'No, I guess it is not. The truth is not often reassuring. It can be harsh. It can be cruel. It can be more terrifying than staring into the abyss and realising that there is something staring back. Or that nothing is staring back. It can be all those things. Such is the way of truth. Such is the way of life.'

'And death,' another of the women called from Ake's right.

'And death,' the leader agreed. 'Now, give me your hands.'

After a slight hesitation, Ariel held out her shaking hands. Aleister felt his own twitch towards the hilt of his sword. Better to be prepared for the worst than to live with the regret.

Ake took the hands and held them in her own, turning them over and inspecting them closely through her golden mask. 'You have the mark of a great leader. And you will be an even greater mother.'

'I don't think—'

'The babe quickens inside you even as we speak. It is early, but I am of no doubt you are carrying a strong and healthy daughter. A powerful woman to continue your leadership.'

Aleister tried to pull his jaw back up but it was stuck.

Usually he would have laughed at the colour draining from Bathos' face. The big man swayed where he stood until Buhle smiled and held her arm out for him. He took it with relief, his eyes unseeing as they blinked over and over again. Aleister turned back to his sister. She was staring at the wise woman, not willing to look away.

'I'm carrying a daughter inside me?' She pressed a hand protectively against her stomach. 'How can you be sure?'

'Our ways are ancient. Our methods sharpened to a deadly point over time. Trust me,' Mother Ake said. 'Or do not trust me. Either way, you are with child and your shape will soon give that fact away.'

'Thank you, thank you so much!' Ariel squealed, the news finally settling in. She leapt to her feet and into her lover's arms. Bathos had just enough time to return to his senses and steady his feet. He caught her with his trunk-like arms and laughed along with her, amazed and overjoyed with the unexpected news. They kissed and laughed and kissed again.

Aleister strode over to them and pulled them both into a hug of his own. 'Congratulations. This is joyous news. A fourth member of our team!' he kissed Ariel on the head and shook his friend's hand before Bathos pulled him in for a bear hug and swung him around ecstatically, ignoring the groans for release.

'It is your turn now, Aleister of the Red Sons.' Ake's voice drifted over, throwing a damp sheet over his sudden joy. His smile faded as he walked cautiously over to the strange woman, unable to muster up his usual confidence and swagger.

'Let me guess, I'm with child too?' he smirked, trying hard snap into his old mindset. 'I have been growing rounder by the day.' He caressed his own belly but Ake's wry smile showed no hint of humour.

'You carry something else entirely.' A hint of malice edged her soulful voice and put the warrior on guard. Not for the first time, his fingers twitched longingly for his blade. Voices sang from the weapon, pleading for an opportunity for blood. *No. Not now.*

'And what do I carry?'

'Buhle Tunya. Perhaps our guests would like some fresh air. You and Sister Nahla may escort them to the Gods' Eye. A beautiful place with one of the best views in all of Takaara.' Aleister nodded grimly to his allies before forcing a smile onto his face as Bathos and Ariel were escorted from the circle and past the golden head to the back of the cavern. Buhle and one of the wise women flanked them, guiding them in the low light and leaving Aleister with Mother Ake and the three remaining women. 'Now we may speak more frankly,' she said when the others had left.

Aleister's heart quickened as even the wry smile faded from the older woman's face. 'I would want nothing less.'

'You are broken.' Blunt, and to the point.

A simple statement but it stabbed at Aleister's heart with a dagger of truth. It was something he knew to be true but his instincts fought against the words like a man flailing against the powerful current, unwilling to admit that the end was near. 'I have been broken. The pieces are being put back together one at a time. Soon, I will be as good as new.'

'Sister Mahlaka is as blind as the cave walls and yet she can see through that lie.' The woman to Ake's left shrugged and gave a little smile of her own. 'You are sitting amongst strangers who expect nothing of you, Aleister. In a world far removed from your own. Release the shroud of pride or you will carry this burden of truth with you wherever you go.'

He sniffed and turned away from the women, nodding and smiling to himself. 'I've seen similar things before. Back in Archania. In the East. Smoke and riddles. Words that aren't words and false truths spoken as fact. Have your fun down here in the cave but know that I'm not gonna fall for this shit.'

'This *shit*,' Ake hissed, 'is what can keep you alive in the wars to come. Do not be so hasty to throw away our help.'

'We're trying to stop a war. That is why we came all the way to this place. Suffering in the heat and melting every day. We lost good men and women to get here. A war is coming if we don't make it to the capital. The Boy King is the one we need to be focusing on. Stifling his need for blood.'

'Blood.' Ake tilted her head towards the vial to Aleister's side. 'That is what he craves. What he needs. Your goal is ours, Aleister. Believe that. If you fail, everything we work for fades into dust and shall not return in a thousand generations of women. We are not cheap tricksters with the aim of amusing ourselves by fooling pink idiots from the North!' The anger and frustration grew with each word and Aleister retreated into his shell, physically shifted away from the furious woman. Even the candles flickered in fear as she continued. 'We sit here in the dark with masks to obscure the world from our eyes because we have seen the terrors to come and we are frightened. We do not wish to see anything ever again if it means we must see that which we fear the most. You have a slim chance of preventing such horrors and yet you are still too busy wallowing in self-doubt and self-pity to do anything worthwhile.'

Aleister bristled at the insinuation. 'I have witnessed horrors too.'

'The dead woman who was married to another? The one you left to seek fame and glory with a large dose of honour?' Ake laughed as Aleister's face dropped, all bravado fading away. The words hit like a slap to the face. 'What about the hundreds you have killed on the way? The men, women, and, yes, *children* who were murdered in the idea of progress Did you stop and think about what you were doing in the Heartlands? In the East? You listened to the story of men and women with tears as false as a second sun and you were blinded by the light. The arrogance of youth has meant that you never took a moment to think about what you were doing. You have seen horror, Aleister of the Red Sons. You have seen it because you were its architect.'

The accusation hit harder than a hammer to the chest. Aleister had to keep from falling back as his body instinctively fought away from Mother Ake. It felt as though the words were a crash of water hitting his face to wake himself up from a long dream. As much as he may have argued against it, he knew the words to be true. He'd fled Archania and Ella in the belief that he would become greater than both of them. He'd chased dreams of glory and clutched at the fragments of opportunity handed to him by any who passed him by. Why should he question what they were saying? There was an opportunity to prove his ability and that was all that mattered. Life was cruel and he was the fighting embodiment of justice. That's all there was to it.

'We have many tales in the South,' Ake said, her voice softening as she reached out a hand and placed it on Aleister's leg. 'There is one truth that can be found buried in all of them.'

'And what is that?' Aleister asked, fighting against the wave of sadness threatening to drown him.

'The bad guy always believes he is the hero of the story.'

'So I am the bad guy?'

'Sometimes. Not always. But sometimes. Enough for you to know that you must do a lot to repair the damage.'

'What must I do?' he asked, defeated.

'To prevent the Great War from destroying Takaara, you must do whatever it takes to ensure the Boy King does not leave the South. He must be here when the darkness arrives. He has made difficult decisions; decisions that have painted him as a monster to some. Yet, he is one of the few who can fight against what is to come.' Aleister nodded weakly. It was his aim to stop the Boy King leaving the South anyway, nothing had changed. But then again, everything had. 'You must use any means necessary, Aleister of the Red Sons. Even at the cost of your life.'

'I will do whatever it takes,' he agreed, feeling a weight lift from his shoulders at the thought of doing something that was irrefutably good.

'You will be helped on your journey. I will send a sister with you and your allies so that you can enter the capital and arrange a meeting with the Boy King. She is quite resourceful and has history of dealing with leaders...'

One of the women stood and took Aleister's hand, helping him to his feet. Beneath the golden mask, Aleister scanned her sharp cheekbones and unblemished, dark skin. Her golden lips curled into a smile that was oddly familiar to him.

'I did say that we would meet again one day, Aleister of the Red Sons. I have been looking forward to it since our incident in the East...' The voice sang to him like only one other ever had.

A magical song that wrapped itself around him like a warm blanket on a cold Northern night.

'Sister Ife will be your guide.' Mother Ake smirked, obviously amused with the reunion. 'I trust that you will take good care of her.'

'I've seen her fight, Mother Ake,' Aleister said with a snort. 'I don't think she is the one who needs looking after.'

Ife picked up the ebony daggers from the ground and spun them with a casual ease before slipping them into her belt. 'Those who plead for our wisdom offer gifts, tokens of their appreciation.' She glanced at the remaining items on the cave floor.

'Aleister does not need to leave a gift, Sister,' Ake informed her. She turned to him and licked her golden lips. 'He is willing to sacrifice his life for Takaara. We can ask no more.'

THE SHIELD IN THE EAST

K ane checked her bags for the tenth time. She knew she had everything ready but there wasn't much else to do unless she was to just sit and wait for Istari to finish his own preparations to depart. Sitting with nothing to do but worry and fret over the previous night wasn't going to do anyone much good.

Drayke had taken it well, all things considered. He'd laughed. He'd cried. He'd almost fallen over in shock. He'd drank and he'd jumped from his seat and paced over the whole tent muttering to himself, drawing conclusions from events long in the past that he felt were connected to the simple phrase Kane had spoken.

'You are my son.'

Four words.

Four words capable of turning a world upside down and inside out.

Four words that could drive him away forever.

Four words with a deadlier edge than most weapons Kane had faced over the years.

Four words.

The young man had sat back down in silence, eyes staring into space as his lips moved together and then apart, his forehead creased with concentration. He had asked for time and she was willing to give it to him. Her own mission was not yet finished and as much as she wanted to stick around to discover the next steps for the mercenary group, Istari was not willing to delay their departure to Darakeche any longer.

'Check that damn bag one more time and I will throw it in the river,' the grumpy warrior growled as he rushed around, picking up a shirt and sniffing it before cramming it into his own pack. The levity brought on through alcohol had left the famed warrior with the rising of the sun.

'You might not like me as a friend yet, but you damn sure do not want me as an enemy…' Kane warned with a raised eyebrow. The warrior just smirked back and finally tied the end of his bag and threw the strap over his shoulder.

'It would be a fight for the ages,' he scratched his beard and surveyed her under his bushy brows. 'I'm almost tempted…'

'Save it,' Kane said, jumping to her feet and heading for the exit. 'We have things to do. More important things than seeing who would win in a swordfight.'

Istari shrugged. 'No skin off my nose. Another time.'

'Another time,' Kane agreed, rolling her eyes and holding the flap of the exit open for him to crouch under. He passed her with a wink and she followed him out into the bright morning light. Already the horizon shimmered with the heat of the sun. Ben stood by the edge of the camp, speaking with two of his men preparing the camels. He gave Istari and Kane a huge smile and opened his arms as he lay eyes on them.

'A parting gift for my new friends!' he called out and pointed at the two strange beasts. Kane accepted a small hug from the tall warrior and Istari a hesitant handshake. 'These camels will guide you to Darakeche with all haste. Misunderstood beasts with hearts of gold. They are the ships of the sea of sand and you could ask for nothing better to finish your journey towards the Sultan and the city of Mughabir.'

'Thank you, Ben,' Kane said earnestly. 'You have been all that Aleister promised and more.'

'It was good to hear from him – even if his words spoke of darkness. Be careful on your journey. The Sultan has fought the Empire all his life, but he is a complex man and one who loves the scent of power. He delivers harsh punishments for those who do not amuse him. He is indeed a shield in the East but the constant barrage from the Empire has dulled his understanding of generosity and kindness to outsiders. There is a reason his son chose exile and disobeyed his father to join us. Keep one eye open at all times.'

'Two, when I can,' Kane winked as Ben helped her up onto her camel. Not as comfortable as a horse but it would have to do. Istari had already mounted his with relative ease, looking as at home on the humped animal as he did back in Causrea. He was rummaging in his breast pocket, searching for the dried, black leaves he loved to chew on his travels. He found a particularly large piece and chucked it into his mouth and began his furious chewing, ignoring the conversation beside him. He spat his black saliva onto the sand. His steed snapped its head back before repeating his action, a larger ball of spit flying further than the first. Two beasts designed for one another, she thought, struggling to hold the laughter inside.

'All the best. I hope The Four watch over you both,' Ben said, slapping the camel's side and making a few strange soothing noises to it. 'I believe a new friend wishes to bid you farewell,' he said, glancing over his shoulder to a cloaked figure approaching from the camp site. 'I will take my leave. Enjoy the East. I hope this isn't the last we see of one another.'

Kane's heart leapt as she saw Drayke's eyes peeking out from between his scarf and hood. 'I didn't think I would see you before I left…'

'Wouldn't be a very good son if I didn't bid farewell to my own mother…' Drayke said the words with light humour but Kane knew it must have been difficult for him to say. He'd had a mother when he was very young. Since her death, he had been told about her and learnt to love the woman who had missed out on so much of his life. Now there was another claiming to be his mother who had been there all the time, waiting in the shadows.

'I'm sorry.' Sorry for what? A stupid phrase but one she felt compelled to say.

'You have nothing to be sorry for,' Drayke said, his sad

eyes staring up at her. 'You and Braego were always there when I needed it. I never noticed that until last night. I lay awake thinking of all the little moments we had. Better than some folk. I would not change any of those moments for the crown. I may not be a prince but I've been rich with friends and family and for that I am grateful.'

'We can speak more on this when I return. Who knows, you could be leading The Red Sons!'

'Who knows?' Drayke laughed. 'Either way, it will be good to spend time with you and listen to more stories about my father. Braego always knew how to make me smile. He was a good man.'

'So was Mikkael,' Kane reminded her son. 'They were both fathers, great ones, in their own ways.'

Drayke nodded, melancholy showing even in the small amount of his face on show. 'Safe travels. May The Four watch over you.'

'See you soon, son.'

'Farewell, Mother.'

She was glad that the tears only began their slow journey down her cheeks when the camel had carried her away from the camp and her back was all that Drayke could see. She'd waited more cycles than she could care to acknowledge to hear that simple title.

Mother.

'The Shield of the East, in all its glory,' Istari said as they tethered their beasts. Kane paid the owners of the shelter and together they stepped out onto the main road and into the chaos of the midday rush.

Camels raced past, whipped by small, hairy men with bare feet dangling from one side of the animal. Some of the riders were even smoking long pipes as their beasts dashed past the grumpy crowds of people barging their way through the busy street. Kane had thought Archania to be cramped and overly populated.

She was wrong.

The Summer Road had been designed so that the midday sun sat straight ahead and watched over the length of the wide path. There was no order to the chaos of the movement. Men and women thrashed and punched and kicked past each other, hurrying to get to somewhere or nowhere at all. Children darted between legs as frustrated and disturbed men cried out in a language Kane couldn't understand. She even saw one pair caught up in a heated argument to the side of the road. The man towered over the older woman, spitting and cursing in the strange language. To Kane's amusement, the women bent down and took off her sandal. She smacked the man with all her force across the face with her sandal and pushed forward as he cowered towards one of the corridors between the white buildings.

'You've been here before,' Kane said, marvelling at the ease with which her companion worked his way through the bustle of the crowd and silenced screaming merchants with a glare.

'A few times,' Istari answered. '*Lahk. Na'amba kilzhun,*' he said, waving a hand and shaking his head as a merchant reached out with some back dried berries towards them. A free offer no doubt. A sample to draw the customers in. Istari was too wise for such a simple trick. 'Keep close and make sure you have your hands close to anything valuable. Funnelled streets before prayer time are the worst in places like this. Pickpockets and thieves look out for those who stand out like sheep in a den of wolves. With your skin, you're the sheep tied in a pink bow waiting to be picked off.'

'You speak the language,' Kane said, amused with the ease of how he had spoken to the merchant.

'I can get by,' Istari admitted. 'No point travelling places and relying on your own tongue. Such arrogance can lead to misunderstandings and misunderstandings lead to death in places like this.'

Kane couldn't argue with that. She'd spent enough of her role leading as an Inspector in Archania to know that trouble could be avoided if people just showed a bit more understanding. A sneer to the wrong person, a thoughtless comment. These were the things that often led to a night in the dungeons or even worse, a body lying in a pool of its blood.

'I've no idea how so many people can enjoy the crowds in this heat. It's unbearable!' Kane complained as a sweaty arm brushed against her cheek. A tall, dark-haired man squeezed past her without acknowledgement, pressing forward and towards a large building with a golden dome at its head. Three loud gongs echoed around the street followed by cries from the occupants standing on the balconies of the numerous minarets towering over the city. The rush of the crowd changed in an instant. Suddenly, they all turned as one and faced the same direction as Kane's new sweaty friend. Like a school of fish, they marched as one, no more arguing and dissent. Just a common goal to reach wherever they needed to be. Kane stood motionless as Istari folded his arms across his chest and watched the strange scene unfold. Like moths to a flame, the procession ambled towards the golden dome without the pushing and the shouting that had filled the street only moments earlier.

'We've come at an interesting time, middle of the day, sun's about to hit its peak.'

'And what does that mean?' Kane asked, puzzled by the strange behaviour.

'Prayer time.'

Kane scoffed. 'Prayer time?' she repeated. She'd attended religious events in the United Cities. Praise for The Four and worship to the One God of Light as the Empire began its poisoning of the kingdom. She thought she had witnessed fervour and faith but it was nothing to the blind loyalty of the masses marching to their destination.

'They have always shown complete faith and deference to The Four. Each facet of the Gods is worshipped throughout the day. Four calls to prayer every day to ensure that the Gods are satisfied. Sunrise. Midday. Sundown. Midnight. Four moments for each person in the city to join as one and give their thanks for the guidance of The Four. Most head to the golden temple in the centre of the city, though some prefer to worship in their own ways…' Istari inclined his head towards the market traders holding coloured beads in their hands and rubbing them with their eyes closed, lips moving frantically in prayer. It was as though they were possessed. He nudged Kane and guided her gaze to others in the crowd who were using the opportunity to slip their hands into the pockets of unaware men and women. A perfect chance for thieves and the dishonourable criminals of Mughabir, no doubt.

'It may be different to what you are used to. You may think it mad,' Istari said. 'But beauty is found in the differences we encounter. Those places and moments where we are taken away from the little bubbles we hide inside and tell ourselves that this is the world and I have all I need. Differences often lead to conflict in this world. A shame. I have nothing but admiration for those who live a kind, happy existence different to my own. They have not shed blood in anger. They have not raised a weapon or threatened in a harsh tongue. Do not be quick to mock those who lead different lives, Katerina Kane, to them, you are a stranger in their land.'

'I was not mocking them,' Kane argued, upset at the claim. She prided herself on her ability to welcome those who led different lives to her own. Had she not fallen in love with a man most would have deemed an enemy?

'Good,' Istari said calmly as the last few people drifted from the street and left them alone with the muttering merchants in the now wide and open space. 'Then it is time to meet with the Sultan. His Summer House is quite the spectacle…'

***

Quite the spectacle. That's how Istari Vostor had put it. A palace to rival any that Katerina Kane had laid eyes on. Admittedly, she didn't have much to compare it to, but still, it was a thing of beauty, that was certain.

The Sultan had a specific taste. Gold and white. Gold and white everything. The team of designers must have been given simple instructions. Make everything as beautiful as can be but use only two colours. Gold and white. In every realm, gold denoted status and power and the Sultan must have been well aware of the symbolism when this palace had been created.

'The Eastern nations have been known for their bluster and pride,' Istari explained as they walked down the smooth, white path towards the wide structure. Kane brushed her hands against the golden rail that lined either side of the passage. Opulence embodied in a single setting. 'This is an example of the lengths leaders in this part of the world will go to in order to push their chest out and behave as the peacock does. Put on the best display and prove to the world that you have the prettiest colours, the best feathers. The biggest cock.' Kane snorted at the last phrase, amused that it had left the swordsman's mouth.

'That's what happens when men are left in charge,' she claimed with a wry smile.

'I agree. Though it is an Empress who rules the dark Empire you wish to stop, remember that. Man or woman, each person is capable of terrifying things; men have just had the opportunities to prove their lack of judgement. Women deserve that chance, even if they screw things up worse than before.'

White birds fluttered past and swung around the tall perimeter hedge that enclosed the estate. The Sultan would be pleased to see that even the wildlife had taken a note of his tastes and blended in with the surroundings.

The green perimeter hedge stuck out as odd to Kane as she neared the palace. Since crossing the river that many called the border of the East and West realms, she had barely seen anything green and growing in the amongst the orange and beige. A few prickly, dangerous-looking plants with wide arms sticking out from an odd body but not much else.

Istari caught her curious gaze and surmised her thoughts. 'A true sign of opulence. Greater even than the golden lining and towers of the white palace. In such heat, it takes great effort and money to ensure such greenery thrives in such a harsh land. Only the rich and powerful can have such things and only the Sultan can afford such a large amount. A true display of power in the East.'

Kane stared at the growth with a newfound respect. She had complained about the incessant rain and eternal rolling hills of the North. Now she had been taken away, she felt a hunger and thirst for that which she had once taken for granted. Though she loved the new scenery and the feeling of something different with every step she took in this strange land, she longed for home. It was as a child being given a shiny new toy for their name's day. It may hold their attention in the short term but after a while, they long for the old familiar sights and smells of what they had grown up with.

'Greetings, friends from afar!' Kane halted her march in time with Istari as a small man with a wide, white smile greeted them with open arms. The smile never reached his cold eyes. He was clearly a man used to his role but there was no warmth in his voice, as much as he tried. 'We have been waiting for your arrival ever since we received the letter from the Council of Ten. An unexpected surprise. It is not often that nations welcome a guest from Archania and the Sword of Causrea himself! The Sultan is honoured by such esteemed guests and welcomes you to his summer home. His honour is shared by all of his subjects, myself included.' The man gave a low bow, his light grey robes rustling in the light breeze that passed him. He was bald but wore a big, bushy black beard around his thin lips. Four golden rings hung from his right ear. 'I am Haroon Yil-Haroon. I am the Sultan's most honoured assistant and it is my pleasure to welcome you to the Shield of the East, Mughabir, capital of Darakeche.'

'*Ahknan al assimar,* Haroon.' Istari gave a stiff bow.

The assistant whooped and clapped his hands together, muttering something in his native tongue. 'I had forgotten that you speak our tongue! A delightful surprise. It has been many cycles since you have been here, Istari Vostor. As always, may The Four watch over you,' Haroon said, smile brighter now and more honest. His dark eyes shone in the light of the sun as they turned to Kane. 'As for you, Katerina Kane. I hope you find your first visit in Darakeche to be one that is enlightening. We often appear to be a harsh and guarded people, but I wish for you to see our lighter side, given the chance.'

'It is an honour to be welcomed to the Sultan's

300

residence, Haroon Yil-Haroon,' Kane said, giving what she felt was an awkward bow, but the assistant did not seem to notice. 'In these difficult times, new friendships forged are of more value than the strongest of metals.'

'A reader of Paesus, I see,' Haroon sad, twisting his beard with a finger and thumb and giving an approving nod as he recognised the line. 'I believe we are to become great friends. Come, you must be hungry. The finest dishes of Darakeche are available for such esteemed guests. Let us grow fat and merry and forget for a moment the troubles that bring you to our doorstep.'

'Sounds good to me!' Kane grinned.

Haroon spun on his heel and clicked his fingers. Five guards stepped from their silent positions beside statues in the magnificent garden, alarming Kane as they fell into line beside her and Istari, marching forward and staring straight ahead as they followed the Sultan's assistant. They had been watching all this time without her realising.

'Do not let the smiles and gilded words move you,' Istari muttered so that only she could hear. 'We are walking into a lion's den and one false move will lead to our heads sitting within the beast's jaws. Stay alert. Stay on your guard. And leave the talking to me...'

Kane's throat tightened and glanced at the brown-skinned, bearded warrior to her right. She glanced at the golden ring perched beneath his nose as it glistened in the sunlight. She eyed the thin sword in the golden sheathe and wondered if she would have to face such a weapon before heading home.

She wasn't a religious woman. But in this foreign land, she found herself praying to The Four.

Praying that she would make it back home.

Back home with her son beside her.

'I have been told that my skills with your language are fair enough for you to understand without complaint or issue. If you are confused by any words or phrases that I use, please, let me know and I promise that there will be no hard feelings. I am a Sultan who is proud to be aware that the journey of knowledge and understanding is one which never stops. Even at my old age!' The Sultan's lips curled up on the one side of his mouth, offering a lop-sided smile as he eyed his two guests like a predator surveying its prey.

'Your skills are outstanding, as always, Sultan,' Istari replied with a small, effortless bow.

Lanterns hung from the high ceiling, casting an orange glow around the otherwise dark room, a shock to the eyes after the white and gold exterior. There were no guards in the room; no soldiers to keep watch in case anything happened. The Sultan was either a confident man or a very foolish one. As with most leaders that Kane had been fortunate to meet with, it was usually one or the other. A life of being given everything that your wildest dreams could conjure meant that there was bound to be a personality defect or two. It made her chest swell with pride to think of how her son had managed to turn out to be such a humble and kind young man.

A purple carpet ran the length of the room and up a collection of marble steps. At the top of the steps, the Sultan sat on a platform of cushions and fur as he peered down at the two of them. Haroon patiently waited at the back of the room by the door through which they had entered. A black covering blocked out any light to the side of the room that may have come through where there should be windows. The darkness unnerved her, as she assumed it was designed to do. Entering such a room for a meeting with the infamous leader after being blinded by the opulence and bright colours of the outside would put even the hardiest of men and women off guard. A clever tactic when one was due to negotiate.

'It is not often of late that I have been fortunate to host foreign guests in my home,' the Sultan said, pulling casually at the edge of his white beard. 'These are dark times and Darakeche stands in the shadow of a great beast, one that may be wounded, but a wounded beast can be deadly and unpredictable. I have many matters to attend to as I calm my people since the last quake. What do you have to say that is so important that I should be driven from such matters?'

Kane looked at Istari but the swordsman just stood there, eyes glazed as though bored by the whole meeting. He wasn't one for words. That left Kane with handling the task she had been sent her for. 'You know Istari Vostor, he has been a guest of yours before and he is known across Takaara as a man of honour.' She paused as the Sultan nodded, hopefully in agreement with what she was saying. 'My name, as Haroon so eloquently introduced me, is Katerina Kane. I have spent my whole life serving the people of the United Cities of Archania and I come at a time of great peril. The beast, as you mentioned, is something that I see as a disease; a plague that threatens to destroy Takaara. I have seen the light leave the eyes of dear friends and watched others leave this world engulfed in flames as a crowd of seemingly intelligent people cheered.' She stopped and took a breath, steadying her shaking voice as the nightmares flashed into her mind.

'You've fought tirelessly against the Empire for your whole life. Now, The Republic of Causrea is asking for an alliance. They do not wish for this disease to spread and feel that such a bond would be strong enough to wipe out this damned plague before Takaara is consumed.' Kane stared into the Sultan's narrowed eyes, ensuring that he knew she meant her words. 'I do not wish to see the world consumed by the fire of that Empire. My homeland is unrecognisable. I do not wish that pain upon anyone else.'

The Sultan sat back and reached for a golden cup sitting on a low table next to him. He drained the cup before placing it back on the table and smacked his lips together. Finally, he sighed and turned back to his two guests, as though suddenly realising that they were still there, waiting for his response.

'You are right. The Empire of Light is a disease. They are led by an Empress with advanced delusions of grandeur and the dream of Godhood,' he said calmly, licking his lips. 'Over the cycles, I have sent letter after letter to the kings and queens and councils around Takaara. I informed them of the dangers growing in the East and spoke of the unflinching bravery of my men and women fighting against it. Each letter I sent was followed by the same response. *We understand your difficulties but times are tough at home. Please inform us if things get worse.* They got worse. Much worse. And I informed them. The responses remained unchanged,' the Sultan spat. 'Mikkael sounded regretful but said that his hands were tied. The fool allowed Mason D'Argio, the *brother* of the Empress, to join his council. So I sent no more letters. As the nations around us fell and were swallowed by the Empire, we found ourselves alone. The letters stopped. The Republic of Causrea cared not for our plight. The Boy King in the South spoke in riddles about a greater war to come. The Heartlands did not even respond – too busy bickering over scraps of land. The only letter with any hope I received was from a man called Raven Redbeard. He sent me a long reply from the Borderlands promising fighters if a battle were to come. In return, all he asked is that his warriors be granted permission to travel freely within our borders. Now I hear that he is dead. The one leader willing to help us in our hour of need. So, tell me, Katerina Kane. Why should we help you when you did not help us?'

It was a strong question. Fortunately, Kane had prepared an answer for such an eventuality.

'Because if we don't stand together now, we won't be standing at all.' She delivered the dark statement with all the heart she could muster. Even Istari broke from his statue-like state to stare at her. 'You can hold a grudge for the shit treatment you have received in the past but that won't shield you from the wars to come. Or you can swallow your pride like a great leader and join forces with the West to take down an enemy you have longed to be rid of. The choice is yours, Sultan.'

The silence was all consuming. Kane could hear the blood pumping within her body. She could feel the hairs on the back of her neck stand to attention. Through it all, the Sultan just glared at her, taking his time to mull over her words.

The silence broke only when Haroon pushed the door open following a quiet knock. After a hurried discussion involving words in the Eastern tongue that Kane had no way to decipher, the assistant stepped back into the room looking rather more flustered than he had at any point of the day. The man rushed along the purple carpet and brushed past Kane as he made his way towards the puzzled leader.

'My apologies, Your Majesty,' Haroon called with a low bow as he knelt at the foot of the Sultan's platform. 'We have another guest. I know that this breaks protocol, but he has something that I think you need to see...'

The Sultan nodded and waved a hand to accept the unusual circumstance. He straightened his back and looked past Istari and Kane towards the door as Haroon hurried back and began another rushed conversation. Two armed guards, spears pointing to the ceiling, flanked a man with a devilish smile and intelligent, mischievous eyes. Even in this intimidating room and standing in front of one of the most powerful leaders in all Takaara, Jaxsin Mortella danced in with a swagger that displayed his confidence with his surroundings. He tipped the edge of his tricorn to Kane and Istari and took his place between them, taking another step forward so that he was at the forefront.

Kane's jaw fell slightly but she had to hold back a laugh as she caught the way Istari glared at the flamboyant fighter.

'Jaxsin Mortella, Your Majesty,' Haroon introduced the man. Jaxsin bowed dramatically low, sweeping his hat from his head and crossing it over his chest before placing it back on. 'A member of the Red Sons...'

The Sultan spat into a golden bowl to his left, his face erupting in fury at the words. 'Why would you dare to allow a member of that treacherous, despicable, *kelzeggar* group enter my hall?'

Jaxsin turned to Kane at the description and raised his eyebrows, keeping his lips tight as he snorted with a quiet laughter, clearly amused with the Sultan's rage. Kane peered down at a dark bag tied to the man's waist. Beneath it, a dark liquid dripped ominously onto the same spot of the purple carpet. She glanced behind her as Jaxsin turned away and saw that there were stains that had followed his path towards them.

Jaxsin cleared his throat and coughed loudly into his fist. 'Our group have a troubled history with your nation. We may not have always seen eye-to-eye, though, let me be clear in saying that there have been grievances on both sides...'

Kane marvelled at the sheer audacity of the man to enter the Sultan's room and utter such words.

'Not seen eye to eye?' the Sultan repeated with a venomous fury. 'Your leader stole a great treasure from me and did not return my son to face justice! This dishonourable action means that members of the Red Sons face death just for breathing within my borders. So, tell me why I should not have your head…'

Jax raised a slim finger to the Sultan and twisted his body so that he could untie the strange bag hanging from his waist. 'You should not have *my* head, because, you can have *this* one.' He opened the top of the bag and flung its contents down on the carpet. A round object rolled its way awkwardly towards the Sultan, only stopping as it bounced against the steps.

The Sultan crept forward from his perch and peered down at the object as all eyes in the room stared at the gruesome gift. Haroon darted over and knelt next to it, checking it from all sides. Kane groaned and stared up at the Sultan as she realised the significance of the gift.

'My son…' the Sultan murmured. 'You bring me the head of my son. Adnan Yil-Youssef. The great traitor who dared to defy me…'

Jax gave another flourishing bow and took a step forward, stopping only as he spotted the spears of the two guards inch closer towards him in response. 'Technically, this isn't my gift. You see, the Red Sons have been having a little clear out. We have made some changes since we last had contact with your gloriously golden self. The leaders of old have left us, fleeing to the South,' Jax winked at Kane. A quick, tiny motion but she noticed it, nonetheless. 'Your son, along with me and one other put forth a claim to become leader. Now, I'm not one for war and the glory of battle. I like simple things. But then a proposition was put forward to me, one that I simply could not pass up. One that made *sense*.' Jax punched a fist into his open palm and grinned.

'A proposition?' the Sultan murmured, tearing his eyes away from the disembodied head of his second son as the fires of his rage started to cool with curiosity. 'What kind of proposition?'

'I take the reins of the Red Sons and lead them away from your beautiful lands. Our group will fight in the North to drive out the Empire from the region and ensure that the rightful king sits on that great throne; a king who will become a great ally to Darakeche and will fight whenever you click your fingers…' Jax mimicked the action and fluttered his long eyelashes.

'The rightful king?'

'Oh, you haven't heard?' Jax giggled, enjoying his little drama. Kane suddenly realised that she was holding her breath. 'King Asher passed away last week. His brother, Drayke, has vowed to take the throne, with your help of course.'

Kane felt Istari's hand press against her back as she lost her footing for a moment. 'What?' she muttered to herself, feeling the room sway around her.

'And what proof do I have that this Drayke would be an ally to my people?' the Sultan asked, clearly warming to the idea.

Jax smiled and pointed at the still head beneath the Sultan. 'He's the one who sent the lovely gift. Chopped it off himself. Justice. This new king is all about justice…'

'Does he have the men to drive out the Empire?'

'The might of Darakeche. The numbers of the United Cities of Archania, and,' Jax wagged his finger in the air and paused, 'he has ties to the Borderlands. A united North joining with Darakeche. The Empire will crumble beneath its might.'

The Sultan clapped his hands together and laughed. Odd for a man who kept glancing at the head of his son lying in a pool of blood. Kane felt the nausea crash against her like a tide of infantrymen in a battle she had no reason for being involved in. Had her son really done such a thing, just to see himself on a throne he knew did not belong to him?

'And what do you say to such an alliance?' the Sultan asked, looking at Kane and Istari.

'You'll have the numbers,' Istari said with a shrug. 'A union with the North and West will be difficult to stand against. It is what you always asked for.'

'And you, Katerina Kane? Is this Drayke the rightful

heir to the throne? And can he be trusted to keep his word?'

Kane waited a while, swaying as the bile tasted bitter in her mouth. She winced as she swallowed the acidic spit before feeling as though she could answer without being sick. 'He is Asher's brother. If Asher is dead, he is the king of the United Cities of Archania now, though Mason D'Argio will have something to say about that. As for the question of trust,' she paused again and fought the different ideas in her mind, struggling to find an acceptable answer as all eye turned towards her. 'He will do whatever it takes to bring down the Empire.'

The Sultan grinned wide, a manic gleam entering his dark eyes. 'Then it seems that we have a deal…'

THE HEART OF THE WORLD

Aleister kept a close eye on Ife as she slashed her deadly machete through the growth of the jungle, casually whistling a merry tune. He followed the path she carved through the strange plants, sweat glistening on her dark skin. Her hair was no longer orb-shaped like when Aleister had last seen her. Instead, the hair twisted together and fell low to the middle of her back, each mesmerising wave thick enough to be used as a weapon.

She spun and swept her locks aside, wiped the sweat from her face and smiled that beautiful smile that Aleister remembered from the East.

'How are you coping?' she asked him. Even without the golden orbs, there was a magic about the woman. 'Different to the East. Wild jungles and strange animals everywhere. Danger lurks behind every tree. And there is a different kind of heat. Every movement brings with it a river of sweat that drowns the body.'

'It's a unique place,' Aleister admitted. 'But a beautiful one. Why have you returned South? When we departed, you were still supporting Sultan Youssef Yil-Rahman. You had yourself a fairly comfortable position in that dog's house.'

Ife smirked. 'Youssef is a man hardened by the long fight with the Empire. He makes poor decisions from time to time but he bears the burdens of his position better than most.

Anyway, I find dogs to be great companions…'

'He called for the death of his son,' Aleister reminded her with an incredulous laugh.

Ife shrugged. 'I know people who have done much worse. Leaders and peasants alike. Are you in a position to judge him?' That comment hit him harder than he would have liked. The words of the wise women still echoed in his mind. 'I left before I wore out my welcome. I saw the quake coming and knew that the Sultan would have no use of me once my power waned. I had a vision of the South and knew that I was being guided back for a reason. Seeing you here only strengthens my belief that this is the correct path. The wise women have guided me before and so they did so again. If Takaara is to survive, we must all play a part.'

'Do you know this region well?'

'I grew up close to here. A small town just inside the Eternal Jungle. An old childhood friend left the town to make his name in the Borderlands and I decided a few cycles later to follow. My path led me to the East and Darakeche.'

'And your friend?' Aleister asked.

'I never heard from him again,' Ife replied wistfully. 'We are close to the capital. Be prepared. We like a good fight down South…'

Aleister dropped back and out of earshot of his guide, nodding to Ariel and Bathos to grab their attention. Both looked as exhausted as he felt. Sweat drenched their shirts and their breath came in ragged starts. 'We are close. Ease your pace, we don't want to be caught off-guard and tired again.'

'You trust her?' Ariel asked, flicking her head towards Ife. Her hair stayed plastered to her head, stuck with sweat.

'What else can we do?'

'You're thinking with the wrong part of your body again,' Bathos chuckled, motioning to Aleister's groin.

'You need to focus on other things than my dick,' Aleister argued, doing his best to look offended. 'Give me *some* credit.'

'We will, when you deserve it,' Ariel laughed, placing a sweaty arm around his shoulder and pulling him close. She dragged his head down for a kiss and pushed him away. 'I won't hold my breath.'

The falls had been something. The city of Ad-Alum was another wonder making this journey worth it. Gazing up at the city, Aleister felt like an ant, such was the size of the colossal structures before him. Passing through the high well-guarded gates and entering the city felt like an out of body experience for the warrior. Usually he would be making mental notes of the layout of the soldiers guarding the walls with their longbows, the obsidian armour of the watchful men and women keeping a close eye on those entering the gate as they slipped between the large crowds of smiling people. He would have also marvelled at the black flags with the blue crown waving from all the tall houses and buildings that ran aside the wide streets clustered with market stalls and a whole host of unusual animals. Usually, he would have done all that. Instead his gaze drifted towards another delight of the foreign city.

Aleister had seen the pyramids in the deserts of the East. Forgotten structures, remnants of the past said to have housed old kings and queens from before the time of the Breaking of the World. They had towered over him, casting a shadow in the blistering sun. He had whistled in admiration and wondered how people had been able to build such things. Standing here, in the City of Ad-Alum, he stared out at a stepped pyramid with a flat top. The base levels of the structure appeared to be at least a thousand times the width of the wide street he ambled along. Its peak held the midday sun itself on its head. Reds, yellows and greens painted the structure as it watched over the great city. From this distance, Aleister couldn't make out the finer details, but he thought he could pick out the same black flags waving from poles either side of a separate row of stairs running along the middle of the pyramid, all the way to its peak.

'The Temple of the Sun,' Ife said, her chest puffing out with pride as she smiled at the open mouths of her three companions. 'I've seen it thousands of times but it never ceases to amaze me.'

'How can such a thing have been built by humans?' Bathos asked, shaking his head but never allowing his eyes to leave the pyramid.

'If the stories are true,' Ife said with a dramatic flash of her dark eyes, 'it was not built by humans. Neither were its brothers and sisters...' She clicked her tongue and pointed to their right and left, diverting their gaze to similar structures to the east and west of the city. Then again to two more further in the distance, further south. 'Four smaller temples for each quadrant of the city, built to the service of the Gods.'

The closest temples were still some distance apart, giving away the sheer scale of Ad-Alum. Aleister could barely see the two in the southern part of the city. Just the tips shimmering in the haze of heat in the midday sun.

They continued their walk through the main street, Aleister taking in the wonders. The stone buildings with their bright colours. Children pulling on an iron pump that produced a spout of water from a thin pipe sticking up out from the ground.

Eventually, they reached a crossroads in the city. The path forward arched up and continued over a wide stone bridge where families and couples peered over the edges to watch small canoes race along the clear river that ran from east to west. The crowd around the banks cheered as a young woman took the lead, pulling hard on her oars and grimacing with the effort as she edged in front of her opponent.

Ife paused and joined the onlookers, leaning against a stone guardrail lining the bridge and hollering along with the cheers of the watchers. Aleister stood beside her and found himself laughing along. He felt a sudden pull on the sleeve of his shirt and peered down, smiling at a young girl. She wore her dark hair down, a yellow headband holding it away from her dark, excited face. She gasped as Aleister allowed her to take his hand. She carefully pulled his sleeve up and pressed against his arm, her eyes widening as she laughed with glee and turned to shout something to a group of youngsters nearby. They raced over, each poking and prodding Aleister's arms as he twisted around in amusement.

'They haven't seen someone of your colour before,' Ife explained. 'They see you as something special, a treasure.'

Aleister thought of the way those in the North treated those who look different and he felt himself blush at the thought. If only adults were able to see the world through the eyes of children. Perhaps there would be less hatred and mistrust.

He dropped to his knees as the children motioned for him to come closer. They pulled gently at his cheeks and squeaked joyfully, speaking to one another in amazed tones as Aleister laughed and faked pain with each press of their fingers. He looked out of the corner of his eyes to see three children climbing their way up Bathos who looked bemused but unconcerned with the attention and Ariel holding hands with a young boy and girl as they each smiled up at her, lost in her strangeness.

'This isn't what I was expecting to find...' Aleister admitted, looking up at Ife who was watching the whole scene with amusement. Others now crowded around, smiling at the playful children and showing no sign of hostility towards the outsiders.

'That's the problem,' Ife argued, smile still shining brightly. 'We expect people to treat us how we have seen them be treated. Your people attacked and threw our people in cages. You expect the same.'

'The South has sent assassins to every nation north of its border to destabilise entire regions. They isolate themselves from the world and have closed their borders for as long as I can remember. Can you blame me?'

'Can you blame us?' Ife frowned, smile finally leaving her face. 'You have been told a version of the story that suits your people. Perhaps it is time to see things from another perspective.'

Aleister bit back his reply, focusing instead on the squeals of happiness around him. The children gave him a few final prods on the face before he stood. They each placed a palm across their eyes, blocking him from view before offering a small bow and running away.

'You may want to move to the side,' Ariel said to Aleister, tapping him on the shoulder and pointing at a large procession heading their way.

He could hear them before seeing them.

Drums pounding a quick, upbeat, rhythmic tune that poured over the streets. The people of Ad-Alum came alive with the music, tapping their feet, clapping their hands and breaking into dances with friends and strangers alike. Men, women, and children joined in with the beat as the procession made its way through the city. Bells and flutes joined the cacophony of sound lighting up the city as they drew nearer to the bridge.

Ife held her hands in front of her and twisted them to the beat of the drums before swaying her hips and smacking her rear into Aleister's hip, nearly knocking him into the river. He regained his balance to the music of her laughter as she clapped and gave him a cheeky wink. He shook his head, smiling at her playfulness. The procession was close enough now for him to see the performers.

Drums of all colours and sizes banged with bare hands and wooden sticks. The drums hung from the waists and hips of the joyful drummers who danced as they played. He saw the flutes and the bells, the dancers dressed in an array of colours, and the singers singing a tune that flowed through the air like a gentle breeze, wrapping itself around the crowd and enticing them to join in. Aleister didn't understand the words but he felt a message of hope within the sounds finding their way towards him. He had seen parades in the North but they were nothing like this. Often they had been stiff, loud, pompous affairs to display strength, often used as a way of warning the common people of what the rulers had at their disposal if they put a foot wrong. Here the parade exploded with vibrant colours and sounds, exotic dress (or little dress in truth), and involved the people of the city with the display. Hundreds of people danced through the city, singing, shouting and playing their instruments. The onlookers joined in in any way they could. And through it all, Aleister could only find happy faces.

'I don't know about you but this is not what I was expecting to find in the South…' Ariel muttered to Aleister, clapping along to the beat of the drums before snorting at Bathos' failed attempt at dancing. A few of the locals laughed with her and attempted to guide the big man through the steps. A futile attempt. He obviously had no rhythm but they loved his effort all the same.

'In all the stories I have heard, none have mentioned such joy and energy,' Aleister said, clapping along and bursting into laughter as Bathos averted his gaze from the women bouncing their chests furiously in front of him and twisting around to shake from the other end as well. The large man turned an interesting shade of red and kept his eyes on Ariel through it all, fearing a sharp reprimand should his eyes wander.

'Think I've got to save him,' Ariel said, marching towards him. 'Poor thing. You'd think he's never seen a pair of tits before! The big oaf…'

Aleister grinned, enjoying the moment as his sister grabbed his friend's large hands in her own and guided him through a simple dance as the locals around them cheered and celebrated with them, bouncing, shaking and showing more rhythm with their bodies than Aleister thought humanly possible.

The parade passed over the bridge with many of the men and women pointing at the three outsiders and waving their hands up and down to the crowds for more noise to welcome their unusual guests. Aleister nodded through it all, soaking up the attention as Ariel and Bathos continued their clumsy attempt at dancing. As the procession marched its way deeper into the city, the sounds faded behind them and left an exhausted Bathos breathing heavily and Ariel with a grin that almost reached her ears.

'That,' she said, 'was amazing!'

'I was getting the hang of some of those moves,' Bathos added with a grin of his own, repeating some of his awkward moves to the merriment of the remaining onlookers.

'Not even close! But ten out of ten for effort, my love,' Ariel said, planting a kiss on his lips.

'The final dance is a monthly procession through the city. It is an honour to take part, something many people aspire towards,' Ife said, her smile now a shadow of itself.

'Final dance?' Aleister asked, analysing the melancholy in her face.

'Yes,' Ife said with a sigh. 'Half of those in the procession will be a part of the tomorrow's full moon ceremony. The other half will be sent to the Hundred Islands east of the Black Sea in the hope of calming the warring nations who live in that harsh region.'

The Hundred Islands were a forgotten part of history in the North. Aleister had gone cycles without even hearing the name. A bunch of islands filled with warring nations too far away from the North for anyone to care. The tales of warring tribes bore similarities to those in the Heartlands – vicious feuds fought over scraps of land that dragged on for cycles.

'What does the ceremony involve?' Ariel asked, her own head wrinkled with concern.

Ife swallowed and stared down at the ground. She picked up a stray, emerald feather that must have fallen from the headdress of one of the participants in the passing procession. She rolled it around in her fingers and stared intently at the object. 'Understand that our ways are different to yours. Half of those dancing through the city will never dance again, never smile again, never hug their loved ones again. Tomorrow night, they will give their lives at the top of the Temple of the Sun. A sacrifice for Takaara.'

'She told us to stay in this room,' Ariel argued, hands on hips and doing her best impression of a worried mother annoyed with her fool of a son. Bathos just stood beside her, as he always did, glaring at Aleister for putting him in the awkward position between the siblings.

'I remember what she said. But are we really going to allow all those people to be brainwashed into dying for their bloodthirsty king? You've heard the stories about the Boy King. Can you really forgive yourself if we just sit here twiddling our thumbs whilst those poor people are led to their deaths?' Aleister had her with that one. She hated being on the wrong side of a moral argument. Saving people was what she lived for.

'Well, how are we going to do anything about it?' she said, changing the point of her attack and hoping for more success. 'It is a city that is entirely new to us and a culture that is completely foreign to our understanding. And I am guessing that you do not have a plan.'

'I have a plan,' he lied. 'At least the seed of a plan,' he added at her knowing glare. 'Find them. Speak to them. Convince them that their lives are worth living. Help them escape. There are more details but we can work them out on the way!'

'You are an idiot.'

'You are an idiot,' Bathos agreed.

'You always side with her,' Aleister argued, mocking pain at the betrayal.

'She is not an idiot,' Bathos explained. Difficult to argue with that one.

'And I don't let you sleep with me,' Aleister said with a wink and a chuckle at the way they both rolled their eyes. 'Come on, we have to do something.'

'Yeah, wait for Ife and speak with her about it,' Ariel pleaded. 'We need to focus on the original plan. There are bigger things at play here.'

'Bigger than the lives of those people who smiled and danced with us in the street? Those who welcomed us and brought us joy?'

'Yes,' Ariel snapped, as stubborn as ever.

Aleister growled and spun on his heels, pacing over to the open balcony window and only stopping when he could rest his arms on the iron railing keeping him from falling into the meandering river below.

It was a beautiful city. He had come expecting a ravaged land of savages, people fighting amongst scraps with each other and trouble hiding behind every corner. Instead, he had discovered a people more welcoming than any he had ever met. Smiles and waves seemed mandatory whenever he passed a stranger in the street and the three outsiders were even given free food from a merchant as they passed through a row of market stalls in an open bazaar before they reached the inn. The food looked odd to Aleister, bits of what he thought was chicken slathered in an orange sauce and spiked onto a small, wooden stick along with what looked like a selection of sliced vegetables. A spicy delicacy that almost blew Bathos' head off but Aleister had loved the richness of the flavours and reached for some coin, eager to buy more. The merchant was having none of it. He handed over more and placed his hand over his eyes, bowing just as the children earlier had done.

The uncertainty he had felt since leaving the cave of the Wise Women had only grown during his time in the city. He had always acted with confidence, a self-belief that shielded him from any of the consequences. Now, that confidence lay shattered like tiny shards of glass and each time he stared at the pieces, he only caught grim, broken glimpses of himself, a shadow of the man he thought he was, of the man he wanted to be.

'This isn't just about those people, is it?' Ariel leant with her back against the balcony, folding her arms and turning her head to face him. 'Still struggling with what happened back home?'

Aleister looked out across the magnificent vista on display. Beautiful trees and rivers running through bright and unique buildings. Wide, open spaces filled with happy dancing families and a bustling market free from anger and arguments. And in its centre, one of the greatest structures he would ever see in his lifetime. He'd travelled all the way across Takaara to this wonder in the South and yet it seemed that he couldn't escape his past.

'It's not just that,' he said, swatting away a buzzing fly that landed on his forearm. 'Do you remember what we used to say to each other; before we left home the first time? We used to dream of leading an infamous mercenary band, of righting the wrongs of leaders in the corrupt cities we had read about. We wanted to stand up for those people who couldn't stand up for themselves. We would be the sword and the shield of those who were defenceless.'

'And we were. We are, I mean, look at us now,' Ariel said, unfolding her arms and turning to look out at the city. 'We are standing in the city of Ad-Alum in the hope of preventing a war that could destroy the lives of those innocent people we spoke of as kids.'

'What about the lives of those people we killed? They may have had families. Wives, husbands, kids, mothers, and fathers. Brothers and sisters. Did we ever think about that when we entered battle? When we slipped into cities in the night and ended a life without a second thought?'

Ariel grabbed his shoulders and forcibly turned him so that he could only look into her eyes, eyes that were full of a keen determination. 'There are some things we have done that would have destroyed lives and upset hundreds. That is the sacrifice we must be willing to bear. That is the sacrifice of a warrior. Everything we have done, we have done with the intention of creating a better world. Never question that.'

'But isn't that what everyone thinks?' Aleister asks, realising that this was the question he had been wrestling with since leaving the Falls. 'No one intends to destroy a world. They believe themselves to be right, just like us. What if we were the bad guys?'

'The fact you're asking that means we're not the bad guys.' Bathos joined them on the balcony, stretching one of his colossal arms across his chest and then pulling it down over the back of his head with a groan. 'The bad guys don't question themselves. We do. Sometimes we mess up. Just like anyone, we make mistakes. Just gotta try to not make the same ones twice.'

'Someone's been enjoying the work of Paesus…' Ariel said, pulling Bathos towards her and resting her head against his barrel of a chest.

'The only way we can be certain that we never do something wrong is by doing nothing at all,' Bathos said, enjoying his chance to display his new understanding of war. 'And surely that doesn't sound like much fun?'

Aleister mirrored his friend's smile and slapped a hand on his shoulder. 'Doing nothing is the worst. I suppose that means that you will be joining me in tracking down those poor souls being tricked into this ceremony then?'

Bathos' face dropped and Ariel cursed as they realised the trap that they had fallen into. Aleister sniffed and pulled at his belt, tightening the buckled and grinning at his allies. 'One hour. We'll speak to them and see what they decide to do after that. No harm in a little conversation…'

'Depends who you're talking to,' Ariel growled, pushing Bathos away. 'I'll get ready. One hour, brother. That is all you get.'

The orchestra of the night played its song as Aleister crept along the streets. Even with the sun sleeping and the moon enjoying time in its place, the city was warm and sticky. A few late-night wanderers jumped into the river, splashing about and spraying the cool water over each other. The song of the crickets could be heard wherever Aleister walked; the rest of the city at rest for the night. There were a few lights still burning – in the inns, the taverns, and even a unique circular building with a hole in the roof that Ife had claimed to be a theatre. But the vast majority of the city of Ad-Alum slept in darkness. Something that he was looking to use to his advantage.

'Guards.' Bathos' voice boomed from behind.

Aleister dodged to his right and kept his back close to the tall pillar. He looked over to the opposite pillar and saw his sister mirror his reaction, adding a finger to her lips to remind him to stay silent. Bathos just continued on his path, drawing the attention of the four guards passing through the opening iron door.

'Greetings!' bellowed the large warrior, plastering on his wide smile and waving at the bowing guards. Aleister bit his lip. The guards seemed welcoming but the halberds they held were certainly not just for ceremonial use. 'A visitor to your wondrous city is lost and I wondered if such kind hosts would be able to point me in the right direction to a reputable tavern. Such a long journey has one needing a drink.'

Ariel silently pointed to Aleister as Bathos drew the four guards further away, listening to the instructions of their helpful hosts. Aleister needed no further prompt, the window for such an opportunity may be small and wasting such a chance could put an end to his night. He slipped around the pillar and crept past the distracted guard, squeezing through the open gate and jumping towards the shadows hugging close to the stone perimeter.

The large courtyard was a city within the city. At its heart, the golden Temple of the Sun. It loomed large and intimidating even from this distance. With each step, Aleister had drawn closer to the monolith but the structure was still further away than he had first thought, tricking his mind with its grand size and the way it drew all eyes towards it.

But he wasn't here for that.

Guards patrolled the perimeter of the courtyard, marching along the battlements with a casual ease that made Aleister feel that perhaps the city did not often have to defend itself. They chatted with each other and laughed together, eyes clearly diverted from the courtyard as Aleister watched Ariel pass through the gate and join him in the shadows.

'We'll go on,' she said, keeping an eye on the guards above them. 'Bathos will see what he can do to find us when he can. If not, he'll keep some of the guards distracted while we get in and out.'

Aleister nodded. It was one of the benefits of working in a team; different strategies available to them to achieve their goal. 'Let's go then, don't wanna keep him waiting. He'll be thinking that I owe him a drink now.'

'You owe us both one,' Ariel added, snapping to the wall as a team of six guards crossed the courtyard. They stepped into the light of the hanging lanterns and made their way into a tall, narrow building through an archway covered in writing. The language was foreign to Aleister so he ignored it and pressed on, looking for any sign of the people from the earlier procession.

Keeping close to the boundary, he soon found what he was looking for. A red brick building taller than the palace in Archania stood alone on the east side of the courtyard. Open

Aaron S. Jones

windows faced out with balconies on each wall of the building. He counted at least ten of them running up each side. Hanging from each balcony were huge banners with coloured hearts and hand drawn images of the blue crown and words that Aleister could not understand. At the base of the building running up to the entrance steps were a mass of vivid, colourful flowers of all types.

Aleister tapped his sister on the arm and pointed at the remarkable display. They kept low as they made their way to the edge of the outer section of the flowers. Aleister picked up a small piece of paper that had sat on the closest bunch and turned it over. He couldn't read the words but a small picture adorned the parchment, a crude drawing – most likely a child's – three people drawn with stick bodies and huge, smiling faces. They each had a massive colourful heart where their chest should be and one of the figures wore a blue crown and held a golden dagger.

'This is the place alright.'

'Look at all of these gifts!' Ariel said, astonished by the lavish display. 'The people of Ad-Alum certainly appreciate the sacrifice…'

'These people are giving up their lives,' Aleister muttered. 'I'd want more than flowers and shitty drawings…'

'You always want more,' Ariel admonished him. 'That's your problem. Never satisfied.'

Aleister scanned the front of the building and saw a cluster of guards and more shining halberds. No sign of a patrol though. The main entrance might be off-limits but if there was another way in, he would find it.

They drifted back towards the shadows and circled the building, dropping into their old habits as they scanned for any points of entrance and looked out for any complications that might arise.

'No patrols so far. Not expecting any kind of escape,' Ariel said, examining the rear of the building. 'Easy access to the rooms through the balconies and open windows.'

'Brickwork gives me enough of a chance to climb up

322

without too much difficulty,' Aleister added with a shrug. 'Seems manageable.'

'We've climbed worse,' Ariel said, as though this was a completely normal way to be spending a pleasant evening. 'Remember that night in Denbar? Or the climb in Starik? I swore I would never be dragged into one of your dumb schemes again after that one.'

'Starik,' Aleister grinned, nodding his head and chuckling at the reminder. Just the name alone brought back fond memories. 'Hadn't even made it out of the United Cities and already you were hating my lead. I thought I was done for.'

'Good job the rope held,' Ariel said, glaring at him and pressing the rope to his chest. 'You might need this. Not trusting the brickwork.'

'I assume I'm going first?' Aleister cocked his head to the side before dodging back and away from the light-hearted slap. 'Stupid question.'

'Most of yours are.'

Aleister took the rope, still smiling, and trudged over to the rear of the building. It took a few swings and a snort or two from his sister but eventually, he managed to loop the rope around one of the balcony's bars. He tied the falling piece of rope around his waist as Ariel took the other end.

He pushed one foot against the wall and tested his weight against it, pleased that he wasn't going to drive a boot through shoddy workmanship. He gave a thumbs up to his sister and began his ascent. It was slow going. Many cycles had passed since he had last attempted such a feat, but he knew the steps. Keep a tight grip and trust your body, and your partner. Now wasn't the time for nerves.

Each step brought with it an increased confidence. Aleister licked his lips and kept his eyes on the target as the balcony appeared closer and closer. Easy. Just like riding a horse. No matter how much time you spent away, it all came flooding back once you jumped onto the beast.

'Fuck...' Ariel's curse broke the lovely bubble Aleister had found himself in. He peered over his shoulder and felt his head sway and his vision blur as he saw his sister waving wildly and pointing towards the courtyard. That could mean only one thing.

A patrol.

'Shit,' Aleister added his own curse and pushed himself forward, tensing his body and feeling his muscles ache with the strain as he quickened his pace. Ariel would need to get to the shadows quickly if she were to hide from the oncoming patrol. He had to be quick. She still held his rope, ensuring he would not fall. If it meant her capture, then so be it. She wouldn't let him fall. He knew that.

Just as he knew that she couldn't be captured.

Not now.

He grabbed for his dagger and slashed wildly at the rope. Four powerful hacks and it flew free. He knew what was coming and was ready for it. His fingers burned as they clawed at the wall, skin ripping from their tips before finding a groove. The muscles in his arm ripped as his body jolted, caught between hanging on and falling to his death. He glanced down and blew out a sigh of relief as Ariel caught the falling rope and rushed towards the shadows. She knew that there was nothing more she could do. It was better for her to save herself than to stare helplessly at him and risk capture for them both.

Aleister gritted his teeth with the strain and took a deep breath. He looked up at the balcony and weighed his options. He could hang there a bit longer but sooner or later, there was only one way for him to go. He judged the distance. Perhaps he could make it to the balcony. A risk. But a necessary one.

That was when he heard a conversation beneath him.

He looked down and saw three guards standing together in the darkness of the building's shadow. One of them lit a match and passed it to his colleagues, each lighting a long, black stick hanging from their lips and inhaling, long and slow. He'd seen the things before. Not faze, but something that could be just as addictive. A calming smoke that relaxed the mind and eased the muscles. He pushed the thought of faze out of his mind and tried to focus on his current predicament.

His fingers started to slip from the crevice in the brick and he pulled tighter, praying he would last for long enough to leap up to the balcony. He tried to pull up further but he didn't have the strength. Looking down, he hoped that he would not land on the guards, they were innocents going about their duties. It wasn't their fault that he had been so foolish. Bathos and Ariel were right. He should have stayed in his damn room.

A loud bang sounded off in the distance, distracting the three guards. Instantly, they dropped the sticks and stamped out the fire, all gazing back towards the entrance of the courtyard. They dashed away without a word, halberds glinting as they entered the lantern light.

Aleister breathed a sigh of relief that his fall would not lead to their deaths. He had enough on his conscience right now.

'*Alluhs bay witt ei!*'

Aleister snapped his head up just as his fingers slipped and his breath caught in his chest. A strong hand clutched at his wrist and held him tightly, his legs dangling perilously. 'One moment, my friend,' the voice said in clear Northern.

Aleister gazed up at his saviour. A local with sky blue eyes – an unusual sight, certainly in Aleister's view. He had not seen the dark-skinned people with anything but dark eyes to match. The effect was strange but wondrous. The man pulled hard, straining to pull Aleister towards safety. Aleister finally grasped at the balcony and crawled forwards, joining his saviour on the carpeted floor.

'Well, this is a surprise and a Gods-given delight,' the man said with a joyous chuckle. 'It is not often I find new friends dangling from the walls of my room. And a pink one! A sign that this night is special, indeed. Come, my friend. Join us for one last drink to the Gods and tell us your story. Tell us why you were climbing my wall like a spider in the night.'

Aleister laughed darkly and waited until he had his breath back. He sat up and smiled at his new friend. 'I will tell you my story. But it is yours that I am most interested in.'

'Then that is what you shall have. My name is Mathusi. It means helper in my language. They say the heart of the world can be found in stories, so let us share ours and find this heart together.'

'That sounds good to me.' Aleister accepted the hand offered to him and winced as he was pulled back to his feet. 'My name is Aleister.' He returned the now familiar bow in greeting before chancing his luck. 'Don't suppose you have any Archanian whiskey?'

Mathusi tutted and shook his head, his stunning eyes glinting in the moonlight. 'My friend, after the drink you have tonight, you won't want such horrors to pass your lips ever again…'

UNDERSERVED

'Starik was the lesser of the three cities. A lone city in the middle of the wetlands just south of Archania. A forgotten, little brother of no real importance. It had once been a thriving kingdom with ideas of progression. The Northern Wars had put an end to that. The king of Archania tore through the land, ordering the burning of villages and towns his company passed and killing any who defied him. A fair few of his own men and women tried to help him see sense. A few hangings later and the rest got the message. Stand or swing. It was their choice. A simple one in the end. The king strolled through the proud kingdom and sneered as it fell to its knees, clinging to its last breath in the hope that its death would be a quick and painless one. Instead, the king demanded that the kingdom be named a city. In return, it would be welcomed into the newly christened United Cities of Archania. The greatest kingdom in all Takaara, the king had claimed. What could they do but accept such a deal? Everyone knew the alternative.'

Sly stared across the campfire, doing his best to not show his complete lack of shits for the story. They knew that they needed to get bloody and soak in the red stuff. Didn't need a history lesson to do that. 'Point me to the bastards and I'll cut their fuckin' head off,' he growled.

The red-cloaked bard shrugged and continued playing with the stick in his hand, drawing images in the mud. 'That's your prerogative. History is something we can all learn from. It is only in learning from history that we can ensure that the mistakes of the past are not repeated. They leave scars and we do not wish to open old wounds.'

'Once they are dead, the old wounds don't matter so much,' Sly informed him, pushing his tongue through a gap in his teeth.

'Death is not the end of the story. In this case, it was just the beginning,' the man argued. 'The people of Starik hate Archania. They feel looked down upon. Treated like fools and ignored in the council and left out of all the big decisions. They despise the Empire of Light and hold annual parties celebrating the thought of independence.'

'Then why aren't they the ones storming this prison?' Sly asked as Kiras took a seat between him and Cray, passing them each a cup of ale. A pre-fight drink to calm the nerves. Not that Sly ever had nerves. At least not ones he mentioned out loud.

'I'd been wondering that too,' she added, frowning at the speaker. His name was Danil, or Danar. Or Danvir. Or maybe it was Alan. Sly wasn't great with names. No need to remember them when you expected folk to be dead within a week.

'They are paid well for keeping the rubbish of Archania. A place for all the waste to end up from Norland and Archania. Yet another reason for the locals to hate the leaders of the United Cities but it is difficult to turn away such gold and silver. The people live happy lives, comfortable lives. They just try to ignore the fact that they are a part of the three cities.'

'Couldn't they just use that silver and gold and pay for an army?' Cray asked, speaking his first words in over two days by Sly's calculation. 'Then they could attack Archania and have their revenge.' It was simple in his mind. Make up for the embarrassing loss by destroying your enemy.

'They could. And it has passed the minds of their citizens. But they are not foolish. Why risk their comfortable lives by rolling the dice on something like a battle against a well-defended and most likely, well-trained army?'

'For honour?' Sly argued, giving his own shrug.

'And how much is honour worth?' Danil asked, leaning towards the fire and throwing his stick into the flames.

'Honestly?' Sly grabbed the stick from the fire, not even flinching as the flames tickled his fingers. He dug the pointy end into his teeth and flicked out a bit of meat that had been annoying him all evening. 'It's worth shit. Especially when you're dead.'

'So maybe you do see things from their point of view.'

'Not much I could do with gold and silver,' Sly argued. 'Point me in the direction of the fight and I'll be there with an axe in one hand and a hard cock in the other. Nothing else gets the blood flowing like that.'

Kiras snorted and even Cray displayed the shadow of a smile.

'Not much you can take when you're bones,' Sly continued, enjoying the talk now. 'That's why I spend my time making sure I'm the better fighter. Or, I have the bigger axe.'

The sun wasn't up yet but Sly could see the prison. A day's ride from the city of Starik, it sat between beside a range of mountains, nestled away from the world and able to live its grim life without the interference of others. The prison had obviously been built with the practicalities in mind. A tall, stone rectangle stood as the perimeter boundary of the prison with iron spikes to intimidate anyone daring to escape the fortress. Didn't need to look pretty, even if it was all the folks inside had to look at for the rest of their miserable lives.

'Baldor's somewhere in there…' Kiras said, tense as a bowstring. 'We need to get him out.'

'That's why we're here,' Sly said, cracking his back and swinging his arms to each side, twisting his hips. Best to limber up before a good fight. Cramp could be the difference between life and death in the heat of a battle. 'And why this bunch are here.' He stuck a stubby thumb towards the cloaked warriors standing on the hill, waiting on the edge of the line of trees. 'Still, those walls don't look too promising…' he added, staring at the barriers standing between Baldor and freedom.

'No need to worry about the walls,' Danil said with an air of confidence as he tiled his head up and gazed out at the layout of the fortress. 'That is why we are here. The wall will be of no concern when we march forward.'

Sly had fought in enough skirmishes to know that grand promises were easy in the light of day but were like water slipping through the fingers when the darkness of battle descended. Words were easy. The actual fighting was the hard part. Sly certainly wasn't going to be making any rash claims or believe anything said to him by these newcomers. He had trust in those he had fought alongside and that was it. 'Take that wall down and the prison will be as good as ours.'

'What are the defences like on the inside?' Cray asked, grimly staring at the prison.

'One hundred guards, give or take,' Danil said with a shrug. 'Trained at keeping starving, exhausted prisoners in their chains. When faced with a battle, they will fall apart.'

'And the layout?' Kiras asked, all eyes facing the same way.

'Barracks to the east for the guards. Cells to the western side. Between the two main parts of the prison, there are scattered buildings built for the purpose of keeping the prisoners busy. A food hall, a small area of land for farming, wood chopping, splitting rocks. Pointless work apart from keeping them tired and occupied. The majority of the camp is cramped as the buildings run all the way to the boundaries. A few guards wander the battlements but they never have need to do anything so there will be points when they will be susceptible to an attack. Honestly, they won't be expecting this. We could attack at any time and we would have the element of surprise.'

'Then there isn't any reason for us to wait much longer,' Sly argued. 'Get your men ready and sort that wall out. My axe is crying out for the red and I'm not one to disagree.'

Kiras nodded and turned from the watching group of warriors. 'I'll get Socket.'

Sly growled. He hadn't even looked at the old archer since their falling out. In his mind, the old man was nothing more than dirt. Still, no one could deny that they could use his skills in the battle to come. An expert archer can be priceless in a fight. Useful for taking down targets from afar but also for the way they view the battle. Sly only saw battle from the hot centre as the bodies begin to fall. Archers learned a different way of seeing things. Standing from a distance with a cool perspective as they watched the hacking and slashing of the crude but effective weapons their fellows used. Sly could never do it himself, but he appreciated the art of archery. 'Just tell the fucker to keep out of my way, or he'll be a blind archer by nightfall.'

'There are more than enough enemies for you to keep busy Sly, without attacking one of yer own!' Kiras called back.

'He ain't one of us no more,' Sly muttered under his breath, stalking off towards the woods and leaving a bemused Danil with the stoic Cray.

'Is he always like this?' Danil asked the grim-faced warrior.

Cray shrugged. 'Nah. Sometimes he's a fuckin' nightmare on two legs. You've seen his happy side.'

Sly heard the conversation, even from the distance.

He smiled and trudged off into the shadows of the trees.

***

'Perfect timing,' Kiras said as the sun began its fall over the mountains. The experienced fighter had stayed silent since informing Socket of the attack, keeping to herself as they prepared for the battle. She had daubed her face with the black soil of the earth around her, painting a thick, dark line that crossed all the way from one side of her face to the other, crossing over her eyes and ridding her skin of any glare from light. Sly loved the look. She was ready for blood and the world knew it. The girl looked like a Chaos demon risen to life and they would be all the better for it.

'You're copying me,' Kiras sneered, watching Sly cut his forearm slowly with the edge of his axe and then dab two fingers to the wound. He pressed the red blood with his two fingers under his eyes, creating two red lines under each. He wiped the leftover blood against his teeth and smiled at the beautiful female. 'I should be flattered. But you look fucking disgusting.'

'Then it must be working…' Sly's growl rolling into a barked laugh. 'They won't want to fight this cunt when I'm racing their way with my axes waving wildly. Break their mind and the body will fall.'

'That sounds too intelligent for you.'

'I love to surprise,' Sly said, licking his dry lips and tasting his blood. He paused and caught the distant look in his friend's eyes. 'We're getting him out of there, you know.'

Kiras nodded, sniffing and wiping the back of her hand over her eyes. She nodded frantically and starting biting at her filthy nails. 'Yeah, I know. I'll slaughter the whole lot of them if he has been hurt.'

'We both know that he will have been hurt. No two ways about it. He's a prisoner and a big fucking one at that.' No use masking shit with gold. Shit is shit, anyway you look at it. The smell usually gives it away.

'Then I guess I'm slaughtering the lot of them.'

'Aye. I'm with you on that.'

Kiras clenched a fist and sighed, her head twisting from one side to the next. She scratched her shaved head and tapped her right foot on the ground. Faster. Faster. 'I should have gone south with you. I should have been there for him…'

'You're here for him now ain't ya?' Sly said with an incredulous chuckle. 'Bane fucked us over. It's his fault Baldor is in there. No one else should be carrying that burden. Baldor knows how you feel and he knows that you would have been there if you could have. But you're here now and you can bring the hells with you to get him the fuck out.' Sly surprised himself. He wasn't usually one for speeches but the girlie seemed like now was the time for one. She needed a clear head if she was going to fight to her best so Sly was willing to do whatever he could to keep her on the straight and narrow. Even if it meant saying a few stupid words.

'You're not bad ya know,' Kiras said with a sad grin. 'As much as you might wanna be.'

'Bad at what?'

'This leader shit. Used to think you'd be too much of a mad cunt to follow. Now I'm not so sure…'

Sly frowned and cursed, giving his best snarl as he struggled for the right words. 'Don't get any stupid ideas. I'm a good leader cause we're heading into a fucking prison to slaughter the cunts hurting our friend. Any other time and I'm the mad bastard you always knew.'

'You're always the mad bastard. That's what I need right now.'

'Then that's what you got.' Sly wiped his hands on his shirt and pressed a finger hard against a nostril, blowing out a stream of snot. Kiras had that disgusted look on her face that seemed more familiar to him. That's what he wanted. 'Come on, follow the mad bastard. We got folk to kill.'

***

Seventy warriors draped in red. Not great numbers but enough to give them a fighting chance if Danil's information was right. Probably wasn't. But that was the fun of battles. Shit never goes the way you plan it to, and each fight is different to how you expected. Kept things interesting at least. No other job like it.

The dark of night had fallen now, supporting their cause as they marched towards the prison. Sly watched from the back beside Cray as four groups of the Magi assisting them carried tall ladders between them, rapidly moving down the hill and towards the lightly guarded prison.

'Suppose we better get moving,' Cray said sliding his sword from the sheath and spitting on the floor. 'Care for a wager?'

Sly smirked. 'Drinks for the night on the loser?'

Cray chuckled and started moving forwards, following the ladders on their way to the prison. 'Perfect. No cheating.

Clean kills only. If someone else helps out, it don't count.'

'Fine by me.'

Sly raced down the hill and blew a kiss at Kiras but she couldn't be distracted, so intent was she on the task at hand. She was ready for blood and the Gods wouldn't be able to stop her now. He knew that look and he was staying the hells out of her way.

She'd mess up his kill count if he didn't.

His heart beat loud enough for him to hear it in his ears. The familiar battle lust grew with each pound of his boots on the grassy hill. Ladders slammed against the walls of the prison and he cursed that he wasn't the first to climb them. Still no signs of the enemy though. That had to be a good thing. Made getting in easier.

A faint glow softened the darkness above the walls. As Sly neared the wall, he could hear the cracking of flames. He picked up his pace and leapt against the rungs of the ladder, his boots flying from the ground and finding a rung with ease. He rushed up the ladder, growling as he caught up with the warrior ahead of him. He fought the urge to pull at the man's ankle and chuck him from the wall, reminding himself that there was a battle to be fought and his lust for violence would be sated before the rise of the sun.

Instincts kicking in, he followed the fighters in front of him and threw himself down the rope on the other side of the battlements. He kicked against the wall and slid down, ignoring the burn against his palms and leaping to the ground, dropping into a crouch. He turned and raised his axes high in the air, glaring wildly and looking for the fight.

Only, there was no fight.

The pounding of blood in his body continued but the wild fury slipped from his face, replaced with a confused frown. The red cloaks had their weapons in hand – a mix of swords, spears, bows and shields. They glanced around nervously, walking slowly around a colossal fire burning intensely in the centre of the courtyard. The men and women who had just stormed over the wall with an eager will to kill and maim were now standing around, clueless and baffled. Water had been poured onto the rising heat inside them and left in its place a cool bewilderment.

'Stay together!' Kiras yelled as she surveyed the scene, glaring at the pockets of fighters creeping away from the bulk of the small army and searching for the inhabitants of the prison. 'Stay together until we can work out what the fuck is going on.'

The last remaining warriors dropped over the wall. Kiras called to a few of them, bellowing at them to stay up there and keep an eye out for trouble. Sly caught Socket skulking along the battlement, trusted bow in hand. He felt the disgust burn inside and turned away, looking for something to hit.

Cray almost bumped into him, almost offering him the perfect opportunity.

No, probably for the best if he let this one slide…

'Where the fuck are they?' Sly asked, prowling the courtyard like a trapped animal.

'Something's up…' Cray said, eyes everywhere.

'Boss!' one of the red cloaks screeched, crouching close to the fire. Danil ran over to the man as fast as his long legs could carry him. Sensing something was wrong, Sly followed closely. 'Burned them. Burned them all…'

Sly peered over Danil's shoulder and swore under his breath, turning from the morbid sight and biting his lip. Bodies. So many bodies. This fire wasn't there to keep them warm at night. It was designed to destroy the corpses of the men and women who had been trapped within the prison walls. Men just like Baldor…

Sly looked around for Kiras but she was distracted, lost in conversation with one of the red cloaks. He marched over to her, running a nervous hand through his hair and, for once, thinking hard about what the right words would be.

'What's up?' Kiras asked, noticing the dark look on his face.

'Look, girlie…' Sly began, licking his lips furiously and clearing his throat. That's when he heard it. The rhythmic stomp of boots on stone. The sound of disciplined marching in the distance. 'Draw your fucking weapon, it's time for blood,' he growled, spinning around and roaring to the red cloaks. 'Weapons out! Kill any fucker standing in your way!'

'Sly…' Kiras said, a warning tone edging his name.

'Not now,' he snapped back, spinning his axes and marching forward to the growing sound of the oncoming soldiers. They turned the corner in the distance, marching past a long, wide wooden building. Dressed in shining silver mail with long, gleaming white cloaks and pristine armour and helmets, the soldiers moved as one, making their way towards the red cloaks with steely eyes and grim expressions on their face. The spears and shields gripped tight looked as though they were brand new, shining in the firelight.

Sly stormed over to Danil and dragged the man up from his crouched position, gripping the collar of his cloak and forcing the petrified man to look him in the eyes. 'Untrained guards. That's what you said. A hundred untrained guards.' He kept his voice low so that the others wouldn't hear him. No use spreading more panic than necessary. 'Now, I ain't one for numbers, but that sure don't look like just a hundred. And they damn sure don't look like untrained fucking guards!'

Danil shook with fear, his watery eyes racing from Sly to the army marching towards them. 'The Empire, they made it here first…'

Sly growled and threw the weak man away. He placed two fingers beneath his tongue and blew log and hard, alerting all the red cloaks his way. 'They have the numbers and they are trained soldiers. Give them an inch and they will take a mile. There's only one way we can win this,' he bellowed, staring into the wide eyes and smooth faces of the men and women shaking in the dark. 'Slaughter every last one of them. These fuckers don't seem to take prisoners…' He glanced at the bodies in the fire and looked away, remembering his time in the dark dungeon where he had begged for any scrap of light, anything at all. Back then, he would have cut his own cock off to see a light like this one. 'There's no escape. Hit them before they hit you.'

Cray smirked and twisted his sword through the air as he stepped past Sly, the roar of the red cloaks ringing in their ears.

'Kill the fuckers.'

'Aye, kill the fuckers.'

Sly Stormson's axe pulled free from some poor fucker's head, spraying blood through the air and cutting free from the metal helmet with a piercing wrench. The usual sounds of battle filled the air but Sly was used to it. In fact, he thrived on it. The screams – both rage-fuelled and terrified, blending as one. The crunch of shields diverting what could have been fatal blows from spears, swords, and hammers. Arrows whistling through the air and landing with a cold thud in their targets. Cries of warriors unaware if this could be their last moments alive. He'd been through it all. The trick wasn't to block any of it out, they could be useful to a good warrior. The trick was to use the sounds, use the emotion around you. The trick was to kill them before they killed you.

He leered around at the bloody chaos and licked the blood splattered on his lips. Might be his own. Might not be. Didn't matter either way. Tasted the same. All men had the same taste in their blood. Black, white, tall, short, those who liked men, those who liked women, those who liked both… All tasted the same when their blood splashed over you. He glanced up and caught the sight of a tall pole with a black flag flowing in the wind. A white sun shone in the middle of the waving flag. Standards were important in battle to those raised away from the Borderlands. Sly knew that. Usually held where the most important folk stood – a symbol to rally around in battle and lend courage to those fighting the good fight. Sly had a sudden idea.

He'd take that fucking flag and piss all over it.

That would show the shiny fuckers what it was worth.

He slammed a shoulder against the nearest shield and bought himself the slightest of openings for his axe to slip into it. Aware of the fragile nature of such advantages, he hacked away with his axe, smirking at the pained screams that followed each swing. He shoved his shoulder again and the shield retreated, opening the gap in the line of soldiers and allowing a small charge of red cloaks to rush between the row of enemies with a great cheer. They didn't have the numbers but they had momentum now and that was something all victors needed in a battle. Momentum, luck, and a shit load of pointy weapons.

Sly leapt forward and slammed the butt end of his axe straight between the eyes of the soldier standing fearfully with his shield out wide. The soldier tripped back with the attack and fell to the ground with a grunt, his eyes closed and his spear coming loose from his gloved hand. Sly didn't miss a beat. He swung his axe with precision, cutting straight through the fallen man's throat and opening up a fountain of blood.

'That's four…' he muttered to himself, turning from his latest victim and scanning the battlefield for the next one. Three lines of trained soldiers stood in his way, blocking that bastard standard from him and the piss brewing inside. A daunting task for most men.

Sly grinned.

If battles were contested on which army had the most expensive armour, then the red cloaks would have lost a long time ago. But Sly knew that wasn't how things were done. Firelight bounced off the shiny silver but there was no fire in the eyes of these soldiers. No amount of training could compensate for experience and they were looking at warriors who had looked death in the eyes and sneered. He could see Kiras flying forwards with her twin blades, whipping them forward with a fury that would scare the Gods. No wonder the bastards' knees were shaking as their eyes glanced from the furious woman and then across each side of the lines, as though waiting for the first one to break so that they too could flee without the shame of being the first. Some folk just didn't have the stomach for it. Sly saw one young soldier flinch as he watched Kiras, with her smoky make-up masking her eyes, stab a blade straight through another's throat and spin into the next strike, taking a head clean off the shoulders. Sly went for the one who flinched.

This wasn't the place for pity.

His axe ripped through the shiny helmet easier than hacking through a young tree. The eyes grew wide and then lost their fear, lost their light. Lost everything apart from a cold, dead glare.

'Press forward!' he heard a voice order from the back of the shiny soldiers. Some idiot without a clue as to how the battle was going no doubt. 'Wipe these heathens from the world! For the Empress!'

Sly dodged a spear thrust and ducked towards his attacker. He stamped on the soldier's boot and brought his knee up a moment later, catching him square on the face and opening a stream of blood from the man's nostrils. No time to stop there. The soldier lurched back, throat exposed. Easy. Sly roared, pulling his arm back before launching it forward, axe tearing through the unguarded neck. His next move was to dodge another spear. Then a high block with one of his axes just twisting another high and safely away. He spun to launch his own attack, only to find a spear mere inches from his face. For the first time in the battle, it was Sly's turn to flinch.

He saw the arrow sticking out of his would-be killer's eye. Glancing up on the battlements, he offered the briefest of nods to Socket, the old archer already readying his next attack but still able to grimly nod in return. He may dislike the archer right now but the bastard had just saved his life.

Sly growled and doubled his efforts, ripping through the line of warriors with an increased intensity. He buried an axe deep into the back of the nearest enemy, pulling it free with a kick against the dead man's shoulder and pushing the body onto the bloody ground.

'That was my kill…' Cray said, annoyance clear on his usually impassive face as his bloodied sword hung long in his right hand.

'Don't see your name on it,' Sly laughed, whirling away. 'That's six!'

'Fucking bastard…' he heard Cray mutter as he continued his bloody trail to the flag.

The red cloaks were attacking with confidence now, seeing the fear in their enemies' movements. The spears shaking in their hands and the nervous steps back each line took as the Borderland warriors led the charge forward followed by the fury of the vengeful red cloaked Northerners. Sly was even surprised to see Danil standing and leading his own group of men, a bloody spear in his hand, taken from one of the enemy soldiers. The Northerner roared and thrust the weapon straight into the heart of a defenceless opponent, screaming with delight.

'Attack! Attack for your brothers and sisters!' Danil yelled, voice breaking with the effort. 'Rid your homeland of these monsters from the East!'

The cheer of the red cloaks faded as another sound took its place. Trumpets from the north of the courtyard in the distance. The Eastern soldiers dropped back as one at the sound, the front line dropping to one knee and throwing their shields forward as the line behind inched forward and placed their spears on the shoulders of their allies, creating a wall to stop the steady advance. Sly gazed longingly up at the standard still waving in the night. Then the sound of boots filled the air for the second time that night and he muttered a curse to himself.

'More warriors,' Kiras simply stated. 'A shit load more warriors...'

Cray hobbled over to them, favouring his right leg as Sly spotted a nasty looking wound leaking blood from the other. The warrior waved away the look of concern and stopped beside them. 'Numbers weren't in our favour to begin with. Worse now, even after some killing.'

Couldn't argue with that.

'Gotta do some more killing then,' Sly argued. He scanned the environment, searching for any way to use the cramped structure to their advantage. He waved Danil over, the inkling of a plan in his mind. 'There's no way we win this fight with a head-on assault. Too many of them.'

The three faces staring back at him were pissed off with the admission but none of them argued. They were not fools.

'We are not giving up,' Danil said, the iron coating his voice pleasantly surprising Sly. He thought the man would have been the tail between the legs type but he was happy to be proven wrong. 'I've seen what they do to those they capture in battle.'

'Then that's off the table, if it was ever there in the first place,' Kiras said. 'Any ideas?'

Sly nodded. 'Spread the soldiers we have to all the corners and clog the alleyways. Let them come to us. Numbers mean nothing if we can force them between the buildings, and rotate our own warriors. We can pick them off and limit their advantage. Use our archers to keep them on their toes and pick them off until they give up or die to the last man.'

All three looked to each other and then back at Sly, slight shock on display. He frowned at them, puzzled by their reaction.

'You're sounding more like the chief every time you speak,' Kiras said with a pleased grin on her blood splattered face. The ashen make up had begun to drip and create a horrifying image as she started to chuckle. 'That blood is turning your beard red. Raven would be proud.'

'I'll get the message out,' Danil said, raising a hand in salute and rushing away before Sly could protest the motion. This only increased Kiras' laughter and even Cray joined in.

'Not you too…' Sly growled at him.

'We make it out alive and this will be something to talk about over a drink,' Cray said, marching away to the nearest group of allies to pass on the orders. Only Kiras stayed.

'Girlie…' Sly began before Kiras cut him off, holding a finger up in the air and stopping him.

'Baldor must be in one of those buildings,' she said, looking to the buildings lining the east of the courtyard. 'We go in, the four of us. Including Socket. There's not much more we can do out here. If I'm going to die, I want to see him again. I want to know his fate.'

Sly opened his mouth to respond but couldn't find the right words. Instead, he nodded and rubbed his thumbs along the handles of his weapons, itching for something to kill. It would be easier to do that. Words were too difficult sometimes.

He rubbed his jaw, attempting to stretch out the pain of the last hit. A lucky shot, Sly thought. The spear had caught him side on and he hadn't ducked in time. Still, he had managed to reach the side door and barge his way through. Socket had put down the bastard with the lucky shot so all was right with the world. Or as right as it could be in the middle of a bloody battle.

The four Borderlanders stood together in the dark entrance, the screams and roars of the battle muffled by the thick walls and doors. The sounds faded further as they looked into one another's eyes, their grim determination of what may be at hand silencing anything else.

'We get Baldor,' Kiras reminded them, voice even and unwavering. 'Then we get the hells out of here.'

Three nods. Nothing more needed to be said.

The building ran most of the length of the courtyard. Each side had tiny rooms blocked with iron bars. Sly walked along the corridor, peering into the rooms and grimacing at the sorry state. The first rooms that he looked in were empty. Messages had been scrawled in blood and shit, a warning to any who pass.

THEY ARE COMING!

ONLY THE RIGHTEOUS WILL SURVIVE!

CHAOS IS UPON YOU!

ONLY DARKNESS CAN OVERWHELM THE LIGHT...

Each room had a small bucket with a funky smell that made even Sly wince upon closer inspection. There was nothing else. Nowhere to sleep in comfort. Some of the rooms had manacles against the brick wall and rusted chains dangling free. This was a place of pain and death. Even the dungeons Sly had struggled in when captured in Archania seemed a comfort compared to this.

Further down the corridor, they began to find occupants.

Kiras visibly perked up at first, delighted to clutch at the thought that her best friend could still be here. Then she saw the state they were in. She pushed the iron gate open and it swung without conflict. Just a creaking cry before the gate stopped and allowed a closer look at the poor prisoner. Sly followed as Cray and Socket continued their search.

Kiras knelt beside the woman, wrists still attached to the manacles and pleading eyes locked on her possible saviour. Tears dropped down her skeletal face. Sly wondered how the manacles worked when the woman's frame was that of a skeleton, no meat on her bones, as though she had been starved for weeks. She wore only a ripped dress and each part of her on display was coloured with bruises creating a grim patchwork for onlookers.

'Help me get her out of the chains,' Kiras said, pulling out her waterskin and pointing at it, letting the woman know that they were here to help. The woman's crying intensified and Sly caught a glimpse of the woman's open mouth. Her tongue was missing. Ignoring it, he fought down the fury in his gut and slammed his axe against the chains, freeing her with two determined hits.

'We need to be quick,' Sly said as Kiras gave the bottle to the near-dead woman.

'There is a fight outside. Stay here or leave. It is your choice.' That was all Kiras could do. To burden themselves with her would put all their lives at risks. They had done what they could. Or at least, Sly knew that was what Kiras was convincing herself.

Every other room bore prisoners with similar fates. Sly swung the axe and the chains fell but there was not enough water for them all. Still, they wore grateful looks and some were even able to murmur their thanks. One pleaded for death, unable to live on. Cray dutifully obliged with a short thrust of his sword.

Then they came upon the final room.

Socket stood waiting at the open door, a single tear running down from his good eye. Cray stopped but Sly stepped in front of Kiras and turned to face her. She tried to barge past but he raised his hands and gripped her tight around her arms, holding her in place.

'Wait here.' Kiras fought against his grip but it made him even more determined. He dipped his head and glared until she was forced to look at him directly. 'Give me one moment, and then you come in.' She nodded, her whole body quivering with a nervous energy as though she was about to erupt. Sly nodded back and released her, pleased to see her follow his instruction. He crept past Socket and into the dark room, steadying his breathing to prepare himself for the sight waiting him.

It was Baldor. But not the Baldor Sly knew.

His large frame had withered so that his ribs were on display, threatening to poke out through his paper-thin skin. His shaved head and hollow face bore the cuts and bruises of a beaten man. There was no need for him to be chained to the wall. Sly's eyes followed the wounds along his body, naked but for the thin cloth covering his groin, and found his arms cut from the elbow and legs missing from the knee. The wounds had been crudely treated, fire most likely judging by the damage to the skin. He was barely recognisable. And then his blue eyes found Sly's and there was a spark of life that Sly knew all too well.

'You're late,' Baldor groaned, voice almost a whisper as it struggled its way out from his swollen lips.

'You know me,' Sly chuckled darkly. 'Like to make an entrance.'

Baldor laughed, his body shaking with the action. The sound died down as his eyes narrowed. 'Kiras…'

'The girlie is with us. She'd fight through the hells to get to ya.'

Tears fell silently from Baldor's icy eyes as he nodded slowly. 'That is good.'

Sly turned at the sound of boots. Kiras. She crept into the room, lips forced shut together and eyes fighting back the tears that she did not want to come. Sly allowed her to pass and she knelt next to her friend, caressing his face and gazing into his eyes, together at last.

'You know that I love you,' she said, pushing her face against his forehead and shaking with the sobs forced upon her. Baldor nodded and sniffed, tears quickening their pace. 'I'm so sorry that I wasn't there for you.'

'You're here now. That is what is important, Kiras.

You're here now. I'm so happy that I've been able to see you, one last time…'

Kiras broke into tears, crying as she held her friend close, eyes shut as they remembered the times they had lived together, the love they shared. 'I love you so much.'

'I love you too,' Baldor said. He kissed her on the forehead and she wiped the tears from his face. 'Now, go. And make them pay.'

Kiras nodded and stood. She wiped the tears from her face and gave Baldor one last look. She marched out of the room, giving Sly a knowing nod.

Now it was just the two of them.

'Look after her. She's stronger than any of us, but she cannot be alone,' Baldor asked of Sly. 'Make it quick.'

'May you be one with the ancestors,' Sly said, his axe feeling heavier than at any point in his life. 'We'll miss you, big man.'

Baldor kept his eyes open for it all. The axe took his head from his neck on the second attempt. It fell to the floor with a thud, blood dripping from what was left of the great warrior. He swallowed down the pain and steadied himself before leaving the grim room. The sounds of battle were no longer missing, they returned through the walls and reminded him that his work was not yet over.

Kiras was waiting in between Cray and Socket, the grimmest looking bastards that Sly had ever laid eyes on. Both of her weapons were in hand, ready for blood. There were no tears in her eyes, no tracks on her cheeks anymore. Just a dark hatred and fury that made Sly pause for moment.

'I take it that you have a plan?' he asked her, knowing the answer.

'I'm going to leave this place. And I'm going to kill every last one of those fucking cunts.' Kiras spun and marched down the dark corridor, not waiting for the others. 'How's that for a fucking plan?'

THE SACRIFCE OF THE FEW

It certainly wasn't Archanian Firewhiskey, but Aleister wasn't going to complain.

The colourless liquid swirled around his mouth and delivered tastes he hadn't imagined were possible. It slithered down his throat and he could feel the warm journey it took as it ignited a warmth inside his chest and stomach, his whole body feeling suddenly alive with a renewed life. He placed the drained glass down on the table and gazed around at the waiting, curious faces in the room.

'I think that I would quite like another…'

The four faces in the room shared their laughter and joy at his statement, clapping their hands together and smiling on the lavish sofas. Mathusi snapped to his feet and marched over to the shelf set between two glorious paintings of the God Falls. He pulled the bottle from the shelf and poured another glass for everyone in the room.

'This is a Southern delicacy, the pride of Zakaria,' Bisa informed Aleister. She was a young woman, only a cycle or two older than him if he were to guess. She wore a stunning silver dress that turned gold when she twisted in the light. 'You are lucky to taste such a gift.'

Hasani inched closer to Bisa and nudged her arm with his elbow. 'Do you remember the first time the drink passed your beautiful lips, my dear?' he said with a cheeky wink, moving ever closer to her and giving her a smile that lit up his handsome face. 'You ran around the market telling everyone who would listen that you could fly!'

Bisa slapped his arm playfully and leaned back, tutting. 'I don't recall such a thing…'

'Maybe not, but everyone else does!' Iniko chimed in to great laughter amongst the friends. Iniko was older than the others. Her dark skin wrinkled around her eyes and lips and she had stunning white hair that fell either side of her face in twisted strands.

'We have had some great times together,' Mathusi said as the laughter faded to warm smiles. 'The Gods have blessed us.' He turned to Aleister and raised his glass. 'And we are blessed one final time with a new friend from the North. His skin may be strange but his heart is true. We are blessed to talk and share stories with a new friend from a distant land. Our people are not fortunate enough to have such guests in the South. The timing of such a meeting is most assuredly Gods-given.'

'*Ar-Tulluh se yilwar.*' The four of them chanted together.

Hasani found mirth at Aleister's confused frown. 'The Gods be praised,' he explained in the common tongue.

Aleister drank slowly this time, savouring the Southern drink and allowing it to touch every part of his mouth before allowing it to pass down his throat. Umlilan came from a grape that only grows in the land around the falls. A rarity that was only offered during important ceremonies in the South. He swirled the liquid in his glass and cleared his throat. He looked up to see that Mathusi was staring at him with a sad smile on his young face.

'You came here for a reason, Aleister,' the Southerner said. The rest of the room fell silent and the others all bore the same sad expression as their friend. 'It was quite the feat getting up here to see us. So, please tell us, why are you here? And how can we help you?'

Aleister took a deep breath and pushed his drink away, locking his fingers together and twisting his fingers around one another as he endeavoured to find the right words. 'I am new to this land. As such, I may seem foolish in my assessment of certain events held in this city and the traditions that you must hold dear. Before I continue, I just want each of you to know that I mean no harm with what I say and do not wish to offend you.'

Hasani shared a smile with Bisa and took her hand in his, resting it on her knee. Mathusi nodded and Iniko leaned forward in her seat and took Aleister's hand in her own. 'You know what is happening tomorrow, Aleister. We know what is happening tomorrow. No words can leave those pale lips of yours that could offend the four of us. Please, continue without such a burden weighing upon you.'

Aleister licked his lips and carried on as Iniko tapped his hand with hers and fell back again. 'You seem like such wonderful people and in the small time this evening that we have shared together, it saddens me that I have not been able to enjoy more of this. But through all the laughter and the stories of the past, the shadow of the future is hanging over me, refusing me the chance to truly become lost in the mirth of your new friendship.' Aleister sighed and pushed his hair from his face. 'Tomorrow, all four of you will take your last breath in Takaara and there will be no more laughter. There will be no more friendship. And for what?' He scratched his nails along his forearm as he felt his frustration rise. 'You are giving your lives to something that you don't know will work. You will die because a ruler of your land has told you that he needs you to do that. How can you walk to such a fate with a song on your lips when there is no certainty of the future you crave?'

He waited in the uncomfortable silence that lingered. Mathusi moved next to him and pursed his lips, smacking them together before looking into Aleister's eyes with a fiery intensity. For a moment, Aleister wondered if he had upset his new friend. Then the fire faded and he calmed himself.

'Our ways will be strange to outsiders. Your people felt us savage and believed we were closer to the animals than to them. In hindsight, we take that as a compliment.' A smatter of laughter cracked the tension in the room. 'Our king is... unique. He carries true divinity within him and our people would jump from the falls itself if it meant he would be pleased. What you must understand, Aleister, is that our time in this world is fleeting. We live, we love, we die. Such is the way of things. Whether we are here for one day or a thousand cycles, it is the fragility and finite aspect of life that makes us revel in the beauty of the world around us. In the South, we appreciate the natural beauty of Takaara. We appreciate the beauty of the people we share our lives with. For we understand that any moment may be our last.'

'But why does that mean that you must give up your life?' Aleister asked, unable to comprehend such madness.

'Because we have been warned of what is to come.' Iniko's face had lost the jovial expression and now bore just a grim, stern and determined look. Half-closed eyes peered out at Aleister, ensuring that he was paying attention to her. 'I have seen the way this world has faded in the cycles of my life. You are young and the eyes of the young have not the experience to see such degradation. Our king has knowledge and understanding beyond us and he has told us of how we can combat the evil to come. We place our faith in him so that others may laugh and love. So that others can experience the wonders of life that we have in our time in Takaara. Without our sacrifice, all of that will be lost.'

'Are you certain of that?' Aleister asked.

'No.' Iniko shook her head and smiled that sad smile once more. 'But that is the essence of faith. I trust in my king. I trust in the Gods. I trust that the sacrifice I make tomorrow will lead to a better world. And that is why we sing and dance to our deaths, Aleister of the North. I don't want my final days to be one of sadness. I want to fill the world with joy and laughter. Do you wish to take that experience away from me?'

Aleister shook his head, knowing that his questions were at an end for the evening. 'You are all so very brave. It pains me that this will be the only time that we sit together.'

'We will sit together again,' Mathusi argued. 'We will share a glass of Yuna in the next life. But before then, you must do what you can to improve this world for those we leave behind. Honour our sacrifice. Honour our friendship.'

'I will. I promise.'

The light of the full moon bounced off the wide eyes of the chanting crowds. They danced. They sang. They hugged. They kissed. If Aleister could ignore the truth of the celebration, he could almost pretend that this was the greatest party in all Takaara and they were celebrating the beginning of a new world, one in which men and women of all kinds could be united in hope and joy. Almost. Unfortunately, he could see the line of people waiting to be sacrificed as it wound its way towards the mammoth Temple of the Sun.

'Enjoy the moment,' his sister said, noticing his slumped shoulders and lack of a smile. 'You said yourself, they want this. Don't taint their experience with your thoughts. We may not understand this, but they do.'

He had told Ariel and Bathos of the conversation when he had returned to them. Thankfully, neither had been caught by the guards and they had made it back to their inn without incident. Aleister had been smuggled out with help from his new friends and a couple of guards who felt honoured at escorting an ally of the martyrs. Both Ariel and Bathos were glad to see him safe and well and were excited to hear of his account of the meeting. His story had ended with them both agreeing that this was the choice being made by the people, and not some dark cult with a fixation of death. It all just felt too confusing for Aleister. The disparity between the tales of the torturous Boy King of the South and the way the intelligent, charismatic new friends of his spoke of their time in Ad-Alum was jarring to say the least.

Ife squeezed her way between the sweaty bodies, dancing to the steady beat of the drums and winking as she finally reached them. 'I heard about your little escapade last night. It's a good job you chose that room and not another. They have weapons to defend themselves, you know?'

'I didn't end up having much choice,' Aleister said, rubbing his hands together and looking down at the red mark left by the rope burn.

'Anyway, your foolishness has caused no harm. I hope

you have more of an understanding of where you find yourself. This isn't the world your friends in the North told you about.'

'It is quite different,' Aleister agreed. He snorted as Bathos distracted him from his morbid thoughts. The tall warrior didn't know what to do with himself. With all eyes facing forward towards the Temple, he found himself standing in the way and blocking the view of many of the dancing locals. They did not seem to mind but Bathos felt out of place and his cheeks had turned a violent red. 'Bathos, they don't care. They will tell you to crouch if they want you to. Or to sit down.'

Bathos stood to his full height, forsaking the awkward half-crouch he had found himself attempting. 'I don't want them to miss…' He stopped himself from saying the rest of it. He didn't want them to miss the death? Would that be the right thing to say? 'The thing they are here for...' he finished limply.

The drums came to a sudden halt and the dancing and singing paused, an expectant silence hanging over the thousands of people in the cramped courtyard. A hum broke out as men and women murmured, each covering their eyes with a hand and bowing repeatedly. A wide corridor opened in the middle of the crowd. Aleister shrugged his shoulders in answer to his sister's questioning look.

'He is here,' Ife said, as though that was enough of an explanation.

The parting grew wider but Aleister couldn't see why. He turned and saw Bathos staring with eyes wide open. 'The king…'

He could see it now. A small procession of brightly dressed men and women waving flags and blowing fire from their mouths. Aleister had seen such tricks in the East but it was still a sight to behold. In the middle of the procession, seated upon a grand, open palanquin, was the Boy King himself.

He was older than Aleister had assumed. A few cycles younger than Aleister, perhaps. His skin was a dark black that shimmered in the full moon's light and mixed well with the unique, bright blue crown perched on his head. Black hair poked out in spikes through the crown and displayed vivid colours of bells tied to twisted strands. He wore a long robe that fell sleeveless from shoulders to knees, zigzagging in greens, reds, purples and oranges between thick black lines. He looked like no king that Aleister had ever seen but still reeked with power and majesty.

As the slow procession passed, the wave of people on either side drifted towards him. There were no weapons to deter them. No soldiers to fight them away. The king held out his hands, each displaying unique silver bracelets that wrapped themselves around the top of his hands and ran down his fingers. He touched the people and smiled an easy, white smile that melted their hearts and made them cry with sheer excitement.

It was magical.

'Now do you see why they believe?' Ife asked Aleister, one eyebrow arched. 'For ten cycles he has sat on his throne. He has made mistakes, like everyone does. But he loves his people, and they love him.'

The crowd folded back in as the king made his way to the Temple. He stepped from his palanquin to huge cries and cheers. He acknowledged them with a kiss and a wave before beginning the arduous climb, followed closely by the martyrs, taking their final steps.

'He climbs the steps himself?' Ariel wondered out loud.

'If those giving their lives must do it, then a king must bear that burden to show that he is with them. Anything else would be an offence to his people,' Ife answered. Aleister wondered how many other rulers would put themselves through such an exhausting task. Not many.

Near the top of the Temple, the king finished his ascent, standing on a flat platform cut into the face of the colourful brickwork. The flags continued their waving and fire leapt up cylinders jutting out from each side of the temple. Even from this distance, Aleister could feel the heat of the flames as they danced in the sky and lit up the courtyard. Children gasped as they sat on their parents' shoulders, amazed by the lights and sounds blasting around them. It took a moment for Aleister to remind himself of why they were here.

A gong sounded to the east of the Temple and a hush fell once more on the crowd. The Boy King stood tall on the platform, gazing out across the mass of people all fixed on him and the line of men and women willing to give up their lives. The king spoke to the crowd in small parts, each repeated down the line by broad-chested men holding the black flags adorned with the blue crown that was so familiar in the city. Every other person in the courtyard stood still and listened, keen to hear the words of their leader.

'My glorious people of Ad-Alum, the heart of Zakaria. I, King Zeekial, stand before you in the light of the full moon, ready to do my duty. Not just for the good of our people. But for the good of all people.' More cheers and screams of joy from the masses. Tears rolled down faces and one man fainted and had to be escorted away by one of the guards dotted throughout the crowd. 'Each life is valued in our city, in our home. But we alone are aware of what is coming. The Great Shaking of Takaara ripped the magic from our land but we were waiting, and we were ready. We *are* ready!'

Aleister tapped Ife on the shoulder and leaned closer so that he would not disturb those around him. 'You knew the magic would be ripped from Takaara?'

'We have known for many cycles,' Ife said, nodding but keeping her eyes on the spectacle at the top of the huge pyramid. 'We have prepared for such an eventuality. That is why we are here tonight.'

Aleister pulled away, folding his arms and watching King Zeekial continue.

'Blood is what we need to combat the chaos heading this way. Tonight, we have beloved men and women willingly walking up these famous steps to offer up their blood, their lives, so that the rest of us may stand a chance. We honour them, as we have honoured their predecessors.'

Every Southerner in the courtyard knelt on one knee, even the children. They covered their eyes and lowered their heads in a bow. Ariel tugged on Bathos' sleeve and forced him to follow her to one knee as Aleister did the same. A sign of respect for those about to lose their lives. Whatever the reason, Aleister

353

recognised their bravery and the reasons for their decision.

Drums boomed around the courtyard again, slow this time, leaving long, mournful gaps between each hit. The crowd stood silently, the joyous atmosphere dropping now to one of melancholic respect.

The first martyr stepped up beside the king. Aleister was too far away to make out any of the details but Ife was on hand to explain. 'They will call the name out of the first offering in a moment. They lie on the altar and King Zeekial himself will use the ceremonial blade to end their life. Blood will spill down through a hole on the platform and sink to the depths of the temple.'

The king's voice called out again, repeated by the Mouths of Zeekial. '*Ar-Tulluh se yilwar.*' The crowd repeated the words, chanting it three times in response. Even Aleister found his lips wrapping themselves around the strange sounds, drawn in by the spectacle of it all. 'We thank you for your sacrifice and pray that you find comfort as you wait for the end of days. Rest, Mathusi Anumbar. Your time is now.'

Aleister's breath caught in his throat as he lurched forward at the name. His body naturally strived to make it towards the man, to save him. But his head told him that there was only one thing he could do for the man now. Respect his wishes.

'It is done,' Ife muttered as the drums stopped and then started back up. 'Come, you do not need to watch all of this.'

Aleister stayed where he was, gazing up at where Mathusi would have fallen. 'I'm staying. I will be here for every single one of them.'

Ariel slipped towards him and squeezed his hand, her other still lost in Bathos' fingers. 'We all will.'

'Then we stay,' Ife stated. 'After, we have an important meeting.'

'Who with?' Bathos asked as the next martyr took their place on the altar. Aleister wondered if it was another of his friends from the previous night. Handsome Hasani with his stunning smile. Beautiful Bisa with her melodic laugh. Wise Iniko with her intelligent eyes. He rubbed his chest, hoping the pain would fade.

'King Zeekial himself,' Ife said. 'It is time you are told the truth of the South, and the burden we bear.'

***

The temple's interior was as unlike the temples Aleister had walked around in his youth as he could have imagined. Every inch of the walls and ceiling were carved in intricate patterns: circles, triangles, squares and every other shape that Aleister had ever seen were blended in an intricate display of workmanship that made the interior of the grand pyramid come alive, keeping an eye on the visitors. The shapes wound their ways into monstrous patterns, unknown beasts, and strange insignias that Aleister was not familiar with.

He walked in between Ariel and Bathos, following Ife as she strode down the path lit by low, circular braziers with large fires dancing in the grey, cavernous room. She looked as though she owned the place.

Aleister picked up his own pace to keep up with the enigmatic woman, glancing to each side to appreciate the narrow, stone carvings of huge-fanged beasts standing tall, guarding the path they walked on. The path eventually led to a set of three steps that ran the width of the room, leading up to low platform on which four, identical empty grey, stone thrones sat. They were simple seats, built with large, grey blocks of stone and adorned with simple patterns carved into the arm rests and the head of the seat. Nothing fancy like the thrones Aleister had seen in the North and East. At the end of each side of the platform, a tall, wide bowl stood alone. Wispy trails of smoke glided through the air, floating a woody smell towards Aleister, catching in his nostrils and calming him instantly. In the centre of the thrones, a dark, red and foreboding liquid trickled its way down between the elegant patterns in the wall and meandered its way down a tunnel running from the back of the room towards the centre, straight down the path that Aleister walked. At its end, there was a small hole in the floor.

'What is this place?' he wondered out loud, voice echoing throughout the chamber.

'We stand beneath the platform where the king himself sacrificed those martyrs. It is in here where he sits with his advisors and discusses the ways that the world can be set right in the face of chaos,' Ife answered as though it was the simplest of answers to such a question.

'So that red liquid…' Ariel said with great distaste as she peered down the hole in the centre of the room.

'The blood of those who have been sacrificed.' Aleister opened his mouth to protest but Ife cut him off before the sounds could pass his lips. 'I ask you to think and not speak. He will be with us in a moment. The ceremony bears a heavy toll on the young man. I ask that you listen to him more than you speak. Wisdom enters through the ears and is lost through the lips. Remember that when you stand before greatness.'

'How old is this room?' Bathos asked, stepping past the braziers and running his fingers along the stone walls, a look of amazement on his bold features.

'Honestly?' Ife chewed her cheek and puffed out a few breathes between her lips as she thought about it. 'Some argue about its age. Older than the Gods. Built by the Gods. Pulled from the sea by a great leviathan in the Old Age. Others even whisper that it was sent from the skies by a race of women from a distant world. All we know is that as long as there has been Zakaria, there has stood the Temple at its heart.'

'More interesting tales to be told over warm fires by talented bards with silver tongues,' Aleister chuckled. 'A few centuries old at best,' he said, hands on hips as he craned his neck to follow the pattern work on the ceiling. It was impressive. But every region had their own stories about the Gods and their impact on architecture. The Watcher in the North. The Gods' Bridge. The Falcon's Eye in the East. The Shrine of Souls in the West. Marvels, certainly. But proof of divinity? He wasn't so sure of that.

Ife crept towards him with a dancer's grace, tongue

rubbing gently against her wet lips. She stroked his chin with a single finger and gazed into his unblinking eyes. 'You have seen the work of magic and what happens when it fails. Such a gift can be a curse. Such things are the work of Gods. How else would you explain the wonders around us?'

Aleister took her hand and gently lowered it from his face. 'The work of men and women. Talented men and women with skill that is lost to the modern world. It is too easy to pass off things we do not understand as the work of the Gods.'

'Sometimes the easiest explanation is the correct one,' Ife argued with a delicate shrug. 'Great men, unfortunately, often find easy paths to be the most difficult to take. Too focused on the idea of proving themselves by facing the difficult challenges instead of opening their eyes to what is right in front of them.'

A good argument. But one that Aleister had heard before. 'Discussing this will get us nowhere, I am afraid.'

'Through words alone, no. But you have seen the divine, Aleister of the Red Sons. And before you leave this city, you will see it again.'

'Ah, divinity,' a voice echoed towards them. The four of them spun to face the open door in the far corner of the room, away from the thrones. King Zeekial stepped forward in his ceremonial robes, the vivid colours in sharp contrast to the dark and grim room he entered. 'Has ever there been such a topic to inspire the fury and violence of man. To have stoked the flames of argument between brother and sister and lovers alike? If so, I have yet to hear it.'

'My King…' Ife said with that now familiar bow of the South.

'Zeke is fine in present company,' the king said, taking Ife's hand and bowing before planting a kiss on the top of her wrist. He turned his attention to Ariel, bowing to her and clasping a hand in both of hers. 'The women in our city are honoured above all. The carriers of life and the heart of our people.' He stepped sideways and looked up at the towering frame of Bathos as Ariel was left blushing.

'We respect the warriors who fight for the freedoms of

those less fortunate. We have a special greeting for such people but I shall respect your Northern traditions.' He held out a hand which Bathos gladly accepted with a short shake. He repeated the action with Aleister in silence, his dark eyes drifting to the elegant sword Aleister had on show at his hip. A flicker of annoyance crossed his dark features. For a moment, Aleister thought of apologising in case such weapons brought offence in such an important structure to the king and his people. Before given the chance, the leader turned away and marched up the steps, holding his robes so that he would not trip. He took his place on the inside throne to the left and rested his arms on the side of the seat.

His eyes were red with exhaustion and his slim frame looked weaker than Aleister had thought earlier and he had the look of a man who had been forced to carry more than most would be expected. The look of a weary ruler.

'These are the people I spoke of, Zeke,' Ife said, waving a hand over the silent band. 'Aleister, Ariel and Bathos of the Red Sons. The founders of the mercenary band.'

The king rubbed his eyes with finger and thumb and shook his head, blinking wildly before looking over them all with new eyes. 'I have heard of you. Even from our isolation in the South, the whispers of the North are fed through for us to gnaw at and digest. Great warriors. That is if the tales are true.'

'We come here on an important mission,' Aleister stated bluntly.

'Indeed,' the king replied, straightening up on the throne and trying to force a bit of life back into his frame. 'Every meeting before me is of great importance. I rule the biggest nation in the South and all other nations in the region look to me for guidance. I have not allowed your people to enter my city in the whole of my lifetime and yet here you stand. We both know it is of great importance.' Zeke sighed and cracked his back, pressing his shoulders back with a groan. 'My apologies. The ceremony is draining and takes its toll on me.' He paused and realigned the blue crown on his head so that it sat a little straighter. 'Tell me, warriors of the North. What do you know of the Breaking of Takaara?'

358

Aleister frowned at his sister and Bathos, a look reflected at him. 'A tale told to children to warn about the dangers of arrogance.'

Zeke nodded slowly to himself. 'What details are there in the story? Tell me the details. Not the message.'

'Four of the greatest magic users in the world believed they could create a better world, a better Takaara. One of them turned against the other three and a battle broke out that ripped the land apart, almost destroying Takaara in an instant. The land became scarred and no life would grow where the battle had taken place. It was tainted.'

'And what happened to these magic users, these Magi?' the king asked, almost bored.

Aleister shrugged. 'I don't recall.'

'They disappeared. Never to be seen again,' Bathos' voice surprised both Aleister and Ariel. The big man ignored their shocked looks and stayed focused on the king. 'In the version I have heard, The Four tore them from the world for their folly, punishing them for the destruction they had caused.'

King Zeekial grabbed his crown and set it on the armrest. He rubbed at his forehead where the crown had left a mark against his skin. 'An interesting version. Simpler than the reality and much more concise and preferable to what actually happened.'

Aleister struggled but failed to keep the shocked laughter from escaping. He spread his arms wide at his sister's annoyed glare and looked back at the unmoved king. 'I'm sorry. But how do you know what happened? No one agrees on the correct story. Centuries have passed and there's around a hundred different versions of the event. Each as outlandish as the last.'

'How do I know what happened?' Zeke laughed and pushed himself from his throne. He took the steps slowly until he stood in front of Aleister. Unbuttoning his robe, he held Aleister's stern gaze in his own dark eyes. 'I know. Because I was there.' He pointed at a dark scar lying over his chest. Exactly where his heart would be. 'I stood in the midst of chaos and fought for the fate of Takaara. I fought until I was stabbed through the heart.' His eyes dropped until they fell on the unique sword dangling from Aleister's hip. 'Stabbed through the heart with my lover's sword.' He pointed at the blade and growled. '*That* sword.'

'This sword has been in the line of Darakeche for centuries…' Aleister claimed, shaking his head and taking a cautious step back from the furious king. 'You must be mistaken.'

'I promise you, if you are ever stabbed in the heart, you will not forget the weapon. It was stolen after the battle. Found its way into the hands of the Sultan who claimed it for his own. But I can prove the authenticity of my claim. For this blade is one of two, and I have its sister.' Zeke buttoned up his shirt and turned his back on Aleister. He strode to his throne and caressed the wall beside the stone seat. Aleister stared as the wall seemed to fade away and reveal a small enclosure. The king reached inside and pulled a blade from the shadows.

Aleister stepped forward onto the platform and unsheathed his blade. He held it out in his palms as the king did the same. They were identical but for the colours. One shining white in the firelight. The other repelling all form of light with its beautiful ebony design.

'You claim to be one of the greatest Magi to have ever lived,' Aleister muttered as he glanced from one blade to the other, unable to deny their symmetry.

'To have lived. And died. Follow me, and I will show you the truth.'

A LINE IN THE SAND

Thousands of warriors lined the main crossing of the river. The whole contingent of the Red Sons marched west as one and away from their adopted, eastern home. For three days, Katerina Kane had fought and battled to find more than a minute with her son but with each attempt, she was met with an almost magical resistance that rebuffed her efforts and kept her away from Drayke. The last time they had spoken to one another, she had been filled with a rare, wholesome joy that had given her a spring to each step as she found her way into the city of Mughabir. Now, as she travelled back along the road to her homeland, her son journeying amongst the same group, a shadow of dread loomed large. His recent actions didn't fall in line with the young man she had watched with pride in Archania.

'You beat yourself up over something that is out of your control.' Istari travelled with ease, patting his mare on its side and muttering something to his beast before glancing across again at Kane. She had noticed the way he had kept an eye on her since Mughabir, unable to trust how she may react. 'Your time will come where you can ask for the answers you so crave. Fighting yourself in the meantime will cause nothing but stress. This I know.'

'I had finally found a relationship with my son after all this time,' Kane snapped back, keeping her voice low so that the mercenaries were kept out of hearing range as they followed the tracks. 'And now it is claimed that he chopped the head off an innocent man in the hope of taking a throne in a bloody battle. I think I am allowed a bit of time to rage and fall apart.'

'Perhaps…' Istari replied with an infuriating calmness. 'But do not claim that any man is innocent. He was the son of the Sultan of Darakeche. That man grew up knowing war and blood. He may have denounced his father's chosen path but he was no pure hero killed before his time to make the bards weep and sing of the falling of the stars. He was a killer. Every single one of the men and women in this company are.'

'You have a strange way of viewing the world, you know that?' Kane said, frowning at her travelling companion.

'There is light and darkness in us all Katerina Kane. I look at life through the lens that has been handed to me. Not my fault it is dusty and filth-ridden.'

'Perhaps a clean wipe every now and then would be worthwhile.'

'A lovely thought. One which I decline to act upon.'

'What a surprise.'

Kane accepted the steady rhythm of the horse and scanned the long, meandering trail of warriors as they crossed the river and towards the great forests in the distance. An orange sun hung low in the sky as the shimmer of the eastern haze painted waves on the horizon. The sun was just about to dip below the mountains to the west when she was joined by a solemn-looking Ben.

'I am shocked to see you,' Kane said, not looking at the man as he pulled his horse beside her. 'Every attempt I have made to speak to you or Drayke has been met with a wall of silence or blathering men tripping over their tongues to create some foolish excuse that just wastes my time. And yet, here you are, finally away from your hiding hole as we head to war in the North.'

'My apologies, Katerina Kane,' Ben said. 'The last few days have been… eventful, to say the least.'

She snorted and fixed Ben with a mocking smirk. 'Eventful? It has been a fucking joke. What the hells happened after we left?'

'Madness took its hold on our camp.' Ben chuckled but there was no mirth in the sound, just a puzzled reflection on what had happened. 'The night you left, there were raised voices. Drayke had been in discussion with Jax throughout the day and, at first, I thought that they had fallen out after one too many drinks. As I pushed through the opening of the tent, I froze. Jax stood in the corner, cowering from Drayke's bloodied blade. Adnan's body lay motionless on the floor, a bloody trail soaking the rug and running towards his decapitated head. Drayke wiped the blade clean and calmly told me what would happen next. He gave me no room for argument. Said that Adnan had been the first to draw a blade. Jax backed him up but I saw no other weapon in the room…'

'Are there no consequences for such actions?' Kane asked, terrified and disgusted at the prospect of what could have happened to her son.

'We live by a code of honour,' Ben said before taking a deep breath in and out. 'But at the end of the day, the men and women of the Red Sons saw that Drayke would give us something to fight for. Jax had thrown in his lot with the young man and Adnan was dead. He became the easy choice. We've all killed for things we want. Anyone casting daggers Drayke's way would find a thousand staring straight back.'

Kane thought of Braego and what the honourable warrior would have thought of it all. He had told her stories of the Borderlands that frightened the skin from her bones. The things that he had done in his youth to survive, or just to gain credibility within a tribe. Still, he had grown into a man who chose a path of dignity but was still willing to do what he had to in order to keep his position. He could let words pass but he would never forget them. Even Kane had helped him hide an indiscretion or two in Archania, turning a blind eye to her lover's acts of subtle revenge outside of the city walls. Was Drayke displaying some of the personality traits that his real father had shown?

'And why have you both been finding ways to keep your distance?'

Ben gave an apologetic smile. 'We both know what he has done and the path it has pushed us on. Neither of us were prepared to face your disappointment and anger until we had something else to distract you.'

'A distraction?'

'Two days from now, maybe less,' Ben started, leaning over the side of his mount and spitting into the sand. 'Scouts have seen signs of a small army waiting for us. A small army dressed in the white capes of the Empire of Light...'

'I assume that we will not be taking the long way around,' Kane replied, arching a single eyebrow at the thought.

A thin smile found its way onto Ben's face and a bit of the warmth she knew returned to his whole demeanour. 'We like to take the fastest route. There's no way the Empire's forces are going to just move aside if we ask nicely.'

'Then I guess there will be bloodshed.'

'I guess so,' Ben agreed. 'You can join the Red Sons at the front or hang back with the Darakechean forces. Either way, we ain't expecting you in the heat of the battle. You haven't sworn an oath to us to shed blood in our name. Your path is your own to take, just thought I'd give you the details.'

'How kind of you.' Kane glanced to Istari who gave her the barest of nods. 'We'll be ready when the time comes. The Prince of Darakeche travels near the back of the army. Will you do the honours of explaining our situation to him, or is that my job?'

'I'll leave that with you. You are the one with a history with princes.'

Kane sighed and bit her tongue as she pulled the reigns of her horse. Istari wordlessly followed, calmly riding beside her as they rode against the wave of soldiers. From the top of the sandy hill, she could see the white and gold flags held by the standard bearers displaying the location of the Prince of Darakeche. She had never spoken to the young man but this journey had been one of firsts. What better time than now?

'Have you ever spoken with the prince?' Istari asked, displaying his unique and unnerving talent of reading her thoughts.

'No. Have you?'

'A few times.'

'Any words of wisdom that you wish to impart?'

'You would have more luck getting sense from the head of his brother that sits on the spike outside the Sultan's Summer House. When brains were handed out at the Gates of The Four, this fool must have been lying drunk in a bush somewhere in the distance.'

'I cannot wait to meet him.'

Istari Vostor, for once, had been downplaying the sheer stupidity of the fool riding his gallant horse along the sands. Four standard bearers rode in the corners around him, keeping a respectful distance from their prince whilst two more waved long palm leaves, wafting the warm air straight towards him but allowing him to create a strange, pompous scene of entitlement as his dark hair waved with each fall of the leaves.

'Istari Vostor!' Prince Naseem cried, back straight as if he had one of those flag poles running from his arse and right up his back. 'What a man! The Duel in Ankerra. The Flight of the Seven. The Eye of Vandir. All stories that I devoured as a child. My servants used to pass on the stories with such glee and I ate them up like a hungry wolf. Of course, tales are there to be exaggerated. I look forward to the tales they will tell of this journey as I lead my men and women to war in the North! Father will be so proud. He loves to remind me of the old days when he would lead from the front. That has not happened in a while, of course. Not with the swelling of his ankles. Ghastly illness. Fortunately, he has me to take on the mantle and show Darakeche how it is done.'

'That is good to hear, my Prince,' Kane said, pleased with the eventual gap in the conversation that provided her with a chance to speak. 'You see, scouts have reported that the Empire of Light have soldiers beyond the forest. Soldiers who are ready for a battle.'

'A battle! Did you hear that Jassim?' the prince shouted over to one of his exhausted flag-bearers. 'An opportunity to display the courage and valour that my people are known for. A chance to prove that I am the prince who understands battle and what it entails.' A worried shadow passed over the prince's face as he lowered his voice, almost speaking to himself. 'A chance to prove that Adnan is not the only son who can wield a blade…'

'We shall ride at the back, Your Highness,' Jassim called over, rolling his eyes as sweat drenched his dark features. 'The best position for a commander to lead his people.'

'Nonsense!' Naseem bristled indignantly. 'Real commanders model the behaviour expected of their soldiers. I have read of such things. Charge from the front and they will see the bravery and skill needed to win the battle. Leading from the front will bring me honour and the love of my men. Standing at the back will bring me nothing but boredom and disdain.'

Kane bit her tongue. She had seen what happened to men at the front of a charge. Those who survived were kissed by luck more than skill and bravery. It was a position in the battle that was least desired by those who wished to live out the day. 'It is your decision, my Prince.'

Naseem lit up at this comment. 'I have heard little of you, Katerina Kane. I must admit, I am not a fan of women fighting. There are much more suitable duties to be done in the world for women than fighting. But I have enjoyed this conversation and so I shall allow your presence.'

'You show great kindness.' Kane bowed and scolded herself for the lack of enthusiasm in her dry words. 'Darakeche is lucky to have such a man waiting as next in line to the throne.'

She almost felt sorry for the idiot as he grinned like a little boy being told that he had done well by his mother. 'Yes! That is what I have been saying to Jassim here. Such a lucky nation. I shall inform my soldiers that a battle is near, Katerina Kane. I am sure we shall speak again once the Empire's soldiers are lying on a bloody heap.'

'I am counting down each moment…'

The moments passed too quickly for Katerina Kane. From the vantage point at the edge of the forest, she could see the fires lighting the small camps on the next hill along. Flags of the Empire waved in the gentle midnight wind and the crescent moon lit up the valley between them, shining a light on the patrol heading their way.

'Have you forgiven me?'

Kane startled at the sound of Drayke's voice. She recovered and felt nausea engulf her as her emotions swayed from delight at seeing him to disgust at what he had done. 'For what?' she replied diplomatically, passing the baton to him.

'I killed Adnan. He and Jax had a disagreement and he struck me when I tried to intervene. I used the chance to dispose of the one person who stood in the way of me and my crown. A messenger had informed us only an hour before that my broth—' Drayke caught himself before he finished the word. 'That Asher was dead. The throne sits idle and now is my chance to claim it. I am not proud of my actions. But I know now that the naïve fool who grew up in Archania must be thrown aside if I am to do what is right.'

'I loved that naïve fool,' Kane admitted. 'And he always knew what was right. Better than me. Better than most wise men and women that I had been lucky enough to meet. I hope that he is not lost.'

'Ready your weapon,' was all that Drayke said in response, ignoring the reality of her words. 'There is no use in wasting time.'

Any hope that the Empire's soldiers would be taken off guard was dashed as the hooves pounded down into the valley. Kane watched from the trees as the soldiers readied themselves with an experienced efficiency that impressed her. Tall shields slammed together into a chain and trumpets signalled for the cavalry to flank the rectangle of infantry scrambling together. Archers lined the back of the regiment beside growing flames rising in wide braziers, waiting for their own signal.

In contrast, the Red Sons' charge seemed reckless, a

mass of bodies roaring and banging weapons against shields to create as much noise as possible as riders on horses navigated a treacherous path between the screaming warriors and the treacherous ground. The ground shook with the volume of the warriors' cries, making Kane appreciate the discipline of the Empire's forces as they stood, unmoving in their positions, unaffected by the wave of noise.

'Not their first battle,' Istari said to her, thinking along the same lines. 'They've been preparing for this war for longer than any of us can imagine. Such cheap tricks will not faze them.'

A familiar voice broke Kane's attention from the tense scene before her. A loud, pompous voice slurring the end of sentences.

'Look at the bastards! Not even moving. The fools! We shall wipe them out and be on with our journey before I finish my drink…'

Kane nodded respectfully at the prince as he marched with his retinue of soldiers to the edge of the trees, peering down at the battle with a keen interest. 'Prince Naseem. I thought you were going to be leading the charge?'

'Ah… yes,' the prince stuttered, scratching at a red mark on his neck just below his dark beard and looking unnerved by the question. 'That was the plan! As much as my heart was into leading the first line of attack, I have been convinced by my advisors and dear friends in the Red Sons that there will be a greater fight to come. Keep my men back until needed and surprise the enemy. That is the plan now!' He beat his chest with a golden-gloved fist and the confidence returned as his men roared their affirmation to his words.

'Such bravery,' Istari said, not even attempting to hide the sarcasm. Thankfully, the prince didn't seem to notice. 'Your people will be pleased to hear the tale when you return home.'

'Yes, I believe they will. It is what all great leaders do. Win battles and show other nations the strength they wield. Prevents wars from breaking out. You have to win wars to prevent wars, you see.'

'Such wise words.' Kane had to discreetly nudge Istari

this time, worried that he was pushing his luck with the foolish but not entirely stupid prince.

'I am full of them. Wise words. That is what people tell me.'

Kane turned from the prince and his smug face to the battle. Arrows pierced the sky and ripped a deadly arc through the night, landing on shields, the ground, and in some cases, through flesh. Valiant screams turned to ones of pain as the archers found their range and lit the tips of the arrows, shooting again at the swarm of warriors heading their way. She winced as the crunch of metal on metal filled the air. Spears stabbed through gaps in the shield wall and riders yelled at their horses to quicken their pace and outflank the attackers. Bodies fell and cries sang the song of the dying as the heat of battle consumed the land. Still, the wall held, and the Empire's forces stood strong, not allowing their fear or the chaos of battle to cause them to flee.

She searched for any sign of Drayke amidst the stream of soldiers flooding towards the gleaming wall of enemies. There was no chance that she would be able to pick him out here, of course, but with each fall of a red-cloaked soldier, her hearts ached at the thought that it could be him. Her fingers twitched and brushed against the hilt of her blade, her body eager to join the fray though her mind begged for patience.

'Standing here will do nothing for either of us,' Istari sighed. He pulled his sword from its sheath and pressed the hilt against his forehead, eyes closed and lips moving furiously. His dazzling eyes opened and he flicked his eyebrows up as he caught Kane's curious look. 'Shall we head down and see if we can keep that son of yours alive?'

Kane felt the excitement rise within her. 'I can think of nothing better to do.' She whipped her blade free and suddenly felt twenty cycles younger. The Empire had caused her such pain throughout her life. Now, it was time to pay them back.

'I shall stay here,' Naseem said, raising his voice to ensure that they could both hear him. He peered over his shoulder as his thousands of soldiers stepped towards him in the shadows, armoured and ready for the fight. 'We will be ready when it is time.'

'Stay safe, Prince Naseem,' Istari said to the young prince, impressed that the young leader was able to keep his voice even and calm. 'Darakeche would be a very different place without you.'

Isatri Vostor turned away and stalked off down into the valley where the shield wall had finally broken and a stream of red-cloaked soldiers broke through the gaps provided. Suddenly, the battle shifted into further chaos as each man and woman fought for themselves, swinging weapons and firing arrows in the hope that they would be one of the lucky ones to survive the night.

As Kane trudged after her ally, she wondered if she would be one of the lucky ones.

Kane desperately stabbed at the towering soldier, the tip of her bloody sword finding the narrowest of gaps between collar and jawline. She ripped the blade free along with a smattering of blood and pulled herself up from the ground, knowing that each moment lost could be a step closer to death.

Battles were an odd beast. Sometimes there were moments where you would freeze, such was the grip of fear that held tightly onto your heart. At other times, there was too much chaos and a crush of stinking, frightened bodies to feel fear's touch. Slashing wildly and blocking strikes left and right. You could hope that those behind you were doing their job but it was a fool's hope. Instead, Kane would ensure her eyes darted in every direction, expecting the next blow from all angles and doing her best to stay mobile and stay alive.

The Red Sons outnumbered the Empire's forces. But the enemy had clearly been better trained. As Istari said, this had been what they had prepared for over the cycles. They broke their lines once in a while but soon regained their focus and knew what must be done. As the bodies piled up, it was clear who would win out the day. But the Empire would ensure that each death would be met with two for their attackers. They fought with a cool fury, each attack meticulous and thought out, even in the madness of the battle.

Kane dodged a frightened horse racing through the soldiers and rolled out of the way of another spear strike, feeling the whip of air above her as it barely missed its deadly blow. Her blade snapped behind her and she felt it slash across her attacker's calves. She turned and drove the sword into the screaming mouth, pushing it through the back of his head and then kicking his now silent body away. No time to even feel a sense of relief that she was still alive. Just a pressing need to push forward.

Another trumpet. The Empire's soldiers backed away, shields and weapons raised in defence but no longer pressing onto their attackers. Kane's heart leapt as she saw Drayke, dark, scaled armour over his black shirt. He had a weeping wound across his forearm and was covered in blood which Kane was unable to work out if it was his or those he had slain. No longer did he look like that young boy she had so loved. Now he was a man. So like his father.

'Fall into line!' Drayke roared. Instantly, the Red Sons obeyed his command, snapping together and standing opposite their enemy. Ben stood beside Drayke, giving the much younger man a nod of respect before turning to face the soldiers.

An uncomfortable silence fell over the battlefield, broken only by the groans of the men and women battling against the sweet melody of death calling for them.

'He has them where he wants them,' Istari said, jolting Kane at his sudden appearance. There was no heavy breathing. No limping. No cuts or bruises. Istari stood beside her as though they had bumped into one another in a market and were eager to listen to a merchant argue with an enraged customer. 'He's becoming a leader. Still undecided if he will be a good one, but he is a leader, nonetheless.'

'You look as though you've missed the battle,' Kane hissed, comparing her own filthy, bloody armour to her pristine companion.

'The trick is to not get hit.'

From behind the rows of soldiers with white cloaks, Kane could see two flags bearing the Sun of the Empire waving on large poles making their way to the front of the line, towards the gap that now stood between the two warring sides. The front of the line opened as the flags drew closer and out stepped the two flag bearers, each standing beside a worried soldier, armour pristine despite the battle that had been raging. The soldier's eyes raced across the line of Red Sons, searching for any sign of a leader.

'A harsh battle. As most are,' he said to the crowd before him. 'Each loss of life is an arrow through the heart of our Empress. You have the numbers. Our scouts know about the desert rats waiting on the hill.' He inclined his head towards the trees shielding Prince Naseem's warriors. 'I am Ashfar D'Ernhar. Cousin to the Empress herself. There is no need for a thousand more men and women to die. I ask that there is only one more death. One against one. My finest against your finest. If we win, we shall head to the North and continue our journey. If we lose, you may have our weapons and armour and we shall leave in the peace of the One, back across the desert to our homeland.'

Drayke stepped forward, all eyes turning to him. 'Why would we end the battle when it is so clear that we will win?' he called to Ashfar.

'You will. But fight, and we will we take as many of you as we can. How much do you care for those who fight for you?'

Kane cursed. The question trapped Drayke. To turn down the offer now would make him seem heartless. To accept would be to risk losing face in front of his men and women. She saw Ben lean towards the young man and whisper something in his ear.

'We accept. Your best, against ours.'

Ashfar flashed his eyes and shared a smug grin with the soldiers beside him. 'Call The Butcher. His time has arrived.'

The soldier beside Ashfar blew on his small horn and the lines of soldiers parted. Kane's throat tightened as she stared up at the monstrosity ambling its way towards them. Frightened gasps broke out around her as the colossal man cracked his neck to each side and casually swung a sword that was longer than Kane's body. Nearly eight foot tall, the warrior's muscles rippled as he stretched his sleeveless arms and paused, staring out at the red cloaks, waiting to discover which of them would be his victim.

'Finally, some fun.' Istari squeezed past Kane, pressing a hand on her back and ignoring her pleas to step back. He marched over to Drayke who was lost in a furious discussion with Ben. He pushed the pair of them aside and walked until he alone stood in the wide expanse between the two sides. The Butcher stepped forward to join Istari in the void.

Kane bit her lip, blood pouring from the force as she watched the scene unfold, an eerie silence falling on the battlefield. The Sword of Causrea looked like a small, lost boy who had wandered across a battlefield and found himself next to a smiling giant.

'The Sword of Causrea! Istari Vostor himself,' Ashfar cried, his face lighting up as excited whispers escaped the lips of all the soldiers around Kane. 'What a match this will be. The greatest Eastern warrior facing off against the greatest in the West. I was there for the Battle of Three Hills. I was just a boy then and you were in your prime. Many cycles weigh upon you now, old man. It will be interesting to see how you have handled them. The boundary between the East and West may be more than a line in the sand, but we appreciate beauty and skill. Whatever the outcome, it is an honour to see you dance one last time.'

Ashfar dipped onto one knee and lowered his head. His soldiers did the same. All except the one they called The Butcher. The soldiers stood back up and although there was no other sound, all in attendance knew that the battle had begun.

The Butcher wore no armour but for a leather plate covering his torso. His grim face bore beady eyes and a long, wide nose. His black beard had been tied with bands so that it hung low from his chin down to his collar. He stepped forward with a gleeful smile, confidence pouring from his every movement as he gripped his obscenely huge sword in one hand.

Kane frowned and shook her head as Istari walked forward, untying the belt at his waist. He lifted it in the air, sword still attached and dropped it the floor before continuing on his path towards the monster. 'What the fuck are you doing?' she said to herself, rapidly tapping her foot on the floor and cursing at herself for being unable to look away.

The Butcher growled and marched forward. Istari quickened his steps, still without a weapon as he dipped his head and lowered a shoulder. The old warrior broke into a sprint, arms whipping alongside his body as he threw off his cloak.

Kane's eyes caught a glint of silver strapped to the man's back as the moonlight bounced against the infamous warrior. The Butcher roared as Istari drew closer and raised his weapon. He swung the sword with the might of a monster, whipping it through the air faster than Kane thought possible for such a heavy thing.

But Istari was faster.

The crowd of soldiers took a collective gasp as Istari ducked under the strike and found himself inside the monster's defence. He pressed a boot against the man's great knee and launched himself into the air. He twisted with the grace of a dancer, his hands snapping to the small blades tied to his back. The first tore into The Butcher's neck and ripped across the throat. Istari used the momentum to swing his body around in the air and stab the second weapon straight through his opponent's eye.

Brutal, practiced precision.

The monstrous sword dropped to the ground with a shocking thud that echoed around the awestruck soldiers. The Butcher fell to his knees, massive hands clutching desperately at his throat and face.

Istari landed effortlessly with the lightest of touches on the ground and threw the bloody daggers at his feet. He turned to his opponent, right hip facing the monster. Faster than Kane's eyes could follow, the master warrior shuffled forward and snapped a side kick that cannoned against the downed opponent's face. The Butcher's throat gave a sickening retch as the wound opened further and his head lurched back in an unnatural display of horror. The rest of his body soon fell, the ground shaking as it slammed into the dirt and blood.

Istari brushed himself off and walked back to the line of shocked warriors without even a bead of sweat on his face.

The Red Sons burst into cheers and cries of victory. Horns and trumpets rang out and relieved hugs between the victors could be seen throughout the swarm of red. Kane cursed a final time and shook her head as she caught Istari's eyes. She looked past him and sighed as the Empire's soldiers fell once more to their knees, in awe of the skill of Istari Vostor.

As the cries died down, Ashfar stood, pulling his helmet off and throwing it at Drayke's feet. 'There will be more blood. But today is not that day. Please, accept our surrender.' He ripped the badge of the White Sun from his breast and threw it beside his helmet.

Drayke picked the badge up and eyed it with suspicion as the Empire's soldiers threw their weapons and armour at their feet, accepting defeat. 'Your Empire has caused me great distress over these past few cycles. I was run out of my home and away from people I love.'

Kane narrowed her eyes as Prince Naseem cleared a path through the Red Sons with his soldiers. They circled the Empire's defeated men and women, all grinning at their hated neighbour's loss.

'A hard-fought victory!' Prince Naseem beat his chest as though he had been the architect of his enemy's downfall. 'As Prince of Darakeche, I offer to escort this merry bunch to their deserved destination.'

Ashfar frowned, confused with the change in plans. He looked at Drayke with pleading eyes. 'We had a deal…'

'We did,' Drayke said. 'And it is one I honour. You may leave and the Red Sons will go on without a backwards glance.' Drayke turned away and strode off, back turned on the Empire's soldiers as Naseem marched forward. 'But the Prince of Darakeche was not part of such a deal, and he does not listen to me…'

Kane's stomach churned as Naseem gleefully called out the order. 'Kill them. Every last one of them. In the name of our great nation. For Darakeche!'

'For Darakeche!' the call repeated by the jubilant warriors.

The men and women of the Empire bowed their heads, resigned to their fate.

They did not defend themselves. They could not defend themselves.

Spears lurched into the circle of defeated warriors, jabbing forward with trained thrusts as the warriors of Darakeche slaughtered their defenceless neighbours. It was quick. That was something. Only Ashfar stood, still breathing in front of the mound of bodies of his people.

There were tears in his eyes as he draw a simple, curved dagger from his silk belt. Kane felt her stomach twist as she thought she saw shame on the warrior's face as he grasped the handle and buried the weapon into his stomach, pulling it across with a wrenching jolt to end his own life. He had nothing to be ashamed of. He had fought with honour and struggled to find a way to prevent needless death.

Kane turned with disgust from the scene, eager to remove herself from the horror and speak with her son. Ben stood in her way, grim-faced and staring directly at her.

'There is no honour in this,' she yelled at the soldier. 'No honour.'

'Where is their honour when they burn women and kids?'

'But we are not them,' Kane argued. 'Or at least… I did not think we were.'

'Katerina Kane,' Ben bellowed, so those around could hear him. 'The Red Sons banish you from our company. You are no ally to us anymore. Until this war is over, you are to be guests of the Sultan of Darakeche.'

'Are you arresting me?' Kane asked incredulously, drawing her sword and staring past the men marching towards her. She could see the back of Drayke's head, unconcerned with what was happening.

Ben's face softened as he gazed at Kane, pleading with

her to understand as he breathed out his next words. 'It is for your own safety.'

Ben gasped as he found a dagger resting under his chin, blood dripping from the edge of the blade. 'I do not think you are taking her anywhere...' Istari growled and pushed the blade further against the skin until Ben squirmed and flashed his eyes at his men to stand down. They backed away, hands open in defeat. 'We are leaving and you will regret it if you follow. If you see us again, I will ensure that it is the last thing that you see, understand?'

Ben managed a weak nod, eyes glancing down in an effort to look at the blade still dripping with blood. Istari pushed him away and marched towards Kane, grabbing her arm and spinning her around.

No one followed as they left the battleground. Kane wordlessly marched with Istari as he whistled and two horses bounded over to them. 'Get on,' he commanded to Kane. She did as she was instructed. No time for pride here.

They were an hour's ride to the East before Kane dared to open her mouth. 'Why are we heading to Darakeche?' she eventually dared to ask.

'We are not.'

Kane frowned. 'But, out here, there is only Darakeche, or...'

'The Empire,' Istari finished for her.

She choked on her shock and laughed nervously. 'You cannot be serious? We'll be killed!'

'Maybe.'

'Give me one good reason why we are going there.'

'To see my wife,' Istari answered calmly, 'and try to put an end to this madness.'

'Your wife lives in the Empire?'

'Of course she does,' Istari said. 'She is the Empress.'

THE ONLY WAY

As they took the steps down to the lower chamber, Aleister sniffed at the air. The incense and earthy smells of the throne room shifted and he caught a scent of metal and a choking sense of familiarity with the scent. It was one he knew all too well; one he was accustomed to having been in countless battles over the cycles and stood in makeshift infirmaries and held the hands of people he had fought beside as they breathed their last breaths.

The scent of blood.

An overwhelming smell that gave Aleister a moment to pause and hesitate. He closed his eyes and sniffed again. He recognised the scent but never had he been choked with the sheer ferocity of it. It seeped through his pores and invaded every aspect of his being. Each breath sucked in brought with it a wave of nausea that slowed his pace and made him reach for the wall to his right, steadying himself before he could continue further in towards the lower chambers of the grand temple.

The stone steps finally levelled out onto a narrow corridor. Candlelight crept through the door frame at the end of the corridor and cast dancing shadows as Aleister followed the others into the chamber. It was one large room. One, magnificent, wide, frightening, disturbing room.

'Oh, Gods…' Ariel muttered, placing a hand over her open mouth as she stopped in her tracks. Her other hand reached for Bathos and the big warrior took it and squeezed it tight as he stared around the chamber.

Ife stopped beside Aleister and turned to him after taking a moment to scan the room. 'I haven't been down here in cycles…'

Her words drifted away in Aleister's mind as he struggled to balance the glut of things attacking his senses. The overwhelming smell of blood; the ringing in his ears that just kept growing; the intricately carved statues of strange creatures dotted around the cavernous chamber, and, finally, the room's centrepiece – a wide, lengthy pool filled with a dark red liquid that Aleister most certainly recognised.

'Blood. You've been collecting blood…' He gazed up to the ceiling that seemed quite a distance away and winced as he watched further droplets fall from above and land in the pool before him. 'This is where it all gets collected. From those who sacrifice their lives. Why do you need such a thing?'

The king offered a weak smile at Aleister and pointed at the grim display overpowering the rest of the room. 'This is what will keep Takaara from the hands of our enemies. I asked you earlier what you knew about The Breaking of Takaara. Now, I will tell you what I know. Or at least, the parts pertaining to you.' He gestured to a row of stone seats carved from the wall on one side of the room. Ife went first, followed by a nervous Bathos and Ariel. Aleister gave Zeke an uncomfortable glance before finally following the others and taking a seat between his sister and Ife.

'Takaara has worshipped numerous Gods over the ages. The Old Gods of the North. The One in the East. Mamoon in the South. The Seven in the West. It was the age before the Breaking when the message of The Four became the most powerful. The strongest song in the world that overpowered all others. Light. Darkness. Chaos. Order.' Zeke sighed and knelt beside the pool, wading a couple of his fingers through the blood and then standing. He wiped the residue against the white scars beneath his eyes and continued. 'Magic grew stronger with each cycle, seemingly in line with the growing religion within the world. Old traditions persevered but the world began to worship The Four, aside from a few determined and stubborn folk in each nation. As the magic grew, those of us who could wield such power grew more confident with our application of such power. We created such things of beauty that the Gods themselves would weep!' Zeke paused, suddenly looking frail and weak. 'Alas, it was not to last.'

'What happened?' Ariel asked, leaning closer in her seat, lost in the tale.

Zeke looked from the pool of blood and then back to those sitting patiently and listening to his story, a sad smile on his dark face. 'We flew too close to the sun. There were four of us. Four Magi to complement The Four Gods. The four corners of the world. Anything that we imagined, we could do. There was nothing that stood in our way. We came together and created a world that we believed would never be bettered. But the problem with power, and success, is that you crave more. It becomes an addiction worse than any drug. You just want more.' Aleister shifted nervously in his seat, understanding the feeling all too well. 'We were great friends. We decided that we would create a bridge between ourselves and the Gods. Open the Sky Plane and then we could rule the land of Takaara from our rightful thrones up high. We became obsessed with the idea that *we* were The Four.' Zeke's eyes filled with a fiery intensity that threatened to blind any who stared at him long enough. He unclenched his fists and winced, cocking his head to the side and took a breath to steady himself.

'Are you okay, my King?' Ife asked, voice full of concern as she made to move towards him.

Zeke nodded and waved away her concern before taking another, long, slow breath. 'Gods. What a stupid, foolish idea. We studied and practised with one another, testing the limits of our powers and finding none. It was Harish who first unlocked a great secret. The ability to heal and be reborn. It took time but it could be done, with a strong enough power source. We found using the land of Takaara itself was enough. Eventually, we tested the limits of death itself. Elena was the one who found a way to tie our being to this world, so that we could be called back in another body. She pushed the boundaries. Such an intelligent woman...' Zeke paused, lost in the memories of a time forgotten

380

to most in Takaara. He cleared his throat. 'We trained Magi called Guardians to identify the signature of our powers so that they would be able to find us if we died, find us and aid in our remembering of the past and what we were capable of. We could be reincarnated with each death and live an eternal life. Imagine the possibilities!'

'None are meant to live forever,' Aleister warned, his low voice echoing around the chambers. 'We live. And we die. This is the way of things.'

'It is. We deemed ourselves above such things,' Zeke admitted. 'We tested our theory and it worked. For hundreds of cycles, we lived different lives but always returned together to share what we had discovered. To share and grow. After all we had accomplished, we felt ready to attempt to open a bridge between the planes, to discover other worlds. It was all going exactly as we had planned. But the cycles of living and dying took its toll on our friendship. Bickering and arguing was the way of things. We grew weary of the endless cycles, exhausted by our continued efforts. In secret, Harish and I developed a weapon that could end our lives and cut the tie that kept us tethered to the Takaara. We split the weapon in two. Sister blades. One of which you now own.'

Aleister unsheathed the sword and glanced over it with a new appreciation. A sword that could kill the Gods…

'You created a weapon that would end the lives of your friends?' Bathos asked with a frown. 'Surely you knew that wouldn't end well?'

Zeke sucked his gums and offered a small shrug. 'We were past the realm of reason. We met away from any form of life and started the procedure to open the gates to the other planes, some of us more reluctantly than others. We were close. The land shook and trembled with fear and a great crack snapped wide open in Takaara. Still we pushed on. Then, the youngest of us, Osiron, a complicated individual caught in a maelstrom of conflict between two lives, became overwhelmed by nerves and fear. They called for us to stop but we were too far gone. Osiron ripped away from the three of us and all I remember next is a great, white light. The next thing I recall is being woken by my

Guardian, my memories being restored, over two hundred cycles later…'

'And the gate to other planes?' Aleister asked. 'I've seen them used by capable magic users.' He thought back to seeing Mason D'Argio and his sermons.

'They were open, for those who knew how to find them. Harish, Elena and I searched for ways to close the gates but we needed our final component. Osiron was missing. Eventually, we found them in the last place we looked. On the Sky Plane. Time works differently there. A world of darkness filled only with voices of the dead. Osiron had grown powerful and vengeful but had no way of escaping. We trapped them on the Sky Plane as best we could, knowing that one day Osiron would break free and seek revenge.'

'You trapped your friend in a hell of your making because you feared their vengeance?' Aleister barked. 'No wonder Osiron is feeling vengeful.'

'Understand, my dear friend lived a life feeling trapped between two sides. Trapped in a body that wasn't theirs. Scorned for their choices, clothes, language, partners… everything. The three of us saw past that. We saw the great mage within and took Osiron under our wing. But we could not risk unleashing their fury on the world. It is my biggest regret, not being able to save our dear friend. We should have done more, but we were fools, all of us.'

'Have you tried to fix the mess you created?' Aleister responded, still furious and struggling to hide it. He felt Ariel's cool hand against his own and calmed.

'I have.' Zeke stepped forward and dropped to his knees. 'Every moment of my existence has been spent on working out how we can fix Takaara. The last quake warned me that Osiron has found a way from the Sky Plane. Magic is tethered to Takaara but, long ago, we discovered that blood, given freely, can be a substitute. It is not as volatile and dangerous as blood taken by force. We can use this to strengthen our forces, for the war to end all wars is coming. Osiron does not come alone. There is an imbalance across the planes and the fiends of Chaos will follow the path now open to Takaara and they will destroy all who stand in their way. We must fight.'

'Where are the other two? Will they be rallying against Chaos?'

Zeke raised a single finger to bring a stop to the discussion. A faint bubbling boiled in the centre of the bloody pool, drawing the gaze of all in the room.

Aleister stood from his seat, sword in hand and crept over to the edge of the pool. Zeke rested a hand on his shoulder and pointed at the bubbling growing in intensity.

Aleister jerked back as a head dripping in blood emerged from the surface of the pool. Bathos growled and Ariel gasped as a body emerged from the blood, soaked in the red liquid, naked and shaking as it ascended the steps at the edge of the pool.

Frowning, Aleister stood frozen to the spot as Zeke marched away and grabbed a large, dark cloth and wrapped it around the frightening man. With another cloth he helped the shivering nightmare wipe the blood from his face. A face that Aleister faintly remembered…

'It never gets any easier,' the man's voice shook as his teeth chattered together.

'You had to grow back legs this time,' Zeke laughed, holding the man tight with the cloth wrapped around his bloody form. 'Why you continue to seek out such punishment is beyond my understanding.'

'Mamoon is watching. Only he can understand what must be done.' Then it all clicked. Like the final piece of the puzzle. Aleister had seen this man before.

'You were in Archania. We have spoken. Harish…' Aleister said, disbelieving the words even as he spoke. Ariel and Bathos wandered over, taking a closer look at the man. 'We spoke in the Lower City, a crowd of fools…'

'… were being foolish. Doing as folk have always done across the numerous cycles. Treating those beneath them with disdain,' Harish grinned. 'I wondered where my sword had gone. The last I had heard it was still in the East. Then it was in the North. A long journey, but I wanted another look at it. It has been many cycles since my eyes took in the beauty of my greatest creation.'

'You made this?' Aleister asked, rolling the sword in his palms and holding it out to Harish.

The weak man waved a hand away and smiled softly. 'I made it. But I have sworn against using such things. It is yours. I have seen it.'

Ife stepped between the two men and the three friends, lightly scratching at one of the white scars under her eyes. 'The Wise Women have also seen it. If we are to close the gates, you know what must be done.'

Zeke shared a knowing glance with Harish and both men nodded before turning to the three allies from the North. 'Two blades that can be wielded as one. They sever the ties to Takaara that we worked so hard to create. Chaos is coming and there is only one way to save this world.' The king glared at Aleister and patted a hand on his own blade before pointing at the one in Aleister's hand. 'Use them to kill the four Magi who believed themselves to be Gods. Only then can Chaos be stopped.'

Ariel's distressed face told Aleister that she wasn't impressed with this idea. 'You want to die?'

'We have lived too many lives, Ariel of the Red Sons. We wish to rest,' Zeke said with a weary sigh. 'I am tired.'

'And we can rest, once we know that Takaara is safe,' Harish added.

'So, we kill the two of you,' Bathos said, counting them on his fingers. 'We kill this Osiron. That's three.' He pointedly displayed three fingers to them all. 'Where is the fourth?'

'The same place Elena has been since she gave up her search for Osiron,' Zeke said, more than a hint of disgust layered into his words. 'Sitting on the throne in the East.'

Aleister laughed incredulously and stared around at the grim faces surrounding him. 'You want us to kill the Empress of the East? The most protected leader in all Takaara?'

Harish and Zeke nodded together as though it was as simple a task as buttoning up a shirt.

Aleister cursed and stared at his sword. The vengeful weapon cried for blood, pleading for its thirst to be quenched. He looked at the grim but determined faces of his sister and his best friend, remembering the words offered to him by the Wise Women. 'Didn't come all this way for nothing. Killing Gods. Fighting an Empire. Fuck.' He blew out his cheeks and plastered a winning smile onto his face. 'Anything else you want while we're here? I'm feeling like a challenge…'

THE END IS COMING

Sly allowed himself a moment amongst the carnage to take a breath and wait on one knee. His arms were an inferno of aches and pains and blood dripped from at least three open wounds on his body. He pushed himself up with his axe, groaning with the effort and ignoring the squelch as his weapon dug deeper into the body of his latest victim. Back on two feet, he pulled his axe free and scanned the pile of bodies around him. The white cloaks were soaked in the blood and filth of battle. Most folk wouldn't have believed it if you said they were white to begin with, so covered were they in the shit of battle.

'Can't do this for much longer?' Cray wheezed, pushing his shoulders back and releasing a harsh breath from between his teeth as his back cracked with the effort. 'Can barely lift my sword.' He waded through the bodies mounting up between the walls of the buildings on either side and gave an admiring glance at Sly's efforts.

'Don't think we have much choice,' Sly said, rubbing his forehead and checking his hand to see if the blood was still pouring from the earlier wound. 'Only way out of this is by killing the bastards. Even if we made it out of the gate, do you think they would just let us go?'

Cray shrugged his broad shoulders and sniffed, wiping a sleeve across his face before replying. 'Not likely.'

'So we keep going.' It hurt to hold both his axes but Sly

made sure not to show it. Looking fearsome was half the job. He clapped a hand against his ally's torn sleeve and marched past, towards the relentless sound of battle. The narrow corridor between the two buildings opened back out into what had been a wide, spacious courtyard. Now the effects of the battle had twisted the area into a mix of motionless bodies and squirming, screaming soldiers crawling their way to what they hoped would be safety. The two sides had attempted to regain some measure of composure following their leader's calls for unity and discipline.

The Empire's fighters had finally realised that their efforts were better concentrated out in the open where they could use their advantage of numbers. The red cloaks stood depleted and exhausted. Danil stood at the head of their forces, one arm hanging uselessly at his side, clearly popped out from its socket whilst an unfortunate wound wept blood from his temple. Still, Sly had to give the warrior credit. He held a sword in his good arm and gritted his teeth, glaring at the enemy and not giving an inch.

'One last stand!' Danil cried to his fellows. He reached behind his back and grabbed a black mask. He placed the mask on his face, the circular eyes gleaming red with blood from the fighting. The rest of his followers copied his actions, hiding their fear, their anger, hiding everything with the odd black masks with the long, beak-like noses. 'Let's wipe this plague from the face of Takaara!'

Sly took his place beside Socket with a curt nod, Cray joining them with a grunt of his own. Kiras just stood, eyes lighting with a calm fury as she scanned the wave of soldiers standing in her way. 'Looks like this is it,' he said to her, spitting at his foot and twisting the axes in his hands. 'I'm on thirty-three, by the way,' he added with a grin to Cray.

'Thirty-five.'

Sly spun on his ally, incensed. '*Thirty-five!*' he growled and took a step towards the enemy. 'Fuck this. I ain't losing out today.'

'Nothing has changed,' Kiras said. There was no emotion in her voice. She announced it with a calm certainty. 'We kill every. Last. One. Of. Them.'

'Aye,' Socket agreed, running a hand along the shaft of an arrow. 'For Baldor.'

The Empire's soldiers marched together, each step booming around the courtyard as they pressed forward, certain of victory against the meagre force defending itself. A few of the soldiers around Sly twitched or switched their stance but, to their credit, they held their ground to a man. Knowing death is on its way can do strange things to a person. Some might run or cry their final minutes away but others will know a calmness with understanding that the end is coming. A serene tranquillity that does not compare with anything else known in this world.

Or at least that is what Sly had been told. In his mind, he had already picked out the three fuckers he was going to behead so that he could beat Cray.

'You have fought well!' one of the soldiers called as the Empire's line halted. His jacket bore a hundred different pompous badges and ribbons that made Sly's head ached just by looking at the various colours and letters. 'Much better than we expected. You have earned honour in your defiance. We shall not take prisoners. But we will offer a quick death if you surrender now.'

No sign of movement. No response.

Sly peered in the chasm between the two warring sides and smirked as he spotted a torn flag lying in amongst the dirt, the bodies and the blood. A flag bearing that white fucking sun. Without another thought, he stepped forward, all eyes turning to him. He pulled down his trousers, baring his pale arse to his allies and smiling as the enemy's soldiers turned away in disgust at the sight of his cock in hand. He rocked back and forth, smiling with glee as his piss landed on the flag, steam rising from the ground. A few groans broke out in front of him. Laughter from behind. He shook away the last few drops before pulling his trousers back up and returning to his position.

Even Kiras had the shadow of a smile on her face.

'I think that's your fucking answer!' he shouted, revelling in the soldier's fury as the pompous prick waved his hand to his fellow men and rushed towards the back of the line. Coward.

The Empire's front line took a step forward, eager to get the whole thing over with and make Sly pay for the offence against their people.

Then the world shook.

Softly to begin with. A low rumble as the buildings around them rocked. Archers on the battlements gripped the edges of the wall and steadied themselves to keep from falling. Nervous glances circulated the Empire's soldiers. Sly had no clue what his own side were doing. One good thing about the masks. Hides the uncertainty.

The rumbling grew until Sly's ears hurt with the sound. Kiras pushed her arms out to balance herself and stay on her feet, and Cray bounced into him as soldiers dropped to the ground, unable to keep up. A huge crack developed in the gap separating the armies and Sly found himself pushing Socket and Kiras back, keeping them away from the gaping hole that had suddenly opened in front of them. The Empire's soldiers fell to their knees and gazed up at the sky, making frantic signs with their hands and screaming in their own language to the sky above. Sly couldn't understand the words but he got the message.

They were shitting themselves.

As sudden as it had started, the quake stopped. A silence pervaded the battlefield as nervous soldiers glanced towards the newly formed hole in the courtyard. Two of the buildings collapsed around them in the chaos and lay in a pile of rubble and debris. A few groans and cries could be heard in amongst the destruction. Poor bastards caught up in the madness.

Then *he* appeared.

Purple robe with black edging. Hood pulled up tight, casting an ominous shadow over one side of his face. Strange, black eyes sparkled with the light of stars… The being was an odd one but Sly recognised him in an instant.

'Kid… you're alive.' Sly choked out the words before turning to see the horror on Cray's face and the worry lining Kiras' and Socket's. 'How?'

Arden marched forward with a new confidence, no longer the kid who had begged Sly for advice in the Borderlands.

'It's a long story.' He stopped and placed a hand on Sly's shoulder. 'I never thought I would see you again. Thank you.' His voice sounded distance and layered with the melody of a thousand others. Sly just nodded as Arden moved on and found himself in Kiras' arms. 'I know what happened with Baldor and I'm sorry that I couldn't stop it. They will pay.' Finally, he stepped in front of Socket. A single tear ran down from Socket's good eye.

'You know what I'm about to say,' the old man croaked, resignation lining his wrinkled face. For the first time since Sly had known the man, the archer looked relieved, like a weight had been taken from him and he was able to breathe easily after a long period of suffocation.

Arden nodded and smiled. 'I forgive you, old man. For stabbing me in the back. That is something I would never do.'

Socket's eye flashed wide as he let out a sharp grunt. Arden fell with him to the ground, guiding his fall and keeping his own, strange eyes on that of his mentor. 'But stabbing you in the front, where you can see exactly what I am capable of. That is something that I would do.'

The young archer stood, turning from Socket's twitching body and choked groans and smiling at the rest of the waiting soldiers, admiring their masks as they watched his every move. 'I like this look. Wiping out the plague... makes sense. You will be cared for, once this is all over. I do not forget those who stand beside me. Who stand beside *us*.'

Kiras dropped to the ground, holding Socket's scarred hand in her own and glancing from the weeping wound to his frightened face. His old body shook with repeated spasms but Kiras did her best to comfort him.

'Arden,' Sly said, cocking his head towards the Empire's soldiers as Arden smiled at him. 'We're in the middle of something here...'

Arden Leifhand grinned. It wasn't the nervous, excited smile that Sly had seen before. It was cold. Confident. Assured. It was the smile of death itself.

'Do not worry. My new friends will deal with them.'

Arden's eyes lost the sparkle of the stars as the black clouds above cracked with lightning, unleashing rain upon the battlefield. Sly jerked back as dark shadows poured from the chasm in the courtyard. The Empire's soldiers forgot all their training and discipline as they fought one another and scrambled to get away from the shadows, crying and clawing their way towards the back of the courtyard and doing anything they could to put some distance between them and the nightmarish creatures ascending from the hells.

Some of the red cloaks backed away. Others pulled off their masks and wept, unable to watch the horror unfold before them. Sly watched the shadows carefully. They were men and women but unlike any he had ever seen. They wore all black, blending in with the night's darkness except for flashes of red as their eyes widened. Some swung swords or stabbed spears. Other held no weapon but tore at the soldiers with claws longer than Sly's axes and ripped at throats with their sharpened teeth. They were no normal soldiers, that much was certain.

Arden just watched it all with a casual amusement.

'Kid, what are you doing?' Sly asked, frowning at the young man as Danil turned and vomited, weeping between each lurch onto the ground.

'Creating a better world. For us all.'

THE OFFER

Cypher had thought about turning it down. The bastard didn't deserve his time or company. That much was true. But Cypher was nothing if not curious. And now he had some powerful friends. Friends that even Mason D'Argio should be worried about. Friends who had killed that little prick King Asher without leaving a trace behind.

So, he found himself whistling a merry tune as he made his way through the palace, nodding at the guards who had been told to look sad, even though most of them had thought Asher had got what was coming to him. Some members of the staff, young maids and a fair few servants had even been caught throwing an impromptu party after the unloved king's funeral. They were the ones who had been treated like shit throughout the little bastard's life though Cypher doubted things would get much better. Uncertainty reigned over the United Cities of Archania now.

He knocked on the door to the throne room and was unsurprised to see the familiar stony expression of Mason's dog.

'T'Chai. How wonderful to see you again.'

'He is waiting.'

'Then I best hurry.'

Nothing had changed in the room. Well, except for the one big change. Mason sat on the throne, a smug smile etched on his face.

'You look like someone who has seen their plan go off without a hitch,' Cypher said to the preacher.

'Not without a hitch,' Mason said, sticking out his bottom lip and rubbing a hand along the armrest. 'But how can I complain when I am sitting on the throne of the United Cities of Archania? I must play the hand that I am dealt. And this hand suits me so well…'

'No arguing from me.'

'I have to say, I am slightly surprised at the ease of your acceptance. I expected more resistance when the offer was given for you to meet me here. We have,' Mason studied his perfect nails with raised eyebrows before returning his gaze to Cypher, 'a troubled history.'

'That is one way of putting it,' Cypher agreed. 'But things have changed of late. I'm a new man.' He presented a wide smile to reinforce his point and flashed his eyes.

'I sincerely hope not. The reason for me bringing you here is wholly entwined with the fact that I know who you are and I know what you want.' Mason leered wildly at Cypher and then chuckled at the raised eyebrow. 'Oh yes, I know. You want me dead. That much is clear even to the dead. No, I know something else about you. You, Cypher Zellin, crave *notoriety*. You have killed and thrive on the power and the rush of pride in the skill you show.'

Cypher shrugged. A fair point. 'You got me there. What about it?'

'I am here to offer you the chance to fulfil your wildest dreams. Nay, I am offering you the chance to do something that you wouldn't have even dreamt of!'

'I'm listening.' He struggled to hide his interest in the preacher's words. Cypher knew what lies could be woven and unleashed by a forked, silver tongue.

Mason stood from the throne and stepped only an arm's length from Cypher, still towering over him and scanning him with those metal grey eyes. 'I know who you have been speaking to and I know why you have been playing your part. Who would dare to argue against a God? Believe me, I understand that more than you know.' The words hung heavily in the space between them, waiting to be unlocked further but Cypher knew when to hold his tongue. 'Only a fool would argue against such power.'

'My thoughts exactly,' Cypher said, licking his lips and staring right back at Mason. 'And I'm no fool.'

'That, I am aware of. Still, I have knowledge that you do not. My position, along with that of my sister's, grants me access to things that would brighten even your grim face.'

'Time to get to the point preacher, I'm getting bored.'

'The offer that I bring to you is one that no one else can give. You, who has killed for fun and revelled in the art of pain. Cypher Zellin, join me and I offer you something that even you would not be able to turn down.'

'And just what might that be?' As much as he hated admitting it to himself, he was intrigued and ready to bite.

'I offer you the chance,' Mason D'Argio said, licking his lips with that forked tongue, 'to kill a God.'

Acknowledgements

The space between books one and two has been a strange one. A worldwide pandemic means that the release for Paths of Chaos is in a world that looks very different to the one in which Flames of Rebellion burst forth. Whilst most of book two was outlined with key scenes already in place, the events of 2020 definitely had an impact regarding themes and the ways in which some of the characters interact with one another. Hopefully reading the books brings as much of a distraction from the difficulties of current events as writing them has been for me.

A big thank you to Grimdark Readers and Writers Facebook group where I have been able to share ideas and be inspired by a range of wonderful and talented people.

To Jon Oliver for his ruthless editing and for ensuring the stupid mistakes I am sometimes blind to get spotted before print. It is a great feeling to be able to work with an editor whom you can trust and Jon is one of the best.

To all of the readers who have reviewed my books or messaged me to tell me about a favourite scene or character, you are amazing and I hope Paths of Chaos provides you with just as much enjoyment!

To my friends and family, especially Sarah and Kiwi – thanks for all the support with my writing. You make this a lot easier than it should be and I hope I can pay you back with more interesting stories over the coming years!

One more book to go and that is the trilogy done!

Until next time, Embrace the Chaos…

If you liked *Paths of Chaos*, then dive back into the world of *The Broken Gods* with:

A Long Way from Home – Short stories from the world of The Broken Gods

By Aaron S. Jones

Blood feuds in the Borderlands. Murder mysteries in the United Cities. A heist gone wrong in the East. Meet some of the weird and wonderful characters of the world of Takaara and they fight, love and survive in A LONG WAY FROM HOME.

THE ARSE END OF NOWHERE

Business was slow. Always was this far out in the Borderlands.

Kiras continued wiping over the cups, unaware that the cloth was now far dirtier than the object she aimed to clean. Just the one patron tonight – a huge hulking figure sat nursing a jug of mead in the corner of the room. At first, she had thought the strange man to be a Barbarian but that would have been stupid. Crossing into the Borderlands would have just meant trouble and they certainly wouldn't be sitting there as calm as the man with the hair spiked in the middle of an otherwise shaved head. She flicked her own braided, blonde hair and continued with the cleaning, now aware that she needed a new cloth.

She glanced over her shoulder into the candlelit backroom. Cagen lay back in his chair, holding up his new book on the history of the Southern Kingdoms. Strange guy. Always yapping on about what life was like everywhere but never really caring about what was in front of him. Still, it was good of him to give Kiras the job. There wasn't much to do in the Borderlands, especially this far north and yet he had taken her on without a second thought. A good man, if a little too lazy.

The tavern stood alone in the snow, a couple of miles away from any village. Kiras liked it like that. Most folk couldn't be bothered to make the harsh journey there and the ones who did were usually decent enough people just desperate for a good drink and a warm fire. Not often would a tavern in the Borderlands be able to go weeks without a good scrap but Kiras had lucked out here. Weren't enough patrons for any such incidents. She felt safe. In a land full of bloodthirsty warriors, a woman needs to feel safe. She checked the two daggers hidden at the back of her belt beneath her flowing navy shirt. She felt safer with a sharp weapon or two. That was certain. A woman can't expect a man to be around at all times. She had to look after herself and that was just the way of things.

'Want another?' she called over to the large man in the corner.

He jerked slightly at her voice as though she had caught him by surprise before recovering and nodding, holding his jug out for her as she strolled over to him. He had a gentle face, for a big man. His shirt had no sleeves, showcasing two pale, rippling trunk-like arms. A large warhammer rested against the wall behind him, almost the size of Kiras. Most warriors wouldn't be able to lift that beast up, let alone swing it with any accuracy but she'd bet her last scrap of food that this guy could.

Strange thing was, with his size and the intimidating weapon he carried, she didn't feel scared around him. Most men put her on edge. You never knew when they might make a pass or get offended by a rejection. Too many women she knew had ended up as bones all on account of a man with a bruised ego. This guy seemed different. A child in a giant's body. Looks could be deceiving.

She poured the man's drink and carefully carried it over to him. He gave her a soft smile and his cheeks turned redder than an evening sun as he took the jug, his eyes averted to the scuffed, wooden table. So strange.

'Want me to put more wood on the fire?' she asked him. 'Gets pretty damn cold up here this time of year. Or any time of year to be honest.'

'I'm fine, thank you,' the strange man responded, clearing his throat. 'I'm used to the cold.'

'What tribe you a part of?' Only a few of the men in the Borderlands were rogues, men of no tribe. For safety and security, it was always better to be part of a group. The lone wolf dies in places like this, but the pack survives. It had always been the way.

'Herick's.' His grin grew as he felt more comfortable with the conversation. 'Further north of here.' That explained it. Herick's tribe lived closer to the Barbarian hordes than any other. Cut away on a small island as far north as you can get in the Borderlands, they were a different breed. She'd heard good things Herick even had a lot of women warriors in his tribe from what Kiras had heard. Good for him.

'I'm Kiras by the way.'

'Baldor. Nice to meet you Kiras,' the warrior said with a

booming voice, smile wider than ever now.

'So, I have to know,' Kiras said, taking a seat next to Baldor. There were no other customers to serve. May as well have a seat and see what the guy's about. 'Can you actually swing that thing in a fight?' She motioned to the Warhammer with a slight nod. It gleamed in the firelight of the tavern. No dried blood on it as far as she could see.

'With ease,' Baldor informed her, taking another sip of his drink and looking awfully proud of himself. 'Gifted my first hammer when I was three cycles. They seem to get bigger each time I get a new one.'

'Bet you can do some real damage with that. I prefer daggers myself. Better for speed.'

'Remind me not to get on your bad side then!' Baldor laughed. It warmed the tavern and put Kiras further at ease. No one with a laugh like that could be a threat to her. She liked this Baldor guy.

'I er… I'm just popping outside,' the warrior said rather sheepishly, again looking away from her gaze. 'Too much drink in a short space of time…'

'You need a piss,' Kiras said with a laugh of her own. 'Got ya! Well, I'll be here when you're back.'

Baldor rushed out of the tavern, pushing open the door and allowing Kiras a glimpse of the growing snowstorm outside. Always seemed to be snowing lately. She grabbed a couple of the smaller logs and chucked them into the fire, pausing to embrace the heat of the rising flames.

Behind her, she heard the door swing open again.

'That was—' she turned, expecting to see the giant warrior returned from his piss. Instead, there were three road-weary men with hoods pulled up over their wild hair. The one standing in front lowered his tattered, brown hood and shook his dark, wild mane before releasing a long breath.

'This is a warm welcome,' he said, eyes running over Kiras like she was a piece of meat left out for a hungry wolf. It was a look that she was used to. 'An unexpected surprise. Usually we only have the ugly mug of Cagen to greet us after a long ride in the snow. I feel warmer already with such a *beauty* standing before me.'

'You three want a drink?' Kiras asked, ignoring the comment. You could dress a pig in a skirt and most the men around here would find it beautiful. Their brains were somewhere a bit lower than their skulls when it came to women. Or just to things that move.

'That would be delightful!' The man said, clapping his hands and glancing at his two grinning fools beside him. They lowered their own hoods to reveal their fiery red hair. Brothers most likely by the way they each had the same crooked nose and dark beady eyes. 'Some mead whilst we wait for our old friend Cagen…'

'I know that voice!' Kiras slipped behind the bar to grab the three drinks as Cagen shuffled out from the back, face slightly pink as he rubbed his knuckles nervously. 'Garren, as always it is a pleasure to see you and your associates,' Cagen said, voice breaking slightly as he held out a hand to the dark-haired man.

Garren's smile dropped as he stared at the hand, not making a move to accept it. 'It's been two moons, Cagen, my friend. Do you have the money? He's getting impatient. Feels like you're taking the piss with him now…'

Kiras peered up from the bar, keeping an eye on the proceedings as she placed one of the drinks on the table in front of her. She'd never seen Cagen look this nervous. Whoever these men were, they were trouble.

Cagen pulled his hand away and wiped his sweaty palms on his black shirt before scratching his short, greying hair. 'It's been a slow cycle. Not many travellers have been coming this far since the incident with the Barbarians at the start of the cycle. Now the weather's getting worse too. I'm a bit short on what I owe…'

'A bit *short?*' Garren repeated, looking at his cronies who grimaced in response. 'Now I *know* that he isn't going to like that. And when he gets upset, there's problems for us all Cagen. You know that. You know how… *angry* he can get. Would hate for anyone to get hurt just because you're a bit *short.*'

'I can sell some things,' Cagen offered, voice growing higher with each word as Kiras finally finished pouring the drinks. 'I promise, I can sort this out. I just need a bit of time.'

Kiras scooped up the three cups of mead and quietly placed them on the table next to the newcomers. One of the brothers followed her every step, winking as she bent over to place the drinks down. She sighed and cursed under her breath. It had been a good run. A whole moon without an incident. Got to be happy with the little things.

'Time,' Garren said, tutting as he let out a long breath from the corner of his mouth and placed his hands on his hips. Kiras spotted the leather handle of a longsword hanging loosely at his side. 'I'm just not sure we have the time, Cagen. Still…' His dark eyes landed on Kiras as she made to head back to the bar. Flashing forward, he gripped her braids and pulled down, jerking her back so that she was looking up into his leering face. Her scalp burnt with agony as her hair clung onto the skin. She groaned but didn't fight back. Not yet. 'I'm sure we can come to some arrangement.'

'Leave her alone!' Kiras was shocked to hear the steel return to Cagen's voice. Didn't think he had it in him. 'She's not part of this!'

'But with her, we could consider the debt paid for half a cycle. That's me being very generous…' Garren snarled, blowing a kiss down to Kiras and tightening his grip on her hair. Stupid hair. Made it too easy for him to control her.

'Anything but that, Garren. Please…' Cage pleaded.

'Take her boys. I want her alive once you're done. Our boss will not be pleased if we head home empty handed.' Garren threw Kiras to the brothers. One of them caught her with a tight grip around her shoulders. Close up, she could see a small scar crossed over his pale lips. The other brother pulled at her hair and leaned in close enough for her to smell his stale breath.

'I won't have this!' She heard a thump followed by a groan and the thud of a body hitting the ground. Poor Cagen. Brave, but foolish. If she was going to get out of this, it would be up to her to act. Can't wait for a man.

Slipping a hand behind her back, she pulled out one of her daggers and thrust straight up, catching one of her attackers in the throat. The grip on her hair lessened as her victim released a shocked, gurgled cry, eyes panicked and darting in every direction as he struggled to work out what had happened. His blood poured over his cloak and onto Kiras but she wasn't waiting. She twisted her lithe body to the left, welcoming the looser grip on her in the madness of the moment and slashed expertly across the scarred brother's throat. Another scar for his collection.

He clutched at his neck, desperately attempting to staunch the flow of blood before stumbling back into one of the wooden tables.

Kiras spun, both daggers now in hand, one soaked in red and the other glistening in the firelight and ready for action.

'You dumb fucking bitch! Do you know who you're messing with?' Garren cried, seething with rage as he watched his two allies drop to the floor in puddles of blood. Cagen had sat up, leaning against his bar with one hand resting on his swollen cheek.

'I've no idea,' Kiras spat back. 'And I couldn't give a shit.'

Garren lunged forward clumsily, sword stabbing for her heart. Kiras dodged it with ease, spinning to the side of the attack and slashing down the man's forearm, forcing him to drop the weapon. She kicked at his legs and dropped him to his knees, snapping forward so that she stood behind him, dagger pressed so hard against his throat that she could feel his pulse against the weapon.

'Who sent you?' she asked calmly, pulling on his hair to force his eyes up to focus on her. 'My patience is wearing thin.'

'Magnar! He keeps these places protected. Messing with him is a bad decision girlie! How old are you? Sixteen cycles? Seventeen?'

'Fifteen.' Kiras bit her lip and dug her knee deep into the man's back, enjoying him squirm. 'Where can I find this Magnar?'

'Two days ride to the east. A small village. Can't miss it. Now let me go!' Garren screamed, struggling against her hold.

'Sure.' She made certain that the cut was slow, painful. She ignored the screams and the feeling of warmth as the blood dripped over her hand. The dagger was sharp enough to cut through his throat with ease.

She released the body once it stopped twitching, sure he was dead. Garren fell to the floor with a thud just as a tall figure returned to the tavern, stooping low under the door frame.

Baldor was covered in blood, his hands especially dripping with the red stuff. He entered the room breathing heavily, staring at the three bodies on the floor, then to Kiras with her bloodied daggers, Cagen squirming next to the bar and finally at his forgotten warhammer in the corner of the room.

'You've been busy,' he said.

'So have you.'

Baldor looked down at his bloodied hands and uselessly wiped them on his already filthy trousers. 'Had a disagreement. Think they were friends of his.' He pointed at Garren's lifeless body.

'You up for a ride?' Kiras asked, sheathing her weapons and strolling over to the giant warrior. 'I quite fancy seeing you wield that bastard thing.' She pointed at the warhammer as Baldor grinned.

'Lead the way.'

The ride wasn't too bad. Baldor didn't complain once. Hardly spoke at all really. The perfect companion in her eyes.

They kept an easy pace and rested when they wanted. There was no need to rush. No one would be racing ahead to warn Magnar and his men. They had time and revenge was never something to be rushed. Patience is a virtue necessary for any warrior wanting to survive to a reasonable age. Not enough of them seemed to know that.

The snow had died down by the time the village was in sight. Shame really. Could have used the cover.

The village of Tofthund wasn't much. Built in the arse

end of nowhere, it was a beacon for those wanting to keep away from prying eyes and out of the light. Had to be tough to live there, this close to the Far North and Barbarians. It wouldn't be easy getting to Magnar. There'd have to be more blood spilled than his.

A wooden perimeter sharpened to spikes at the top acted as a deterrent to any passers-by with a wish to cause mischief. The only way into the village was through the guarded entrance at the front. Kiras spotted six men with spears – two of them asleep on chairs. They wore no armour; content with the thought that any outsiders would be dissuaded from causing trouble.

'What's the plan?' Baldor asked, following her gaze to the guards. Smoke rose over the village from the numerous fires that would be heating the longhouses, taverns and faze dens within.

'He won't be hard to find. Let's just ask if we can go in. Two weary travellers wanting a drink. Shouldn't be much of a problem. Once we're in, we find him and ask a few questions.' She liked the way Baldor's lips curled on the one side at the suggestion of this ending without blood. 'Can't see any harm in it.' She ensured her daggers were tucked inside the back of her belt as she bounced down the hill towards the village, followed closely by the giant footsteps of her new companion.

'Halt and state your business!' one of the guards shouted as they drew near. All eyes stayed fixed on Baldor, nervous glances at the giant and his ungodly weapon.

'My name is Kiras. This is my friend, Baldor. We are both of Herick's tribe. No villages around here for days so we want a bite to eat and some rest for ourselves and our horses. Then we'll be on our way!'

They listened to her. One of the guards even glanced her way for a moment before returning to Baldor. Men don't like feeling small and in the giant's shadow, that's all a man could feel.

'Inn's on the left as you head in. There's some spaces,' the guard said, cautiously ending his scan of Baldor and turning to Kiras. 'We'll call for someone to take the horses to the stables.

404

They'll be looked after.'

'That's so kind. Isn't it, Baldor?' she fluttered her eyelids up at the big man who grunted back, eyes fixed on the spears in front of him. He was enjoying this. Just like her.

The guards parted to allow them entry into the village, eyes never leaving them, even as they walked on the rough, dirt path covered in the week's snow.

Kiras snorted and thumped her ally on the arm. 'Easy! Told ya!'

'Long way to go yet...' Baldor warned. He wasn't stupid. A good sign. Had his head screwed on. Being the size of a small house and carrying a weapon like that would be dangerous if he didn't have at least a bit of intelligence.

She'd suggest keeping to the shadows but her companion didn't seem like one for keeping out of sight. Best thing to do would be to embrace it. She strode down the middle of the street like she owned the place. Winked at a few of the grim-faced onlookers and returned scowls with warm smiles. No one seemed impressed but they eventually looked away, eager to keep from causing trouble with the beast at her side. They didn't need to know how gentle he could be.

A bunch of revellers stumbled out onto the street, clearly many cups deep and struggling to keep on their feet. Kiras paused as one of the happy gang fell into Baldor, his face dropping as his sudden motion was stopped by the huge man.

'What the f—' He was ready to begin his tirade before his eyes found Baldor's stomach and then slowly drifted up to the warrior's face. Kiras enjoyed watching the blood fade from the drunken fool's face, leaving him almost as white as the snow that his three friends had fallen into behind him. 'Must have slipped on the wet ground...'

Baldor nodded and growled, his whole body tensing, ready for an altercation.

It never came.

They were drunk but they had enough sense to leave this one alone. Kiras waved them away as they scrambled towards whatever hole they were staying in.

'I take it you don't want to be staying here long?' Kiras asked the big man as he tore his eyes away from the group and towards the large tavern they had fallen from.

'Too many people. Let's do what we have to and go.'

She wasn't going to argue with that.

Blowing out her cheeks, she pulled her trousers up and tightened the wolf-fur wrapped around her shoulders before heading towards the music emanating from the tavern.

The heat of the room hit her first, followed closely by the smell. A packed room of sweat drenched thieves, merchants and warriors all drinking and gambling away. In every town and village in the Borderlands, it was always the taverns that did the best business. Even the poorest of folk seemed to be able to find a coin for a drink or two.

The buzz of conversation died down only a fraction as they entered. She tried her hardest not to snort with laughter as most of the men struggled to decide whether they needed to stare at the woman walking into their hovel or at the giant who had to bend down to even fit through the doorway. Nervous glances towards the warhammer slung over Baldor's back told them all they needed to know as they returned to their talk and mead and the volume resumed at its usual level.

Kiras sauntered over to the bar, squeezing past some of the more ignorant patrons unwilling to get out of her way. She smiled as Baldor towered over them. They soon moved.

'What can I get the two of you?' the barman asked Kiras with a smile that said he'd worked in this business a long time. Probably seen it all in a place like this.

'Two meads. Big one for the big guy,' Kiras answered before leaning closer over the bar. 'Where can I find Magnar? I have some business with him. I've a message from Garren for him.'

The barman's suspicious frown switched to relieved smile at the name. 'In the back, playing cards with a select few. Shouldn't be long. I can let you know when he's done?'

'That would be perfect,' Kiras flashed her best smile and paid for the drinks. She spun around to keep an eye on the room.

Better to be safe than sorry. Showing your back to a room full of drunken men is a one-way street to being bones. Thankfully, she had Baldor to look out for her.

'There's a guy who's been staring at us since the moment we walked in,' he told her. 'In the corner. Back to the wall.'

'Messy beard? Flicking the dagger around his fingers?' she asked, eyeing the unkempt warrior in the corner of the room. He looked a right mess. Baldor was right though. His eyes were fixed on the two of them. 'Keep an eye on him. We won't be long.'

All tables were full of men and a few women lost in conversation and dropping their drinks over each other as they laughed and argued with one another. In the corner closest to them, a few of the patrons were throwing their daggers at a red and black board, aiming for the centre target and betting whatever items they had available. A few others were doing their best to win a game of cards. Cheating was encouraged if you could get away with it in the Borderlands. Though, she'd seen enough brawls break out in her time to know that getting caught wasn't fun.

'He's ready, miss,' the barman called over.

Kiras downed her drink and smirked at the impressed look on Baldor's face before he followed suit.

The barman led them through a closed purple curtain that separated the main bar from a quieter room.

The room was the complete opposite to the bare bar next door. Opulence was the first word that snapped into her mind though she had no clue how it had got there in the first place.

The walls were covered with paintings of bloody battles and stuffed heads of a variety of animals that could be found in the wild Borderlands. Some of the animals must have been foreign as she'd never seen them before. Huge red heads with fangs longer than her forearm. Soft cushions lay scattered around the edges of the room where a few men smoked faze from small pipes, the mist filling the room and creating a thin fog that made things a bit more difficult to see in. Scantily clad women not much older than Kiras lay with them, cups of red wine in hand and dizzy smiles on their faces. In the centre of the room was a large, round table.

Eight men sat on chairs that looked like they were made from bone with red cushions pushed against the backs. The largest of the men sat opposite the entrance to the room. He had broad shoulders, a closely trimmed dark beard and intelligent eyes that scanned the two of them as they moved further into the room.

Magnar.

'My assistant tells me that you have a message from Garren.' His voice was strong and deep. Kiras felt a sudden flash of stupidity for coming here but she shook it away. Confidence was key.

'Yeah,' she said, clearing her throat and feeling some confidence return as all the seated men stared up in wonder at Baldor next to her. 'The message is, he's dead.'

The mood in the room could be cut with a dagger. Seven of the men broke into dark mutterings with one another, their hands twitching to weapons beneath the table but not Magnar. He just sat there. Staring.

'I assume your companion had something to do with Garren's... passing,' Magnar said, glancing at Baldor before his eyes returned to Kiras.

'Actually, it was me.' A few laughs broke out around the table but they stopped as Kiras glared at the perpetrators. 'Along with the two brothers with the fiery beards. My friend here killed the rest.'

There was no laughing now.

'I assume that is not your only message, girl?'

'My boss, Cagen. He doesn't owe you a thing. So leave him alone and we won't have any more of this *unpleasantness*.' Her heart quickened as she said the words. The chairs scraped against the floor as seven men stood as one, staring at the two of them. Still Magnar just sat there, unmoving.

'I shall leave him,' he said to stunned silence. 'But I will take you as a gift in return.'

'Your friends already tried that,' Kiras snapped. 'Didn't turn out too well for them…'

'I'm sure it didn't. Too bad,' he yawned and waved a hand, finally standing from his seat. 'Kill them.'

Baldor moved faster than the North wind. His great warhammer was in his meaty hands quicker than she could realise what was happening and grasp for her daggers.

A rather angry thug whipped his sword her way, eyes wild and violent. Before she could raise one of her daggers, his head exploded before her eyes with the weight of a perfect swing of that mighty hammer. Blood sprayed all over the room along with bits of what she assumed was flesh and bone. The headless body crumpled to the floor, watched by all in the room. A tense silence filled the air as all Magnar's men stared at Baldor and his weapon. A calm before the storm. Kiras used it to her advantage.

Whipping forward, she slashed a dagger across the back of one of the men before thrusting the other into his throat and throwing him out of her way.

The room erupted with cries as all the men rushed towards them. All except Magnar. He just stood patiently. Waiting.

Baldor was a sight to see. Between her ducking and diving to escape the wild lunges and swipes of the swords and daggers heading her way, Kiras could see the giant weaving his way through the room in a beautiful red dance. He decorated the room with the men stupid enough to step in his way as Kiras stabbed and slashed to keep the rest from getting too close.

She was fast but not fast enough. The edge of a blade caught her hip and snapped her out of focus. Barely blocking the next strike, she rolled to the ground, cutting across the man's thigh in one motion before jumping up behind him and delivering a killing blow straight into his heart.

'That was close…'

'Not as close as this.' Cursing, she felt a sword pressed against her throat and warm breath on her ear. 'A good fight but it ends now. Tell him to drop that lovely hammer of his…'

Magnar.

Soaked in blood, Baldor loomed over one final opponent. The poor guy was staring up at the warrior like he was a god, his breathing quick and panicked.

'Kill him, big guy. Kill them both,' she urged, praying that Baldor wouldn't do anything stupid. Her face dropped in time with the hammer. It fell to the floor with loud bang that shook the room. 'Shit…'

'Wise decision,' Magnar muttered. 'I could do with fighters like the two of you. Better than seven of my men apparently. What do y—'

Kiras flinched as an axe whipped past her face and buried itself deep into Magnar's. She slipped from his grasp and joined Baldor, both staring at the fallen leader as the blood began to pour from a wound that ran from his forehead all the way down to his chin.

Baldor picked his hammer up and stared at the man walking into the room. The one who had thrown the axe.

The newcomer sniffed and snapped his head to both sides, producing a loud cracking noise.

'You could have killed me!' Kiras yelled, recognising the man who had been watching them in the bar. He had a foul smell that followed him into the room and his eyes were like that of a wild animal.

'*Could*…' the warrior repeated. 'Remember that girlie.' He pulled another axe from the holster on his hip and swung it absently across the kneeling man at Baldor's feet. They were all dead.

Not done, the warrior paced over to Magnar and placed a filthy, hole-riddled boot onto the dead man's shoulder. He pulled the axe free with a squelch and wiped the weapon against his tattered olive-green shirt.

'Why did you do that?' she asked him.

'Been wanting to kill that fucker for ages,' he shrugged in return. 'Heard the commotion and thought now was as good a time as ever. There's a way out back. Wouldn't recommend going out the front. Too many eyes.'

Kiras exchanged a questioning glance with Baldor who took his turn to shrug.

'Who are you?' she asked.

'Sly. Sly Stormson.' He hocked up a great load of saliva and spat on Magnar before stepping nonchalantly over the corpse. 'You two coming or not?'

'Where you going?'

'Reaver's son is calling for warriors. Putting a group together,' Sly frowned, looking up and down at Baldor. 'Looks like your momma fucked a bear. Reaver could use a big bastard like you.' He turned to Kiras and licked his cracked lips. 'I'm assuming by your bloodied blades that bearboy over here didn't kill 'em all. Could use you too, though not sure if he likes fighting girls. That's Herick's deal.'

He left without another word.

Kiras turned to Baldor, biting her lip as she weighed up her options.

'What do you reckon? Should we go?'

Baldor shrugged his huge shoulders again. 'Wherever you go, I'll follow.'

That was all she needed to hear. Ignoring the blood and bone, she stood up on the tips of her toes as the giant leant down. She kissed him briefly on his cheek and laughed as he went that amazing shade of red.

'Looks like we're going with that mad bastard.'